Conundra

Conundra

h d munro

h d munro

Part One:

Break Stick

Break Stick

i

'Spoke to Screwloose today?'

'Nah bruv, keepin' out of his way innit, fuckin' nutter man since he got that fuckin' piece.'

'I smell what you're cookin' bruv, but he's a bruv too innit, can't just diss him like that, got to keep him tight, innit?'

'S'pose.'

'We don't want him driftin' off to Seven, keep him close man, or he'll be pissin' in the tent instead of out of it, innit.'

The Pope brothers were walking up the Walworth Road. It was late and they moved fast, having dumped the wheels three streets back on another estate. What the older of the two had just said was bang on the money, and the younger one knew it. Driss had always lived under the shadow of Kribz and didn't mind one bit. There was only eighteen months between them but to Driss it felt like as many years.

They were not alone; each had in his hand the end of a strong leather leash, and at the end of each leash was a very strong dog. Lois and Ciara were mature American pit bull sisters that the brothers had bought several months previously for a serious lump of money. Their purchase and possession of the animals were criminal offences, but the law enforcement agencies in the swamp never bothered much about such minor infractions; the daily shitstorm of knife and gun crime saw to that.

The foursome had been out for several hours and, as they neared home, the dogs started to pull, particularly Lois who had six weeks earlier given birth to five pups that she was now keen to be with. The lift was out as usual, not that they ever used that tin toilet on strings. They plodded up the equally acrid concrete stairs and walked along the balcony walkway on the fourth floor of the 1920s block.

They weren't talking and saw it together. The door of the flat was ajar, and splintered wood showed why.

They slowed, bitches straining but remaining silent. Driss was the first to speak.

'Shit, bruv, we've been done, what the…?'

'Quiet,' hissed Kribz. 'They might be still in there.'

They paused for a few seconds. Kribz was surveying the scene, including the car park below. Driss was watching him, waiting for orders.

'Okay, fuck it!' Kribz kicked the door fully open and marched in with Driss and the dogs right behind him. Lois barked and lunged forward, pulling Driss inside. Ciara growled her support.

'The pups!' Driss turned to check the other rooms.

'Shit, fuck man, the pups've gone! They've taken the fuckin' pups!'

Driss was still shouting as he bounded back into the living room. Lois was yelping, frantically searching the flat. Ciara sloped into the kitchen in search of food. She also had pups but they were still in her belly.

'How'd they do this?'

'What in Holy Jesus' name happened now!?' It was their mother, Molly.

The boys stood still as she appeared at the door of the living room, both hands full of shopping and cleaning kit. She held down two scrubbing jobs and did all the chores too. Old before her forty years, Molly's face was battered by work and worry.

'Don't worry, Mum, we got it under control. Somebody's t'ieved the pups, that's all.'

'Did the pups have chips in them?'

'No, course not, Mum, you don't 'ave to do it till they're older.'

'Well, you better get chips put into these two before the same 'appens to them. It's the law, it's a crime not to 'ave your dogs chipped.'

Despite the circumstances they sneaked a smile at each other. They loved their mum and her naivety; try to get an unlicensed pit bull micro-chipped and you lose the dog and cop a big fine – or even jail time – for having it in the first place.

'Can you feed the girls please, bro?' Kribz left Driss to this and left the room. A few seconds later he was back. 'Didn't you see this?' He was holding a piece of paper.

Driss looked up at it. 'Where was that?'

'Stuck to the wall, you dick. Good job I checked in there.' He handed it to his brother.

'Fuckin' Seven innit, gotta be.'

On the note was scrawled 'Want your dogs back follow the Snap 7.'

Kribz was already on his phone, thumbing through social media, including Snapchat. 'Yeah, man, fuckin' cunts blackmailin' us innit, they're wantin' a grand up front. Each.'

'We playin' ball?'

'Like fuck we are, not by their fuckin' rules anyway.'

Driss was trying to pacify Lois; the dog was very distressed, refusing to eat. 'Get onto Screwloose, get him over here, fast as he likes.'

2

'What you catchin' Screw?'

The brothers and their third member Screwloose were sat on the floor on their phones. Molly had fried some chicken and the empty plates were strewn on the threadbare carpet.

'Fuck all man, gone quiet.'

'Yeah, lull before the storm innit, waitin' for us to make contact innit, they'll 'av a long fuckin' wait.'

But the three kept thumbing away, hoping to pick up some tittle tattle on the media, some clue about the pups.

'One of you's gonna fix the door?' enquired Molly from the kitchen.

'Yeah Mum, in the morning, nobody's comin' tonight.'

'Nah, not with me fuckin' here they ain't,' chipped in Screwloose, and they all laughed with deep voices, like men.

And then they fell silent. Lois had settled a bit but was still confused and irritable. The boys all stared at her, poor animal.

'Wonder if she knows?' said Driss.

'What, knows they're gone? She ain't fuckin' blind bruv, innit.'

'What makes those cunts think we're gonna give up two grand when there's another bellyful gonna get popped out any time soon?'

'Not the point fam. We just took a serious dissing, can't go unanswered.'

'Too true bruv, too true.' Screwloose smelt blood. 'You seen Massive 'bout?'

'Nah, not lately, fedz on 'im innit, not us he's fearin', layin' low innit.'

'He's gotta be behind this though.'

'Yeah, no doubt 'bout that, always gotta be 'avin' a pop at us, even from his hideout, wherever the fuck that is.'

'He'll surface soon enough tho', all we gotta do is wait.'

'Nah, waitin' ain't for me, bruv. We gonna flush him, him an' that Buzzcock fuckin' wanker…. hey, bet they'll be at the Aspect gig tomorrow!'

It was always Kribz with the ideas, and Driss was always first to agree.

'Yeah man, too right. We gonna rock up?' Screwloose perked right up at this one.

'Fuckin' too fuckin' right man, can't miss the opportunity. We gotta get in there fast, strike while the steel's hot innit.'

'Iron.'

'What?'

'Don't matter, whatever, nobody gonna fuck wid Braganza like dis!'

3

It was Tom Rankin's favourite time of day: 4 a.m. And the first hint of daylight had the birds vocalising their own approval. *Aye*, thought Rankin, best part of the day. The early part, *before I get found out.*

He walked unsteadily down the wide staircase – bad knees – and into the huge kitchen with its marble floor and chandelier which would rattle when the first Boeing hurtled over the rooftops within the next hour. That would wake Marlene, still asleep with her blindfold and earplugs on the other side of the king-size bed he'd just left.

The house had been built on unwanted land to the immediate west of Heathrow's Runway Two. The village itself, Stanwell Moor, had been there long before the airport, but nobody cared about that. It had a certain charm though, an outlaw quality which council planning officers did well to respect. Respect rather than *inspect,* might as well have been their motto; the latter led to confrontations that were well above their paygrades.

Rankin's house was an indescribable folly overlooking, to its rear, three acres of land from which the 73-year-old ran his various businesses, including dog breeding kennels. He'd got the plot for next to nothing and the building materials for less. The rest had been easy; from good Irish Traveller stock Rankin knew how to build and how to get builders to build, without too much attention to regulatory detail.

That had been twenty years ago, the first ten of which had been good, the remainder less so.

The planned runway realignment meant that, before too long, the Rankin homestead would no longer be in the flight path; the value of his land had consequently quadrupled, and predators were circling.

Rankin had no intention of selling up voluntarily and had made his position clear. But those sharks weren't going away;

they'd had a whiff of the old man's blood and he could see no way out.

'I don't see what the trouble is. I bought the chipping franchise six years ago, the business is making money and I'm paying off the loan Mr Jackson, at the agreed rate. What's the feckin' problem?'

Jackson was there on behalf of Royal Bank and was getting paid well for his job which, basically, was to steal Tom Rankin's money – all of it. As an insolvency practitioner with an odious reputation, he was very busy, so desperate were the banks to ruin, fillet and devour their own customers. A decade of reckless lending had led to the crisis, but the borrowers were being made to pay – through their noses and sometimes even with their lives, the mounting bankrupts' suicide rate being proof of that.

'I'm sorry Tom, the bank's calling it in – with immediate effect, and I'm going to make sure your business is properly restructured to take the hit and trade through your problems.'

'But I haven't got any feckin' problems – or I didn't have till you came on the feckin' scene! We're trading fine, never miss a monthly payment. What's the panic?'

'It's not a panic Tom, but the loan is payable on demand, and the bank's demanding, so, unless you can come up with the cash now, which I know you can't, my company will come in and restructure. It's not a problem Tom, we do it all the time.'

Rankin was deeply suspicious. This shiny suited spiv reeked of perfume and wore cufflinks; never trust a man with cufflinks, Tom had been advised by his father half a century previously.

'I still don't get it. If it's not a problem, why are you even here?'

'Just a friendly visit mate. We're not going to do anything today, but I'll be bringing my colleague next time, so I'll give you plenty notice, we'll go through a few details then, okay?'

Not waiting for an answer, he started walking to the door.

'Great place you've got here. Must be worth a fortune with the airport re-alignment. Your noise levels'll plummet.'

An Airbus screamed overhead. The two men were just emerging from the front door and they looked up. The plane was so low they could see the tread on the tyres.

'See you soon, Tom,' said Jackson chirpily as he got into his 7 Series Beemer. Rankin watched as the big car turned and sped off through the oily mud and gravel of the unkempt front driveway. He stood there for a full thirty seconds and surveyed his world. The house was rambling with extensions of differing styles, the doors of the detached garages, with one exception, were open, revealing his hotchpotch of vehicles: three ageing cars and a Ford Transit van, all scruffy and in need of a wash. But he loved it; it was a home, a working home. Marlene was out the back, and he could hear the dogs barking as she hung out washing. Then another plane thundered and crackled above him, shaking his buildings and reverie. Those things, he reflected, had saved him up to now, they had been his real guard dogs, and soon they would be diverted. The anticipated increase in the value of the land had sprung the hyenas.

4

Driss picked up the car from the rental company that afternoon. A dark blue Vauxhall: nothing flash. His driving licence was clean, and his manners were good.

'Bring it back in one piece, won't you,' laughed Julie, the rental manager.

'As always Julie, no worries.' Driss shot her his best smile.

He picked up Kribz and Screwloose from the gates of Myatt Fields as arranged, and the crew began its day of maneuvers.

Their main enterprise was the safe and pre-arranged delivery of controlled drugs to purchasers, mainly cannabis at night and cocaine in the mornings between eight and midday when they knew the Q cars would be resting. They would typically buy an ounce of coke for £1000, good quality gear, largely uncut. There are just over 28 grams to the ounce and the boys had no trouble getting seventy-five quid a gram. They were high enough up the food chain to be selling five-gram bags between five and ten times a week, and there was no shortage of customers calling their regularly changing burner phone numbers. So, 110% profit margin, less a few overheads such as car hire and stashing costs. Then mix the coke fifty-fifty with baking powder or creatine and the margin jumps two-fold.

They had their stashes at various places: lock-up garages, friends' kids' bedrooms, gym lockers. It was tedious work with lots of precautions. For instance, they could only hire each car for a few days at a time because of the ANPR.

Automatic Number Plate Recognition cameras are positioned on all the main London corridors and then some. The police have the capacity to view the footage retrospectively so that when a suspect car comes to their attention, they can scan the system to see which cameras had recorded its plate: where, when, what speed and what direction. The cameras can even see vehicle occupants if the light is right.

Only one of the boys would carry the 'food' and Screwloose's piece was wrapped in a towel under the front passenger seat, nice and clean, no prints. If pulled, only one boy would get nicked for possession of a sufficiently small amount for him to say it was 'personal' and the gun would of course have been there, unbeknownst to them, when they'd picked up the motor. Likewise with the bigger stash inside the false fire extinguisher masquerading as part of the safety kit in the boot; that also came with the car.

It wasn't only the fedz they had to worry about. D7 and other rival gangs had to be looked out for, especially when they strayed out of the Elephant into neighbouring Brixton or Peckham. Brixton was D7's manor, but Braganza had business there and the boys' eyes were peeled as Driss drove carefully along Coldharbour Lane.

5

Kribz's phone buzzed and he picked up.

'Yo!'

Screwloose watched Kribz's face grow dark in the rear-view mirror.

'You go fuck your mother,' he snarled before cutting the call.

'Who the fuck was that?' asked Driss, not unreasonably.

'Spin round! Seven's on us innit, get outta here fam!'

Driss slowed and looked for a turning point.

Then they got hit. The impact wasn't particularly hard, just like when an old lady hits you up the chuff, but it did the trick and Driss put his foot down. He recognised the faces in the pursuing car in his mirror and Kribz and Screwloose twisted round to mouth obscenities through the rear windscreen. Screwloose knew better than to reach for the gun – just yet – but was donning his gloves. Drill music blared out of the speakers as Driss did lefts and rights across Brixton with the Sevens finding it easy to keep up in their higher spec wheels. They were up for it and Massive was the front passenger directing the driver. They weren't going to back off; this wasn't a warning.

'Okay, right, fuck 'em, if they want it they can 'ave it!' shouted Kribz. Driss knew what this meant and slammed on the anchors.

The second impact was bigger and louder and the B Boys felt it bad. Screwloose came out of the whiplash, went down to the floor and grabbed the gun. The Sevens were out and all around, banging on the motor, dancing and shouting.

'We got your dogs B Boys, now we got you!' yelled Massive, before Screwloose calmly leaned out and shot him in the leg.

The bullet went into Massive's thigh without hitting any bone or main pipelines, but the shock of the assault stunned the big thug. He looked down at the wound and the blood and the enormity of the event; he'd taken a cap, become a drill lyric, he was on the map, but just stood there, looking down at his leg and wondering why it didn't hurt all that much and why he was still standing.

Time froze over; the thwack of the gunshot had halted proceedings and the Sevens retreated into their car. They looked a bit crestfallen, a sense of injustice enveloping them, like they'd just been beaten at football by cheating opponents and a bent ref.

Driss revved up the engine and the B Boys shot off speechless, the speakers still delivering the soundtrack to the action.

They covered three blocks before Kribz spoke. 'Get rid of the piece, man.'

'No.' The speed of Screwloose's response meant he'd anticipated the order.

'What ya mean fuckin' no? You just shot a guy, now sling it or get outta this car, innit!'

'No, Kribz, man, this cost me three hundred sheets innit an' they ain't easy to come by!'

Screwloose was right. It wasn't just the money; it still wasn't easy to get a decent shooter in London, not overly difficult, but not easy either - no matter how many Lithuanians you knew, and Screwloose hadn't know any, so he'd had to start from scratch and take risks, and didn't fancy having to go through all that again.

6

'Okay, so a few stressed out poor bastards hang themselves.

Unfortunate, yes, but missed opportunities are missed bonuses, peeps, and we're in this filthy business to make money. Except,' and Claude Jackson paused for effect, 'except that you can't really make money. What you have to do is divert it, attract it, siphon it off and channel it into places from where it bestows its benefits in your direction.'

The audience was less than thirty strong and consisted of the fledgling Rebuilding Group, the selection of its members based on their reputations for ruthlessness. Jackson paused again to wipe a fleck of spit from the corner of his mouth.

'If we don't call this dosh in double-quick, we're fucked, all of us! The government's as slow as arseholes, their bailouts'll come, maybe, eventually, but far too late. In the meantime, you guys've got to do the dirty work and pull that money back to where it belongs – in our clients' bank and our personal accounts!'

'Too right boss!'

'Leave it to us!'

Jackson raised his palms to stop further nonsense, 'Oh yes, it'll be left to you alright. But are you up to it? Have you got the balls to be cruel? Sadistic, even?'

'Fucking right we have!'

'I certainly hope so, because the very survival of the bank and our other sponsors is in your hands and your hands alone, so get out there and strip!'

A spontaneous cheer erupted, but not all of them contributed. Jackson's eyes swiveled and made an instantaneous mental note of who was less than delirious. He then looked to his right where Larssen sat motionless in her leather trouser suit. He often wondered why she insisted on dressing like this. The firm had various names for her – Catwoman, Latex Girl, Dom – but none were spoken to her face. She could permanently destroy a reputation with the click of a mouse and enjoy the experience. She was Jackson's subordinate in name only.

Having graduated with high honours from Aalborg University, the 21-year-old Freda Larssen had won a scholarship to do a one-year master's degree at Trinity College, Cambridge. She lasted less than three months and went back to Denmark. Throughout her late teens she had been experiencing episodes of oscillatory mood swings the extremities of which – and the damage they caused – progressively increasing. Her one and only marriage had started when she was twenty-three and ended acrimoniously three years later, with her husband getting sole custody of their infant daughter. The further deterioration of her mental health found expression in sulphuric venom; focused, laser-like. Doctors prescribed various courses of medication to no avail, one psychiatrist noting that the patient exhibited very serious anger issues which appeared to strip her of empathy and any sense of social or interpersonal justice.

Her English was fluent and her eventual transition from Copenhagen to London, at the age of thirty, was effortless. She glided from one job to the next, maintaining an upward trajectory, a bulging deposit account, and a lengthening list of enemies.

The work was predatory and, to Larssen, satisfyingly hurtful. She found no trouble admitting to herself that she enjoyed separating stupid people from their hard-earned money.

Jackson hadn't really been looking for anyone when she breezed into his office one fine morning. Larssen had done a little homework and, before he'd recovered from the momentarily stunning effect of her looks, she hit him with 'You need me for the Copenhagen job.'

Jackson had been mentioned in the City press as being tangentially involved in stripping a Danish firm's UK assets. That had been Larssen's key to his door and the rest quickly ensued.

She was just waiting for her time to come and he would be unseated from the chair of the board. He lived in perpetual fear; when the time came, the damage would be permanent.

The meeting ended and the gatherers filed out of the room, muttering their intentions to one another, hoping to be overheard: 'I've got one waiting to drop', 'I've got a dozen little piggies lined up', 'One of mine's in hospital with an overdose, so I've nailed his insurers!'

'Dogs of war, eh?' said Jackson to Larssen, hoping for her blessing. He was disappointed.

'Puppies more like. No, correction. Fucking pussies.' She rose to stand at her full six feet two inches, stretched, and walked out.

7

'I'm his brother, innit. Just checkin' him out Doc, that's all.'

Kribz had found it easy to get into St Thomas' Hospital and knew there was no way the Sevens would have involved the police. At the same time, he knew Massive would not have been stupid enough not to seek medical attention and Saint Tommy's was the nearest.

'Okay, he's in that side room, but we've called the police as it's a gunshot wound. They'll probably kick you out when they get here.'

The B Boy knew he only had a narrow window. He slid into the room. Massive's eyes widened.

'Don't panic, big boy, I ain't here to finish the job. Just want to know where my pups are.'

'You must be mad man, comin' in here, the fedz'll be all over me anytime now!'

'You gonna grass?'

'Nah, fuckin' course not, but there was no need for that, man, your boy's a fuckin' nutter, you got a fuckin' war on now Kribzy, just you fuckin' wait bro!'

14

Kribz sneered at this; Massive's leg was pressure bandaged up to his balls and here he was threatening a war.

'You tell me where those pups are now or I'll send in my man to pop you another cap and he don't give a fuck. Now spit it out big boy, you ain't got no choice.'

Massive relaxed, closed his eyes and took a deep breath. The drip in his arm probably had more than saline on board.

'Kennels at Heathrow, place called Stanwell Moor, Gypsy called Rankin. Round one to you Kribzy, you won this battle but the Sevens'll win the fuckin' war…'

He opened his eyes; Kribz had gone.

8

Rankin was busy feeding the dogs. There were about thirty in all, mostly bull terrier variations, from Staffs to hybrid American pit bulls, plus a smattering of the more exotic breeds of fighting beast. The pups were together, thankfully, keeping each other company in a hostile environment. They were in a metal cage about six feet square and three feet deep. At just over eight weeks old they were eating solids and seemed well nourished, if a bit dirty.

As Rankin gave them their food, he wondered about the boy who'd brought them to him. He didn't like black people and trusted them less, but this very big black boy had seemed polite enough and had paid him cash up front and very well indeed for the kennel services – twice the asking price and a tip on top. Rankin had asked no questions, knowing that the dogs were illegal, along with probably most of the other activities of his new client.

Massive had been alone when he'd taken the pups out to Stanwell Moor and had had a hard job finding the place. Rankin's homestead had no specific postcode so the satnav in the hire van had been useless. Like most south London gang boys, Massive didn't like the countryside or anything with a rural whiff; he'd made sure he was clean of drugs, weapons or brothers as he reckoned the chance of getting a pull by bored cops not used to seeing young spades was high. He needn't have worried; Skyport security concerns sucked in police resources like a black hole and the surrounding motley collection of villages and council estates were scarcely patrolled during daylight hours.

Kribz and Driss knew this and hadn't worried themselves about travelling in a rented Beemer. But they knew better than to be carrying anything and Screwloose had been rested for the day. They got out of the car and stood together for a few seconds, surveying the sprawling hotchpotch of outbuildings which surrounded the shambolic Rankin residence. Oily water from the poorly tarmacked drive soaked up into their three-hundred-quid trainers as a 737 blasted over them. Driss actually ducked. 'Jesus Christ! How can any cunt live here man?!' He looked up and around like he'd just landed on another planet.

Kribz ignored him, his narrowed eyes in search of signs of life or danger. The open front drive belied the security which surrounded the inner sanctum of the estate; the face of the rambling house sported at least two cameras, and on each of its two sides was evidence of a fifteen-foot double ply wire mesh fence which obviously encircled the property and whatever lay to its rear.

Having finished most of the morning's routine, Rankin had gone into the house through one of the back doors to put the kettle on. He happened to look out the front and, seeing the brothers standing by their car, thought of getting one of his shotguns out of the secure cabinet in the living room. He incorrectly surmised that these two would be friends of the big one who'd brought him the pups, and correctly, but for the wrong reasons, surmised that there could be some more money coming his way. It was a close call, but he decided to leave the weapon where it was.

'Can I help you gentlemen?' Rankin was polite as he stepped out of the front door.

'You Mr Rankin?' Kribz's question was put respectfully.

'That's me. What can I do for you lads?'

Driss couldn't wait to get in on the act. 'You got our pups man, innit?'

Rankin made out he hadn't understood the diction, but he knew exactly what the boy was talking about. He shrugged his shoulders and showed his palms, 'Sorry, can you explain?'

Kribz inhaled deeply and stepped forward with his eyes lowered, unthreatening, thoughtful.

'Look, Mr Rankin, we had some pups stolen from us and the thief says he took them to you. We need them back but we'll pay you for your trouble. Ain't no big deal, we just need back what's ours.'

Rankin nodded slightly, acknowledging the reasoned approach.

'Right, I've a lot of dogs back there,' he jerked his head towards the house and the land behind it, 'but I think I know the ones you're talking about. Would the fella that brought them look a bit like you, if you know what I mean?'

'Yeah,' said Kribz, his lip curling a little at the racial reference.

Driss sucked his chops: 'Tssssch.'

'Okay, come through,' said the old man.

The brothers could not help being impressed by what they saw. Although a bit untidy looking, the place was secure and the configuration of sturdily built kennels, exercise pens and a refrigerated food storage shed had a professional edge to it. Rankin led the boys to the little cage. Driss grinned when he saw the pups lolloping about together in clean straw with fat bellies. They seemed happy and contented.

'Wow man, they look great!' enthused the younger brother. Kribz was more restrained but equally pleased.

'These the ones boys?'

'Yeah, these are ours, Mr Rankin. How much do we owe you?'

'Nothing lads, just take them. I don't need to be involved in any shenanigans with you lot.'

Driss walked towards the pen, looking for the door latch.

'Hang on a minute bruv,' said Kribz, before turning to Rankin. 'D'you do microchippin'?'

'Yes, I do, but then we'll have to talk some money, forty quid a shot.'

'And what if we were to leave them in your care, what're the kennel fees?'

Rankin wasn't sure if he wanted this; if ownership was disputed he might have pitch battles kicking off on his land. It had happened before on several occasions, but between his own kind, third generation Travellers, who he'd been easily able to quell. These blackies might be a different kettle of fish.

'Well, to be honest with you boys, I'm not sure how long I'm goin' to be here. Got trouble with the bank, so it can't be a long term deal.' He paused, looking down at the pups. 'How long did you have in mind for me to look after them?'

Kribz was assured by the old man's transparency. 'Ah, jus' a few weeks man, not long innit, jus' till we find them better homes, innit.'

'Okay, we'll go a week at a time then. Let's say a hundred a week, how does that sound?'

'Yeah, okay, and one other thing, when you get them chipped could you have them registered in your name? We done some checkin' on the net and found out you're licensed, badged up to keep these kinda dogs.'

Kribz had indeed done his homework and it was Rankin's turn to be impressed, but not without a hint of trepidation; he felt he was being recruited to something he might later regret. But he smelled money, and cash at that. The gathering clouds on his financial horizon put paid to caution.

'That'll need to cost you extra lads, quite a bit if I'm honest. I've got other dogs registered in my name, it's like being a foster parent to naughty kids.' He laughed as he said this, trying to lighten the mood and ease the passage of his requirement. But the brothers didn't get the joke and remained stony faced.

'Don't matter,' said Driss quietly. 'Whatever it costs, we need them taken care of.'

Rankin nodded and was about to respond when Kribz continued from where his brother had left off. 'And that includes protecting them from t'ieves man, you know what I mean? Including the guys what t'ieved them from us and brought 'em here in the first place.'

This flustered Rankin. 'So they might come here for them?'

'No, doubt it, we've got an arrangement now and they shouldn't come back here. But if they do, or anyone else, we need to know you can fend 'em off.'

Rankin made a show of looking around at the high fences and walls surrounding his hacienda castle. 'Well, if they get past the fence, they set off an alarm in the house and they get me with a twelve-bore shotgun. Is that enough for you?'

'Sounds good, Mr Rankin.' Kribz allowed himself to smile.

'Okay lads, let's have a mug of tea and talk about money.'

9

Jackson and Larssen were going over some paperwork.

'It's even better than I thought. The runway realignment turns that land from unusable to premium hotel site quality,' said Jackson.

Larssen listened and nodded, frowning at the documents. Jackson was right. What he was forgetting was that it was the tall Dane who'd originally found out that the Rankin land was unadopted by any local authority. They would have to move fast: it had to be assumed that they weren't the only ones looking at this substantial opportunity.

'We need to get that land registered in our name before the bank moves in ahead of us. We'll take a hit on the fee and go for the development rights. The bank'll have our hand off if we reduce our price sufficiently.' It infuriated Jackson that the bloody woman was always one step ahead of him. Larssen paused before dictating the next step, 'We're going to take another drive out there today.'

'What for? We've already put him on notice of the bank calling the loan in. It's up to Rankin to raise the money if he can – and we know he can't.'

'We have no way of knowing that. He could obtain the money from an unknown source, which would lead us to being fucked, kicked out of the picture. The bank will have no further fucking need of us.'

The way in which Larssen combined her accented but near-perfect diction with a smattering of obscenities struck Jackson as almost erotic.

She went on. 'Come on, make some calls, pull in some favours, make sure nobody else lends to him. I'm going to ensure that the fucker is thoroughly discredited.'

10

The following morning saw Kribz and Driss driving out once again to Stanwell Moor. They'd chopped the Beemer in for a small van, in the back of which were now two very worried looking pit bull bitches.

They'd done the deal and Rankin was for the foreseeable future to be their licensed breeder. Both boys were a bit concerned about the effect the move would have on the dogs, especially Ciara, the pregnant one, but they were sure Rankin knew what he was doing and had decided that the risk was worth it. They couldn't take any visits from the police.

'So, these are the two lovely ladies, eh?'

Rankin was full of his usual bonhomie and the kettle was already boiling. The three of them took the dogs through the house and out the back where a detached kennel with its own secure playpen had already been prepared. A canine cacophony welcomed them as the thirty-odd residents got a whiff of the newcomers. The noise soon subsided and the brothers continued to be impressed by their new associate. They watched as the dogs were served a good introductory meal and seemed to settle but started barking when the brothers turned to walk back into the house. Driss made to return to soothe them; Kribz stopped him.

'No bruv, walk away, c'mon, they got to get used to it innit.'

'Lois must be able to smell her pups,' said Driss, looking across the estate to where the youngsters were being kept separately and well out of the way.

'Nah, not a chance fella,' assured Rankin. 'There's a million smells around here, I've got three dozen dogs on this place. We'll keep the pups separate, they're well past weaning age anyway.'

The pair of them followed Rankin into his sprawling kitchen where the tea was brewing.

They'd already discussed money on the previous day but it hadn't been bottomed out as to how long the arrangement was to last. Rankin broached it. 'So how long then, boys?'

The brothers glanced at each other. 'A few months,' ventured Driss.

'And if you get buyers for the pups we want the agreed share within a week of you getting paid.' This was from Kribz, who wanted to keep the business angle pinned down.

'That's already agreed,' said their host, a bit tersely for Kribz's liking. Rankin appeared worried by something. He sighed before going on.

'Look, lads, you need to know more about my problems.'

Break Stick

Neither brother could remember a time in their lives when they'd seen a white man looking embarrassed and perhaps a bit furtive. Maybe the odd schoolteacher or outreach worker had patronisingly feigned sensitivity to gain their confidence, but this was a businessman – well, sort of, after a fashion.

'The sharks are after me. It looks like I might lose my place and everything I've got.'

Driss and Kribz looked at each other and back at Rankin. They had not a clue what he was talking about. The old man read their faces and knew he had to elaborate.

'I had to take a loan out a few years ago. The place needed rewiring and the kennels had to have a lot of money spent on them to make them legal. I was getting inspected by the RSPCA and the trading standards people and I had to pass those inspections to get my licence, especially for the microchipping business.' The boys began to nod slowly in unison. 'I need to raise a hundred thousand pounds within six months or I'm out on the bones of me arse. This place has suddenly become valuable because of changes to the runways which'll reduce the air traffic noise. The bastards want shot of me so they can pull my house down and build hotels and feckin' offices.'

'A hundred grand? Where you gonna get that from, Mr Rankin?' Driss asked the question.

'I haven't a clue son, short answer is that I haven't a chance of raising it. None of the other banks'll touch me, the liquidators have made sure of that.'

'What are The Liquidators?' It was Kribz's turn to ask a question and Rankin sighed again; it was going to be a long conversation, but the old man felt an acute need to share his torture, use these boys as a sort of lightning conductor, and instinct told him that maybe, just maybe, they could become useful to him. There was something solid about them; a hunger, a willingness to listen and learn. They were not the run of the mill darkies he'd come across in Acton and the Bush before he'd moved out west.

Rankin enjoyed talking to the boys, he liked their attentiveness and apparent respect for him. He relaxed and made more tea as he recounted his purchase of the land twenty years earlier; before then he'd rented it from a distantly related family who'd merely squatted on the homestead for the entirety of a generation.

Relieved by having someone to talk to, he relaxed into drinking mode and began to self-administer large shots of Black Bush whiskey into his tea mug. He offered the boys some; they politely declined. Driss wished he could roll and light a spliff but correctly assumed the old Irishman wouldn't approve.

'D'you mind if I have a walk around the place for some fresh air, Mr Rankin?' asked Kribz, interrupting a particularly long monologue about how the banks were systematically fleecing small businesses up and down the country.

'Sure son, you go ahead, fill yer boots, but don't try to get too friendly with the dogs, they won't be used to…' Rankin stopped himself just in time, sensing any racial reference would not be appreciated. Driss glared at him. '…strangers on the place.'

Kribz stepped out of the back door, leaving his brother to be solely entertained. He gathered speed as he made for what he'd earlier identified as an unused outhouse located about seventy yards from the rear of the house. It was solid, brick-built, about five feet in height with a wooden, felt covered roof set at a slope to provide a run-off for rain. Without any difficulty Kribz reached in through the open door, angled his arm upwards and blindly discovered a very convenient rafter where the sturdy roof was attached to the brick wall. It was in between this and the roof that he carefully wedged a tightly wrapped package containing a kilogram of very pure cocaine which had been concealed in a belt bag at the small of his back. It was the Braganza Boys' main stash and had cost them a cool twenty grand. He was taking a chance putting it here, but the prevailing heat in the swamp made the risk necessary.

Concerned about CCTV coverage, he gave credence to his tarrying by taking a piss. Zipping up, he sauntered back to the house to find Rankin now slurring his way through an explanation of asset stripping to a moon-eyed Driss. The old man had an accountant of sorts, another Irishman with a run-down office in nearby Staines who'd done nothing but explain to his client what was happening to him and that there was bugger all he could do about it except come up with the money.

'Best we get going, bruv.' Driss nodded eagerly.

Rankin's eyes dropped, thinking he'd bored the boys. 'Okay lads, I can tell you've had enough,' he laughed, faking more embarrassment than he felt.

11

Massive walked out of St Thomas' Hospital with the aid of two crutches. He'd been warned by the medics not to put too much weight on his heavily bandaged leg. Foremost on his mind was the damage to his pride and his reputation. He'd had a few visitors but not many. One or two desultory pop-ins by nervous fellow Sevens and, of course, the po-po wanting a statement from him. He'd given them all short shrift, the latter for obvious reasons – rule one of gang life: no engagement with the police, the former because he was disgusted with them. The Sevens were all youngsters, full of wind and piss and he was sick of carrying them. Now that he'd taken a cap, he reckoned it was time to move on.

'Just fuck off and lay low man,' he'd told Spacer. 'Go an' concentrate on your drill, innit, youz not up to fightin'.'

Spacer was a talented musician and was relieved he'd not been asked to help with the retaliation job. The gunshot had been the first he'd witnessed and had scared the shit out of him.

Not so with Gence. He'd really been up for it. 'What you want us to do, Mass? They ain't getting' away with this, coulda killed you, lucky you ain't lost that leg!'

Massive had shushed him. 'Up to me bruv, all in good time. Just go an' keep your head down, the fedz'll be waitin', prob'ly have Bs' places plotted up waitin' for us. Nothin's gonna 'appen for a good time, so go an' chill.'

Massive had dealt with the situation as it stood. Oh, he had no intention of letting the Braganza Boys away with this; his time would come.

12

Screwloose was sulking. Academically dim and no good at football, he'd struggled at school; been excluded at 14 before doing time in Feltham YOI for a bungled knifepoint robbery and possession of some crack cocaine that he hadn't known what to do with. Six months later he'd been out and about feeling all rough and tough with delusions of adequacy. Kribz and Driss had taken him in to stop him joining another gang; better the fucking idiot was pissing from inside the tent than into it from outside, blah blah. For they knew he'd do anything – anything – for acceptance. And now he felt like a leper, although he knew it was temporary and necessary. Screwloose liked blaming himself, almost enjoyed being the fuck-up, relished the motivation it gave him to make amends. He also had an eye for the future and a vivid imagination.

Kribz had assured him that Massive had learned his lesson and wouldn't be coming back for more, but Screwloose chose not to believe a word of that. As he stewed in his trashy room watching gangster movies and smoking weed, he formed the solid conclusion that he was in big danger. He knew Massive from schooldays and had always thought the big boy had never really been gang material, more of a lone wolf. He guessed with some accuracy that the shooting would probably split the 7s, at least for a while. And he knew Massive was quite bright and wouldn't just come blazing back like a mad bastard. But he would be back somehow, sometime, he had to be, he had nowhere else to go; the shooting would not go unanswered. And he, Screwloose – *the* Screwloose – would be getting that answer.

13

The big black Beemer crunched to a slushy halt in the oil, shit and gravel. The boys' van didn't look out of place at the front of the house. Larssen had driven and Jackson had had time to take in the bleak, disconnected landscape of broken villages, dual carriageways and grey steel business parks that lay around the south and west perimeters of one of the busiest international airports on the planet.

'What a fucking shit'ole,' sighed Larssen, looking around as she stuck the gearshift into park.

'Where there's muck there's money.' Jackson's trite reply caused the Dane to clench her teeth and close her eyes in irritation. She was not overly familiar with English euphemisms but was instinctively bored by Jackson's contribution.

Just then the front door of the house swung open and the liquidators suddenly had something new to think about. As the boys bounced down the front steps they both turned back, bidding their farewells to Rankin. But he wasn't paying attention, focused instead on something ahead of them. They looked forward, following his gaze, and stopped dead, making the connection between what they had just heard and what they now saw.

'Go on lads, off you go now, don't get feckin' involved in this.' Rankin urged this without taking his eyes off Jackson and Larssen, now emerging from their car.

'This them?' hissed Driss, his neck thickening.

'Come on bruv, the man wants us outta here.' Kribz was keenly aware of Rankin's discomfort.

'Aye boys, jest get in your van and feck off without a word, please.'

The brothers did as Rankin asked but glared at Jackson and Larssen as they walked to their vehicle. Larssen returned their glare; Jackson averted his eyes.

Kribz made the mistake of letting Driss take the wheel. The younger boy gunned the van's engine and spun it round with maximum effect, deliberately hitting a puddle to send a sheet of greasy water in the parked Beemer's direction, just missing the immaculately dressed pair who stood beside it.

Having watched the brothers disappear out of the gate, the asset strippers turned to Rankin who was still standing at the top of the doorsteps.

'Interesting friends you have, Mr Rankin,' said Larssen cheerfully as she strode up to the old man, her hand held out. Jackson struggled to keep up with her but was not about to be outdone.

'Customers of yours, or were they trying to rob you?'

What a fool, thought Rankin. 'Rob me, Mr Jackson? Not them, I thought that was your job and you're certainly in no need of help doing it.' He turned and went into the big house having ignored Larssen's hand, leaving the door open for them to follow.

14

After a few minutes of driving in silence the boys spoke about the parcel that was now in Rankin's unwitting possession.

'What if he fuckin' finds it fam?' The question from Driss was not unreasonable.

'I doubt it but it's a chance we gotta take innit, can't risk 'avin' it at home or in the Arch just now, too much heat, 'specially with Massive getting hassle from the fedz to come up with names.'

'D'you think he'll squeal?'

'Doubt it, but there's always a risk an' then it'll be scorched earth innit.'

Another silent minute, and then:

'Poor fucker, man, how can they just do that? Steam in an' take his livin' an' his house like that? Robbery man, they're fuckin' gangsters, like the fuckin' mafia bruv, jeez....' Driss was in a state of excitable disbelief as he hurled the wheels round the bends and roundabouts too angrily for his brother's liking.

'Business, innit, we ain't the only ones to play rough, them suits do it far worse, jus' without the violence.'

Kribz's mature summing up quietened the younger brother, and the van slowed down a bit. After a couple of miles Kribz continued.

'You know bruv, we don't know fuckin' nuttin', we fuck about down there on the turf, shootin' an' shankin' an' dealin', but we don't know fuck all about anythin' outside our own back fuckin' yard.'

Driss was now driving quite sedately, with a frown on his face. 'But ain't that how it is bruv, you know, we ain't ever been taught anythin', what with Dad fuckin' off an' Mum 'avin' to work all the fuckin' time, it's how we are bruv, jus' survivin' innit.'

'Yeah, s'pose.' Kribz was looking ahead through the windscreen, but his eyes were glazed, thoughts elsewhere. The journey was completed in silence.

15

Police Constable Doug Napper swiped his ID through the card reader and the bolt sprung open. He pushed at the heavy steel door and it yielded, reluctantly. Once inside the compound he tapped a number into the back door of the building and went inside.

Kennington Police Station was virtually derelict. Only a handful of coppers worked there now: the site had been sold and was awaiting possession by its new oligarch owners. In the meantime Napper and a few others were allowed to use it for a bit of screenwork and the coffee machine and toilets. That was about all that went on in the place.

Napper took it all in his stride. He worked four twelve-hour shifts and then had four days off – *ad nauseam*. He was part of the Safer Neighbourhoods Team, but the 'team' part of the title meant nothing as he was on his own ninety percent of the time, and that was the way he liked it.

Nine years in the army had not made him a team player. He was unmarried and lived alone, didn't have any real hobbies; his only interest was his job. *The* job. The patch of the swamp between Kennington and the Elephant was all his to play with and what he didn't know about what went on in his manor could sit inside a frog's ear with room to spare.

He had short hair, a hipster beard and hadn't been seen in uniform for as long as anyone could remember; jeans, trainers and an assortment of hoodies comprised his wardrobe. But nobody complained: his return of work was formidable. People joked that he had his own server on the Crimint system, the Metropolitan Police Criminal Intelligence Database which bulged at the seams with information, the vast majority of which went stale through absence of use but was promptly replenished and refreshed by the likes of Napper, only to often atrophy again within days or just hours. It wasn't Napper's problem. As an SNT officer his job was to bring in the intel; if the lazy bastards on the crime squads or borough CID couldn't get round to using it, that was their problem.

Well, most of the time. Now and again he would get a bee in his bonnet about something and try to force his indolent colleagues into a bit of action.

29

Break Stick

'It's going to kick aaf big stoile down there if you don't do something, Aaron. Massive's got a hole in his fuckin' leg and the B Boys' dags are missing. The grapevoine's fuckin' buzzin' about a serious shootout loomin' up.'

'Yeah, I heard about this nonsense,' lied Aaron Briggs, after the couple of seconds it took him to decipher the Cornishman's accent. Briggs was a graduate entry Detective Constable who spent most of his time studying for the sergeant's exam. The call had found him at the police training establishment in Hendon, north London, where he was attending a three-day course on asset confiscation. Consequently, his head was even further away from practical policing than usual.

When Napper got cross his accent grew stronger. 'You can roit it aaf as nonsense if you loik, Aaron, but I'm sendin' you an email with this on it so if you do fuck all an' the wheel comes aaf its down to you mate!'

Napper hung up and the university boy was left wondering if he shouldn't perhaps apply for a search warrant. But he didn't wonder for long and joined his colleagues back in the classroom to hear more about the Proceeds of Crime Act and how the Met had become increasingly dependent upon the seizure of criminals' ill-gotten gains to bolster its dwindling budget.

Napper sat and seethed, staring blankly at the filthy, antiquated screen he'd chosen to sit in front of. The big, cold room was littered with broken chairs and decommissioned workstations. He and a few other cops and PCSOs had cobbled together a few bits of hardware to fashion an environment from which they could do the odd bit of work. They all had force issue tablets of course, along with instructions from the higher ranks to use them in cafes and public spaces, thereby saving costs, increasing efficiency and being more shoulder to shoulder with members of the esteemed public. Yeah, all right in Belgravia or Islington perhaps, but you log on from a greasy spoon in John Ruskin Street and you'll be deploying your CS canister pronto.

Napper's bitter thoughts were interrupted by McAdam, a civvy investigator in his sixties. He was one of a few dozen old guys brought back from retirement to help with researching the intel vaults and putting together briefing packs for the troops. They were all retired detectives with pensions, keen for a bit of beer money and to get away from their wives for a few hours a day.

'Wassamatter Doug, job getting' t'ya?'

McAdam didn't wait for an answer.

'Don't let it mate, s'not worth it, do your time, take your pension an' fuck off.'

'S'alright for you mate, you got your pension. It's all changed now, don't get mine till I'm sixty.'

Silence followed, neither man wanting to get into a moan-up; it was boring. They both knew they worked for a near zombie organisation, a patchwork of repairs, disconnects and gaping holes. The only thing the Metropolitan Police did with any semblance of efficiency was change, constantly. A mirage of smoke and mirrors that contorted and morphed according to who was watching and which senior officer's career path was momentarily under scrutiny.

16

Had Kribz benefitted from more than a rudimentary education he may have been able to give voice to his thoughts, or even thoughts to his emotions. His mood, sporadic and fleeting, was that of a young man perceiving not an alternative but the possibility of an alternative way of seeing things. His recent association with Rankin was of course not his first with an established white man. He'd had many not entirely unpleasant dealings with teachers, lawyers, social workers, customers, cops even, but these had all been forms of benign conflict or necessary business.

Break Stick

The relationship with Rankin was emerging as something different altogether. Had Kribz been able to elucidate his feelings he would have adduced that there was a bridge, a continuum, across which men and their positions were a matter of degree and that those positions existed or were gained by a combination of both their own influence and external forces. Like that of most intelligent uneducated men, his brain joined the dots of its own accord, and then patched through the message to his persona. *Hey, opportunity knocks man. Relax, get alongside, keep your options open in case you have to jump, but chill for now and go with the flow. Innit.*

The bottom line was that he found himself identifying with Rankin, an old white Gypsy who he knew would have called him a nigger at the drop of a hat. It wasn't that he trusted Rankin – he certainly didn't – but then he didn't trust anyone apart from his mother and brother and the B Boys – and the latter only some of the time. It wasn't about trust, it was about kinship, affinity. The man was being fucked over by *The* Man, The System, Babylon, and therein he felt a shared problem. And a problem shared is a problem halved, as Mum would say.

Him and Driss were sitting in the sunshine on the roof of their block.

'What you cookin' bruv?' Driss always wanted to know what his brother was thinking, especially after long spells of silence, like the one he'd just interrupted.

They had been discussing their recent acquisition of a proper headquarters, the loft of an old church which had become a makeshift mosque. The boys had decided to call it the Arch because of the rafters that supported the roof. And it was a good name because it was where they could go and *be arch*, and plan stuff. Not many knew about it yet; it was going to be strictly the Braganzas' inner sanctum, to be used operationally, not casually. So, for now they just sat on their roof of their block and enjoyed the cold south London sunshine.

'Nuttin' much bruv, just 'bout Rankin. I reckon we got a good offer there; we could do some stuff widdim innit.'

A pause, then he added: 'I been thinking 'bout what he was sayin', maybe us an' 'im could help one another.'

Driss was frowning. 'Got to be honest bruv, I didn't understand a lot of what he was on about.'

Kribz concurred. 'Me neither fam, but I got the gist of it, can smell what he's cookin', see somethin' there an' I think he sees somethin' too.'

'Let's jus' hope he don't find that package though. Maybe we shoulda arksed 'is permission first.'

'Nah bruv, if he'd said no we'd 'ave had nowhere to go, an' if he finds it I'm pretty sure he won't call the fedz. He'll know it was us and he'll want a piece of the action, which we'll be more than happy to give. In the meantime the food is safe as 'ouses innit.'

'S'pose.' Kribz was right, as usual.

They were interrupted when Screwloose and another Braganza boy called Numbers appeared.

'Yo?' Screwloose included the question mark to enquire if they could join the brothers.

'Yo,' Kribz admitted them. 'How's it going bruvs?'

'Good,' said Screwloose as he turned to Numbers, a wiry sixteen-year-old with a face of twenty-five. 'Numbers here 'as a result for us innit.'

The brothers looked up at the youngster. 'Sit down guys,' said Driss.

'What you got Numbers?' said Kribz.

'He got himself an Albo!' Screwloose was keen not to give Numbers centre stage, but the brothers' eyes were on the kid, side-lining the gunman.

Numbers milked it, sitting down with his back to an air vent cover, sagely savouring the moments leading up to his announcement. He knew not to wait too long though, and not take the piss, so he cleared his throat and spoke.

'I got this connection with an Albanian kid. He wants to do some business.'

Driss asked the obvious. 'You know him? Can you vouch for him?'

Numbers was honest. 'Not really man, never seen 'im before, he came outta the blue. But I think he's genuine, says he got a carwash near Crystal Palace.'

'What, that place that's always gettin' raided by the po-po?'

'Yeah, that's the one.'

Driss sucked his teeth and shook his head.

Kribz wanted to know more. 'That's interestin' man, no G boys go there much, how'd you meet 'im?'

'My sister,' explained Numbers. 'She knows his sister from school, that's all, nuttin' sinister.'

'Tell 'em what he's got man.' Screwloose was keen to move things on, get to the point. Numbers looked at the brothers for permission to proceed. Kribz raised his eyebrows and gave his head a little backward jerk.

'He needs to move some high quality food. He's holdin' it for someone who got nicked, put in custody. He's scared the guy'll fold an' sing so he needs to get rid, an' quick.'

'How much?' Again, Driss asked the obvious one.

'Two Keys, eighty per cent pure, and more to come if he can get a market.'

Kribz was delighted. 'Get a market? Get a fuckin' market?! Tell 'im he don't 'ave to look no further my bro!'

Screwloose grinned from ear to ear. Numbers felt he'd just risen a few notches in the Braganza hierarchy, which he certainly had.

17

There was a subsidiary of Rankin enterprises that the old

Gypsy kept quiet about. He was engagingly quite open about most of his business strands and kept them as legal as he could. But this one was well naughty and very private.

'Tell him it's Tom.'

The big gatekeeper raised his short-range walkie-talkie and growled something which Rankin couldn't understand, apart from his own name.

18

'What's occurring then Eric? Anything tasty for me?'

Napper was sick of being fed morsels of shit by so called 'sources' who were only after a quick few quid. Most of the spades were like that but Eric was a bit different, like he had a mission, like he believed in something. Napper's perception was that Eric went out looking for stuff, proactive, not just doing it for the money. His current task was to find a gun, a real gun, one that was in working order. And that would fetch a grand. Eric would get a monkey and Napper would take the other five hundred.

'Ain't gonna lie to you, Mr Napper, all a bit quiet jus' now. Nuttin' much 'apnin', mainly coz of the shootin' innit, but stuff should warm up soon, innit. Just gimme a lickle bitta time, know what ah mean?'

Napper assumed Eric was referring to the bullet Massive had taken in the leg, but it could have been any one of several pop-pops in the swamp over the previous week or so.

'Okay Eric, no sweat mate, keep at it, stay safe, fella.'

19

'Eric' put his phone down and reflected. *Stay safe, fella*, As if he fucking cared. Then he tapped out a number that wasn't on his favourites list; that he knew off by heart.

'You okay?'

'Not sure if I can do this much longer.'

'Nobody's asking you to.'

'It ain't the danger or the risk – that's no prob – and it's not me having a touch of the guilts either, I don't give a fuck about those losers, so called fam an' bruvs an blud, it's well, I've got a problem with the po-po to be honest. I don't like working for them.'

'Nobody's asking you to.'

'I know, but I'm gonna be a winnernigger, a token black what's gonna do well', innit. And I can do it without tossin' off these creeps, these pussies that hide in uniforms and clever talk about communities.' He paused, waited for a reaction.

'Go on, I'm listening.'

'An' I hate bein' called fuckin' Eric! My name's Michael, Michael Brooker. AKA Screwloose.'

'Tell me something I don't know.'

'Eric Talea, my arse, sounds African. Anyways, it's only Napper that calls me Eric Talea…'

'There's a reason for that,' came the interruption.

'Yeah, I know, but I wanna cut loose' innit, be free of this shit…'

'I've been telling you to do that for months.'

'I know, but the wonga comes in handy, two or three hundred jus' to keep me sweet. Cash, always in a white envelope. Napper's good like that, even though I'm sure he skims a bit. Be fuckin' mad not to, innit.'

'Suppose.'

'You gonna help me cut loose?'

'You know I can't do that.'

'These gangsta boys are stupid. I could see them comin' through school, coulda named 'em then from the age of ten. I played along, suited me, made me feel big an' part of somethin', put me on the map, then I got my piece and loadsa respect, but they still think I'm thick an' a loser. But they'ze the losers, I'ze gonna show them, when the time comes, when it suits me, innit.'

'Is that time coming soon?'

'Maybe, yeah, you gonna gimme support?'

'Like I keep telling you, I can't get involved, no way on God's earth can I get involved, neither of us can risk what would happen if the truth got out, especially you, they'd kill you.'

'So when I come close to getting' rumbled, which'll 'appen for definite, Napper'll put me in a, whaddaya call it, witness protection, fit me out with a new ID and a nice pad, maybe in Birmingham or Manchester?' give me a better name than Eric fucking Talea?'

'I don't know, maybe, maybe not, but you can do that all yourself, just walk.'

'Where fuckin' to? Who with? I duuno…'

And then the line went dead.

20

A few days later Screwloose was in the back seat of a hire car, sweating as usual about the gun at his feet. 'Surprise we ain't had a fuckin' pull yet.'

'You know what, you would have thought so but I don't think so, it's weird but it's like the fedz've got bigger stuff to do round these places, innit.'

Kribz was driving carefully as he said this, Driss at his side, eyes everywhere. The three boys were in an E Class Merc, picked up that morning from Avis, two hundred quid for 36 hours, plus five hundred deposit. Business was good and they could afford to look good.

Beside Screwloose on the back seat was a briefcase full of papers that Kribz had concocted on his Apple. They related to musical events, musicians' draft contracts, potential venues, minutes of meetings that had never taken place, photos of drill artists, etc. The Braganza boys had even got themselves a drop address in a virtual office in the Walworth Road. Braganza Events Company was their 'merch' tag, and the two brothers

– not Screwloose – knew how to talk the talk of the music business with a well-dressed and convincing enthusiasm which would bore the tits off any inquisitive cop.

Add to that the fact that they were in Knightsbridge; those places never got 'section sixtied'. Section 60 of the Criminal Justice and Public Order Act gives police the power to stop and search any person and/or vehicle if it is reasonably anticipated that violence is about to occur in any given 24-hour period in a given area. The 'given areas' were obviously those with the most notorious postcodes in which gang tensions often bubbled over into the use of knives and guns. Places like Knightsbridge didn't fit the bill.

'We gonna do this tonight then?' Screwloose was sweating, adrenalin pumping, mixing with the line he'd snorted before they'd left the Elephant.

'Yup, if we get the chance bruv.' Kribz was matter of fact.

'You gettin' the seconds, Screw?' Driss asked, knowing the answer.

'Course fuckin' not bruv. From what you tell me the cunt deserves it big style, needs a lesson, innit.'

'Yup,' confirmed Kribz.

'That's the place.' Driss pointed ahead to the low canopy slung over the restaurant doorway with a bouncer in top hat and tails in attendance.

Screwloose leaned forward, eyes agog between the two front seats. 'What the fuck is he wearing man, looks like a fucking penguin!' The brothers laughed, a bit nervously; it was getting near show-time.

It was pushing midnight and the traffic was light. Kribz found a parking space without any problem, with a clear view of the doorway. 'This is the hard bit bruvs, the waitin'.'

'Yer,' said Screwloose and Driss in unison, before all three fell silent. Screwloose reached down, took hold of the gun and checked it over by sense of touch.

21

Inside the restaurant the evening was drawing to a close. The diners had peaked and were now getting jaded: combinations of a long week, rich food and alcohol. Several lines of Peruvian consumed during periodic visits to the lavatories had helped sustain their enthusiasm, but they were all so exhausted that even the returns on that were diminishing.

'Right, I'm off,' announced Jackson. He'd already footed the bill. He twisted around in his chair, got the attention of a waiter and signalled that he needed a cab. The doorman would presently get a buzz in his earpiece and the wait would be less than a minute.

'Anybody need a lift?' asked the firm's CEO, quietly pleased there were no takers.

'I'm not sharing a cab with you,' chuckled Larssen. 'You've been looking at my tits all evening.'

Jackson frowned at the Dane's chest. 'Call those tits? I've seen a bigger pair on a hamster.'

'What is a hamster?' It was a rhetorical question, but she wanted to push this one as far as it would go.

Palmer, an outspoken member of the team, objectionable at the best of times, contributed: 'A small rodent that homosexuals put up their arses.'

Jackson at once regretted his choice of mammal. Larssen grabbed the prompt. 'Obviously a Freudian slip there Jacko.'

Jackson looked down, stood up and took his coat from the waiter.

22

They say every man has his weakness. Rankin's was somewhat surprising, for an essentially nice guy. The sights and sounds of extreme violence, spurting blood and painful death gave him such extraordinary pleasure that even Marlene had suggested he seek help.

'It's just animals, love, they live to fight and die, it's in their feckin' blood.'

'They haven't got any feckin' blood left by the time you's lot've finished with the poor blighters!'

'Ah, away widchya, you don't know feck all!'

'You should see one of them psychiatrists, you sicko!'

And that was how it went on the subject of dogfighting, Rankin's weakness.

Maybe she was right, thought the travelling man as he walked into the derelict pump room barely half a mile from Stanwell Moor.

About thirty men stood around in bunches in the huge brick and steel Victorian building which dwarfed them all. In the centre of the space was a fight pit, caged off with makeshift steel fencing sections, like the ones that form public order cordons at *legal* sporting events. They were supported by bales of straw, a few of which had been deliberately broken and scattered around the pit, serving to make the combatants unsure of foot – and soak up the shit, piss and blood.

Money was changing hands as the owners and their minders paid the bookies for their slips.

'*Pershendetty*,' said Rankin to one of the stewards. It was the only Albanian word he knew.

The fat middle-aged Gheg nodded and jerked his head. Rankin followed him, regarding Kemal Gozit's thick, pockmarked neck. *How did these animals get into this country?* he found himself thinking. Rankin knew a lot of bad men in the so-called travelling community, but they were models of good citizenship compared to the Albos.

23

'That's 'im!' Kribz and Driss blurted in unison as Jackson stepped unsteadily out onto the pavement. They watched him exchange a word with the doorman and hand him a tip as the cab pulled up, obscuring the boys' view from the other side of the street.

They got out of the car in a second, three pairs of feral eyes fixed on their quarry through ski-mask slits. Screwloose released his safety catch. Semi-crouched, they weaved around the cab as Jackson began to climb in.

The doorman saw them and knew something was wrong. 'Sir!' But the warning was too late. As Jackson slid into the vehicle his trailing left leg took the bullet just below the knee. The doorman, an out of condition ex-soldier, saw his chance to be a hero and lunged at Screwloose, but Driss had seen that coming and delivered a superb upward kick to the man's midriff. Kribz followed up with a crashing strike of a knuckle-duster-clad fist into his neck.

Jackson screamed. 'Drive! Drive!' The driver put his foot down just as the spiv used both hands to haul his shattered leg on board. And then the boys were back across the street, into their car and away. It had taken less than seventeen seconds.

And it took Kribz everything he had not to turn south across the river. Instead, he followed the plan and went north, up through Shepherd's Bush and onwards as far as he dared. Driss and Screwloose bailed within a few hundred yards of the attack and dropped underground at Ken High Street. Bastards would be home by now, thought Kribz, as he pulled onto a patch of waste ground in Harlesden. The story would be that they'd been carjacked by the Church Road Soldiers, and Harlesden was their turf.

Kribz jumped onto a bus with an unregistered travelcard. He sat on the upper deck and reflected. How wrong he'd been to tell Screwloose to dump his piece: sign of panic, overthinking stuff. He'd have to work on that.

24

Jackson was crying like a baby as the cab driver helped him into A&E at St Tommy's. He gripped his trouser leg to form a sort of tourniquet but could still feel warm blood squelching in his shoe. What worried him most was that he could not feel his lower leg: no pain at all. A pair of world-weary nurses got him onto a gurney, cut off his lower clothing and stuck a drip feed into his arm. A call went out for an emergency surgeon; the patient would go into shock before long and that was where the danger lay.

'Any idea who did this?' asked one of the nurses, more out of curiosity than any genuine need for information. Well-dressed white geezers didn't often get shot in the leg.

'No, probably after my Rolex, black bastards!'

The nurse saw that Jackson was still wearing his watch. 'Well, at least they didn't get it, it's a nice one.' She was now trying to keep him talking and conscious.

'Oh, thanks, they could have had the fucking watch if they'd just asked! Am I going to lose my leg?'

'Course not, you'll be fine, I'm sure,' – which she wasn't. 'We're going to have to call the police, Mr Jackson. Is there anyone else you'd like us to inform?'

Jackson was a divorcee and his teenage son lived with his ex-wife. The boy suffered with depression.

'No, no thank you, I'll let people know when I'm ready.' As he spoke the nurse whacked a dose of morphine through the canular in his arm as a young houseman bounded up and helped push the gurney into a side ward.

25

'Gimme that feckin' break stick, quick!' roared Rankin at Gozit who was supposed to be making sure of things. The betting had all been on a black pit bull the size of a pig, but the poor creature had met his match against Rankin's dog, a much smaller animal with a bigger heart and a fiercer temper that had its jaws locked on the back of its opponent's neck. The match was won and the Irishman wanted to save his fighter's energy for the next bout; he'd be quids in on a double or nothing bet.

He caught the stick that was tossed to him, a two-foot length of well chewed oak which he expertly rammed between the jaws of his winning animal, prising it free of its victim which, once loose, scuttled off to the other side of the pit, whimpering.

Rankin dragged his charge away, praising it loudly. 'Well done me beauty, feckin' good girl, the next bastard'll be a piece of piss!' He was getting on a roll; it wasn't difficult against this stupid bunch. They didn't care properly for their dogs, didn't feed, exercise, or rest them like they should. Rankin invariably started like this; on top. But then, just as invariably, he got ahead of himself and became less risk-averse, doubling down on his betting, chasing the money.

26

'Fucking Church Road Soldiers?!' Napper was on the phone to DC Aaron Briggs who'd the misfortune to have been allocated to the Knightsbridge shooting of an insolvency practitioner. Some rapid ANPR analysis, and an enquiry of the database that reputable car hire firms had to keep updated with their daily transactions had come up with the Braganza Boys. But the 'word on the street'– disseminated in coded lingo by Kribz via Snapchat from the upper deck of the bus he'd boarded – had countered that the car had been hijacked by a rival gang, the Church Road Soldiers of Harlesden, before the pop-pop.

This rumour had been carefully disseminated via some unconnected loudmouths to a few uniformed beat Bobbies and PCSOs who'd dutifully logged it on the Crimint system. It had also been given a big dose of credence when Driss called into the car hire office the next morning and gave Julie the rehearsed story that the motor had been forcibly nicked from him by a bunch of crazies, just after he'd dropped his mum off at her sister's place.

'They couldn't take on Braganza, especially if that fuckin' Screwloose was on board, would 'ave been a bloodbath mate, an' none of the blood would have been the B Boys'.' Napper spoke as if the Braganza gang was his favourite team, like he was a supporter with a scarf and an eye for the weekly league table of violence.

'What do you suggest then?' Briggs was out of his depth.

'This Church Road Soldiers shit is a load of bollocks. If that's the word on the street then it's smoke an' mirrors put about by the Bs, no doubt about it.'

'Gotcha, Naps,' said Briggs in what he thought was the appropriate vernacular.

Prat, thought Napper as he cut the call. The Cornishman sat back and rubbed his brow.

27

The thwack of Screwloose's shooter had gone unnoticed inside the restaurant: car backfire, blowout, or even a gunshot, so what? Whatever: the revellers were so caught up in themselves that they couldn't have given a collective fuck what had just occurred out in the real world. It was only when a stressed-out doorman had crashed in and bolted the doors behind him, feebly advising everyone to remain calm.

'Why, what's happened?' Palmer had asked. With half of Colombia up his hooter he was looking for action.

'There's been an incident outside, nothing to worry about,' hyperventilated the concierge, who had then shouted, 'Call the police!' to one of his colleagues.

Larssen made the obvious connection. *What had that arsehole done now?* Jackson couldn't even leave a restaurant without fucking up. She rose to investigate. The doorman collected himself.

'Sit down madam, your friend has just been shot but he's alright, got away in a cab. Nobody can leave here now, not until the police have attended.'

'What?!'

'Sit down, madam!'

By then Palmer was on his feet. This was exciting, too good to be missed.

Larssen, for once, had done as she was told, and Palmer followed suit. A semblance of discipline descended, brandies and coffees suddenly forgotten. Phones came out, calls were made. 'I may be late honey,' etc., etc.

Within minutes a minibus full of armed cops had rocked up. They didn't have far to come with the attentively patrolled Kensington Palace just down the road. The premises were secured, and full details of potential witnesses were taken from all the diners before they were allowed to leave. Nobody was under arrest of course, but the gravity of the situation encouraged compliance – and there was a reluctance to rock the boat; it's stupid to annoy a team of rozzers when you've got a couple of wraps in your back pocket or handbag.

Larssen had been first to volunteer her particulars and made sure she watched carefully as the others did so.

28

'Happy now? Cruel bastard.'

Oh, here we go, thought Rankin, always the same after a nice little evening of sport. Payback time. 'Ah, shut the feck up woman. We won, didn't we?'

'How much?'

The Irishman, lying on his back, allowed his belly to laugh. 'Aha! Gotcha missus! How much? You ask! Animal liberation gone out the feckin' window now, eh?'

'No, feck off Tom.' She could barely suppress a giggle. 'It's wrong what you're doin', but, you know, we need a new kitchen…'

'We don't need a feckin' new feckin' kitchen! Besides, if those feckin' asset strippers get their way we'll be after a caravan in Lyne, but don't worry, they come with *fitted* kitchens!'

Lyne was a Travellers' village not far away with permanently parked mobile homes, a tarmacked access road and quite posh facilities.

'I don't want to live in Lyne, I'd rather die. What will my sister—'

Then, to Rankin's relief, the Irish jig ringtone of his phone put paid to the bickering and the need for his lies – he hadn't won; he'd come away just under two grand down on the night, which had been nearly five at one point, so his recovery of three thousand quid on the final fight had restored some self-delusion.

'Feck, who the feck can that be?' It was not a question, more an announcement of his departure from the king-size bed. It was only 5 a.m. so probably not the bank or Jackson or any other arsehole intent on fucking him over.

'Hello?'

'Mr Rankin, you're a free man now, we done it.'

'Who's this?'

'You owe us man, big style. It's a pleasure doin' business wid you.'

And the line went dead.

'Who was that?' came Marlene's predictable question.

'Nobody, wrong number love,' replied her frowning husband.

29

Having spent the early morning distractedly going through various crib sheets and texts on interview techniques, Briggs now sat nervously at Jackson's bedside.

'Any ideas Mr Jackson?'

The morphine in Jackson's system did little to quell his irritation. 'Yes, many, the foremost of which is to tell you to fuck off.'

'I understand how you must be…'

'How I feel is irrelevant. What is relevant is that you lot have lost control of the streets. I was shot in the middle of Knightsbridge, not the Bronx, so my question is what are you going to do about it?'

'We've located the vehicle. Your attackers were members of a notorious gang known for drugs, violence and robbery….'

'Oh, good gracious, I'm shocked, I thought they were Boy Scouts. Have you arrested them?'

'Sorry?'

'Have you arrested them?'

'Not yet, Mr Jackson, we're still gathering and collating evidence.'

'Are arrests imminent?'

'Well, what I can say is that the investigation is ongoing and you can be assured that—'

'Look, I'm not really interested, to be honest. I've given your colleagues full descriptions of those scum, for what they were worth, they wore masks but they were black, that's for certain. You say you have their car and the incident on CCTV, so I'm sure you'll pick them up some time or another.' He sighed, reflecting on Briggs' question. 'As for ideas, no, I've got a lot of enemies, that's for sure, but none of them drive around in cars wearing masks and shooting people.'

'Don't be so sure.' The two men were startled. Neither had seen Larssen enter the room.

'Well, hello there, dear colleague, come to help me with my last will and testament?'

Briggs made a mental note of Jackson's sarcasm.

'It's just a scratch you pussy, a peashooter would have done more damage.' Larssen grinned as she said this, grabbing the opportunity for a bit of cruelty dressed up as black humour.

'They haven't assured me that I won't lose my leg, I'll have you know.' Jackson didn't expect sympathy but wanted it on record that he was quite worried and miffed by the recent turn of events. People like him lived in constant fear of being sued, harassed, arrested for fraud even, but being shot in the leg was definitely *off fucking piste*.

'Look on the bright side Jacko, you didn't lose your balls. Not literally anyway.'

'What do you mean?'

'Only joking.' The Dane then adopted a serious tone. 'I need you to sign these.' And with that she presented her prostrate colleague with a sheaf of papers.

'Are you being serious? I'm on fucking morphine and you're asking me to sign stuff!'

Even Briggs was incredulous. 'Excuse me madam, I was talking to Mr Jackson. I need you to leave.'

Larssen ignored the officer. 'These are important. Foreclosure documents against Rankin. We get this over the line and you'll be able to afford a diamond studded prosthetic.'

'Fuck off! Get her out of here officer, go on, prevent another offence – she's trying to fucking kill me!'

Briggs did as requested and Larssen cackled as she was ushered out of the room. 'I'll be back tomorrow to see what's left of you. Just don't let them amputate your hands, you need to hold a pen.'

'See what I have to put up with.' Jackson spoke to Briggs in a man-to-man manner once Larssen was gone. Not that he considered this besuited apology for a copper a man, but hey, any port in a storm.

'You work with her?' was all Briggs could offer.

'Purportedly. More like I work despite her. She fucking hates my guts.' Jackson was suddenly exhausted and seemed to drift off into an opioid world of his own. Briggs couldn't help thinking that a bullet in the leg wasn't all this man had to worry about. Numerous courses at detective training school told him to press on.

'I have to ask, Mr Jackson, could the woman who just visited you have anything to do with this?'

This jolted the wounded man. 'Don't be ridiculous officer, I was gunned down by a bunch of fucking blacks after my watch or wallet – and they fucked it up big style. If she wanted me dead you'd be speaking to the coroner and my next of kin.'

The detective nodded sagely. Jackson corrected himself.

'Actually no, you'd be on a missing person enquiry. There wouldn't even be a body to examine.'

The patient appeared to drift away again and Briggs thought it best to leave. The written statement could wait. As he walked out of the hospital, he couldn't help feeling that he was missing a trick. Something wasn't right, especially in the light of what Napper had told him. He felt like he was being tantalised by a shadow in the mist. *Come on,* it said to him, *forget detective training school, follow your guts mate, your feelings.*

Wow, he thought. Maybe I am a tecko after all.

30

Kribz, Driss and Screwloose were on the roof again, listening to Numbers prattling on about his Albanian mate. Except that Kribz wasn't really listening.

'Kribz, you listening bro? This boy's onto sumtin!' Driss immediately realised he'd made the mistake of raising his voice, attracting a glare from his senior and better. He backed down. 'Sorry, I just—'

Kribz decided on the pastoral approach. 'You gotta unnerstand, young brother, that there's a lotta other 'tings going on. We can't just drop everything to do your shit innit. Take it easy, just give it time fam.'

The po-po would come crashing into their mum's flat with a firearms search warrant and a quiz about what they'd been doing two nights earlier. It had to come. But he had all the answers and Driss was well briefed. It was just a matter of keeping Screwloose out of the picture. The lunatic could not be trusted to keep his cool with the fedz.

'Man, he got loads to unload, innit,' pressed Numbers, 'When you want to meet up?'

'Numbers, that's all, leave it.' Kribz voice had the edge of finality; the boy zipped his mouth.

Driss knew what his brother was thinking about. 'Any word yet bruv?'

'Nah, I put a call in yesterday, he ain't called me back. I'm thinking we was maybe too quick off the fuckin' mark.'

'Oh, fuckin' great!' chimed in Screwloose. 'I capped a suit for fuck all, innit, thought it would be worth the risk from what you said, what the—'

'Shut the fuck up Screwy, it's all under control innit. Rankin'll pay us one way or the other, we just saved his fuckin' skin. Those fuckers'll leave 'im be now, truss me.'

A silence descended. A little breeze whipped up, blowing dust and debris across the rough bitumen roof surface. Numbers tried again, 'Like I was saying—'

Screwloose lost it. 'Shut the fuck up bruv, or you'll go down the street the quick way!' The boy complied, convinced this time.

31

Rankin rarely watched television or listened to the radio or read newspapers. It was either shit or other people's problems and he had plenty of both of his own. So, the new day found him grinding through routines: feeding, repairing, moving stuff around and trying to avoid having ideas for the future. The last one was a relatively recent addition, and by far the most difficult.

It had occurred to him that throughout his life a huge proportion of his time had been spent planning, having ideas, setting himself future tasks and projects, all revolving around his home and business. No point anymore: best try not to think about it. No use trying again and again to accomplish the impossible.

He fed his most recently acquired guests. They were settling in fine and the pregnant bitch looked particularly healthy; she would probably drop within three weeks. His thoughts turned to their owners and the hostility they'd shown towards Jackson and Larssen. Then the phone in his pocket played its silly tune. He looked at the screen: withheld number.

'Hello?'

'Mr Rankin, you okay?' It was him again.

Without his wife nearby the Irishman could speak more openly. 'I'm fine son, and how are you on this bright morning?'

Kribz ignored the question. 'You heard the news?'

'What news, son?'

'The man called Jackson; word is that he got shot the other night.'

'What?!' Rankin felt an urge to insist that he had not been off his homestead for over a week, but he managed not to blurt.

'Yeah, the fedz think it was a robbery gone wrong. He took a bullet in the leg.' Kribz stopped there.

'Couldn't have happened to a nicer fella. Can't say I'm not pleased by this; wish they'd got him in the feckin' head. How do you know it was him anyway? There must be more than one feckin' thievin' trickster called Jackson in London.'

'Cos it 'appened at that restaurant innit, the one you was talking' about, where they all go on Friday nights to spend the money 'dey've t'ieved.'

Rankin genuinely appreciated the call. 'Okay son, thanks for letting me know, you've cheered me up, don't know how it's gonna help me though... hey, was that you on the phone yesterday mornin'?'

'Dunno what you're talkin' about, Mr Rankin.' Kribz said this deliberately quickly so that the answer was in the affirmative.

Rankin had to pause whilst a 737 roared not three hundred feet above his head. The ten second interruption was sufficient.

'Hey, if you boys did this, I want feck all to do with it. Not in my name.'

'Dunno what you're talkin' about Mr Rankin,' repeated Kribz, before he cut the call.

'Fuck man, is he fuckin' thick or what?' Kribz said to the others. 'Beginnin' to 'tink dis is gonna be harder than I thought.'

'You better be fuckin' jokin' bruv!' This was from Screwloose. He was sat with them in the Elephant flat and it was the first time that he'd seen Kribz doubting himself.

Kribz took a toke of his very big joint, and Driss did the same with his. Neither were bothered about Screwloose's moan-up, but both thought it was justified.

The gunman went on. 'You 'ad me use my piece on 'im, that was a big job innit. I need compensation innit.'

Driss saw the opportunity to take offence, be the big guy. He jumped to his feet.

'What d'yo mean fuckin' compensation? You're a Braganza Boy, remember, that's your fuckin' com-pen-sation, don' you forget it—'

'Ah, sit the fuck down bro, the man's right, we was quick enough to use 'im and 'is shooter so now we got to reassure 'im, innit.'

Driss sat down. Kribz went on. 'Hey Screw, youz a big member man, a bruv, an' we truss you innit, jus' give me a lickle time. The Gypsy'll come on board, trust me man.'

This had been unnecessary. Screwloose had already relaxed; he'd said his piece, put his displeasure on record, and that was enough, for now.

32

Larssen did her power walk into the open-plan office. 'He's fine,' she announced to quell the enquiries, most of which would have been malevolent. 'Might be losing some weight soon though, like a leg's worth.'

One of the secretaries audibly winced; another, braver, vocalised: 'What?!'

'Nah, only joking, he's fine. Attention seeking behaviour is what I think you call it in this nanny state of yours.'

The deskers looked around at each other. They weren't exactly close friends but were always united against this bitch.

Their eyes followed the Dane into her sound-proofed glass box and watched her throw herself into her chair and pick up her phone. The sprung door closed behind her, so they could hear nothing.

'I need a power of attorney done,' she ordered. The startled recipient of the call had to collect himself but did so willingly and very quickly. There were big bucks in this. It sounded like an in-house take-over, not to be missed.

'I take it that's Ms Larssen. Okay, I need some sort of scrawl, not much, won't be a problem.'

Larssen retained a stable of lawyers to whom she often outsourced the numerous grubby ends of the business. Form-filling, process serving, dots and commas boys, they queued to get up her arse. The firm paid well, so these guys jumped through hoops and broke rules.

But the lawyer on this occasion was Stuart Blake, and he never queued for anybody's arse – just made them think so – and could break not only the rules, but also the law. The call he'd just taken had been short but informative. Larssen had given the basic facts, tilted her way of course. Her business partner had had an attempt made on his life, no knowing when the next one would be, she had to protect her clients. Having gently replaced the receiver of the desk phone he fished his mobile from his tracksuit bottoms.

'Hey, you cunt, best you buy me a pint mate. There was a shooting in Knightsbridge, not your manor I know, but I might have a lead for you.'

Blake had become acquainted with his buddy within the cloistered surrounds of Oxford University. The tubby Oriel College law undergraduate hated the social confines of academia and preferred to do his drinking in the grittier parts of town, as did one of the college gardeners, a Cornish former soldier called Douglas Napper. The pair shared a liking for monstrous swilling sessions. A punch-up with the local pond life – yes, Oxford has plenty – often rounded off the evening.

They were kindred spirits: single, scruffy, bright; loners whose positions on various mental calibration spectrums licensed them to operate on the fringes of society. Neither minded one bit, perversely enjoying the isolation, the freedom of not giving a fuck.

Often when the pints were in double figures, Blake would try to cajole Napper into applying for a place as a student and studying law. Apart from not having any A-levels, the ex-squaddie wasn't interested. But he was bored with mowing lawns and pruning rose bushes and, when Blake graduated and departed Oxford, Napper applied to join the Metropolitan Police. They'd kept in touch and their friendship not only endured but developed, the legalistics of their respective professions providing a regular harvest of talking points and arguments. Before striking out on his own as a civil litigation fixer, Blake had been a trainee at a West End firm of crime solicitors whose portfolio of practices included representing bent coppers in court and at discipline proceedings. Napper had never fallen into that category, possibly because he'd always had his lawyer friend to advise him how to avoid it.

Anyway, the unlikely twosome were always looking for mischief of some sort, usually quite harmless but often teetering on the edge of becoming anything but. It was only a matter of time.

The Cornishman was in a greasy spoon in the Walworth Road. Apart from him and the staff it was empty. It was one of those places which was always empty. The cash receipts would tell a different story, for sure. The owners were eastern European and their taciturn ilk came and went regularly, but never tarried for cream teas and gossip.

The sound of Blake's voice always cheered him up a bit, a nice distraction on this occasion from thinking about Albanian money launderers.

'Hey, Stu, good to hear your insulting tones, me ol' mate! What could you possibly know about a shooting in Knightsbridge? And what makes you think I'd be remotely interested?'

The cop was of course very interested, and the strange possibility that a civil litigation solicitor knew something made him very much more so.

'My client works for the same company as the victim and not only is she not upset by what happened, she seems a bit miffed that her colleague didn't take the bullet between his fucking eyes, instead of in his leg.'

Napper's interest waned, remembering that Blake was possessed of a vivid imagination. He played along though.

'You suggesting your client had something to do with it?'

'Wouldn't put it past her, Doug, she's a fucking psycho. I can't tell you the things she gets me to do…'

'No, don't,' interrupted Napper. 'Look, I need a drink anyway so let's blow the froth off a few tonight and you can bore my tits off with your latest conspiracy theory.'

'Done. I like watching you yawn. Usual place, eight o'clock.'

'Done.'

33

'You did feckin' what? So, it *was* feckin' you!'

Kribz and Driss had decided to pay Rankin a visit, otherwise he wasn't going to appreciate what they'd done for him.

The old man could barely believe it. His immediate reaction was to put some serious distance between himself and these sun-kissed lunatics.

'It works Mr Rankin, trust us. All we need to do now is have 'im know where the message came from.'

'And get me feckin' arrested for attempted murder! I've a good mind to call the police on you myself!'

'You know you won't do that Mr Rankin.' Driss served this one up with a garnish of menace.

'You's threatenin' me now?' Rankin's disbelief climbed.

Kribz took over. 'No, Mr Rankin, we're helping you innit. I know this is 'orrible shit but it works and there's no way the fedz'll make a connection between us an' you.'

'Except that you're sittin' in my feckin' house at this very feckin' minute.'

'In the middle of nowhere.'

'What happens if you get followed here? And anyway, Jackson and that feckin' woman seen you here the other day.'

The boys had already thought this one through and had assessed the risk as negligible. 'Don't prove nuthin'. You're lookin' after our dogs, so what?' Driss made the point well. Kribz sought to summarise.

'Look, Mr Rankin. Let's be honest and up front about this. You're in deep shit, but you don't seem to be used to it. We're always in deep shit an' we fuckin' deal with it, every fuckin' day of our black fuckin' lives. It's the air we breev man innit. But let's be straight here, we're figuring if we can save your bacon, we can go on to do some cool business, you an' us, innit.'

It had long since dawned on Rankin that these blackies were deadly serious. He'd talked – too much, as usual – about his problems, about Jackson and his asset stripping outfit who, according to his otherwise useless accountant, liked going to a certain Knightsbridge restaurant every Friday night to gloat over the skins they'd ripped off their victims, how he suspected the banks and the lawyers and the fucking judges were all in on it... yes, he'd talked too much by far, and these boys had soaked up every word. And then acted. Because action was what these boys were about every day of their desperate lives. Rankin sat back in his kitchen chair and looked at the brothers. They regarded him with a sort of detached interest, like he was an animal they'd just infected with an experimental virus and were watching the disease develop.

The old Irishman knew it was his call. 'Okay, I suppose I've got two options. I can either kick the pair of you out now, kill and bury your dogs and deny ever feckin' settin' eyes on you, or I can say game on, let's go for it, nothin' to lose.'

Kribz smiled. 'The first one won't work, Mr Rankin.'

'The second one will though,' added Driss. 'Trust us Mr Rankin, we could swing this for you.'

'And us,' added Kribz, just to tie things up nicely.

Rankin considered the two young men, who may as well have been from outer space. He could barely believe they were sitting in his house. It was fortunate that whenever they came Marlene was out shopping in Staines; she would freak if she knew he was involving himself in these shenanigans.

'So, you're sayin' – and let me get this straight – if Jackson is persuaded to believe that gettin' shot was because what him and his firm is doin' to me, then he'll think twice, leave me alone and move on to shaftin' some other poor cunt.'

'Couldn't put it better myself Mr Rankin. Violence makes people listen, think, an' move on.' Kribz smiled almost sweetly as he said this. His tone had the sincerity of world-weary conviction. 'You gotta remember that the likes of Jackson are jus' grazers, grass eaters, they ain't meat eaters like us. Any sign of trub – an' he's had a fuckin' big one – an' they're off to the next field man. Like we keep sayin', trust us.'

Rankin nodded and swallowed, hard.

34

Even with her Machiavellian imagination, Larssen could not have guessed what was going down in Stanwell Moor. And had anyone told her she would not have believed it. Black boys trying to save a Gypsy? Nah, she knew enough about London sub-culture to know that didn't happen and besides, it would take a lot more than street kids with pop guns to stop what she was up to. In fact, Jackson's little leg wound had helped her leaps and bounds because leaps and bounds were what he could do none of now. Or ever again – they'd amputated his leg from just above the knee.

Feigning sympathy, the woman had visited. 'I'm sorry Jacko, we all are. I've spoken to the team and they agree that you will of course be given every support necessary, including a share of everyone's bonuses whilst you recover. This is terrible, what's happened to you. Terrible.'

Jackson could not even look at her. He just stared up at the ceiling, a huge frame supporting the bedcovers over his body, making his head appear small and vulnerable. He'd been crying. 'Okay, thanks, you can go now, before you start asking me to sign anything.'

'I wouldn't do that to you. You've had too much morphine.'

She was right of course and he was getting a steady dosage via the drip feed in his arm. Then Jackson's ex-wife and their teenage son walked in and the Dane made her excuses.

Having left the hospital Larssen called Blake. 'Have you done it yet?'

The lawyer was relieved that he had. 'Yes, of course, all ready for you, I'll have it sent over this afternoon.'

'Okay, well done.' They were talking about a set of papers – forged, of course – which effectively put Larssen in charge of the organisation pending Jackson's recovery. She now had full control. Missed opportunities were missed bonuses, she assured herself, and the bonus from the Rankin job would be a very big one. The Rankin homestead covered about 8,000 square metres. At current prices, once the runway realignment was signed, it would fetch £13 million. JLP Restructuring PLC had negotiated a 17.5% commission for the successful seizure of the plot. That was a nice £2.3 million coming their way. Take off a mill for expenses and staff bonuses and you were still left with 1.3 million – and Larssen wanted all of it.

35

Napper shook off his hangover with a three-mile jog, showered and took the train to Kennington. Once inside the faded shell of the copshop he logged on to the Crimint system, moving straight to the Knightsbridge shooting file. Briggs had done a predictably thorough job on the crime report, including a follow-up to the effect that the victim had lost his leg. The crime was classified as attempted murder stroke GBH.

Napper pondered on whether to input the intel he'd got from Blake the previous evening. It was so outlandish as to be almost plausible, but he would be pressed to reveal his source, which of course he would refuse to do. The ensuing palaver would attract attention he didn't want. Better leave it, he decided, perhaps work out some other way to have the line of enquiry included, without the risk of scrutiny.

But he called Briggs anyway, from his private phone.

'Hi Doug,' said the CID man. 'What you got for me?'

Napper gritted his teeth; he disliked the jumped-up little university knobber.

'The Knightsbridge shooting, word is that it was an inside job.'

'Whose word was that? Have you updated Crimint?'

'Confidential source and no, it's not good enough for a Crimint report yet, I'm still workin' on gettin' supportin' intel. As it stands it's too vague and single-stranded.'

'There's no such thing as a confidential source these days, Doug. You're living the past. All informants must be registered; you know that as well as I do. Now, who fed you this shit? I need to know.'

Arseholes like Briggs pulling rank never bothered the Cornishman. 'Yeah, okay, not sure of the geezer's proper identity yet, he calls me anonymous loike, but I know what 'is voice sounds like and he's given me intrestin' stuff before. I'll get back to you. Boi now!'

Napper giggled as he cut the call. That would scatter the pigeons. He knew Briggs would feel compelled to run checks on Jackson's company and any names of people who worked there. Probably a waste of time but at least it was now a waste of someone else's.

His next call was to Eric.

'Yo.'

'Yo.'

'What d'ya know?'

'What about, Mr Napper?'

'The Knightsbridge shooting.'

'Church Road Soldiers, innit. They stuck up the B Boys, nicked their car, done the job and dumped it. Simple as that.'

'Bollocks.'

'How d'you mean?'

'I don't buy that, Eric. The Soldiers could never take on the Bs. Come on, why are you feeding me this? Don't insult me, it's disrespectful. I need to have faith in you.'

Napper had his snout registered as Eric Talea, a 23-year-old with no previous convictions, born in London of Somalian refugee parents. He knew of course that Eric was no such person, and that was his business. Napper knew exactly who Eric was – unbeknownst to Eric.

'I'm gonna call you Eric. Eric Talea. You're as clean as a whistle with no form, no convictions. This is the way it works, goddit?' That was how it had gone.

The newly recruited informant had nodded and accepted his first white envelope. Napper had been watching the boy on and off for over a year and the kid fitted the bill. An outsider, keen to be accepted by any gang that came by, but never quite making the grade. The Cornishman had got alongside the boy in a backstreet pawn shop, the kind that sells burner phones and knocked off electrical gear. He'd got chatting and told him he had a little job for him, a quick fifty cash for delivering a parcel to a geezer in one of the tower blocks. Eric had been taken in by Napper's appearance; thought he was just a druggy vagrant scared of highrise estates heaving with gangsta boys, so he agreed, and a meeting was arranged in a café off the manor in adjacent Battersea. It was then that Napper had showed his warrant card and popped the question. It could have gone either way, fifty-fifty at best, and the cop was pleasantly surprised when the kid who he knew to be the one and only Screwloose, agreed.

He'd given him a leg up in the form of twenty wraps of variously graded cocaine he'd pilfered from equally various seizures. It would only have been burned, shame to waste it. 'Eric' had snorted half of it and used the rest as a currency to buy some credence, sold it off cheaply to become the 'go to' guy for a while.

Eric was only one part of the little world Napper lived in. But it wasn't a particularly little one. More like lots of little ones all joined up. That's what Napper did – join things up, join dots which had no real obvious connections. He knew very well that what Blake had fed him was probably wide of the mark: probably. But not definitely.

Break Stick

There was no such thing as 'couldn't' in Doug Napper's elliptical view of the world. There was no such thing as a road that led nowhere. Growing up in Cornwall with a penchant for organic substances, strange music and an expectation of exclusion, he had throughout his nineteen years before joining the army fashioned a glazed but colourfully stained view of the universe; subtle hues, refractions and reflections imbued and enhanced his perceptions. As an intelligent man he had insight, yes, but he congratulated himself on having what he privately called his 'outsight'. Some spreadsheet monkey in a human resources department would probably label it as 'breadth of perspective' or 'an ability to think laterally'. Napper knew better; 'breadth' and 'lateral' were measurable on scales; he was way off any scale.

It wasn't difficult. Devote every fibre of your being to something, no matter what it was, and everyone and everything else involved in that something – competitors, victims, detractors, whatever you want to call them – will fall away, clutching at their systems, their procedures, their norms, their calibrated standards. These things comprised the beds they slept in, the mattresses of their comfort zones.

Napper stayed free of all this. The likes of Briggs and the rest of the Metropolitan Police hierarchy provided him with not so much a backdrop, but more of a blank canvas on which to paint his expression, or impression... whatever. What the fuck ever.

Barking up the wrong tree never got anybody anywhere, but *climb* that wrong tree and you never know what you might see from the top of it; you can get a very good view of the right tree, for instance, and from an interesting angle. So, despite the high possibility that the Blake-Larssen tree itself bore nothing but white elephants and red herrings, Napper started climbing.

'Get your nose to the ground, Eric, and I'll get you something to sniff with it.'

They were standing in the entrance of the British Library, the sort of place where wannabe gangsters and eccentric cops looked like students and sociology tutors.

'That shooting was an inside job, whoever did it was paid by a Danish woman called Larssen. She was inside the restaurant when it happened, probably tipped off the shooter when their target was leaving.'

Eric just gawped and blinked a few times, at a loss as to how to react to this.

'Get weavin' son, find out who's been cavorting with tall, good looking white women, and I'm not talkin' about fuckin' baby mothers or brasses. This bitch is high class pussy an' somebody'll know somebody who'll start braggin' sooner or fuckin' later.'

Eric remained speechless as he stared at the paperback book Napper then handed to him. It was a used reference text on African architecture and wedged in its pages was a white envelope.

The pair parted company. Napper went into the library and Eric went out onto the street and away towards Kings Cross from where he would get the Tube back to the swamp. As he walked his pace quickened and by the time he got to the underground station it was all he could do not to run. But he didn't run, of course – that would end badly and probably in the boob. Encounters with Napper had thus far been interesting and profitable, but this recent development had sent the boy's small but complex mind reeling. He spent the journey home trying and failing to get his head around the possibilities. His recurring thought was that he'd been had over, short changed, used and duped. Same old, eh?

36

Rankin was preoccupied, to say the least; his initial horror had subsided, giving way to careful consideration and risk assessment. The possibility that the police would make a connection between himself and the Knightsbridge shooting was real, but his rudimentary knowledge of the rules of evidence told him that connections by association alone proved nothing.

His only persistent worry was that the boys themselves would get pulled in, roll over and drop him in the shit. *'He made us do it, said he'd kill our dogs if we didn't, innit.'* No, that wouldn't do it; street blackies don't take orders or threats from old white men. *'He paid us good cash; said he needed the dude taken out to save his business.'* Hardly; it would mean them having to plead guilty to use that weak excuse. And anyway, whichever scenario Rankin considered, it was their word against his. Bottom line: it was done, too late now, he would just have to grit his teeth and hope that Jackson had enemies queuing up to take him out and that the police would choose other roads to go down. So, he'd decided to look for ways to add to their range of choices; build a Spaghetti Junction, add some smoke and mirrors.

The old Irishman's thoughts, oiled by the bottle of Black Bush he'd been helping himself from before his wife got back from seeing her sister, were interrupted by the sound of a familiar vehicle. He hadn't heard it for a while and it always meant a challenge.

The huge Hummer still had its engine running as Rankin emerged resignedly from his front door. It was 7pm and already getting dark. The vehicle's occupants would not disembark until they were sure he was alone.

'Aye, come on, it's all clear.'

The driver shut the engine down and both front doors opened simultaneously. The two Albanians kept looking around as they walked slowly from the vehicle to where Rankin stood. It was like they were always expecting an ambush. Rankin shoved his fists in his trouser pockets and regarded the approaching pair with disdain. Christ on a bike, the giant flat screens they got along with their other ill-gotten benefits must have been pumping out the gangster shit big style.

'Pershendetty, boys.'

'*Pershendetje*, Tom, how are you?' It was the passenger, Kemal Gozit, who Rankin of course knew well; he'd never clapped eyes on the driver before.

'No feckin' better for seein' you Kemal. Who's this feckin' thug? Your brother, or your mother's latest boyfriend, or both?'

Rankin had no time for the Albo community's reputation. It was all a myth, like that of his own kind had been. They were scum; again, like a lot of his own kind, and deserved no respect – which they only treated as weakness anyway.

Kemal Gozit was used to Rankin's insults. And he knew it was all bluff. He had the gypsy by the bollocks and the streams of abuse were just the old man's way of keeping face, retaining a bit of self-respect.

'I need a dog, Tom, a good one.' The two had stopped five yards short of the front door. The Hummer driver kept looking sideways at his boss for cues, not wanting to fall out of step.

'Come in Kemal but tell your gorilla to get back in that ridiculous feckin' vehicle.'

Gozit jerked his head at the driver, who shrugged and complied. Rankin turned and walked into the house, the Gheg followed.

'Tea or whiskey?'

'Both.'

'Sit down, I might have something for you.'

Mugs were filled with fortified brew and chair legs scraped on the marble floor as the two men took seats facing each other across the kitchen table.

Rankin had not expected this visit, but knew he was due one and had not been looking forward to it. But the afternoon's whiskey and recent events had given him a fluidity of thought.

'Aye Kemal, I might have a dog for you, but it'll be at a price.'

'A price? And what kind of price would that be Tom?'

'Well, I know it won't cover the money I owe you, but it'll go a good way towards it. She's a good fresh bitch, hungry as fuck, not long since had a litter.'

'Sounds good,' nodded the Gheg, 'I want you to set up another fight night also, within the next few weeks.'

Rankin didn't need this, there had been complaints after the last event at the old waterworks and he knew the venue would not be available for many months to come, if at all.

'Can't do that Kemal, you lot didn't clean up after you last time and my contact at the place is not speaking to me, it'll be months before we can get back in there.'

'So, what are you going to do about then Tom?' The Albanian let some menace creep into his voice.

'I'm going to do feck all about it you feckin' Albo bastard, I'll have you know...'

'Whoa! Stop right there Tom my friend, that ten thousand pounds you owe me is overdue, very overdue, here's your chance to clear it one day!' Gozit's raised voice unnerved Rankin for a second; the Gheg was excited; he had a plan.

Quickly composing himself, Rankin replied, 'What have you got in mind?'

We use your place. Right here. You've got plenty space and the noise of the jets will drown the noise – I've worked it all out.'

Rankin chucked another couple of slugs of whiskey into the mugs, smiling ruefully as he did so to mask his rising anger.

'You *have* been thinking, haven't you, you sly fucker.'

'I also have problems Tom', was the Gheg's quick response, 'I need a tournament, and soon, or I'm going to need that money back from you even sooner.'

Rankin was at a crossroads. He could lose his Irish temper, kick this foreigner out and let the worst come to the worst, or he could give some breathing space to the crazy idea that was working its way to the front of his alcohol-addled mind.

He sat back in his chair. Stretched, clasped his hands behind his bald head and surveyed the ceiling. The crazy idea was having a life-or-death fight with an established principle – *if you give in to threats from Albos they'll be back for more, they'll bever leave you alone.*

'Okay, give me a week or two, I'll see what I can do.'

He was still leaning backwards, talking like he was reading from a fresco on the plasterwork above him.

The Albanian leaned forward, putting his elbows on the table. 'No Tom, I need agreement now, this minute, will you do it or will you not do it? The exact date can wait for a few days, but I need you to agree… how d'you say… in principle.'

Rankin mirrored Gozit's move, leaning forward to put his own elbows on the table, squaring up. He was twenty years older than the Albanian but that didn't bother him. He let some whiskey-driven menace put an edge to his own voice.

'Your command of the English language is getting better Kemal.' A short pause. 'Okay, you've got a deal, I'll fix it up.'

That softened things a little. Gozit nodded and hauled himself to his feet with his fat fists on the table for assistance.

'Okay Tom, now show me the dog.'

37

'It was all a waste of time bro, we put our necks on the line for nuthin', fuck all.'

'What d'you mean Screw? What you talkin' about? Stop chattin' shit man.'

They'd been discussing, in a desultory sort of way, the Knightsbridge job, as it was now known. A week had passed and Driss was concentrating on giving his brother time to think whilst at the same time keeping Screwloose focused and patient.

His response to the latest moan came out in a tired, unconvincing voice. The pair were waiting for Kribz who was out picking up a bag of sample wraps from the Albanian introduced by Numbers. It had been a condition that he'd go alone, and such conditions were never broken.

'We shoulda gone with 'im bro, innit. Could be takin' a cap from the Seven by now. We don't even know that Numbers well enough to have Kribz rock up on a meet on his own. Might be all a trick, man, he could be one of them...'

'Ah shut the fuck up! My brother – our brother – can take care of himself, and he don't need a piece, neither.'

Screwloose took this badly. 'What d'yo fuckin' mean by that bro? You sayin' I can't fight without a piece, that it?'

The pair were sitting in Screwloose's squalid room, slumped at either end of the unmade bed. Driss was rolling a spliff and paused, gritted his teeth and closed his eyes. The question was a good one; he'd spoken without thinking. He sighed, opened his eyes and sought to make good.

'Sorry bruv, I didn't mean it personal, all I'm sayin' is that sometimes you gotta be cool, relaxed, not go blazin' in.'

'What? Like we did the other night?'

Another fair question.

'That had to be done, it was an opportunity that couldn't be missed and the payday'll come. You gotta 'ave faith bruv.'

But he wasn't convincing, and Screwloose sucked his chops. 'Tchsssst.'

38

Kribz's meeting with Numbers and his Albo went okay. The guy's name was Mergin and was just a kid, a Gheg version of Numbers. The three met on the mezzanine balcony at Waterloo Station and Kribz greeted them with the bonhomie of a fellow student on a visit to the UK capital. He had on his back a rucksack and on his head an Alitalia baseball cap.

'Hey guys!' he whooped. 'Whaddaya know?'

Numbers and Mergin cottoned on and exchanged high fives with their 'old buddy'. The CCTV cameras glazed – bored – and swiveled away inside their opaque black semi-domes. Hidden in full view was the name of the game.

The three boys bounced into the Sports Bar at the end of the walkway. Arsenal were playing and all eyes were on the screens. The exchange was easy, over three bottles of Peroni and the purportedly shared fascination of some pictures on Kribz's phone. They parted company within ten minutes, high fives again.

Kribz plunged the wraps inside his rucksack; it was newly bought and contained nothing but some shabby clothes and travel books from a charity shop in the Old Kent Road. The whole shabang could be dumped in a trice. But no such need arose and the gang leader tapped quietly on the door of the flat Screwloose shared with someone he called his sister but who'd never been seen. Once inside he unshouldered the little rucksack and fished out the bag of wraps. A bit of quality control ensued, rather too enthusiastically on Screwloose's part. Driss nodded his approval – as if his brother needed it – and there followed affirmative grunts all round about continuing the association with Numbers and his new Albo buddy.

But this was all run-of-the-mill stuff, just another day in the office; there was a great big stinking elephant in the room that needed to–be dealt with – they had to move quickly, take the initiative, or the Knightsbridge job would be wasted, along with the chance to get into bed with Rankin. A plan emerged, painfully.

39

The wheels of the day was a modest Astra, grey, no trimmings: *stealth, bruv, innit*. Having picked it up from the rental shop about an hour earlier Kribz had driven back home and collected his brother, and the pair had gone off for Screwloose. It had been a bit of a debate as to whether to take the gunman. They'd decided 'for', but without the gun bit. The three were now sat up in a loading bay over the road from the main entrance of St Thomas' Hospital, expecting to get moved on any minute. Screwloose had followed instructions and left his piece at home. He was there for the ride only, to make him feel included, and sat as usual in the back.

'Is he deffo in there bruv?' asked Driss.

'Yeah, just about certain; Mum told me.'

The younger brother nearly choked on the cigarette he was smoking. 'Mum?! What the fuck 'as *she* got to do with it?' He coughed it as loud as he could whilst trying to catch his breath.

'One of her jobs is in there innit, twice a week. Calm down, I just mentioned if she knew of any shooting victim recently, since Massive, that had been taken in an' she said yeah but told me that it was a fat white dude, *nuttin' to do wid dem stupid boys an' their guns shooting at one another'*. The last part of this came out as an impersonation of Molly's Jamaican twang.

Driss had recovered his breathing and sat back, blinking. 'Oh well, s'pose it's handy havin' family in high places.'

'Yeah,' agreed Kribz. Screwloose remained silent, keeping watch through the rear windscreen. Until he said, 'Hey, bruvs, I think we gonna get a tap.'

A PSCO was approaching on foot, no doubt summoning her nerve to ask the boys to move their illegally parked vehicle. She didn't have to: Kribz started the engine. He was just about to move off when Driss piped up. 'Hey, wait, look what's just come out!'

Kribz followed his brother's sightline and saw her. 'Fuck, it's that bitch what was wid 'im. She must have just visited him, innit.'

They hung back and observed Larssen stride to the kerb and hail a black cab. Screwloose was watching too, wide eyed, mouth shut.

The PCSO had her knuckle tentatively raised to rap on the window, but that was as far as she got. The car moved off, joining the traffic about three cars behind the cab which now carried the Dane.

'What are we gonna do bruv?' asked Driss.

'See where she goes innit. This might just be an answer to the problem. There was no way we was gonna get into that 'ospital man, too much risk.' Kribz was right, of course. They'd thought about fronting it, just barging in, but that would have been reckless. They'd discussed getting some cleaners' outfits to wear and slip in under cover, but again, dodgy. The chances of finding the patient without raising suspicion were low. This was a real break.

The gap between them and the cab shortened to just one vehicle and Kribz was keen to keep it like that. He needn't have worried. Larssen had no reason to suspect she was being tailed and was too busy on the phone to notice anything untoward.

'I've just been to see him. He's fuckin' livid,' she laughed.

On the other end was Blake, who did not laugh. 'I'm not surprised. He's just been reduced to the status of monopod *and ex*-boss of his own company. I wouldn't be too happy either.'

She spoke through a sneer. 'We all deal in unhappiness, Stuart, it's our *raison d'etre*.'

Blake was about to say 'Speak for yourself,' but Larssen cut the call and leaned forward to instruct the driver. She was home.

'Stop here, please.'

They were in Notting Hill and the B boys, still one car behind, were inconspicuous. The gentrification of the village had not eradicated its still significant black population and three spades in a Vauxhall Astra, although always worth a routine stop, didn't warrant urgent police attention. Unlike what happened next.

The boys were masked up and out of the car as one. It took about three seconds and they were all around her on the stone steps of her Georgian terraced number. Even the ice queen Larssen was alarmed. She didn't scream though – just froze, like ice queens do.

'Leave the Gypsy alone!' Kribz spat the words into her face. Driss and Screw rasped 'Yeah!' and 'Heed!' close into her ears. She just stood there, rictus grin on face, Yale key in hand. And they were gone, in half a dozen leaps and bounces, down the steps, across the pavement, into the Astra and gone. Ten seconds, tops.

The engine had been left running, the risk had been high. The boys tossed out their black balaclavas; they were going to get stopped for sure.

Kribz hurled the car round the first few corners and then slowed, steadied, sedated his driving. Nothing was said until they were up on the Harrow Road, in heavy traffic, heading out north-west to Harlesden. Kribz had the Church Road Soldiers in mind if anything went wrong. Just delivering a car to them, or some smoke and mirrors shit like that. If the Astra's reg number had been clocked by that bitch it sure wasn't gonna be seen heading south of the fucking river, was his thinking. They would park up in NW10, head home separately on public transport and have a young bro recover the car *manyana*.

'Fuck, man, that should get tings movin' innit,' laughed Driss, breaking the silence.

His brother agreed, laughing. 'Yeah, bruv, like we told the old man, we do stuff there and then, on impulse, no overthinkin' innit!'

The brothers were pumping, high on that gear called adrenalin. Screwloose sat in the back, eyes still bulging, mind boggling.

'You okay, Screw?' It was Kribz, eyeing his quiet passenger in the rear-view mirror.

Driss answered for him. 'He's fine bruv, prob'ly jus' wishin' he'd 'ad his piece.'

'Thank fuck he didn't!' roared Kribz, and both brothers were suddenly in stitches. Screwloose grinned, laughed along a bit, but didn't join the banter.

40

'May I speak to Muz Larssen please?' The caller's attention to politically correct detail did nothing for his pronunciation. But the receptionist at JLP, a pleasant lassie with a degree in theatre studies, thought him rather cool, especially when he identified himself as *Detective* Aaron Briggs.

Briggs was politely put through. 'Larssen.'

'Hello Muz Larssen, I think we met last week at St Thomas's Hospital, I'm Detective Briggs, Metropolitan Police C.I.D., Violent Crime Task Force.' He never included his full title which featured the lowly rank of 'Constable'.

'Yes, go on,' replied Larssen, cagily.

'I'm investigating the brutal attack on your colleague Mr Jackson, and I need to see you in the course of my enquiries. When would it be convenient for us to meet?'

Larssen had not reported the previous day's incident on the steps of her home; she was still trying and failing to find a mental silo in which to drop and forget it. The morning had been conveniently preoccupied with all sorts of other nastiness, mostly with her as the instigator. This call dragged the small law and order issue to the front of her mind.

'Oh, right. Okay, come here when you like, I suppose.'

Briggs was about to suggest a time and date, but didn't get in.

'Actually, yes, come today at 3pm please. There's something else I'd like to tell you about, probably not connected but I need something done about it.'

41

Massive was in the gym. He'd given up thinking about being a lone wolf and shedding the gang game. He'd tried, but success would have meant moving out of Brixton and there was no way he could see himself ever doing that.

A couple of the elder D7 men got alongside him and the three of them dabbled in some peripheral business. Staying away from drugs, they found themselves concentrating on firearms. Not good things to get caught with but dealing in weapons didn't involve the complex supply chain that white powder and weed demanded. You got a piece, held it, got a buyer, sold it, simple as that. Only your supplier, your buyer and you – three people. And no youngers involved, that was another bonus. Kids were necessary to shift drugs, but they were a real liability, the weak links who always found out more than they needed to know, and then could never keep their mouths shut. But you didn't need them in the armaments business, nor did you need a big gang of nutters to protect your turf. Just a couple of real brothers to have your back, that was all.

The D7 boys had given lip service to loyalty but had inevitably drifted off. Formed loose affiliations elsewhere on the pretext of widening business interests, started up little 'sub-gangs', recruited school kids for county lines: the same old morphing of allegiances, promises and *'Yeah, I'll get back t'ya bruv,'* etcetera. Yeah, right.

The big negro pumped the iron. Yes, that was it, Massive was a negro. He had always felt that his African genes, transported from Ghana to Jamaica a hundred and fifty years previously, had remained pure. The wound in his leg had healed perfectly, and the muscle he'd piled on in the process of rehabilitation was significant. The motivation for doing so was even bigger. The concentration required by the intensity of his workouts had energized his thoughts, realisations, insights.

42

Three days later the pups were born. Rankin had known it was coming and had made sure Ciara had plenty of fresh bedding and clean water. He looked down into the little enclosure where she lay, exhausted but vigilant. There were five of them, little beauties, top class brindle American pit bulls. Their eyes were barely open, their faces pictures of blissful innocence as they suckled their mother's teats.

Rankin set about cleaning up what was left of the placenta – mum had eaten most of it – and provided the new kids on the block with fresh bedding, food and water. He reckoned that, once weaned, the pups would fetch a grand apiece, maybe two. There would have to be a discussion about how that money would be divvied up but that was way down on the Gypsy's list of priorities. He went back into the house and put the kettle on, looking furtively at the half-empty bottle of Black Bush before averting his gaze. Far too early.

He burned his lips on the first sip of Tetley, put down the mug and picked up his phone.

'Hello son, you have five new gang members.'

'Yeah? Are they okay?' Normally, Kribz would have been annoyed by the gang reference, but the good news was more important.

'They're fine. Come over and have a look for yourself.'

'Yeah, tomorrow maybe, that okay?'

'Come about two, after my old lady's gone out, then we can have a chat.'

'Okay Mr Rankin, see you 'bout two tomorrow.'

'Fine, and feckin' call me Tom, will you.'

'Okay Tom.' Kribz was chuckling. The two cut the call simultaneously.

Rankin exchanged the phone for the mug and walked back out onto his land. It was just after ten and all his jobs were done. He understood canine noises and the odd smattering of barks and yelps were nothing but jousting and bickering. Occasionally fights broke out in the collective pens and separations had to be enforced, solitary confinements imposed. The old Gypsy was the alpha male, his word irrefutable law.

He walked, stiffly through age, to where an injured animal was recovering in what he called his sickbay. The dog was a big Staff-Husky cross breed with sharpened teeth. His name was Nero; a misnomer, for an albino.

'How are you this fine morning, me ol' fella?' enquired the alpha male.

The dog got slowly to his feet and limped to where Rankin stood on the other side of the wire mesh fence. The two regarded each other for a few seconds, looked each other up and down. Then the animal turned and limped back to its straw bed, greetings exchanged.

'Aye, I wish all the animals were like you Nero. Honest. Specially the feckin' two-legged kind.'

43

Kemal Gozit spat the lump of tobacco he'd been chewing, followed by a short stream of brown saliva, onto the kerbside of Askew Road, Shepherd's Bush. He walked into the shed which had once housed a tyre shop but was now a car wash where customers paid a range of prices for a range of services, from full valet at fifteen quid down to quick rinse for a fiver. The five workers did one car at a time, each working on different parts of the vehicle. It looked impressive. What would have also been impressive to even the most indolent investigator was the throughput of hard cash. It would look like the hard-working but under-qualified staff were consultant brain surgeons, not sponge-wielding Albanians.

Nail bars, greasy spoons and car washes were among the favourite street level money rinsing conduits in the UK. Of course, at nowhere near the dizzy heights of the banks and accountancy firms, but the principle was the same: an inflow of ill-begotten gains got mixed in with legal income, tax would be paid on the total and then the apparently spotlessly clean bottom line would be carved up, invested in foreign accounts, or disbursed on respectably receipted purchases.

'*Pershendetje*!' shouted Gozit at everyone – it was a demand for respect, rather than a greeting. The workforce responded with lowered eyelids, nods and mumbled replies. They were terrified of him. Their cowed body language was that of a bunch of slaves, trafficked by a man who had their balls – and passports – in the grasp of his meaty hand.

Gozit marched through the shed and into what passed as a rear office. He drew out a bunch of keys that was nearly the size of his fist and let himself into the inner sanctum of his operations. Closing the door behind him he pulled out his phone and called Rankin.

'Kemal.'

'Hello Tom, how are you?'

'Fine, what d'you want?'

Gozit reddened: when would this Irish piece of shit start showing some respect?

'I need the show put together for next week. That dog you loaned me needs blooding.'

'Is that the only reason?'

'No Tom, it is not the only reason, there are other reasons, which I don't have to give you.'

Rankin knew he was on the back foot here; the deal had been struck and he had no choice. To save some face he tried to bully the Albanian with fancy English. 'Would any particular day and time meet with your approval?'

Gozit digested this before replying. 'Any time next week, or I will *disapprove*.'

The Gypsy couldn't help liking this riposte and struggled to suppress a chuckle.

'Okay Kemal, call it done. Oh, hey, would you be interested in looking at a litter of pups to invest in? The owners are clients of mine. They might be up for getting rid of them quick, if the price is right.'

The Albanian was pleasantly surprised by Rankin's approach; requests to do business were usually the other way round – how the tables had turned for the better.

'Er, yeah, okay, maybe, so long as you can take care of them.'

'That goes without saying you fat fecker,' said the Gypsy, saving more face with the insult.

Gozit gritted his teeth and remained polite as he ended the call. Taking a deep breath, he opened a battered filing cabinet and took out a bunch of grubby unpaid invoices to have sight of what lay beneath them: a 9mm Luger semi-automatic pistol, fully loaded. Something told him it was about time he started carrying it.

44

Larssen looked at the clock and began mentally preparing for the police officer's visit. What would he know that could help her? That was her angle. Certainly not how she could help him. It didn't occur to her that this was any more than a routine visit by a thick policeman ticking the boxes. She had been at the restaurant at the time of the shooting and therefore had to be visited. It didn't matter one jot that she had seen nothing. The cops in Denmark were the same: plodders with routines, shift patterns, salaries and pensions. She'd occasionally wondered why such people engendered so much traditional respect. But the recent encounter on her doorstep had been difficult to pigeonhole; the incident had bothered her, so she was on the hunt for answers.

Gypsy. What Gypsy? She was sufficiently conversant with the English language to know what a Gypsy was – the Danish equivalent was the *sigøjner*; a musical and colourful travelling culture that had suffered murderous official discrimination, almost on a par with their kindred Roma in Nazi Germany. But what had that to do with her? She had had no dealings with Gypsies, and with good reason: they were invariably poor, itinerate scum who owned nothing but horse-drawn caravans, mandolins, and hordes of filthy children.

But it had to be *them*: the young black men she'd seen at Rankin's homestead! They had a fucking share in the place! They'd shot Jackson! Her next thought was that if she wasn't careful, she'd be next… they knew where she lived!

Larssen didn't do fear; it was an emotion she preferred to instil in others – big style and proper – but a shiver went down her long spine. Suddenly, she looked forward to seeing this police officer who stressed the word *detective* at the front of his name.

45

Sat on his unmade bed in his tiny room, Screwloose was cleaning his piece, caressing it lovingly, like he was administering a massage. It was a Beretta 9000, fitted with a twelve-round magazine for 9x19mm cartridges. He'd acquired it from the 'go to' source of weapons: the Lithuanians in Canning Town. It had been difficult. Not that getting hold of a gun in London was very difficult, because if you knew what you were doing it wasn't, but because Screwloose didn't really know what he was doing, and found doing things by himself difficult, and therefore buying a shooter more so.

It had cost him three hundred quid and he reckoned it was the best investment ever. The dividends, in terms of respect, power and self-confidence, were enormous. From being passed around from one gang to the next like an unwanted orphan, he'd become a valued asset, albeit one which had to be kept on a tight leash. And he was tight with the Braganza Boys – for the time being at least. It didn't matter if they dumped him. He was safe in the knowledge that he could move onwards – and perhaps even upwards – any time he chose to.

The gun had given way to a new insight for Screwloose, a clarity of thought which invigorated him. He watched a lot of movies and had even taken to a modicum of reading. Nothing too heavy of course – it would take him months to get through a three-hundred-page crime yarn – but he took it all on board, his vivid imagination transporting him into the plot sequences. This stuff was fact, man, about real people, and he, Screwloose, was real. Innit.

46

Jackson was in a bad way. He'd been shifted to a rehabilitation ward and his main attendants were now not doctors but physiotherapists and prosthetic technicians. He was in constant discomfort which regularly gave way to pain, sometimes severe. To quell the tears, he tried to console himself; he was still alive. He'd given little thought to the shooting, having wholeheartedly attributed it to a botched robbery. Whether or not he was in some sort of denial didn't occur to him.

His phone vibrated on the bedside cabinet. He painfully reached for it; the screen said 'Bitch'.

'Yes, I'm still alive and no, you're not in my fucking will.'

'I know who did it.'

'Why, because you paid them?'

Larssen ignored this. 'It has something to do with that fucking Irishman, those black guys we saw at his place. I'm sure it was them and now they know where I *live*!'

Absorbing this would have been hard enough, but the disorientating effect of hearing a distinct tone of worry in Larssen's voice further muddled his cognizance.

Silence.

'Did you hear what I just said?' The Dane's voice was still slightly raised, in both volume and pitch.

'Yeah, I heard you.'

'Tell me something then; does Rankin know any Gypsies?'

Jackson wasn't sure how to respond to this, so he just co-operated: 'Yes, probably, given that he fucking *is* one.'

'How the hell do you know that?'

'I don't know how I know, but it's obvious, he's what they call a settled traveller, there's loads of them in that area.' Jackson paused, but then added, 'Don't you know any anything? Don't you ever do any research?'

Larssen ignored the weak dig. 'That confirms it then; the same ones attacked me outside my door yesterday, threatened me, told me to leave the Gypsy alone, so what do you think we should do about it?'

'Oh, it's back to *we* now, is it? Funny that, I thought I'd become surplus to requirements.'

'That's business, this is different....'

Jackson was warming to this, 'No, it's not different. Rankin is one great big cash cow which, if you're right, has grown teeth and is coming round to bite our arses – actually, no – from now on, *your* fucking arse!' He winced as the exertion of this exchange sent a wave of pain down his left leg, including the missing bottom half of it. 'Have you notified the police?' he continued, after it had passed.

'Not yet, but I have a detective coming to see me this afternoon, about what happened at the restaurant'

God help the poor sod, thought Jackson. 'Right, just be careful what you say to this *detective*... if it's a chap called Briggs he's a total prat, wouldn't be able to find his own arsehole with a mirror, but just stay onside. We're the victims of this shit, remember. What we do makes us unpopular, but we're still entitled to police protection. These animals are killers.'

Larssen was slightly soothed by Jackson's instinctive common sense, and her respect for him rocketed upwards to the dizzy heights of zero. He was right: these lunatics needed to be arrested and if Rankin was involved, which he surely was, then he should go to prison with them. Wouldn't do the asset-stripping of his business any harm at all, she thought. Probably make it easier, in fact. Wouldn't have a leg to stand on.

That last of these venomous thoughts made her nostrils flare; she couldn't resist vocalising. 'For once I agree with you. This is an opportunity. We get the Irishman locked away and he won't have a leg to stand on.'

The invalid heard the spiteful smile. 'Very funny,' he said, and hit the red icon.

47

'Mr Napper, we need to meet up, maybe I got sumthin' for yuh.' Eric made the call from one of his numerous burners, number withheld to make double sure.

Doug Napper had been busy with other stuff and this caught him flat footed.

'Oh, hi Eric, nice one mate, okay, er, two o'clock today, same place as before?'

'See you there Mr Napper.' End of call.

The policeman was becoming more impressed by his snout. He'd never really had much hope for him: an outside bet – a long shot, so to speak. But the boy seemed to be rising to the occasion.

Same routine; tutor-stroke-mentor meets struggling student at British Library, well clear of the swamp. They sat on high stools, facing each other across a bench table in the public cafeteria.

'Whatcha got then Eric?'

'The tall woman, you said she was Danish or German or sumtin', the word is that a couple of dudes are gonna whack her, an' she ain't no brass or baby mother, bruv – er, sorry, Mr Napper.'

'I don't mind 'bruv', Eric,' said Napper, waving away the apology. 'Tell me more.'

'Well, like I say, a couple of gangsta boys is after her, sumtin' 'bout a deal goin' wrong, innit. I ain't got close enough yet, but the whole ting's kinda strange, sumtin' to do wid dogs goin' missin' an' stuff. Like I say, I ain't got to the bottom yet, an' I gotta stay cool, innit, the boys I'm chattin' 'bout are into some serious stuff.'

This sounded like a string-along to Napper, but he played the game. He was happy that Eric wasn't making it up – he knew the boy well enough to make that risk assessment – but he was getting held back on, not getting the full story, no doubt about it.

'Okay Eric, this sounds like good stuff. When's the next instalment?'

'Eh?'

'When you gonna drip feed me the next fuckin' episode son?'

'I ain't drippin' you, man, dis is all I got jus' now, that's all, but there'll be more to come, truss me innit.'

'What d'you know about dogs, Eric?'

'Fuck all man.'

'What kind of dogs d'you think this is all about?'

'Pitbulls prob'ly, I dunno.'

'There, you see, you *do* know, you know enough to know that your koind down in the swamp don't fuck about with poodles or spaniels.'

The kid's eyes were down, lids hooded. Napper knew there was a lot more going on in that little ebony head than its owner was letting on about.

The cop passed over a shabby paperback novel, charity shop number about British slavery in the Victorian era. He noticed the boy's hand tremble as he took it carefully, deliberately, without snatching. 'Go on, fuck off.'

Eric slid off his stool and made a hash of leaving, faltering before finding the right door.

Napper stayed put for a few minutes, toying with his empty coffee cup. Dogs? Pit bulls? Hmmm.

His left nipple told him someone wanted to talk. Absentmindedly, he took the vibrating phone out of his shirt pocket and looked at the screen. It was Briggs.

'Aaron.'

'Doug, how's it going, you okay?'

'Yes. Aaron, I'm good. What may I do for you on this foine afternoon?'

'Was just wondering if you'd picked anything up about the Church Road Soldiers on your labyrinthine network.'

Napper liked that: *labyrinthine*, nice one. 'No, but I've just picked up some info to the effect it had nuthin' to do with that bunch of Harlesden halfwits.' The Cornishman paused, gathered some patience. 'Look, somethin' might be comin' through. I got a source on our manor who says the shooting had something to do with dogs, prob'ly pit bulls.'

Briggs suddenly found himself questioning Napper's sanity. The guy had always been known as a bit of an eccentric, but this was off the map. Either that or he was having the piss ripped out of him.

'Yes, right, okay Doug, let me know about the next bit of red-hot info. I'll wait to hear from you. Bye!' The educated detective was not rude by nature but ended the call abruptly. Putting up with idiots on his side of the fence was not a box he was expected to tick. He looked at his watch: time to head for Notting Hill, a pleasant change from south London, the shithole they called the swamp.

48

'What the fuck did you do that for, you blithering idiot?'

Blake knew Jackson, had helped him set up his company, before Larssen had arrived on the scene, and had been expecting this call. He'd forged Jackson's signature, several times, on the power of attorney papers. Totally deniable, of course, as would be Jackson's denial of having signed them himself. But the denials of a man about something he did whilst on a morphine drip could never amount to reliable testimony.

'What are you talking about?'

'You've given her full control of my company and in particular a multi-million pound deal. I'm banged up here minus a leg and facing fucking bankruptcy. I hope you're fucking proud of yourself!'

The lawyer, alone in his shambolic office, gathered himself. These barking calls were always worse than their bites. He possessed a natural nimbleness, an instinctive readiness to dodge and parry.

'You signed the papers old chap; all I did was lodge at court.'

'Bollocks, you fat bastard—'

Blake took control. 'No, no, no, Jacko, don't fucking start all that crap, think it through. If you allege that I forged your signature you'll get nowhere. If you perhaps say that, just possibly, you may have signed those papers when you were off your tits on morphine while they were busy hacking your leg off, then you may just get somewhere.'

Jackson absorbed this. The fat bastard was right. With a bit of care he could turn this round, overturn the POA, take back what was his and move on.

'Who'll help me with this?'

'Well, *I* obviously can't. Clear conflict of interest. You've got to find yourself another lawyer, me ol' mate.'

'Who do you recommend to get me out of the shit you've got me into, then?'

'I can't recommend anyone. Like I say, conflict of interest. Larssen would sue me.'

'Pity for fucking *you* Blakey.'

'Ta-ta Jacko.'

Blake had had enough and ended the call. He cracked open a Stella Artois, smirking. These animals were all the same, bright but desensitised by greed. The upside was that they never complained, never went squealing to the authorities. They effortlessly accepted that all was fair in their filthy business, that loyalties chopped and changed like squally weather. They stabbed one another in the back and constantly expected to get stabbed back.

With his free hand he called Napper. 'Can you talk?'

'Yep.'

'That inside job I was telling you about. There's been a development.'

'Oh yeah? In what direction, backwards?'

'No, sort of sideways I suppose. The one-legged man is going to fight it in court.'

'Fight what in court?'

'The power of attorney shit. He's going to sue the woman to get his company back.'

'Why should I be interested in this?'

'Well, put it this way, he stands a very good chance of success under the circumstances, and I'll have to advise her to that effect. If she was behind the shooting then she'll have another go, and it won't be a leg-shot next time, get my drift?'

'Hmmm, suppose, if she *is* behind all this—'

The lawyer interrupted. 'Should be a copper, shouldn't I!'

'God fuckin' forbid! Look, Jackson doesn't think she was behind the shooting, otherwise he would have told the investigating officer, DC Briggs, so this is still a hell of a long shot mate, and what you're givin' me now amounts to a *threats to life* warning, which means I've got to put it in fucking writing.'

'So then what happens?'

'Risk assessment nonsense. Jackson'll get a visit from some tosspot inspector with a clipboard wanting to know the ins and outs of a cat's arsehole and, if I know the sort of bloke Jackson is, he'll tell him to fuck off and not be stupid.'

'So? I don't understand mate. At least your arse'll be covered—'

'And I'll look a proper cunt an' all.' Napper scratched his bushy beard, irritably, before going on. 'Okay Stu, I'm only thinkin' aloud. It's just that this idea of yours, on the one hand it's bollocks, on the other hand it might be growing a pair of legs—'

'Which is more than fucking Jackson's got!' bellowed Blake, roaring and slapping his thigh at his own joke, tears suddenly trickling down his contorted, unshaven face.

Napper tried to interject, but there was no stopping the crazy brief.

'And what's all this about my idea being bollocks with a pair of legs growing out of its hand?' Blake blurted through a short pause in his delirium, and then, several octaves higher, 'You've been having anatomy lessons from some cunt on drugs!'

Napper resigned himself to a spell of patient tolerance; he knew what Blake was like when he got on one of his humour rolls. He sat it out.

'Finished?'

'Yeah, good now. Thanks mate. Cor, needed that, relieves the stress a bit.'

'Well, good, but it hasn't relieved mine.' A second's silence followed as the cop mulled a move. 'Right, I've decided to keep schtum about this and I need you to as well. You never told me about this, okay?'

'Cost ya.'

Napper sighed. 'Okay, where and when?'

'Same place, same time tomorrow.'

'Fine.'

And that was the end of the latest of their seemingly pointless conversations, or alternating monologues, like verbal Pollock paintings: numerous desultory splurts punctuated by random splodges of gibberish. But Napper knew these little chats with his good friend were never pointless. The Pollock analogy held; stand back a few yards and sometimes, just sometimes, the shit would merge, and the semblance of a picture would emerge.

Neither man knew quite where they wanted to be heading, but the unspoken spirit of their fuzzy logic was that it would be somewhere scary – and, vitally, it would be fun.

The Cornish cop now knew he had to do something about the Danish woman. Napper figured that the only thing that Jackson and the Dane had in common was their business. She was probably involved, but as a potential co-victim, not a perp. There was a third party in the loop, had to be, against both Jackson and the Dane, and Napper reckoned Eric was his route forward.

49

Briggs climbed the steps of the Notting Hill townhouse with unattributable trepidation. There had been something in this woman's tone, a distinct whiff of danger, nebulous but threatening.

He pressed the intercom button and a light came on beside a camera lens. Three seconds elapsed; he was being examined. 'Come in, officer,' and then a loud crack of the bolt being released.

He pushed the heavy door and walked in. It closed behind him automatically, and the thud of the bolt re-engaging had a nasty ring of finality to it.

The hallway was white, totally, floor to ceiling.

'Come through officer, door to your left.'

He did as instructed. She was stood at the window as he entered the large, minimally furnished room, so all he saw was the silhouette.

'Come and sit, *Detective* Briggs. Tea or coffee?'

'Oh, er, no thank you, this shouldn't take long.'

'You've got *that* right. I've a hair appointment in forty minutes.' Larssen moved away from the window, lowered herself onto a dining table chair and pointed at the adjacent sofa.

Briggs' mouth was dry. The woman exuded a feline menace; he wished he wasn't alone with her.

The sofa was very low. She sat on the edge of her chosen perch, endless legs crossed sideways, hands clasped on knees, looking down at him condescendingly.

'Okay, *Detective* Briggs, what can you do for me?'

'I need to take a statement from you regarding the shooting of your friend last week.'

'Why?'

'Standard procedure, Muz Larssen. I'll be seeing everyone who was at the restaurant that evening.'

'But nobody actually saw what happened.'

'I'm aware of that, but—'

'Wouldn't you rather I told you who did it?'

Suddenly, the source of Briggs' uneasiness revealed itself: the woman was fucking mad. Slightly relieved by this insight, he made a show of considering the offer, pursing his lips and frowning at a spot on the spotless carpet.

'Probably,' he said, 'except I'd worry about how you knew.'

Larssen nodded and lit a very long cigarette with a miniature flame thrower. She didn't inhale, instead expelling a mouthful of blue smoke in a single puff which billowed across the room between them.

'It was personal. And now they're after *me*.' The second sentence was almost offhand, an aside.

Briggs didn't respond; let the witness volunteer, no leading questions: training. He sensed she no longer had the better of him. It didn't last long.

'I'm going to give you the name and address of the man responsible for shooting Claude Jackson and for threatening me.' She paused for effect, and to unleash another cloud of smoke into the already toxic atmosphere.

Briggs maintained silence, but it was no longer deliberate; words had deserted him.

'And I want action.' Another puff. 'And quickly.'

50

'There's sumtin' goin' on wid dat boy, bro.'

Kribz was toying with a ruminative spliff, examining the roach end as he spoke.

'Which boy bro?' Driss was struggling at the ironing board; the lads pitched in occasionally to give Molly a break.

'Screwloose, he ain't right lately. Sumtin' on 'is mind, innit.'

Driss stopped faffing about with a shirt and half turned towards his brother. 'So, what you sayin' bro, you think he's rattin'?'

'Can't think what else it could be. Either that or he's workin' for another posse.'

'What, like the Sevens?'

Kribz sometimes questioned his brother's parentage, which was the same as his, as far as he knew, but occasionally he wondered about the ability margin.

'Don't be fuckin' stupid bro, wouldn't be surprised if Massive is out there lookin' for him now.'

Driss resumed his wrestling match with shirt and iron. 'Yeah, okay, see what you mean bro, but rat? Screwloose? Nah, don't buy it innit. Anyway, I ain't noticed nuttin' 'bout 'is behavior. What you smellin'?'

'He's holdin' back on us, knows sumtin' and ain't letting on. I'm fuckin' sure of it.'

'Like you just said though, Massive'll be lookin' for 'im soon. He's prob'ly jus' shittin' 'imself an' scared to admit it to us, so he's tinkin' of nuttin' else, innit.'

Kribz had to admit to himself that his brother, for once, had a point.

The younger boy gave up on the domestics and put down the iron on the cork end of the board. He turned and looked down at the sibling he'd always looked up to. 'Fuck, man, if you're right, we got to get rid, an' fuckin' quick. He could do a deal wid the Sevens to save 'is own skin, then we'd be fucked, innit!'

Kribz's eyes were still on the spliff which he was attempting to repair with a torn off sticky part of a Rizla paper. Driss went on.

'He could tell the Sevens about the Arch man, then they would ambush us for sure.' Driss was milking this for all it was worth: nagging his big bruv, calling the shots, didn't happen often – and never lasted long.

'Shut the fuck up my brother, don't you think I gotta plan?' The repair job was on pause as Kribz shot an icy glare at the boy he'd carried, and loved, since they were toddlers.

Seven seconds, about average. Driss was back in his place but kept up the motions, albeit with his chin retracted half an inch. 'Yeah, well, tell me 'bout your fuckin' plan, it's my black arse on the line too bro.'

Kribz fired up his spliff anew with a disposable lighter. He inhaled and eyed his brother, holding his breath to put the cannabinoid boot in good and proper.

'No disrespect bro, just let's call it a 'need to know' situation, an' you don't need to know what my plan is.'

Driss felt his knees weaken. The hurt visibly shrank him. 'Fuck man, what you sayin', you don't truss me?!'

Kribz calmly put the spliff onto a saucer on the arm of the sofa and rose assertively to his feet. He took his brother by the shoulders, arms outstretched, and engaged him with very meaningful eye contact.

'This has never happened before my brother, but I need you to not take it personal. What you don't know won't hurt you, innit. Jus' have my back while I do my ting, then if sumtin' goes wrong you'll still be here for Mum. D'you catch my drift my brother?'

Driss nodded, eyes down. 'I got your back bro.'

51

Two days later JLP were instructed by the Royal Bank to serve a statutory declaration and eviction notice on Thomas Rankin, together with an application for a charging order against the old man's homestead. Once the papers were served on the Gypsy he would have little time to appeal and little chance of that appeal being successful before the eviction notice was executed.

The firm, now effectively controlled by Larssen, passed on these instructions to her retained, no-questions-asking lawyer.

How do these people achieve such professional success whilst being motivated by such unprofessional greed and spite? Blake entertained this pointless, academic question as he listened to the gloating tone of Larssen's clear orders. He had the answer: the money was obviously important, but the satisfaction of a sadistic need to bully, hurt and ultimately destroy fellow human beings was core to the motivation. Psychopaths.

Having put Blake on notice by telephone, Larssen lounged in her chair and lit a cigarette, openly visible to her employees in her soundproof glass reptile tank. One of those deskers, Palmer, watched with loathing. A friend of neither Larssen nor Jackson, he hated the woman more and, possessed of a modicum of empathy (not much, though), felt a tad sorry for the recently unseated chairman.

For some time, Palmer had been collecting facts and figures on the Dane, one figure being the four-digit code of the keypad lock on her office door. He often stayed late and had done this, whilst alone, by depositing a miniscule splodge of his semen on each of its ten digits. At the end of the following day, alone again, he shone an ultraviolet torch onto the keypad and made a note of the four numbers on which the product of his gonads no longer appeared. 1,7,8,9. He tried 1987, the Year of the Bitch. Wrong, too obvious. So, backwards: 7,8,9,1. Nope. Semi-backwards? 8,7,1,9? Bingo! Third time lucky. Thanks, CSI.

The mood of the staff was always laced with fear, but of late that constant unease had been relieved – replaced, even – by a general atmosphere of resignation, almost liberation. They sensed that Larssen's recent monopolisation of power would conclude badly, would probably be the end of the firm and their jobs. But, to a man and woman, they weren't all that bothered. For it was exhausting; no matter how lucrative the dividends, the daily pretence and sycophancy wears down even the hardiest of predators because, instinctively, they want to do their own thing, be in charge, lead the pack.

In the case of Colin Palmer, ambition and conscience had become unlikely bedfellows. He reckoned Jackson would eventually come out on top after this, so he was aligning himself accordingly – and looking forward to perhaps getting the poor bastard a bit of justice.

52

'Screw, man, we gonna have to whack the woman. You up for it, bruv?'

'Suppose.' The response was muttered, unenthusiastic.

'You don't sound too sure bro.' Kribz, not for the first time in recent days, sensed something, saw a lizard's tail of fear flick across the gunman's face.

'Yeah, I'm sure enough bro, but why, you know, what for?'

'They're hurting our new business partner bro, you know that, messin' wid our dogs innit, I told you. You give the dude a nice cap, now that bitch has to get the same. They ain't heedin', innit.'

Kribz watched as the same shadow he'd seen in the rear-view mirror in Notting Hill darken Screwloose's visage. He pounced. 'Okay bruv, give me the gun an' I'll fuckin' do it.'

Screwloose didn't like this. Lose his piece and he'd lose his identity, everything he'd worked for. The two were in his room, no one else in the flat, and Kribz had made his mind up he wasn't leaving without that gun.

'No way bro, you ain't 'avin' it. Get your own piece, you ain't sidelinin' me like dis!' As Screwloose spoke his eyes, for a split second, flicked to a place on a high shelf on the wall behind Kribz. That was enough. The gang leader was on his feet and reaching up for a Nike shoebox. Screwloose was on his back and trying to snatch it away, but Kribz had the gun out and pointed at its owner in under two seconds.

Screwloose backed off, staring at the little black hole at the end of the barrel. 'It ain't loaded.'

'You sure, bro?'

He wasn't.

53

'Who's this?' Jackson hated withheld numbers, rarely answered them but hey, not much to lose these days.

'Mr Jackson, it's Colin Palmer. How are you?'

His guard immediately up, Jackson's default aggression kicked in. 'What the fuck do *you* want Palmer?'

'Well, not to do you any harm. That's already been done, I would say.'

'Big style. I'm fucked, nothing left of me so you might as well fuck off and leave me alone.' Even as he said this Jackson knew he didn't sound convincing; he was just going through the tough guy banter motions.

'We're all going to be fucked pretty soon Mr Jackson, so I've nothing much to lose. Just thought you might like to know something, that's all.'

'Yeah, and what's in it for you?'

'Perhaps a nice feeling that I've evened the odds a bit. Levelled the playing field.'

Jackson kept it up, but he was hooked.

'Hah, even up the odds? Level playing field? Not the way I've raised you son, you on the turn or something?' A degree of humour had softened Jackson's tone, and he was all ears.

Palmer got to the point. 'They're serving on Rankin sixteen hundred hours next Tuesday 24th. She's going for eviction and immediate occupation of the land, probably before you manage to appeal against the power of attorney stuff.'

Lying flat out with his stump elevated, the unshaven Jackson took a few seconds to absorb the information. 'How d'*you* know? She can't have trusted you with this.'

'She didn't. I'm in her office now.' It was nine fifteen in the evening and Palmer was in the glass cubicle perusing a file with surgically gloved fingers.

'Well fucking get out of there, she'll have you arrested!'

'Leaving now Mr Jackson.'

'Look, sorry to be rude Colin and – er – thanks.' Saying this nearly made Jackson choke.

54

'This feeling of warmth, is it in any way sexual?' Dr Nigel Privette hadn't been looking forward to asking this question, but the base had to be covered. The patient remained calm.

'No, it's emotional, like happiness, joy, satisfaction, not sexual at all.' Her eyes were hooded as she spoke, unfocused; she was concentrating.

'What kind of—?'

'But it can work the other way round. Good sex can bring on the warmth if I've...' She trailed off.

'If you've what?'

'Dominated.'

'Caused pain?'

'Not necessarily, but – er – discomfort, certainly.'

'Physical discomfort?'

'I prefer the emotional kind.'

'Why?'

'It fascinates me.' She remained motionless, hands on the armrests of the chair, eyes now quite glazed, like she was in a semi-trance. Privette scribbled a note; the disposition was self- induced; he hadn't hypnotised Freda Larssen – she was in total control.

55

Kribz took the gun to the Arch. No way was he having the thing in his mother's flat. He had left Screwloose in a bit of a state and was worried that the boy would do something predictably unpredictable. He gave him a call.

'Hey, look bro, I'm sorry, you'll get it back as soon as the job's done, I promise.'

'That ain't the fuckin' point man, you'ze sidelinin' me. I'm a brother innit, don't force me out like dis.'

'Okay.' Kribz sounded conciliatory and made the compromise. 'Look, nobody is forcing you out, an' besides, I need you alongside me to have my back. Driss can't make it, so I need you, bro. You up for it?'

Screwloose frowned down the phone. 'Yeah, course bruv, whatever. You want me to take aim for you too?'

The leader made a sound of finding this funny. 'Fuck off man, I was popping these 'tings when you was still in nappies.'

Relieved to be in the plan, the gunman accepted the peripheral role. 'Okay man, when do we do it?'

'I'll let you know, but we travel there separately, so if one of us gets nicked he doesn't know where the other is, get my drift bro?'

'Yeah, sure, course.' He didn't really, but there was no point in arguing.

Kribz felt elaboration was needed. 'I ain't usin' wheels. Gonna rock up on foot and then dive underground. The wheels man, they're a fuckin' toil, they bind you down, more trub than they'ze worth.'

Screwloose was convinced.

56

The incongruous pair sat at a quiet table in the back room of the Hercules pub in Kennington, Napper hoping that nobody he knew would come in and see him with this twerp.

Briggs was nervous, clearly needing help. 'I went to see Jackson's business partner yesterday. She's as mad as a snake, says she was accosted by three masked IC3s two days ago and reckons they were the ones responsible for the shooting.'

Napper promptly stopped worrying about appearances as he tried to take this on board. 'We talking about a tall woman, Danish or German or somethin' like that?'

'Yes, Freda Larssen. She's demanding we arrest a Gypsy who has dog kennels out near Heathrow.' The detective looked down as he said this, slightly embarrassed and expecting a volley of ridicule from his scruffy colleague.

None came. Briggs looked up to see Napper frowning at the table. 'You got the address of this place, and the name of the Gypsy?'

'Yes, of course, and I've logged everything on the Crimint system before you ask. Had to – this woman will have the fuckin' DPS's number in her favourites!'

The Directorate of Professional Standards went through the motions of taking every complaint seriously, and Briggs knew that if they got one from Larssen they would dance to whatever tune she whistled.

'I've also prepared a POCA application.' Briggs didn't expect Napper to have a clue what he was talking about.

'What the fuck are you talking about?'

'Proceeds of Crime Act. If Rankin's engaged in criminal activity, on behalf of himself or anyone else, then the Assets Confiscation Unit will want to know about it, so I'm going to ask the CPS to apply to restrain his property.'

Briggs' smugness irritated Napper, but he supposed the graduate CID man was right. The Met budget, although senior management would never allude to the fact, was indirectly but significantly enhanced by proceeds of crime sequestrations. Bright young things like Briggs were always ahead on this sort of game, keen to ingratiate themselves with the purse string holders.

57

Napper was tired of the British Library – too much of a habit, and the statue of Isaac Newton was getting on his nerves – so when he and Eric next met it was on the steps of St Paul's Cathedral. They sat side by side, the cold from the stone numbing their buttocks, and pretended to people-watch and chat idly.

'She's gettin' it on Monday, outside 'er office at 7 o'clock in the morning, or as soon as she gets there innit.'

'What if she's got a security guard? Some Lithuanian with a Mac 10 under his belt? There'll be one hell of a shootout Eric.'

The boy considered this, gazing ahead. 'That'll be your problem, Mr Napper.'

'Where did you get this from?'

'You can't expect me to tell you that Mr Napper.'

'I know, but I've got to ask anyway.'

'I'm good on Snapchat. I follow it using three phones at the same time, you can build up a picture that way. Plus I got my ears to the ground innit. I don't miss a fuckin' ting, Mr Napper.'

'Any more stuff about these dogs, they still in the picture?'

'Nah, not really, the only ting I heard 'bout dogs is that the D7 gang are into them, breedin' them innit.'

'D7?'

'Yeah, D7.'

Napper obviously knew that Massive, the D7 leader, had recently taken a bullet in the leg but had refused to speak to the police. If all this involved pit bulls then it was a good line that that shooting had been about dogs as well. Or perhaps not; these shootings went off all the time for all sorts of random reasons, mostly territorial or disrespect.

All the same, the cop made a mental note to find out how the ballistics work was progressing. Bullets from both Jackson and Massive had been recovered and sent for examination. In themselves they said nothing, but together they could paint a picture.

The white envelope was inside a Pret sandwich bag which Napper shoved onto Eric's lap. The boy nodded and rose, stuffing the bag into the big front pocket of his hoody.

'Give me a call on Sunday Eric, even if there's no more news. I want to be sure you're okay.' The boy he called Eric nodded and bounced down the steps onto the street below.

Napper pulled out his phone and called Briggs, recounted to him a sexed-up version of what he'd just been told, and the clunky wheels of London's finest were coaxed into reluctant motion.

58

'I can assure you, Mr Tremayne, that site will be in your hands and under your total control within three weeks, a month at most. The papers are all in order and repossession has been fast tracked, the bailiffs are poised and ready.'

Larssen sat forward at her desk to deliver this news to the billionaire conglomerate buyer's extremely expensive lawyer. Her head was turned towards the wall to avoid being lip-read by eyes in the outer office.

'Thank you, Miss Larssen. We have the upmost faith in you. Our client is delighted by the speed at which you have expedited this acquisition.'

'And thank *you*, Mr Tremayne, for your valued custom. Oh, and, er, please note that as of today our company has undergone a name change. We will henceforth be known as JLP Restructuring Denmark PLC, with the Denmark bit in brackets. This is of course just an administrative move following Brexit, nothing fundamental has changed and I'll inform you formally on paper in due course.' She didn't mention that she was now the effective owner of this new entity.

'Good move, Miss Larssen, it is a refreshing pleasure to do business with a progressive company.'

'Thank you again, Mr Tremayne, and bye for now.' Larssen ended the call, sat back and licked her lips, slowly.

59

'They're serving the eviction order on Rankin next Tuesday, at 4pm.'

'Why are you telling me this Jacko?' Blake was genuinely confused by this call. He was in the Coach and Horses in Soho waiting for Napper and had already downed two pints of San Miguel. He was busy paying for his third when the call came through.

'Well, no point in me appealing against the power of attorney nonsense now, is there? Too late I suppose.'

Blake hadn't quite finished his transaction with the barmaid and had to multi-task his way through the conversation. 'Not really, you could always contest it later and recover losses sustained because of the ensuing unfairness. But like I've already told you mate; I can't represent you.'

Jackson was sitting in a wheelchair in the hospital dayroom. He looked dreadful: bereft of his leg, livelihood and self-respect, his mental health was in freefall.

'I know you can't fucking represent me, but I just need someone to talk to occasionally!'

Blake suddenly felt guilty; he had after all been part of all this and it was astonishing that Jackson had nowhere else to turn but to someone who'd been working for the other side.

'Listen, Jacko mate, are you sure that bitch had nothing to do with you getting shot?'

'Totally. It's given her an opportunity for sure, but trust me, she hasn't got connections with those scumbags. She wouldn't give them the time of day.'

The lawyer then got a tap on the shoulder. He looked in the mirror behind the bar to see a very tired Doug Napper standing behind him.

'Look, Jacko, gotta go now mate, I'll give you a call in the morning.'

'Please Stu, be sure to.' Jackson's voice trembled.

'I will.' And the call ended with the lawyer feeling decidedly uncomfortable.

'Jackson, eh?' Napper had caught the tail end.

'Yeah, he's a bit out of sorts, to say the fucking least.' Blake blinked unseeingly at the carpet. 'They're serving eviction papers on Tom Rankin next Tuesday if you're remotely interested.'

'I might just be very fuckin' interested – are you goin' to buy me a pint or what?'

60

Napper could have done it as part of his duties and taken an unmarked police car; it was, after all, part of a criminal investigation. But his chosen line of enquiry was well off piste, even for him, and consequently he was in his own time and his own vehicle, a thirteen-year-old Land Rover he'd got for next to nothing.

The location given him by Briggs was very accurate as it had originated from Larssen and had in turn come from the Land Registry, complete with Ordnance Survey map co-ordinates. Napper parked up about a quarter of a mile away and embarked on his favourite method, a CROPS approach. He'd never been in the Special Forces but had done some Covert Rural Operations training in his regiment and liked to deploy it whenever he could. This usually amounted to hunkering down under a condom-strewn gorse bush in some south London dog-shit park whilst observing a social housing block or car park. But on this lovely morning he was in the real countryside, albeit punctuated every ninety seconds by the shattering noise of several hundred tons of steel and human flesh screaming overhead.

He approached the homestead from what he correctly calculated was its rear and entered, his titanium bolt cutters making short work of the double-ply chain link fence. He had full view of the rear of the Rankin house. In his foreground was a collection of sheds and outhouses, some apparently more secure than others.

It was just after 6 a.m. and most of the dogs were awake and either eating or awaiting their breakfasts. Tom Rankin had been up and about for two hours, preparing food, drinking tea and trying not to think about either his troubles or the bottle of whiskey on the kitchen table. He was now in the biggest of the 'back sheds' as he called them, located at the very rear of the rambling estate, as far away as possible from Marlene's prying eyes. The dog was a Presa Canario, a huge animal, rare in the UK and prized as a fighter. His name was Franco and he was Rankin's secret weapon. The old Gypsy was putting him through his paces.

61

The big outbuilding was built solidly of breezeblock with a corrugated tin roof. It backed onto the perimeter fence and its back wall featured a high, unglazed window. It permitted natural light and ventilation, but nothing else. It was certainly not there to be looked through, which was exactly why Police Constable Douglas Napper was doing just that. Instinctively drawn to it, he'd quickly dumped his bolt-cutters and fashioned a makeshift ladder from a forty-gallon oil barrel and two wooden pallets. Had Tom Rankin looked up at the window he would have seen the silhouette of a bearded head observing the ongoing cruelty.

Franco was strapped into a sturdy leather harness which was an integral part of an electrically powered treadmill, the rubberised track of which was being propelled at an alarming rate. The dog was sprinting, both to keep up with the track and, vainly, to try to get its jaws around a lump of steak which hung tantalisingly before it. The animal was massive, square and powerful with cropped ears crowning a huge, brachycephalic skull. It was very lean, straining muscles rippling visibly through its gleaming pelt. The downward traverse of the saliva streaming from its jowls accentuated the fact that the poor beast was getting nowhere fast. Its eyes expressed pain, confusion, and total determination.

'C'mon you lovely fecker, one more minute and that meat is yours, me beauty!'

Napper heard this and decided to use that minute effectively. He dropped down to the ground and sloped off, staying close to the perimeter fence and heading for a collection of rusty old fairground machines parked at the southernmost side of the estate. He knew the meaning of what he'd just seen. That Rankin was in the dogfighting game did not surprise the Cornishman.

He edged closer to the house, his knowledge of Rankin's whereabouts relieving his concern regarding any CCTV cameras; there had been no screens in that shed. He surveyed the scene and made the assumption that the place was an illegal dog farm.

He started taking photographs with his phone: kennels, foodstores, exercise pens, the rear of the rambling house; he needed to build some evidence.

'Put that feckin' thing down and turn around slowly.' A rural Irish accent usually has a jolly intonation, but when laced with menace it's bloodcurdling. Napper did exactly as he was told and found himself facing a double-barrelled Purdy twelve-gauge shotgun.

'Sit down on the ground and put your hands behind your feckin' neck.'

Napper complied.

'Now, you're either a copper or a feckin' thief. Which is it to be?'

'The first one. Put the gun down, Mr Rankin.'

'Shut the feck up! Let me see your ID – slowly.'

Again, compliance.

'Throw it over here, and the phone.'

Napper was looking up at the Irishman and saw a man very near the edge. So, *strict* compliance.

Gun still aimed at his prisoner's face, Rankin stooped slowly to pick up the officer's warrant card and phone.

'Douglas Napper, Police Constable eh? Metropolitan Police, eh?'

Napper nodded eagerly and tried to smile. His mouth had gone dry. A huge Boeing hurtled overhead, the near-deafening clatter suspending the one-way conversation for a very long ten seconds.

'Strip.'

'What?'

'Strip. Take off your feckin' clothes, now – and slowly.'

Napper had never been taken by the IRA, but had heard all the stories, some firsthand from a few lucky survivors. He didn't think Rankin had ever been a Provo man, but the Gypsy was doing a good impression. He slowly got to his feet and undressed, occasionally glancing at the unfaltering Purdy which, once he was totally naked, jerked in the direction of the big shed.

'Go inside. Somebody wants to meet you.' The instruction was almost nonchalant.

Napper of course knew exactly who this 'somebody' was and the low, guttural growl that greeted him when he entered the outbuilding sent his hands to his exposed genitals. He tried to calculate the length of the chain which tethered the dog to the wall; it was long enough and lay in an untidy pile beside the exhausted beast.

'He won't touch you unless I invite him to and, yes, that chain has plenty feckin' length to it. Sit yourself down.'

Napper did so, slowly, on the cold, hard concrete. He seriously feared for his life; this was one bad man he was dealing with and he had no doubt that shooting and quickly disposing of the body of a police officer were tasks well within his capabilities. Not that he would even have to do that:

Napper's appearance and the nature of his unauthorised entry made him fair game to be shot on sight by an elderly and vulnerable landowner.

'Right,' went on the Gypsy, 'tell me why you're here.'

The cop hadn't prepared for this, but the urge to play what he hoped would be his winning card was too strong to resist and the news he then gave Rankin had the desired effect of making him more use alive than dead. The old man looked him squarely in the eye. 'How do you know all this?'

'I've a friend in the legal profession',

'So why didn't you just knock on the front feckin' door, then?' came the reasonable question, 'instead of sneakin' about like a feckin' ferret?'

Napper was accustomed to answering questions about his propensity to act alone. 'It's in my nature, my training. I always sneak about to be one step ahead; I can't help it.'

Rankin liked this and sagely nodded his approval. 'So, a lone wolf, eh?'

'Suppose so,' replied the policeman, before hastily adding, 'but if I go missing there'll be a massive search party sent out.'

Rankin picked up on the panicky tone of the cop's warning, continuing to regard his prisoner coolly. 'D'you know son, my guess is that not a feckin' soul knows you're here, and if your buddies manage to track you down, well, let them come, I'm gonna keep your I.D. card so if they find you I'll just say you refused to identify yourself.' Another pause: Napper relaxed – he wasn't going to get murdered, just yet anyway. Rankin sighed and continued, asserting his authority. 'Right, you're not one step ahead now, son.'

Napper nodded agreement.

'Okay young man, now you must do exactly as I say. You're my guest here for a few days and you'll be treated well, but you're not feckin' leavin'. If you try to, I'll blow your bollocks off like I'm entitled to – you're a trespasser, remember that, and I'm an old man, so stand up and go through that door, turn left and go into the next shed on your right – slowly.'

This reality of the situation stunned Napper; he was being held hostage and there was nothing he could do about it.

'Don't worry, you'll be fed and watered. I'll even give you a drop of whiskey to keep out the cold at night, but you're goin' feckin' nowhere 'till this shite is done an' settled. Is that clear to you, son?'

By this time Napper had entered what were to be his quarters for the following 36 very long hours: a small brick and breezeblock outhouse which had evidently once been home to some valuable machinery, such was its sturdiness. Once inside he turned to face Rankin but only got a glimpse of the Gypsy before the steel door was closed, plunging him into almost total darkness. The cop then heard two bolts being secured with hefty padlocks.

62

Screwloose had done his Google Maps homework and had just about memorised the layout of the streets around the offices of JLP Restructuring PLC. He was a fish out of water in the West End, especially at seven o'clock on a Monday morning.

He felt vulnerable without his gun, but relieved that a stop and search would yield nothing but half a reefer in his pocket which he fired up occasionally to quell his nerves. He looked for Kribz as he took up position in a doorway opposite the block where JLP was housed. Seven a.m. came and went and the street was awash with pedestrian traffic. He checked his phone for messages, missed calls, Snapchat postings – zilch.

He watched the people like they were from another planet. He couldn't remember ever meeting any person like any one of them in his entire life. They were smart, in a hurry and white – all of them. It struck him that *he* was the one from another planet. He lit the spliff and took a furtive draw before quickly nipping it out. He held his breath for full effect and worried about the smell. Then he saw Kribz across the road. *What was he doin' just standin' there like that? Like he was doin' his best to look fuckin' suspicious?*

Then a cab pulled up and the tall woman alighted; she was about to step smartly across the pavement and through the door of the office when Kribz approached and spoke to her. Screwloose couldn't hear what was said but the conversation was very brief, being briskly interrupted by the swift action of a team of armed cops rudely pouncing from a nearby van. In four seconds Kribz was face down on the pavement, hands cuffed behind his back. He offered no resistance; it was like he'd expected it. A female officer escorted the tall woman through the entrance of her place of work.

Screwloose decamped, unseen.

63

'You got your show; next Tuesday afternoon, startin' at three o'clock.'

The Albanian was relieved the match was going ahead, but had wanted it earlier.

'Okay Tom, sounds okay I suppose, but why not this week?'

'You wouldn't understand this, but some people in this country aren't too keen on our idea of fun – and my lady wife is one of them. She just happens to be away in Ireland next week, so I've a free run of the place for a change.' This was true.

He was right: Kemal Gozit did not understand that, nor would he understand anything like it, including why the opinion of a woman would ever matter anyway. Or even that a woman would have an opinion.

'I want to put the dog you've lent me against one of mine. How would you feel about that?'

'Fine by me Kemal. That animal needs a good bloodin'. Besides, if she doesn't come out of it alive I'm not too feckin' worried. She's on loan to you so you'll be getting' rid of the carcass.'

'Oh, so you've lent me a pig then?'

'No, but she's not too fit. Not long had a litter though, and if she thinks the pups are in danger, she'll fight like a feckin' tiger. You gonna rig the bettin', I suppose?'

'That's my business Tom and I'll be bringing along some brave gamers.'

'Bring along as many as you like, Kemal, but I won't be betting on anything, I'm wanting to wipe my slate, not get into more debt to you.' The old man paused, before adding, 'Tell them to park up in roads around the place. I don't want my drive full of feckin' Hummers and people-traffickin' wagons.' It was like he had to have at least part of the deal on his terms, even though the arrangement was very much the opposite.

'That's fine,' said Gozit.

It was gone three by the time the call ended, and the sun was over the yard arm in his book. He reached for the bottle of Black Bush and thumbing through the contact list on his phone, stabbed the number that Kribz had given him.

'Hello son, Tom here.'

'I know,' said Kribz. 'Are you okay Mr Rankin?'

'For the feckin' love o' Christ, will you call me Tom?'

'Sorry Tom, what can I do for you?'

'We got a problem. I need you to come over, it's a bit urgent and not for the telephone.'

'Okay, we're on our way, Tom.'

'No, just you, son, leave your brother at home for a change, this one's for guv'nors only.'

Kribz didn't like the sound of this, but agreed anyway: the Gypsy sounded worried, vulnerable. He told Driss he was popping out for a couple of hours to clear his head. He left the flat and walked to where the car that hadn't been used that morning was parked. It still had two days left on the rental agreement. 3.15pm: he would just about beat the west-bound rush hour.

64

There was to be seven fights on the main bill, five of them pretty much pre-ordained; the betting on those would not so much be on which dog won, but how long that winning took and whether the outcome was fatal.

Rankin's two best dogs were Nero (injured but angry) and Franco (fit and raring to go). Amongst Gozit's animals included a Presa Canario which looked like it carried the genes of a wolverine, and a very frightened Ciara, taken by him from Rankin for a spell of heavy training the week before.

This was part of the itinerary that Gozit and Rankin were now discussing over whiskey-laced Tetley in the Stanwell Moor house. The show, as the Irishman liked to call it, was going to be a 'merry and fulsome afternoon of sport'.

65

Several other people were making plans for the following Tuesday. Larssen was on the phone to Stuart Blake.

'Have you lodged the charge with Land Registry yet?'

The lawyer was a bit stumped here. 'Er – there was a slight problem at court. The district judge was in one of his awkward moods, wanted to see more papers in respect of you, rather than your client bank's claim of beneficial ownership of the property. So, er, the charge hasn't been actually registered yet, but don't worry, he's signed the eviction order and it's ready for service and execution.'

This worried Larssen very much indeed and she immediately became furious. 'I gave you strict instructions,' she spat. 'The bank has assigned ownership to my company on the undertaking that we will deal with the subsequent conveyance, therefore it must follow that the registered charge in the paltry sum of two hundred thousand pounds be in our name.' Her voice was controlled, menacing.

'Wrong judge, wrong day, these things happen but we'll—
'

'No, not *we*, fucking *you* will put this right by the end of this week. I want that charge properly registered, do I make myself clear, Mr Stuart soon-to-be-struck-off fucking Blake?'

'Crystal.'

'Good.' Larssen cut the call.

66

'They're making me have the show at my place and they're using one of your bitches son. I had no choice – a gamblin' debt I owe them. If you want to stop the fight I suggest you come out here and lay claim to the animal yourself. I told them she wasn't mine but they don't give a fuck. They could see she'd just had the pups and there's no better fightin' dog than a bitch tryin' to protect her youngsters. The show's next Tuesday, be here at four o'clock but don't come before that or they'll suss you out and keep her in one of their vans and deny havin' her, then you'll lose her forever.'

Rankin rattled off this story to Kribz with just the right amount of contrition in his voice. Kribz felt his blood rise. A bunch of fucking Albanians were going to put Ciara in a fucking fight pit! There was no way that was going to happen. Okay, so it looked like it was Rankin's fault, but the guy sounded scared and there was more to this than he was telling. He still had Screwloose's gun, but it was in the Arch, so he would have to go back to the swamp.

'When did all this 'appen Tom?' asked the gang leader calmly.

'Oh, only a few days ago. They came and took her. I couldn't do anything about it, there's only two barrels on a

111

shotgun and there were five of them, tooled up with hatchets. They said they would bring her back on the day of the show to give her a sniff of the pups an' then blood her, and then my slate would be clean. I've been feedin' them with a bottle since. The poor bitch'll be frantic.'

'How much do you owe them?'

'Ten grand, but they want it back now if I don't do as they say, either that or they'll get nasty and be wantin' blood.'

Kribz understood this; Albanians regarded prevarication on debt repayments as disrespect, they liked clean slates – one way or another.

'Okay Tom,' nodded the gang leader, 'I'm getting' your drift.'

The gypsy went on; 'Jesus Christ, as if I didn't have enough trouble with the feckin' bank I've got this bunch of animals to contend with an' all!'

The old Irishman was nearly in tears; although sympathetic, Kribz wasn't entirely impressed.

'And here's us thinkin' you was a man in charge of your castle Tom. What the fuck went wrong?'

Rankin was slumped at the kitchen table, clearly with a lot of whiskey on board. 'Ah son, you don't know the feckin' half of it. I've been dealin' with these bastards for a long time, and yes, it's all my fault, but at least you have a chance to come an' put it right. Can you raise some of your own soldiers?'

'Yeah, suppose so, but it ain't endin' here Tom. Once we get our dog back in one piece and see these fuckin' Albos off for you then you and us is in business, big style. Is that clear bruv?'

'Yes, clear enough, better you fellas than them animals, at least you're predictable,' Rankin said, before adding 'but I'm not your feckin' brother!'

Kribz smiled at this last bit of defiance from a man on the brink of defeat. 'Maybe not, Tom, but you're family now innit, without a fuckin' doubt.'

67

On the way back into London Kribz pulled over and made four calls. The first two got negative responses, the third got him the number he wanted, which became the fourth call – to a big man called Massive.

'Do you want 'im bro?'

Silence.

'It's Kribz bro, d'you want 'im?'

Massive knew what his purported arch enemy was talking about. 'Course I fuckin' want him, but what's the fuckin' catch bro? I ain't got no turf to give you, I'm out of the fuckin' food game in case you hadn't heard.'

'Well, I've got a way for you to get back into it.'

Massive was sitting in a Brixton cafe, resting after a long, hard workout. With him were his two remaining D7 members, a couple of hoods called Shanker and Gillie. He wasn't keen on either of them, but they were muscle and after taking that bullet from Screwloose, Massive liked muscle with him. And guns.

'I don't want fuckin' back into the food game, but I want your fuckin' shit-for-brains cunt that put that cap in me.'

'You'll 'ave 'im, but in return—'

'What d'you want?'

'Hoods.'

'Where and when?'

'An' guns.'

'Where and when?'

Shanker and Gillie, although able to hear only one side of this, sensed action in the offing. Things had been too quiet.

Against all protocol, Kribz then gave Massive the location of the Arch, along with an invite to be nearby in an hour, and to bring along as much beef and hardware as he could muster.

'Fuck man, we gonna be alright goin' in there? From what I hear the place is crawlin' wid fuckin' Taliban dudes. Are they safe?'

'Safe as 'ouses bruv, but don't go near it till I get there. You won't get in without me, get my drift?'

'Yeah, right, in a bit.'

'One hour from now bruv, an' then we'll move forward like a proper outfit.' Thus, an alliance was formed. It was like that in the swamp: the wind would change and suddenly sworn enemies would become blood brothers – and just as often the opposite happened.

68

Massive and his two lieutenants had been loitering nervously near the building for over ten minutes before Kribz parked up in a loading bay and walked casually towards them, hands in full view. He'd been taking a chance doing this, alone, without cover.

'Okay my brothers, let's go make peace with Allah,' he said cheerfully. The three D7s regarded him balefully, although their nervousness showed through.

Kribz led them to a door with Koranic scrawls above it and a rough translation about it leading into a Muslim community centre. He pressed a grubby intercom box which hung loose on its connecting wires.

'Yes?'

'*Salam Alaikum,*' Kribz spoke the words in a lowered tone close up to the box. Gillie and Shanker looked at Massive as if to say, 'What the fuck?'

Access achieved, Kribz led his new cohorts inside and up several flights of filthy, creaking stairs, at the top of which was a surprisingly clean room under a high, vaulted ceiling.

'Welcome to the Arch.' Kribz announced, inviting his guests to choose from an eclectic array of shabby chairs.

The three relaxed and the contents of Massive's rucksack were carefully laid out on the grubby floor. The big negro had clearly been busy on his change of vocation and the display was notable: an array of guns, zombie knives and a certain fist-sized object that made Kribz shudder and swallow hard.

'Fuck, man, you really come prepared, innit.'

69

The vehicles began to arrive just after midday. Rankin, dressed in overalls, sturdy boots and a trilby hat, directed traffic and chastised Kemal Gozit with a stream of expletives.

'I feckin' told you not to bring these feckin' things into this driveway, you Albanian bastard. Now get them out of here and down that road – the feckin' cunts can walk back. I don't want this place looking like a fairground feckin' car park!'

Gozit gritted his teeth and conformed. Rankin had not been so stupid as to speak to Gozit like this within earshot of the other Ghegs who were rocking up thick and fast – that would have pushed his overstretched luck.

So, the two of them made sure that the array of Hummers, Jeeps and high track Toyotas, once relieved of their canine cargos, were scattered around the tatty village where blind eyes were turned as a matter of convention.

The dogs were taken around to the back of the homestead and placed in cages which had been set out in readiness.

Napper sat in his prison and listened intently to the gathering drama, the barking, growling and excited voices speaking a language he recognised as Albanian. He was in no doubt that what was being prepared explained his incarceration. Releasing him would have risked him returning with his colleagues to spoil the fun. He'd spent the preceding thirty-odd hours dozing and exercising, track of time barely kept by his receipt of silently delivered meals, blankets, water and whiskey. Rankin didn't speak when pushing these supplies through a three-inch gap under the door: he was treating Napper like a dog.

But there was something else he was grateful for, and which he was pretty sure Rankin didn't know about. He'd failed to find even the hint of an escape route from the cramped little jail, but his search had revealed a well–wrapped polythene package, about the size of a jam jar, rammed between the rafters and low-slung roof of the building. A few modest but regularly snorted samples of its contents had relieved him of the need to sleep deeply.

70

The treadmill had been put away out of sight, along with various other contraptions, tools and sundry debris. The back shed now featured a cleared space enclosed by a fence of chicken mesh stretched around metre-high posts with heavy concrete feet. The fight pit was oval with no gates or openings: the combatants would simply be thrown in.

It was by now three thirty and the Braganza Boys and their barely trusted D7 transferees sat in their vehicles, waiting for instructions from Kribz. Six of them sat in a low spec car and a small van, both freshly rented that morning. Screwloose had not been invited.

'What the fuck's this all about bro?' It wasn't the first time Driss had asked this question. He'd driven out to Stanwell Moor and was rapping a tattoo on the steering wheel; they were parked up three hundred yards from Rankin's place.

'I told you bruv, our man might be 'avin' a bit of trub with some Albos. Jus' wants us on standby, that's all.'

'Yeah, I know, you told me that, but what's it got to do with us man? We got shit of our own, innit, all you're givin' me is a load of crap man. Standby my fuckin' arse, why are we carryin' all this firepower just to be on stand-fuckin'-by? You're givin' me a load of fuckery man, an' I'm sick of it innit, I—'

'Shut the fuck up fam.' Kribz did not need his brother's out-loud thinking when *he* was trying to think, but Driss was undeterred.

'No. I won't shut the fuck up bro, stop dissin' me. An' what are we doing out here with these three cunts? What if they use this to turn on us? It was only a few months ago we was trying to fuckin' kill them, and them us bro, an' now we'ze trussin' them on a tooled-up job?'

Kribz could not believe he was hearing this. Reason: Massive was sat in the back seat listening to every word. Not unreasonably, the big African saw fit to object.

'Cos I'm providin' the fuckin' tools an' the muscle, you cunt, an' any more of that shit an' I'm pullin' my boys outta here and you cunts can do this alone – if you got the balls!'

Although it hurt, Kribz took Massive's side. 'Yeah bruv, take it easy, less of your shit man. These dudes are 'elpin us now, we've joined forces innit. Tings 'ave changed bro, innit, an' if you don't like it get out the car and fuck right off!'

Kribz had turned sideways to deliver this, close up and personal into his brother's ear. Driss fell silent. Kribz relaxed a little, caught Massive's eye in the rear view and winked. Then he sighed and continued in a more conciliatory tone.

'Think about it bro, we got dogs in that place, includin' two litters of pups, we got assets to protect and a good deal going forward, not to mention that stash what Rankin don't know about.'

'So why are we hangin' back here then? What we waitin' for, let's just go in, get the dogs and the food outta there for a while.'

'Ain't that simple bro, there's another side to it. He wants a show of strength and if we're gonna keep him onside then we oblige, an' it keeps 'im warned as well, so he know what we can draw together. Get my meanin' bro?'

Driss thought for second and nodded. 'Yeah, s'pose.' Then, 'Why no Screwloose then?'

Kribz had anticipated this. 'Coz I ain't wantin' a fucking bullet-fest man.'

Massive pitched in. 'Yeah, an' he don't want me drillin' the fucker's leg like he done to me!'

Driss suddenly felt stupid for digging that one up. He fell silent again, apart from the drumming on the steering wheel.

'Pack that fuckin' noise in!' shouted Kribz. 'You fuckin' nervous or sumtin'?'

'No. Well, a bit. Off our manor, innit,' mumbled the disgruntled younger Pope.

'Well fuckin' turn it in bro, nerves is contagious, catchin', innit!'

71

Numbers was sat in the passenger seat of the van around the corner. Behind the wheel was Shanker who had refused to let the youngster drive. Of mixed race with muscles on his spit, he'd never been a full D7 member but was always ready to be called up by Massive for a bit of action. Plus, he'd nothing much against the B boys; Kribz had taken the rap for him when they'd been kids, done a spell in Feltham YOI on his behalf, and the redskin had never forgotten it.

'Fuckin' don't like it round here, fuckin' creepy.' Young Numbers felt out of his depth, which he most certainly was.

'Just shut the fuck up and stay behind me. If this fuckin' kicks off I don't wanna be 'avin' to have your back all the time.' Then, after a pause, 'Anyways, I thought you 'ad the measure of these fuckin' Albos. You said they wasn't up to much, always drunk an' stuff.'

'Most of the time they is, but they get fuckin' nasty if they fuckin' want to, truss me.'

'Not as fuckin' nasty as I can get bruv,' hissed Shanker as he touched the loaded weapon tucked inside his puffer jacket. It was a .44 calibre Russian number, originally built to fire rubber pellets, its barrel now modified to deliver the real deal.

'Tchsssst!' The tut and toothsuck came from the back of the van where lay the other ex-D7 dude, on his back, with his hands clasped behind his head. Numbers twisted around, concerned by the attitude. Shanker viewed the source of the noise through the rear-view mirror.

'Whassamatter wid you Gillie, what you fuckin' sneerin' at?'

'You'ze cunts are full of bullshit, man, that's what's the matter. You dunno what's cookin' till we fuckin' get there, innit.'

Gillie was older than them and had not long come out of prison after a three year stretch for GBH and possession of a firearm. Numbers decided to assert himself.

'You ain't so fuckin' good as to say that to us bro. You just come outta the fuckin' boob, so you ain't that hot at plannin' stuff.'

'Oh, so you done all the plannin' for this did ya? Nuttin' to do wid Kribz 'n' Driss eh?'

The boy swivelled forwards again, put in his place by the man of experience, who went on. 'Don't worry though, I'll have your backs – ah'z fuckin' sure I ain't goin' anywhere in front of you'ze!'

And then Number's phone buzzed.

72

The brief event of the previous morning had troubled Larssen not one bit. The young black man had only asked her for a cigarette before he was set upon by a bunch of idiot cops not much older than himself.

She'd received a call less than an hour later to say that the 'suspect' had been released without charge, having been in possession of nothing but a snotty handkerchief and a gym membership card bearing a name unknown to the police, who had decided not to treat the incident as significant. Neither Napper – otherwise engaged – nor Briggs had been present, and none of the cops in the van had recognised either Kribz or another black youth seen briefly skulking across the street. But she wasn't mollified, not being able to discount a possible connection between the occurrence and previous events.

She decided to put the matter to the back of her mind and now drove calmly out on the M4 motorway, slipping down onto the Hayes bypass. The bailiffs had agreed to be there at 4pm; she would meet them at the Stanwell service station to give them a pep talk about the consequences of failure.

Right, this is just an old guy with an old wife but be careful, he's got a lot of dogs and he's in a desperate mood. Or something like that, she would say. Her whole body tingled with anticipation: this had been over a year in preparation but now she was about to make serious progress towards becoming rich. The only fly in the ointment was Blake's failure to secure the charging order against the property, but that would come within days. In the meantime, the old man could pack up his stuff and get the fuck off the very valuable real estate of which she would soon have beneficial and legal ownership.

73

Rankin had stayed off the whiskey all day and was feeling the pressure. It was all coming together though, after a fashion, and instinct told him that all this could do no harm. All his life he'd hated inaction: do or die and then move on, come what may, but whatever you do, don't take anything lying down.

Napper heard the padlocks being unfastened and was not especially pleased. He'd got used to his safe and sturdy little jail and wasn't overly keen on being part of whatever was about to go down outside of it.

'Come on Officer Nappy, or whatever your feckin' name is, time for you to spring into action, my son.'

The cop got to his feet, shakily. 'What are you talking about?' He saw that the Gypsy was not carrying his shotgun.

'C'mon, yer a feckin' copper aren't you? You'll need to see what's going on here and I suggest you call for help – as soon as I give you your feckin' phone back. Now, you're gonna walk with me to the big shed to join our party. What you're about to see will get you a nice promotion I reckon son, and don't try to run for it. I can still get to my gun before you reach the fence. Now walk, slowly.'

Napper, stiff and sore and in no fit state to run anyway, did as he was told and as he was led into the big shed, he relaxed a notch; he was not about to become the centre of attention. It had been several hours since he'd had a snort of the stash he'd found in his temporary home and residual fatigue was all he now felt. Drained, he surveyed the scene. He knew a bit about dogfighting, having seen it portrayed on screen, but he'd never witnessed the savage fixation on the faces of this bunch of thugs whose love of violence had reduced them to salivating perverts, gleefully inspecting snarling caged dogs before placing bets on those they fancied to inflict the most death and serious injury. If any of them had noticed Napper enter with their host, they would have assumed he was one of the Gypsy's gophers. They wouldn't have been far wrong.

Kemal Gozit carried the cage containing the five very young pups into the shed. All eyes were on him, including those of the six or seven muzzled dogs, either in cages or being held on very short leashes. The entry of the pups got lots of attention; a new spectacle, something to be relished, like a rare wine or a plate of truffles. Gozit heaved the cage up onto a shelf at the far end of the shed, just beneath the high, unglazed window. The pups stood in the cage and shivered, looking down at the fight pit, wide-eyed, confused, scared.

Tom Rankin wanted to get the show on the road – and over with. He was not sure how it would end, other than messily. He just hoped that some good would emerge from the mess and was working on the basis that more mess equalled more good.

'Right!' He had their attention. 'First up is number 45 against number 72. Can we have owners and agreed referee please!' His shouts were clear above the background noise of barking and betting. Both dogs were owned by Albanians, although in 72's case this ownership was nominal as 72 was Ciara who had caught sight of her pups in the elevated cage at the far end of the pit and was yelping and straining so hard at the leash her handler had a battle to restrain her. Between Ciara and her whimpering offspring was 45, an experienced Presa Canario in the process of being given an idiotic stream of instructions by its handler, a young shaven-headed Albo with a facial tattoo.

'Gents,' Rankin addressed both handlers loudly enough for all to hear, 'have both dogs been weighed and washed to your satisfaction?' The men nodded, happy that neither animal significantly outweighed the other, or had toxin-laced pelts or claws.

'Carry on referee!' ordered the show host, who then stepped out of the pit as quickly as his bad knees would allow.

The instant Ciara was un-muzzled and unleashed she made a dash for the other side of the pit in a doomed attempt to reach her pups. The Presa only had to wait for her, upending the poor bitch with one lunge and an upward jerk of its huge head. Ciara recovered and retaliated, managing to turn on the beast bravely to sink her teeth into its hind leg. The crowd roared – and Tom Rankin sent a text from his own phone, before tossing Napper his.

The Presa rolled over and spun away, expertly dislodging its opponent before swiftly counter attacking with another upward thrust, knocking Ciara over and then sinking its teeth into her neck, locking its mighty jaws and bearing down with its full body weight. The terror and confusion did not deter Ciara from her mission, her eyes, though misted with agony, were fixed on her pups a few yards away. But she couldn't deal with the dog on her back and the match looked like it would be over sooner than was profitable. In-fight bets were being placed, so the agony had to be prolonged. The referee called in the handlers and the combatants were separated; a breakstick was rammed between the Presa's jaws, forcing it to release its grip before being dragged off Ciara who then made another lunge towards her offspring. Her handler caught her with a stick-collar and drove her harshly back to the centre of the pit, not releasing her until the now furious Presa was between her and the pups.

'Fight on!' shouted the referee, and this time Ciara went for Presa directly, her rage and desperation suddenly evening the odds. The men roared, betting escalated – and the shed door crashed open.

74

Kribz led his ski-masked soldiers in with all the aplomb of a military commander, Screwloose's loaded gun in the front of his belt and clearly visible. For this to work it had to look good, and the gang leader's surging adrenalin expunged any trace of nerves or self-doubt.

Despite the absence of specific instructions from Rankin, Kribz knew the required outcomes. Firstly, rid his new business partner of these Albanians once and for all; they were nothing but trouble and were obviously planning some kind of takeover of the old man's business. Secondly, although he knew nothing about the real estate game, the drugs business had taught him that contamination affected price, so turning the place into a war zone would do no harm at all. From what Rankin had told him he reasoned that the old man's hold on his homestead would be stronger if its value took a serious turn for the worse.

'What the fuck is going on in this shithole?!' He roared the rhetorical question, flashing menacing glares at as many of the startled occupants as he could make eye contact with. There was no reply.

'Stop that fuckin' fight – now!' He pulled the weapon out and made a show of cocking it whilst marching straight up to the nearest Albo and pointing the barrel at his head. He'd unwittingly made the right choice – it was Kemal Gozit.

'Any fuckin' shit from any one of you and this cunt is dead! We've all got fuckin' guns!'

And indeed they had. Driss stood at Kribz's side whilst the other four boys spread to the left and right, circling behind the astonished crowd, their guns out and swiveling ominously.

The fighting dogs had re-engaged, with Ciara trying to pull her front paw out of the Presa's jaws. The break stick was deployed again; the dogs pulled apart and dragged into separate cages.

'Get your hands behind your heads and kneel on the floor!' Kribz was really getting into role – and Driss was really getting worried: it was like his brother wanted to use that piece.

Larssen's Beemer rolled quietly into Rankin's front driveway, followed by the two bailiffs in their shiny black van. There was no sign of life at the front of the house, no reply to the doorbell, but the door was ajar. She led the way inside.

One of the bailiffs shouted, procedurally, 'Anyone at home?' Silence. He and his partner looked around the hallway and then at each other, then they noticed that Larssen had gone on ahead of them, into the kitchen and towards the lounge and the rear of the house.

She stepped out onto the patio and surveyed what appeared to be the deserted homestead. *Fuck*, she thought. Was she to be deprived of her pleasure, the sight of that Irish pig being told to vacate what would soon be her land? A Boeing screamed overhead.

The ragtag bunch of blood-thirsters was on its collective knees, as instructed by Captain Fuckin' Kribz of the Braganza Brigade. All apart from Gozit who remained standing, seemingly mesmerised by the gun held to his head from a few feet away. And apart from Tom Rankin who moved slowly, cautiously, to the side of the shed.

'Oi, cunt!' shouted Shanker. 'On your fuckin' knees!'

Rankin looked at Kribz who ignored him, pointedly. The old man did as ordered, lest he gave the game away. But he had almost got to the wall and was within reaching distance of the Purdy which lay hidden beneath a piece of sacking.

Then Kribz turned to Gozit. 'And you!' That was when Gozit went for his weapon.

Larssen froze at the sound of the gunshot. Both bailiffs instinctively bobbed their heads and shrank back into the house; this was way above their paygrade. The Dane focused on the back shed, over a hundred yards away.

The bullet had missed its target and Gozit's head was still intact. But the Gheg lay with both hands to his throat, trying to quell the spurting blood whilst staring at Kribz who couldn't believe what he'd just done. The shed would have fallen completely silent, had it not been for the dogs. The eruption of barking and howling did nothing for an occasion that should have been enthralling, sombre at least: a man was about to die.

Frantic in their cages, the animals provided movement and noise in contrast to the surrounding human stasis. The B Boys, guns still raised, were wide eyed and motionless, as if waiting for a signal, a prompt. Then came the sound of police sirens.

'Time we was outta here bruv!' Driss shouted this without taking his eyes off the two or three Albanians who were sharing the aim of his gun.

'Yeah bro, come on, wadda we gonna do, we can't fuckin'—' Numbers was voicing the concern felt by all. He was interrupted.

'Get the pups an' the bitch bro,' said Kribz to Driss as he kicked Gozit's gun away from its dying owner.

'Fuck that man, c'mon, we gotta get outta here!'

'None of you's are goin' feckin' anywhere.'

All heads turned to see Rankin, the Purdy raised stock to shoulder and pointing directly at Kribz. The distance between them was over ten yards and Rankin had just seen that the gang leader was no marksman; couldn't even hit a fat Albo's head at point blank range.

'Drop your guns, the feckin' lot of you, or your boss man gets his block blown off.'

Kribz made a show of obeying and let Screwloose's weapon clatter onto the concrete floor. The sound of the sirens gave way to the overhead scream of the next flight to God knew where. When this subsided, the sirens sounded much closer.

'C'mon! All of you, I'm not feckin' jokin', you'ze got three seconds.'

More pistols hit the concrete. Napper sent a text, his movement distracting Rankin for half a second, enough time for the suddenly desperate Shanker to make his move – he had to get out of there or he was going back to boob for sure – he raised his gun and fired in one skillful movement. The bullet hit the Gypsy in the leg, just above the knee. As Rankin fell he impulsively returned fire but Shanker rolled away, catching only a few of the searing pellets from the Purdy. The two blasts sent the dogs into further uproar and the kneeling gunpoint captives down onto their faces.

Rankin turned again, but both Kribz and Driss were on the floor. Kribz recovered his gun and fired twice at Rankin, deliberately missing, as did the Irishman as he discharged the Purdy's remaining barrel. The pellets flew over the heads of both brothers and the Gypsy surrendered.

On receiving information that firearms were being used the police held back, pulling up in the narrow suburban streets and staying at least a hundred metres clear of the homestead. The airwaves crackled with code words for procedural instructions whilst a hierarchical chain of command fell into place and armed units were summoned from the nearby airport.

Larssen and her bailiffs had wisely stayed near the house, the racket from the back shed and the sound of approaching emergency services telling them to remain as spectators and nothing more.

Kribz and Driss were back on their feet, the older brother barking orders. 'Keep your guns on them and back off to the door, come on, we gotta get the fuck outta here!'

'What about the pups?' asked Driss.

'Fuck the pups bro, we gonna get fuckin' capped or nicked or fuckin' both if we don't fuck off real quick, now come on bros, keep your eyes on these fuckers and back yourselves towards the door.'

Napper was at Rankin's side and applying his belt as a tourniquet to the wounded man's leg. 'Don't fuckin' tell them who I am,' he hissed into the contorted red face, 'or I'll loosen this and you'll fuckin' bleed to death.' Rankin managed a brief nod of his head as he forced himself not to scream.

Then, despite his agony, Rankin yelled advice. 'Go round behind this shed, there's a hole in the feckin' fence, then a path to the reservoir, follow that and you won't have to...argh!' Napper tugged the tourniquet hard and forced a thumb into Rankin's left eye socket.

'Hey, right, you wid the beard, what's your fuckin' game?' Kribz was addressing Napper who wasn't acting like he was scared.

'He's okay,' wheezed Rankin, 'He's one of my own.'

'Okay beardy, get your boss outta here, rapid.'

Napper took the old man under the armpits and dragged him across the floor and out of the door.

The Braganza Boys had heard enough. 'Okay you heard him innit, let's go!' shouted Kribz.

Shanker dawdled, hesitated, his eyes on Rankin's Purdy; he fancied owning it.

'Come on Shanker, move it!' Kribz immediately regretted the use of his man's name. And then they all bundled out of the shed, wide eyed and colliding with each other, panicking that the Albos would be up and taking aim – but they needn't have worried: the brave dogfighters were only too glad to see the backs of their lunatic masked visitors. Like good captains, Kribz and Massive were last to leave, covering their boys as they dashed out into the bright sun before turning to the rear of the building and the hole in the fence kindly made by a certain trespasser a couple of days earlier.

Before following, Kribz slammed the door shut and bolted it. 'Get him and yourself well away from this fuckin' shed!' he shouted to Napper. The cop did as advised.

With Driss and the rest of them already gone, Kribz and Massive made for the escape route. On reaching the back of the shed Kribz started to give Massive the go-ahead but there was no need: the big man was already priming the grenade and two seconds later it was sailing through the unglazed window.

The Police Armed Response Team pulled up on location. Larssen and the bailiffs emerged from the front door of the house to be confronted by two personnel carriers parked across the gates, an assortment of cops pointing guns and a negotiator with a megaphone.

'Stay exactly where you are and keep your hands in full view!' The three of them just stood on the steps and gawped. Larssen attempted to be helpful. 'It's not us you're after, there's something going on around the back. We're here to serve court papers.' She managed to shout this clearly before the next monstrous Boeing intervened. The usual surreal ten seconds elapsed before communication could continue.

'Walk slowly towards us, stay well apart from each other and prepare to be searched. This is purely precautionary, once your identities have been verified, you'll be taken to a place of safety.' The instructions were loud, clear, and rehearsed.

75

Napper was still crouching over Rankin when he was hit by the shed door, blown off its hinges by the force of the explosion. It knocked him down and onto the puce-faced injured Irishman whose sense of humour had amazingly not deserted him. 'For feck's *sake!* What's happenin' feckin' *now!?*'

The cop straightened up with some effort, shrugging off a large chunk of splintered wood. He turned and peered through the gaping entrance – and then came the screams.

The police officers at the front of the house heard the grenade explode, and the negotiator hastened the process of getting Larssen and her bailiffs to the safe side of the cordon, searched, and into police vehicles where they would be detained for their own protection. The senior officer wasn't totally satisfied that the Dane and her men weren't involved. He'd already dispatched three of his officers to the rear of the house and within minutes they were cautiously approaching the opening in the fence just behind the shed, still unable to see Napper and the wounded Rankin, but within clear earshot of the wailing, barking and shouting coming from within. They climbed through the fence and into the compound, gingerly circling the shed.

'Give me my warrant card!' murmured Napper through gritted teeth, as he leaned over Rankin. 'It's in my top pocket, get it your feckin' self,' wheezed the old man.

The approaching police team came upon the pair, to find Napper slowly dragging Rankin towards the house.

The lead officer pointed his weapon at them both. 'Stay where you are and raise your arms. Make your hands visible!'

'I'm a police officer!' shouted Napper, vainly attempting to make himself heard above the Airbus which seemed to be hovering directly overhead for maximum effect. But he had heard the order, or at least knew what was expected of him, and did as bade. Rankin, suddenly unsupported, slumped and, still in great pain, involuntarily moved his hand quickly towards the tourniquet around his thigh. An officer fired a single shot. The bullet grazed Rankin's shoulder before hitting Napper's arm, just above the elbow, and then the wounded pair were overpowered, spread-eagled and searched by two of the armed cops, leaving the third to cover the gaping smoke-filled doorway of the shed, whilst shouting into his radio for reinforcements. The Airbus was suddenly gone, according precedence to the agonised human and canine din. Radios crackled and within a few more seconds the outhouse was surrounded, instructions were loud-hailed and the Albanians who were able walked slowly out into the sunlight, hands raised, heads down. A clearance tactic was deployed and the shed was carefully but theatrically entered by the armed response team with halogen flashlights, voices and weapons raised.

76

The road out of the back of the village was easy to find and the posse had no need to drive anywhere near the Rankin place to reach it. Kribz thumbed his phone. He'd missed several calls from Screwloose – that was another thing that had to be dealt with. It hadn't quite hit him yet that he'd just become a murderer; there was no way the Albo he'd shot would survive. He'd shot and injured before, but this would be the first time he'd dispatched another human being. As things to be tackled went, it should have been top of the list. No doubt at some point it would be, but for now it was mere detail. The job was done and Rankin was surely now in front – for the time being, anyway. The Branganza Boys had seen to that. His Braganza Boys. Kribz felt good.

He called the rested gunman.

'Yo Kribz, what the fuck's 'apnin' man?'

'Nuthin' much bro, you cool?'

'Never mind about me bruv, I saw youz getting swifted man, you in the boob now? They let you 'ave your phone?'

'I'm fine innit, they let me go. I was lucky, man, just casin' the place and they swooped. I wasn't carryin' your piece so they had nuttin' on me.'

'Where's my fuckin' piece then bruv?'

'Don't worry, it's safe man.'

Screwloose could hear his leader was in a vehicle.

'So what's cookin' now bro? You comin' to pick me up? I'm goin' stir crazy innit, stuck home alone.'

'Nah, let's give it few days man, a lot of 'eat about jus' now. I'll see you at the weekend.'

'The weekend? What's fuckin' goin' on man? I ain't a weekend fuckin' member, fuck man—'

Kribz interrupted. 'Gotta go bro, laters.' And that was it.

Screwloose knew something was seriously wrong and that he was losing control. He stared down at his phone and tried to call Kribz back but got declined. He slung the device onto his bed and it bounced. He kicked a book that was lying on the floor. It hit the wardrobe door and also bounced; back to his feet, front cover up: 'Victorian Slavery – the Shame of the British'.

77

Briggs had got wind of the 'major incident' by way of a call from the police control room at Heathrow; his name and number had popped up on numerous screens during the frantic risk assessment conducted at the start of the deployment.

'Yes, I've been investigating intel on that premises for some time. What's the problem?'

Having been told of the mounting operation he seconded a young officer called Rebecca Mason to drive him to Stanwell Moor.

'Shouldn't we seek authority before attending a fucking armed incident unarmed?' she asked.

'Don't worry, we're not getting involved, I just want to be there at the aftermath. There's a lot more to this than meets the eye.'

Forty minutes later they arrived and showed their warrant cards to the cordon controller.

'I can't let you pass yet mate,' said the bored lad with the clipboard. 'The ARU are still securing the place; we're waiting on the dog handlers to come and there's a load of fuckin' pit bulls in there. Personally, I'd just shoot the fuckin' things and….'

But Briggs wasn't listening; he was looking past and behind the officer at the tall woman striding towards them.

'Well, well, it's none other than *Detective* Briggs. I think you missed the action, *Detective*.'

Briggs did not like the sarcasm, especially in front of his female colleague.

'It certainly seems like *you're* always near the action, *Muz* Larssen, a little bit worryingly so, I might add.'

Briggs was immediately proud of his riposte and glanced at young Mason who didn't know the history but smirked approvingly anyway. Emboldened, he continued to address the Dane, who stood only feet away on the other side of the cordon.

'We'll probably need to get another statement from you now, *Muz* Larssen, as you obviously have some sort of season ticket to these events.' He was on a roll and the accented *Muz* was a returned compliment.

'Oh, stop showing off to your girlfriend, Mr Briggs, you're clearly not up to your job or you'd have been here earlier for the firework display—'

'All right madam, that'll be enough of that. Please return to the witness holding area.'

The Dane did as the cop with the clipboard requested, but not before giving both Briggs and Mason withering looks.

'Who's your fucking friend?' asked Mason. A curled lip had replaced the smirk and the expletive was a regular feature of her speech.

'She's a liquidator and she's trying to take possession of this place.' Briggs' answer did nothing to enlighten Mason.

The cop with the clipboard made an unsolicited contribution. 'She's a pain in the fuckin' arse, that's for sure. I'm surprised she hasn't been slapped in fuckin' cuffs by now, the trouble she's been causing.'

A team of paramedics needed to be checked out of the cordon to unload two stretchers into one of the nearby ambulances. The first to go through was Rankin; the cop with the clipboard looked at his watch and noted the departure from the cordon of one injured white male, yet unidentified and in need of a police escort. The second stretcher bore an extremely pissed off looking PC Douglas Napper with a heavily bandaged arm.

Briggs was astonished. 'Doug! What the fuck! The world and his wife have been looking for you!'

'Been unavoidably detained,' wheezed the exhausted Cornishman.

Briggs walked alongside the stretcher. 'What in God's name happened?'

'Watchin' a fuckin' war kick aaf. Let's just say I was a guest with a ringside fuckin' seat.' The paramedics prepared to haul the stretcher into the ambulance, making it difficult for Briggs to stay close, but he persevered. 'Is there anything I should know about?'

'Plenty. Make sure the whole place is searched, including for drugs.' And then the prostrate Napper disappeared behind slamming ambulance doors.

78

The blast had put paid to the electric lighting, allowing the darkness, thick smoke and stench of roasted flesh inside the shed to mercifully disorientate the search party cops, some of whom were youngsters in their twenties. But only for about thirty seconds. Then their eyes and throats adjusted to the smoke, their ears to the wailing and howling, and their minds reeled at what they beheld. Two Albanians – or what was left of them – were obviously beyond help. The other two of those who had remained in the building were writhing and mewling charred contortionists who looked like they were suffering from the bends. One, rocking back and forth on naked buttocks, his clothing blown off by the blast, was trying repeatedly to re-attach his left arm which was hanging from its empty shoulder socket by a single tendon.

The grenade had landed on the cage containing Ciara's pups; they had promptly disappeared together with most of their mother. The cage itself had become a bomb burst of searing shrapnel, inflicting hideous injuries on anything made of flesh and blood. One of the officers heard an incongruous sound. Investigating with her flashlight she found a relatively uninjured pit bull, starved to be fighting fit, tucking into a large lump of flesh. Fighting her own gagging reflex, the young cop couldn't bear what she was looking at and put a bullet into the animal's head. The crash of the shot attracted a blaze of halogen from his startled colleagues and the place fell deadly silent for a full three seconds.

'It was just a dog!' shouted the officer, and the job resumed. Then the paramedics were allowed in, and the clean-up began, subject to instructions on the preservation of the crime scene pending arrival of the Counter-terrorism Squad who would, over the following days, painstakingly collect, package and record every bullet, shotgun pellet and grenade fragment that had not found a soft target.

79

Having finished dismissing Screwloose over the phone Kribz thought it best to console Massive who, curled up on the back seat, was hugging his arm and shoulder. The Purdy pellets had not done serious damage, but the big negro was still very irritated that that he was going to have to seek medical assistance to get the little lumps of lead tweezered out.

'We can't take you to a hospital round here bruv, that's for fuckin' sure.' Kribz unnecessarily made this clear as he twisted round to inspect the wounded passenger. 'Are you sure you need a hospital? Can't you wrap up tight, stop the bleedin' till we get away from here?'

'Yeah, suppose, but you owe me big Kribzy and I'm needin' paid fuckin' soon.'

Both vehicles were on the M25 with the van four or five cars behind the car Driss was driving. Kribz made a decision and called Numbers whose phone was on speaker, 'Pull off somewhere, split up an' take fuckin' trains back, we'll see you at the Arch inna cuppla hours. We need to ditch these wheels, there's fuckin' cameras everywhere innit.'

'Okay bro,' said Shanker at the wheel, nodding his agreement. They pulled off at the first junction and into the town of Staines, dumped the van in a quiet back street and quickly found the railway station. But they didn't board a train, instead making for the local cab office and taking separate cars back to the swamp.

Kribz and Driss took more of a risk and kept driving around the orbital motorway, not pulling off until Leatherhead. The traffic was heavy and the journey nerve-racking, but they were shy of leaving the car with the injured Massive in tow. Sleepy Leatherhead was unsuspecting, though, and the cab firm they chose obliged with a tinted windowed people carrier, no questions asked.

The A&E Department at Ashford Hospital, the nearest to Heathrow, was mayhem. The wounded Albanians were displaying a range of reactions depending on the degree of pain and shock they were in. But all were by nature and habit less than co-operative with their police escorts, providing the scantest of personal details and accounts of what had happened. Two were very seriously injured and incapable of giving any co-operation, whether they wanted to or not.

Rankin was on a gurney in a corridor, stable and staring at the ceiling, the cannula in his arm delivering a steady flow of morphine-laced saline. Anyone with time to look may have detected a faint smile playing on the old man's lips, like he was thinking, *two birds with one feckin' stone - seen off the Albanian feckers and turned the place into a crime scene - that'll put the cat amongst the pigeons.*

On the next gurney was Napper. Briggs and Mason had followed the ambulance and stood beside the Cornishman, who was lucid but detached, fighting fatigue and trying to measure the information he was parting with.

'Got some info from a snout, got hooked, couldn't leave it alone, heard the property owner was plannin' a dogfight and that the Braganza Boys was involved. Did some snoopin' around while I was in there—'

'What, without a warrant?' Typical fucking Briggs: even Mason looked at him and tutted. 'Time and place Briggsy, fuck's sake.'

'Found some coke in one of the sheds, a small brick built one near the big shed. It wasn't actually a search; I was lookin' for somewhere to hoid.'

'Why didn't you call for assistance earlier?'

Mason tutted again and intervened. 'Let him talk Aaron, for fuck's sake.'

But Napper had the answer. 'There was a lot of activity an' I had to lay low, in a place where there wasn't a mobile signal. I was stuck there, an' then it all kicked aaf big stoil.'

'You can say that again Doug,' said Briggs before turning away to make a call.

'Wanker, isn't he,' said Mason to the injured cop as she squeezed his hand. Napper winked at her.

80

The following days saw the Rankin homestead receive the attention of many species of police life. Dog handling teams, with the help of the RSPCA, took away much of the canine population; over twenty animals were shipped to various establishments to be tested and tagged and, in some cases, destroyed if the beast was showing signs of disease or being dangerously uncontrollable. The Terrorist Squad did a full forensic search of the entire estate as it had been the scene of an explosives attack. They found nothing to indicate a danger to national security and the exhibits they collected were handed over to the Major Incident Team set up to investigate the murders of three Albanians, including Kemal Gozit, and several GBHs, along with a host of firearms and explosives offences. Many weeks of work would follow. The package of cocaine was of course quickly located in the small shed that had been Napper's prison, or rather where he'd claimed to have hidden. Both Briggs and Napper found this to be by far the most interesting aspect of the case as it was a clear indication of the involvement of the south London gangbangers.

More particularly, Briggs was fired up by the opportunity the drugs find presented. The breeding and fighting of illegal dogs were certainly criminal activities, but not compelling ammunition for restraining property under the Proceeds of Crime Act - unlike a nice twenty grand's worth of high purity cocaine. Possession of Class A Drugs with Intent to Supply was weapons-grade evidence in support of POCA applications and the courts invariably granted seizure of assets that had been even tangentially accrued by the commission of this offence. The documents Briggs had been carefully preparing were amended and enhanced. He obtained the signature of a senior officer and submitted by email his application to the Crown Prosecution Service which then made a quick and successful application to a judge at

Southwark Crown Court and the restraining order was obtained. Tom Rankin was now unable to sell or otherwise dispose of his possessions or real estate until criminal proceedings were finished and then, unless it had not been proved that he had made gains from serious criminal activity, the Crown could take the lot. The process could take months, years even.

81

Claude Jackson was just starting his day of painful physio when Stuart Blake's name came up on the screen of his vibrating phone. Having given up any hope of ever receiving good news about anything ever again, he toyed with ignoring it, but someone to talk to about something other than the shade of pink the latest prosthetics came in would be a welcome change. He stepped shakily out of the walking frame, picked up the device and hit the green icon.

'Morning Jacko,' laughed Blake. 'Have I got fucking news for you, me old mate!'

'Go on,' said Jackson, flatly, not expecting to be impressed.

'That Gypsy farm place out near Heathrow that you lot were trying to get your grubby hands on, it's been raided by the Old Bill!'

It annoyed Jackson that Blake was laughing. The lawyer went on. 'There was some sort of riot with people getting blown away and grenades going off, and then the cops steamed in and found twenty grand's worth of Charlie. You couldn't make it up, mate!'

The brief's exuberance tailed off, Jackson's silence deflating him. 'Are you listening Jacko?'

'Yes, I'm listening, and wondering why the fuck you're telling me this.'

'Because this little turn of events has shafted your bitch former business partner right up the fucking arse, that's why.

The police have got the CPS to restrain the property and everything in it, so now the lovely Larssen can't get anywhere near it, now do you understand?'

And now Jackson got it. 'Yeah, I suppose it's sinking in, but what's this to do with me?'

'Well, for a start it stops me from getting a charge put on the property in her favour.'

'I thought you'd already done that.'

'I tried but, as luck would have it, the judge got arsey and sent me packing. I was due to go back tomorrow – I still will 'cos I shouldn't know about what's happened – but my application is bound to fail now. The property has effectively been seized by the Crown pending POCA proceedings.'

'I'm still looking at a lump of plastic where my left leg should be.'

'Point taken mate, but there's something else. When all this kicked off at that fucking farm yesterday, she was there! Now, what's that all about?'

'She was probably serving the eviction order. What happened? Was the place booby trapped or something?'

'Nah, there was all sorts of shit going on, Albanians and spades battling over God knows what. Like I say, you couldn't make it up mate.'

'Okay Stuart, thanks for the call. At least I know she hasn't profited from my loss, not yet anyway.'

'And not any time soon mate. Ciao!'

Blake ended the call, a little disappointed by Jackson's lack of enthusiasm. *Ah, what the fuck*? he thought. *The one-legged wanker was up to his throat in it – what goes round comes round, my son.* And with that the lawyer cracked a Stella, his first of the day.

82

Tom Rankin lay in a side ward, his bed next to the window. Swathed in bandages and sporting several cannulas with bleeping attachments, he was not in a good way. He had just finished a video call with his wife, a nurse having propped his phone on his chest to facilitate the conversation. Marlene was not happy, nor overly sympathetic.

'I told you all this dog fighting would end badly and when I get back home I'm putting that place up for sale. We're getting chased out anyway so we might as well jump before we're pushed.'

'Leave it to me my dear, it's all under control.' The Irishman couldn't see what his wife's screen showed, otherwise he would have put more effort into being convincing.

The call had ended with Marlene threatening to return to Ireland for good if things didn't change for the better. Blah, blah, he'd heard it all before.

83

The D7 boys left the Arch quietly and separately, first Gillie then twenty minutes later, Shanker. Numbers had tried to hang around longer but was dismissed soon afterwards.

An hour then passed in which the conversation between Kribz, Driss and Massive was forced and desultory. It was mostly about their collective past, the one they shared growing up in the swamp. They laughed about school, getting nicked, Feltham YOI, the parties, the money, the girls, and lots more stuff that avoided making direct or even oblique references to more recent history. Kribz was particularly keen to keep the chat light and on shit: he didn't want Driss knowing about his deal with Massive. Thankfully, the big man picked up on this and played along.

'I need to go, innit,' he eventually said to the Braganza leader. 'Will you see me out bro?'

'Sure bro, stairs are dodgy.' Kribz was on his feet and leading the way. Driss sat still, low down on a scrapyard car seat, constructing a spliff.

140

Kribz turned to face Massive before he opened the street door at the bottom of the staircase. 'Okay, I'm keepin' my word, don't worry. You'll 'ave 'im tomorrow.'

Massive nodded but looked down.

'What's up, bro?'

'Lost ma piece man, innit, it's still on the floor in that fuckin' shed man.'

'Fuck, man, why didn't you say somethin' before now?' Kribz knew the answer but got it anyway.

'Fuckin' embarrassed bro, ashamed innit.'

'Did it 'ave your dabs on it?'

'No, it's safe, wiped it down with my gloves on, still gutted though, it was a beauty.'

Kribz knew why Massive had divulged the mishap. He put on his own gloves, pulled Screwloose's pistol from the small of his back and handed it over.

'Thanks bro, you'll get it back.'

'Nah, keep it Mass, I'm done wid the fuckin' thing.'

Then, more for affect than confidentiality - there was no one within earshot - Kribz leaned forward and murmured. The parting sentence into the big man's ear contained a time and a location. Massive nodded, stowed the weapon and was gone.

84

Screwloose left his place at five o'clock sharp the next morning and set off to Myatts Fields to meet Kribz, as instructed by his leader six hours previously. He was getting a job to do, and he was getting his piece back, so he had a spring in his step.

His journey took him through Cobalt Gardens, a particularly rundown square surrounded by derelict flats and garages. Abandoned cars littered the place, along with used syringes and piles of fly-tipped rubbish.

It was still dark, but he recognised the masked figure that suddenly appeared before him.

'Kribz told me to give this to you.' Massive's unmistakable voice was calm, almost melodic. Screwloose stopped walking and felt his knees weaken. 'So here it is.'

The gunshot may have woken a few slumbering inhabitants of the surrounding sink estate, but not many, and they wouldn't have been interested anyway. It was south London, the swamp.

And then Screwloose felt nothing more, ever again.

Part Two:

Algorithm

85

Tom Rankin discharged himself from hospital three days later and persuaded one of the nurses to call him a cab.

'Are you sure you're wantin' to do this Tom?' she said, her Irish brogue endearing her to the old man.

'Yes, my darlin', you've looked after me well enough, and the doctors've been grand, but I've a business to run and a wife to fret over me.'

'At least let me change your dressings first, it won't take long and then the cab'll be outside waiting by then.'

Having a business to run and a wife to fret over him was a watered-down version of having the fear of God that his place was going to get torched and his wife was going to kill him into the bargain, but Rankin thought it best not to divulge too much detail.

An hour later the Indian cab driver helped his passenger out of the vehicle and into the porch of the house. Having seen the arrival, Marlene opened the door in fury. 'What the feck! You're not supposed to be home Tom, they told me another week at least!' But she helped him in anyway.

'Pay this man please, an' give him a good tip.' Rankin jerked his head at the driver before limping through into the lounge and collapsing into his armchair, looking around to see if there was a bottle of Black Bush handy. There wasn't – no surprise there.

Marlene paid the cabbie and put the kettle on. 'I might've known you'd do this, against the doctor's orders, I might've known.'

She followed him into the lounge and saw he was already asleep. She lifted his feet up onto an old poof, slung a blanket over him and gently took the skew-whiff specs from his face and placed them on the mantlepiece. She stood back a pace and regarded him with a mixture of love and scorn. 'Feck's sake, Thomas Rankin, what am I going to do with you?'

86

Twelve hundred miles away another man was sat in an armchair, but he was very much awake and had slept barely four hours over the preceding three days. Zamir Gozit had been back in Albania for almost three years, most of which had been spent greasing the palms of Albanian cops whilst giving a wide berth to the ones whose palms weren't greasable.

He'd emigrated to the UK as a boy with his family and had listened to his father recite lies of them being Kosovan refugees, a status which afforded rights of residency in the land of *mundësi*. At only twelve years of age with no English he found life hard at first, but the onset of puberty in a school of hard knocks in east London's rough town of Barking had moulded the young Gozit into a teenaged horror story. He didn't need to join a gang: like a dozen or so other boys in the school, he was an Albo, and they were *familje*, as tight knit as if they'd come out of the same womb.

But of course a gang did emerge and by the time Zamir reached his twentieth birthday he was a leading younger of the notorious Hellbanianz, an amorphous outfit with its roots in Barking and tentacles all over London. The Hellbanianz hadn't been a gang as such for very long; the very nature of its members and their natural capacity for organization, loyalty and extreme violence had soon earned them the official tag of OCN – an Organised Crime Network.

Old Kemal Gozit had seen the road his only son was taking and tried and failed to throw him out of the family home before heading west to less lawless Shepherd's Bush where he set up his car wash, leaving his wayward son to stay in the east end of London and do what the hell he liked. That way the old man could maintain a semblance of hard-working law-abidingness without having the constant worry of police raids on the family home. He took with him his semi-literate wife and trainee nurse daughter and made it his mission to keep them well clear of Zamir, whose criminal career was on an upward climb to international cocaine trafficking, kidnapping and contract killing.

So, Gozit senior had been unashamedly relieved on hearing that his son had made a dash back to the motherland when evidence of his involvement in the fatal shooting of a black gang leader had become sufficiently compelling to activate the issue of an international arrest warrant. Zamir had laid low in Tirana for several months but the once anarchic capital city of a country eager for EU membership was now home to an uncomfortably keen state police department which was busy shedding its reputation for endemic corruption. So Zamir had become a pariah in his own hometown, unable to secure safe accommodation no matter how much of his ill-gotten gains he waved in the faces of property developers, hoteliers and estate agents.

It was in a house in the run-down mountain village of Ferraj, five miles to the north of Tirana, that young Zamir was sitting when he got the news that his father had been shot dead by a bunch of *zezaks*. The news had arrived via his encrypted satphone; he just stared at the device after the caller, a contact in Barking, rung off abruptly. He tried to patch together in his mind some sort of picture, any chain of events that could have led to this, a sliver of logic; people didn't get whacked for no reason, not in London.

He'd hardly spoken to his father in years and his mother and sister would have nothing to do with him. His immediate conclusion was that this was a *Kanun* killing and that his father's murder was a settling of scores. Still holding the satphone, Zamir burst into tears, briefly of sorrow, then quickly of rage. He hurled the device across the dirty little room, threw his head back and screamed.

87

PC Doug Napper had made an executive decision whilst lying in his hospital bed. He'd only been there for an hour: the bullet had cracked a bone in his elbow and torn a couple of tendons, nothing too serious. He'd been bandaged up with his arm in a sling and discharged with a bottle of painkillers for when the morphine wore off. He prepared himself for the inevitable inquisition. He was in deep shit, whatever happened, and his job was at risk. But those who would question him – and they'd be queuing up – would have to be very lucky to get the truth out of him. He just hoped Rankin would stick to the script.

Fortuitously, their gurneys had been parked side by side once in the A&E department and Napper had managed to get the old man's attention for a few minutes as the frantic nurses coped with the more serious casualties.

'Right Rankin, listen!' he'd hissed.

Rankin hadn't even turned his head. 'Aye son, I'm listening. What've you got in mind?'

'You lockin' me in that shed never happened, right?'

'Right.'

'You never set eyes on me until we were in the big shed, right?'

'Right.'

'Stick to that story and I won't have you prosecuted for fuckin' kidnapping me, right?'

'Right.'

The cop was going to leave it at that, but Rankin was a nosey bastard. 'Why, though?'

Napper had sighed through his exhaustion and decided to come clean. 'Because I'm fuckin' embarrassed, that's why, and I'll lose my job for breakin' into your place without a fuckin' warrant. Is that clear enough for you?'

The logic wasn't lost on the Irishman. 'Lad, crystal feckin' clear.' Napper could almost hear Rankin's cheeky smile and relaxed a bit. Job done, for the time being at least.

And it had been just in time because that was when Briggs and Mason had rocked up.

88

'Do you *know* Doug Napper?' asked Mason, as the pair sat in the canteen at Heathrow Police Station the next morning.

'Not very well, and I'm beginning to wish I'd never met him. He's a good cop but he's a loose cannon.' Briggs was keen not to slag off Napper because he got the impression Mason liked the wretched man, so he gritted his teeth and took the moral high ground. 'Don't get me wrong, it's coppers like Napper who get things done, force issues out into the open.'

Mason nodded wistfully, looking down at her cup of tea.

Briggs went on. 'I expect he'll be in for a torrid time, mind you. He's got a bit of explaining to do about being at the scene of a mini war in the middle of nowhere and fifteen miles from his designated patch.'

'He'll handle it.' Mason was now smiling at her cup.

The conversation was interrupted. 'DC Briggs?' The speaker was one of two suits who'd just walked into the canteen. They had PSD written all over them: a couple of automatons from the uniformed branch who'd had recent visits to Marks and Spencer.

Briggs looked up. 'Yes, that's me.'

'I'm DS Bamber and this is DS Wallace. We're from Professional Standards.'

'You don't say,' replied Briggs, his impertinence impressing Mason, until he lost his bottle and ruined it with a sheepish smile.

Bamber ignored the weak slight. 'We need to have a few words with you Mr Briggs. We've reserved an interview room downstairs.'

Briggs noted the 'Mr' bit: typical plodspeak; these two were definitely wooden-tops in cheap polyester. 'What, now?'

'Yes please, Mr Briggs.'

Briggs' eyes fell to meet Mason's worried gaze. 'Excuse me, Rebecca, catch you later.' He rose with a sigh.

The two rubberheels led him out of the eating area, down to the ground floor and into one of the witness interview rooms. Briggs didn't like their silence: no small talk, no holding the door for him.

'Sit down, please.' This came from Wallace, tersely. Briggs sat, starting to feel a bit worried. He should get some sort of grip on this.

'Do I need a Fed rep?' he asked, as casually as his rising pulse would allow.

'Not really necessary, Mr Briggs, this isn't an interview under caution, but if you insist on a representative of the Police Federation being here, we won't object.'

Briggs felt his nervousness giving way to anger – and liked the feeling. 'Okay, let's just get on with it. What's this about?' Nowhere near as if he didn't know.

All three of them were sat around the small table. There was no visible recording machine, but Briggs didn't trust them not to be wired. It didn't occur to him that these two wouldn't have a clue how to operate covert kit.

'Just an informal chat, Mr Briggs,' said Bamber, formally. 'We want to establish what sort of relationship you have with one PC Douglas Napper.'

'What do you mean, relationship?'

'Well, you know, how well do you know him? Have you worked together long?'

Briggs was beginning to feel at ease, superior even: these two were on a fishing expedition, a pair of numpties sent to test the water.

149

'I've known him for less than a year. He's a top class beat officer, knows his patch like the back of his hand, virtually got his own server on the Crimint system. The intel he gets is always high grade and he keeps me and a lot of other *detectives* busy actioning it.' He watched Bamber's eyes narrow at the emphasis but the PSD man didn't bite.

Although quite pleased with his boldness, Briggs decided to dial it down a bit. 'As regards anything else about PC Napper I'm afraid I can't help you gentlemen. That's really the extent of my relationship with the officer.'

'Does he have any informants?' asked Wallace with a slightly lowered tone, as if moving onto delicate ground.

Briggs was having none of it. 'Not that I know of. I've nothing to do with other cops' registered informants. You'll have to ask him, or go to the DI.'

The two suits regarded him for a few seconds, then Bamber stood up and Wallace did likewise.

'Okay Aaron,' Bamber said chummily, 'thanks for your time. You'll no doubt tell him we've spoken to you and I'm sure he'll understand.'

'Have you seen him yet? Is he in trouble?' Briggs thought it best to ask.

'Two of our colleagues are with him now.'

89

And they most certainly were. Although signed off sick with his arm in a weird plastic sling, Doug Napper was at his place of work in Kennington Police Station. The derelict canteen's fare was limited to vile shit from a vending machine that didn't give change. Three plastic cups of this were on a table at which Napper sat facing his own brace of PSD officers. But these two were different from the pair who'd seen Briggs: DI Colin Reeve and DS Gill Durman were proper, time-served detectives who'd done their shift catching criminals before being transferred under duress to the 'funny firm'. Both awaited promotion and a stint with the PSD was expected of them.

'How're you feeling, Doug?' Reeve's voice was weary: he was fifty and feeling it.

'I'm fine, guv'nor, off me tits on Co-codamol mind you, so me memory's a bit slow.' Reeve and Durman laughed.

'Okay, Doug,' said Durman, 'might as well get down to it. This isn't an interview under caution, nothing you say to us will be used against you.'

Yeah, right, thought Napper.

'We've read the statement you made in your hospital bed,' she took out two copies as she spoke and handed one to him, 'and we just want to go over a few bits and pieces, okay?'

Napper shrugged. 'Yeah, fine, crack on sarge, fire away.'

Reeve sat back and began thumbing his phone absent-mindedly, like he was on the subs' bench. Durman cracked on, as invited.

'Right, paragraph seven, you state that you received information to the effect that indictable criminal offences were being planned or committed at a property in Stanwell Moor, Middlesex, and that you decided to take it upon yourself to investigate, alone and unsupervised. Correct?'

'Correct.'

'Why?'

'The information came from a private contact, my solicitor in fact, and as such unregisterable as a police informant.'

Reeve stopped thumbing his phone. 'Did you put this information onto the Crimint system?'

'You'll know that I didn't. What was the point? It was single strand intel, unverifiable and highly unlikely to be used by anyone but me.'

Reeve smiled wryly: it was an excellent answer.

Durman took up again. 'Why didn't you tell anyone where you were going?'

'I took a chance. I thought I'd be there and back inside just a few hours, and I was on a rest day so no one would miss me.'

'But events overtook you and you felt obliged to remain on the property for two and a half days, even though you say you had no signal on your phone so you couldn't call in.'

'I know, big mistake, but that's me I'm afraid. I sussed there was some action looming and I couldn't leave it alone.' Napper paused, frowning, then said 'Can you understand that?'

'Of course we can Doug, but—'

'It got to the point where I couldn't have got out of there if I'd wanted to. Things were happenin', I had to lie low. It's all in here.' He waved his copy of the statement with his unslung hand.

'You say you couldn't call in, but the CAD system shows a 999 call coming from you. That was the call that got the armed units to attend.'

'Again, like it says in my statement, I was hidin' in some sort of strongroom, in a bit of a low area. There was no signal until I broke cover and looked in the big shed. Could see it all kickin' off, then I had a signal and made the call.'

'And it was in the storage hut – or strongroom, as you're now calling it – that you found the cocaine?'

'Yes, sarge.'

'You've given descriptions of the men you saw – did you recognise any of them?'

'No, sarge, not really, not as such, but I've got a pretty good idea who some of them were.'

'Do you know Tom Rankin, the old guy you dragged out of the shed?'

'No sarge, never seen him before, but I know from my intel that he owns the place.'

Reeve was watching this intently and Napper's overuse of the 'sarge' title told him the weirdo cop was nervous.

The DI took over. 'Doug, there's something not right here and the problem stems from your source. You may be compelled – on pain of discipline proceedings, I must warn you – to reveal his or her identity—'

'Can't do that sir, so I'll 'ave to take my chances.'

Reeve winced at the interruption and felt himself starting to dislike the scruffy constable. But the man did have a point: if his informant was his solicitor then communication between them was arguably confidential, sort of. It could need a court order to get Napper to divulge it, and the DI didn't want to go down that messy road – the adverse publicity would not be welcomed by those who decided on who to promote.

Durman appeared to have finished and looked at her boss.

Reeve smiled. 'Alright Doug, we'll leave it for now. You look fucking knackered mate, thanks for your time.' Reeve's chair scraped on the uncarpeted floor as he stood. Durman followed suit and Napper offered her the statement copy he'd been holding.

'Keep it, Doug, you might need it again.' She smiled and made for the door.

Reeve hung back, put his hand on Napper's shoulder and stooped to be closer to his ear. 'Don't push your luck, Doug.' He straightened suddenly and strode off. Durman was holding the door for him. Napper looked across at her and she winked, before following her boss out of the room.

90

The first thing Tom Rankin saw when he awoke from his nap was Marlene sat opposite him. Behind her were the French windows leading out onto the estate. Light curtains were drawn over them.

'How are you feeling?' she asked. There was a note of sadness in her voice, like she'd been hurt.

'Just tired, and I daren't even feckin' go out there. God knows what they've done.' He'd been made aware of the police search whilst in hospital.

'They finished two days ago, Tom, took the place apart, dismantled all the sheds and a lot of the dogs were taken away by the RSPCA. You've got about a dozen left, that's all.'

He was looking past her at the curtained French windows. He pulled himself painfully to his feet. 'Aye, best I have a look then.'

She got up, drew back the curtains, opened the twin doors and helped him out onto the patio. He blinked in the sunlight. She held his arm to give him support and he relaxed a little.

'Well,' he said chirpily, 'they've tidied it up a bit I suppose. It's not too bad at all.'

'They were very professional Tom. I kept them going in tea and biscuits for three days solid, twelve hour shifts they was on, there was all sorts of experts with their equipment and stuff.'

He started walking, heading for the big shed, but she tugged him back. 'No Tom, come on back into the house. You've got to rest.' Then they both heard the doorbell ring, followed by some rapping on the front door. Marlene went inside to investigate. He heard voices and Marlene reappeared.

'There's two police officers here to see you. They went to the hospital but you were gone.' She helped him back into the living room to meet Briggs and Mason, both displaying their warrant cards.

Marlene told them to sit down and offered them tea. Tea was declined and neither sat. Briggs cut to the chase.

'Mr Rankin, we're not here to arrest you because you aren't fit for custody, er, however...' the young detective paused and glanced in Marlene's direction. Mason's eyes were on the swirly carpet.

'It's alright son, I know I'm in the shit and I don't keep anything from my wife so let's just get it done.' Rankin had not expected the overwhelming evidence of illegal dogfighting to have been ignored, even though he'd already been informed that he wasn't under investigation regarding the gunfight and grenade attack and, for the time being at least, was being treated as a witness. He suspected that his police bullet wound might have had something to do with that decision. But he was fully prepared for his canine affairs to be wound down, and to be prosecuted at some stage for animal cruelty. He was certainly not prepared for what followed.

Briggs took a slightly theatrical deep breath. 'Mr Rankin, I'm here to inform you that during the police search of your premises a quantity of white powder was found in one of your sheds. This has been analysed and comes back as cocaine.' Marlene gasped and Rankin's eyes bulged. Briggs hurried on. 'I must inform you that you are now formally under investigation for the offence of possessing a Class A drug with intent to supply. You do not have to say anything but it may harm your defence if you fail to mention now something that you later seek to rely on—'

'You must be feckin' jokin'!'

'—in court,' finished Briggs. Mason now appeared fascinated by the swirly carpet.

Marlene was suddenly holding her husband's arm again, her face florid. 'He would never have anything to do with drugs. Dogs, and mebbies a bit of chorin', but never drugs!'

Rankin pulled his arm away and made for the nearest armchair, frowning. He sat down heavily and sighed. 'Sit down Marlene and don't start your shouting. These two officers are only doing their jobs.'

'Do you have anything to say Mr Rankin?' Briggs sounded hoarse as he took out his pocketbook.

'No son, I've nothin' to say except that I've no knowledge whatsoever of any drugs, either on this place of mine or anywhere else. Can we leave it at that?'

'Yes,' said Briggs, scribbling.

'What happens now, officer?' was Marlene's question.

Mason decided it was her turn. 'Nothing for the time being, Mrs Rankin. Your husband is now technically on bail and I have a couple of little forms for him to sign to say he'll not skip the country, that's all.' Her attempt to lighten the mood didn't work.

'So, I'm under house arrest then?' Rankin was still frowning, not looking at either officer.

'It's not a term we use but you could put it like that.' Briggs replied almost conversationally, relieved that it hadn't kicked off.

'When will I know if I'm to be charged or not?'

'That'll be up to the Crown Prosecution Service,' said Mason. 'It'll probably be a few weeks, they're rather slow.'

Rankin relaxed back into the armchair. 'The Crown Prosecution Service,' he repeated the name with sarcastic gravity. 'Fine, officers, I'm not goin' anywhere, I'll just wait to hear from you.' He showed his palms. 'Are sure you don't want that cup of tea?'

'We have to be off. Thank you for your time.'

Both cops turned and made for the front door. Marlene showed them out without a word.

91

Molly sat and sobbed. They'd called to say they were in Manchester on a bit of music business and that there was *nuthin' to worry 'bout, Mum.* Then why had the police come crashing in and wrecked the place? She didn't know, so she just sat and sobbed.

She'd done all she could and had nothing more to give. Dying before her time, she was being killed by her own boys,

156

her own flesh and blood. She'd never known anything but how to work and pray; work and pray and just keep doing her best. But she knew all along that her best would never be good enough, not even near it. And praying never did anyone any good.

She looked around herself, at her poverty, her desperation. The police officer, the one in charge of the raid, he'd said that she was better off without 'those two' and that they were in a lot of trouble. They'd always been in a lot of trouble, but this time there was something about the police, their attitude, that made her think it was really very serious.

So Molly just sat and sobbed, because her big salty tears were all she had left to give to the world.

92

It hadn't taken an exercise in quantum physics to put the Braganza Boys at the top of the suspect list for the Stanwell Moor murders, and their arrests were top of the agenda for Trident, the arm of the Metropolitan Police dedicated to the investigations of gang-related violent crime in London, ninety per cent of which was 'black on black'. But being top of the suspect list didn't put the B boys in the dock at the Old Bailey – for that the fedz would need evidence, and a lot of it. Innit.

This was the general topic of desultory conversation between Kribz and Driss as they sat holed up in the Arch wondering what the fuck was going to happen next. The more they thought about it the more shell-shocked they both felt. They kept going over it all.

Oddly, Driss was more sanguine that his older brother. 'They got fuck all, bro. We was all wearin' gloves an' masks innit, an' we all sound the same to those Albos, and the old man won't say nuthin', how can he?'

'Cos he's a fuckin' old man bro. We don't know what they'll threaten him wiv, he's the weak link, innit.' Kribz wasn't going to be mollified. Relaxing too much would stop him thinking and he was scared he might miss something, some detail, some track that should be covered. 'We need to make double sure that all the loose ends is tied up, can't leave nuthin' to chance.' He said this with an air of finality, menace even.

It took a good ten seconds for Driss to react. 'You ain't thinkin' we should pop the old man bro? How the fuck we gonna do that?'

Kribz shook his head thoughtfully. 'Nah, too risky, the fedz'll have the place plotted up, might even 'ave him in protective custody innit, we ain't gonna be able to get to him.'

Driss stood up from his old car seat with some effort, the exertion putting a strain in his voice. 'I can't believe we're even talkin' like this bruv. A gun fight with a bunch of crims is one thing, casualties 'appen, but plannin' a cold blooded fuckin' murder is a whole new fuckin' business, fam.'

'I know that, my brother, an' you don't 'ave to tell me, but loose ends is loose ends and I ain't puttin' my head in the sand.' Kribz didn't like looking up at his younger brother, so he got to his feet also, pretending to stretch to avoid the appearance of confrontation. He looked around the place; three days of pizzas, coke (the liquid stuff) cans and spliff ends littered the floor. The air was acrid and damp and stank of body odour. A sleeping bag moved in the corner.

'And there might just be another problem,' said Kribz, not caring if the seemingly slumbering Numbers heard him.

'Now you're bein' fuckin' ridiculous, innit. Numbers is cool, he was wid us from the start.'

'I'm hearin' ev'ry word of this,' croaked the sleeping bag.

'We're jus' thinkin' aloud bro, nuthin' for you to worry about,' said Driss.

'Yeah, sorry Numbers, me an' Driss talk like this sometimes, it's the way that we cover all bases, get my meaning?' Kribz was keen to diffuse this, nip it in the bud.

Numbers rolled out of the bag and stood up. He was in his boxers, nothing else.

'If you'ze gonna pop me, best you do it now.' Numbers was addressing them both. 'But then nobody'll truss you, then you'll have to go after Shanker an' Gillie an' Massive, an' then it won't end there cos they all got families too.'

What amazed Kribz and Driss was how Numbers said this, actually through a stifled yawn, like he was making a passing comment on the weather or a football match.

'You seem very fuckin' relaxed, bro,' blinked Kribz, rapidly reassessing the youngest B Boy.

'Let's just say I've kinda grown up lately Kribzy, an' maybe's I ain't as stupid as you was thinkin'.' The yawn had evaporated and a sharp edge was in Numbers' voice and the look he was giving the elder brother.

Kribz held the gaze and matched the tone, but said 'Okay my brother, chill, I apologise, full respect to you, brother.' And higher regard was established: Numbers was now a senior player.

All three were fidgety and a bit beside themselves, not least because they didn't have their phones. Kribz had faced no resistance when he decreed that all devices – they had seven between them, including burners and a tablet – had to be switched off and dumped in a safe place, that being a plastic bag on the roof of their home block three streets away. Kribz had led from the front and done the carrying; it had only taken him twenty minutes at around five pm the previous day: busy time, less chance of being pulled. On the way back to the Arch he'd loaded up with fried chicken and the strewn cartons on the floor of the hideout were testimony to full stomachs.

They all sat down and started rolling spliffs, each lost in his own exhausted thoughts. Kribz completed his first and fired up noisily. He took a deep pull and held it for a full five before blasting the smoke out across the space between them, lessening it and re-enforcing the bond.

'We gotta make contact wid 'im though, an' soon.' Kribz said this half to himself, eyes unfocused.

'Yeh, real fuckin' soon bro,' agreed Driss, quickly, like he'd been thinking the same thought at the same time. 'We gotta make ourselves clear to 'im, innit.' A few wordless seconds of puffing and blowing, then Driss added 'An' where the fuck is Screwloose man?'

Kribz was glad he was sat back in an old armchair, his face almost roofwards. He answered as casually as he could. 'Fuck knows bro, it was a good job he wasn't wid' us, the whole ting coulda gone wrong.'

Driss was incredulous. 'Whadaya mean coulda gone fuckin' wrong? You sayin' it went fuckin' *right*?!'

'Coulda bin worse fam, none of us got killed innit.'

Numbers was observing this exchange closely: there was something about Kribz's offhand manner he didn't like.

'Anyways,' continued the senior brother, 'he knows where to come if he needs us, but I think even he'll have the good sense to stay away from us, must be out by now what's 'appened.' A few seconds of silence, then Kribz went on - with a change of subject; 'Fuck man, we need a phone, innit.'

Numbers piped up, 'My siss lives near, she's got loads of phones an' sims, shall I go fetch one?'

The brothers both nodded and Numbers got to his feet and put on a baseball cap with a long peak. It was past midday and there would be loads of foot traffic: it was worth the risk.

'Take a long route man, be careful innit.' Driss drew a disdainful look from the junior member.

'I ain't stupid, bro.'

Kribz followed Numbers out of the space and down the stairs so he could let him out and lock the street door behind him. They passed three floors on the way down and could hear prayers being muttered through the thin walls. It was Friday.

93

'You didn't get the charging order, giving me the excuse that you had the wrong judge sitting in the court and that he was in a bad mood or some such shit. You are unable to explain how this nonsense from the police, proceeds of crime shit, how it can be removed and beaten back, you say you'll have to take advice from a specialist barrister – you're a lawyer, aren't you? Sometimes I'm wondering that maybe you're not, and you're also now telling me that Jackson is looking for ways to overturn the power of attorney and my new company might have problems.' Larssen paused for breath. She was hunched over her desk, snarling into her phone, the veins on her neck standing out like pulley cables, and she was then suddenly aware of the silence on the other end of the line; the recipient of the call was unable to speak.

'Hello? Blake? Are you *there*?!'

Stuart Blake's contact with his chair was limited to the small of his back and his shoulder blades, the dome of his belly accentuated by the concaved arch of his spine, his legs quivering at the strain the position was placing on them. One hand just about held his phone to his ear, the other clutched the edge of his desk. His face was a puce mask of such contorted hilarity that could have easily been mistaken for an expression of excruciating agony. His nostrils, flared to their fullest extent in their eagerness to give passage to an inward flow of air had their owner been capable of breath, instead exuded twin streams of clear mucus which came nowhere near to matching the gush of tears that spurted from the squeezed-shut eyes a few inches above them.

'Blake! Are you fucking listening?!' hissed Larssen.

Blake's utter powerlessness then gave way a little, slightly mitigated by the warmth he felt on the inside of his thigh as a trickle of urine escaped from his penis – he would really have to get a grip.

'Blake, if you're fucking finding this funny, I'll sue the fucking balls off you!'

That did it; the trickle became a full flow and the tubby solicitor managed to catch the breath that had eluded him for at least thirty seconds. The mucus from his nostrils did a rapid reverse manoeuvre, thrust backwards by the sudden rush of the long overdue inhalation.

The loud snort confirmed the caller's suspicion. 'You *are* fucking laughing! Right, that's it, I'm going to file an official complaint against you. You are an incompetent fucking idiot!' She ended the call and threw her phone with such venom that it hit the wall and bounced back onto her desk.

Blake just let his phone drop as he deployed both hands to heave his sweat-drenched carcass back into the semblance of a sitting position. The wheezing laughter that then followed took the form of a rhythmic, high pitched screech, like something out of a demented seagull. Blinking through his tears he looked down to inspect the damage, thankful he was wearing dark trousers.

What Blake found especially funny was the fact that the woman was totally powerless. The Proceeds of Crime Act restraint order that the Rankin property had been swiftly made the subject of was, however, *very* powerful. All the police – DC Aaron Briggs in this case – had had to do was persuade the Judge, via a quick application by the Crown Prosecution Service, that there was reasonable cause to believe that Tom Rankin had benefited from criminal conduct; not really difficult given the evidence the search teams had found on the homestead, without even taking account of the multiple murders and grenade attack for which the old Gypsy would probably not be prosecuted. Even if the cocaine couldn't be pinned on him there was still the very unpopular matter of illegal dogfighting, and the large amounts of cash strewn around the scene of devastation would be enough to support an allegation of lucrative profiteering and money laundering.

The bottom line was that until the investigation and any proceedings against Rankin were complete, the property was unassignable, worthless. If a conviction ensued, all or part of it could then be the subject of a criminal compensation order and, subject to any existing encumbering charges like the one Blake had failed to secure, it would become Crown property.

The rotund solicitor wiped his face, dropped his pants and used the same handkerchief to dab his groins. Then, his sweaty bare buttocks just about gaining traction on the fake leather chair, he cracked a can of Stella and flicked through some emails. The most recent one was from Claude Jackson; still smiling, he picked up his phone.

94

The intercom crackled and Kribz descended the staircase, checked through the spyhole, and re-admitted Numbers. The younger member was sweating, flummoxed, but patted the pocket of his hoody to indicate 'job done'. Back upstairs in the big space under the rafters he addressed the brothers with aplomb, announcing the word he'd just heard.

'Screwloose is dead.'

The Popes just stared at him, waiting for more.

'That's all I know, innit, my sister told me, he got shot an' nobody saw nuthin', not until the po-po set up a crime scene an' started askin' for witnesses to come forward – as fuckin' if.' He was looking back and forth at both Pope brothers, expecting a reaction; he got none, just more of the expectant stares.

'Whadaya lookin' like that at me for, that's all I know innit.'

Kribz broke the brothers' silence. 'How does your siss know? Thought you said she was a clean skin.'

'She *is* a fuckin' clean skin man, but the streets are alive wid the news, and that the fedz are after youze for it, and a whole lot of other stuff which must be about what happened out at the airport, innit.'

'What 'ave you told her?' asked Driss, quietly.

'I've told her fuck all bro, jus' that I lost my phone and need to get back to my girl. She don't even know that I know you.'

'Okay my brother, gimme the phone.' Kribz was satisfied, for the time being at least. He took Numbers' sister's phone, which was unlocked, and thumbed through the apps. He registered on Snapchat and within thirty seconds was getting the griff.

'Fuck me, you're right, Screwloose took a cap an' they're gonna try an' pin it on us. You sure you didn't get followed back here, bro?'

Driss was watching his brother and he'd never seen him so weak: his hands were trembling and there was sweat on the bridge of his nose. 'Why the fuck would they think it was us bro? We'ze part of the same gang innit, ev'rybody knows that! What the...'

Kribz appeared to rally a bit and held up his free hand. 'Okay.' His eyes were still on the phone. 'We need to calm down. They got nuthin' on us, we jus' need to stay here till it blows over, we got no choice.'

'I ain't stayin' here, Kribzy, I need to go to college.' Numbers' protest came out as a whine.

'You'll do as you're fuckin' told.' Driss made to walk forward to the boy.

Kribz intervened. 'No, he's right, we need 'im out there, innit, keepin' 'is ear to the floor. Go on Numbers, fuck off back an' act normal, before your siss puts two an' two together. Tell her you left her phone wid your girlfriend.'

Driss didn't argue but had to have the last word. 'We get rumbled bruv, an' it's down to you, got that?'

'Okay man, fuck, whaddaya tink I is?' protested Numbers as he made for the top of the stairs. Kribz followed him down and locked him out for the second time that day.

95

With the swagger of Brixton royalty, Massive walked into the Coldharbour Lane cafe and joined Gillie and Shanker at their table at the rear. They exchanged fist bumps, grunting solemnly. It was the first time they'd joined up since the Stanwell rumpus.

'All cool?' asked the big man.

'Yer bro,' they muttered, almost together, nodding at him with hooded eyes so as not to show any inner stuff that was going on.

'You sling the piece?' dared Gillie, wanting a quick kill of the elephant in the room. 'The one you whacked Screwloose with.'

'Dunno what you're chattin' 'bout man, shut the fuck up innit.' Massive kept a straight face as he spoke the words, but then a malevolent grin spread across his black face, quite slowly, like a speeded-up film of a hideous white flower opening in the darkness. 'It's safe, blud, truss me, there'll be no comebacks.'

That dealt with, Shanker pitched in. 'You got satisfaction, innit.'

'For sure blud, the boy had to die, he was snitchin' anyways. Kribzy set 'im up for me.'

'Fuck, man,' said Gillie. 'Good job he weren't on the fuckin' airport job.' (As it was now known.)

'The fedz are lookin' for Kribz an' Driss big style,' said Shanker, wanting to move the conversation on. 'What 'appens if they get taken down an' take us wid 'em?'

Massive was shaking his head before Shanker had finished. 'Won't 'appen bro, truss me innit, we've 'ad our differences but dem two would never do that, weeze all the same blood after all, innit.'

The two hoods nodded, lips pursed, accepting the logic. Massive anticipated the outstanding concern and covered it. 'That kid Numbers might be a prob, we'll need to 'ave a quiet word wid 'im maybeez.'

'Wish he'd never been on the job,' grumbled Gillie, flicking a spoon around the saucer of his empty coffee cup.

'Same, bro, but it's done now innit. We just gotta hope he keeps 'is fuckin' mouth tight shut is all.'

96

The Metropolitan Police Firearms Forensics Unit – the 'Lab' – was in the huge basement of an anonymous building just south of the Thames in Lambeth. Guns, bullets, shell casings, shotgun pellets, cartridge wadding and swabbed traces of discharge debris were probably the main occupants of sealed exhibit bags stacked high but in meticulous order on the shelves of the Waiting Room, as the vault leading to the examination areas was known, and the overworked team of scientists kept a rota of twelve-hour shifts to process the incoming tide.

But they were always up against it, having to develop thick skins to objectively prioritise jobs according to a set of rules based on chemical volatility of the subject matter cross referenced with a first come, first served queuing system. Hence the chemical stuff tended to get done first, leapfrogging the hardware which stayed in the slow lane. Memos from senior investigating officers urging precedence for certain jobs were given lip service by the heads-down technicians – they'd heard it all before and, to a man and woman, just concentrated on keeping the production line going as quickly as possible while avoiding mistakes and cross-contamination.

So, when the bullets from the legs of Massive and Jackson were identified as coming from the same Baretta, those which had killed Gozit and Screwloose were still in the pipeline. When Aaron Briggs got news of the positive match, he fired off a report to his supervisors in which he virtually put himself up for a commendation: *...the prompt and efficient submission of the ballistic exhibits by the officer in the case enabled this timely and fruitful examination....* Then he got round to informing Napper.

Briggs was quite getting into the streetwise detective persona so instead of calling or emailing Napper he went for a walk, having heard where the Cornishman habitually enjoyed breakfast. The Madeira Cafe in the Kennington Road was already busy at 7 a.m. as the 'detective', appropriately tieless and wearing jeans and a knowing smirk, sauntered in, hoping to look casual.

'Gotcha!' he said, sitting down opposite Napper, who didn't look exactly pleased.

'Mornin' Aaron, what happened, shit the bed?' The scruffy street cop spoke through a gobful of Portuguese sausage.

'Early bird gets the worm.'

'Yeah, an' the second mouse gets the cheese.'

A waiter was loitering. 'Two poached eggs on toast please, and a filter coffee.' Briggs couldn't have faced anything like the gargantuan mound on Napper's plate.

'Whoever shot Massive shot Jackson.' Briggs issued the headline with a hushed urgency, once the waiter had gone.

'Possibly.' Napper didn't even look up.

Briggs stared. Napper went on. 'The bullets came from a Braganza shooter, I already told you as much. What you need to be gettin' on with is lookin' at the bullets from the Stanwell Moor scene.' A forkful of bacon and beans concluded the sentence. The speaker's eyes were still down as if the conversation was of secondary importance.

'I'm on it.' Briggs' attempted detective vernacular was unconvincing. 'Analysis requisition is in on the hurry-up.'

Napper chewed and gulped, then looked up at Briggs. 'I bet I know what you're not on,' he said with a mischievous glint.

'What?'

'I bet you're not on the small matter of the murder of a lad called Trevor Bayado, nickname Screwloose.'

The CID officer regarded the street cop's smirk with the feeling of a chess player about to be checked, or at least seriously cornered; he felt his sails sag as what little wind they'd had in them departed. Then he was thankful for the distraction as his poached eggs arrived. 'Thank you – er – have you any pepper?'

Napper kept observing his fellow officer, nearly impressed by the avoidance of eye contact and the use of the pepper enquiry to play for time. The waiter went off in search of the condiment and Briggs refocused on his interlocutor.

'No Doug, I'm not on that case, but I'll pass on any info you've got to those who are.'

Napper was back to the job in hand, stacking his fork anew. 'Get that bullet given priority, too. I reckon it'll be linked in with the Stanwell job. Screwloose was a B Boy.'

Even Briggs saw that this didn't stack up. 'What? Are you saying a B Boy got murdered by one of his own?'

Napper wasn't going to get drawn any further down this road, so made light of it. 'Stranger things 'appen Aaron, these twats are always shootin' at each other,' was as far as he was prepared to go.

97

His own phone being on the roof of his home block, Kribz had to Google for Tom Rankin's number on Numbers' sister's phone; it was out of gigs so he had to use the wifi from the mosque downstairs, its use being part of the 'rental agreement'.

'Hello?' answered Marlene with her telephone voice.

'Is Mr Rankin there please?'

Mrs Rankin instinctively knew that this was not a business call – well, not normal business anyway – and woke her husband gently.

Tom Rankin was still exhausted, despite having slept in his armchair for most of the preceding twenty-four hours. 'It's for you,' said his wife with a weary sigh. 'Sounds like trouble.'

'Hello,' Tom's voice was flat, guarded.

'Mr Rankin, its Kribz, you okay boss?'

'Aye, son, but I shouldn't be talking to you, this is probably bein' listened to right now. I'm under investigation, I should tell you.'

'That's cool Mr Rankin, jus' checkin' you're okay, it's good that you're outa hospital an' on the mend, innit.'

'Thanks for calling son.' Rankin cut the call and handed the phone back to Marlene. She correctly thought it best not to say anything to her tired old man.

A 737 lumbered over the house on its descent to Runway Two, its 350 passengers including a very awake Gheg Albanian.

98

To avoid the officialdom that infested Tirana airport, Zamir Gozit had made the arduous road journey to the south of his country and the port of Sarande. From there he had paid cash for the short boat ride to the island of Corfu where his forged Greek passport had been nodded through with a withering smile by a bored Greek border guard. He had waited two days for a flight to Heathrow, spending the downtime making carefully placed calls to contacts in London, Barking in particular.

Algorithm

The young Gozit, chilled by several in-flight vodkas, was nonetheless nervous as he walked unimpeded through the gate at Terminal Three; interpreter assisted spot checks were still occasionally carried out and he spoke not a word of Greek.

Bora Gozit wore a light raincoat which did not entirely conceal her nurse's uniform. She hated using her status and hard-won respectability to provide cover for her brother, but they were Gheg Albanian and, despite his exile, family was family. She smiled thinly as she saw him emerge with his single item of hand luggage.

'You always travelled light, brother. Nothing changes, eh?' Her face was drawn after nearly a week of shock, weeping, and lack of sleep.

There was a quick, cold embrace, then: 'You got a car?'

'Yes, of course, and you're not driving it. Come on.'

Zamir followed his sister out of the arrivals area and into a car park lift. He hadn't seen her in over three years and was struck by how she seemed to have matured; he saw worldliness about her now and, although she carried herself well, a tiredness in the way she walked. Bora took a key from her pocket and pressed the fob, the thump of a deactivating lock and the blink of indicators identifying the car.

Zamir raised an eyebrow at the big Lexus. 'I thought you nurses were underpaid in this country.'

'Yeah, well, let's just say I'm careful with my money, Zammy.'

She drove with confidence and, once on the clockwise carriageway of the M25, at considerable speed.

Apart from some tense exchanges about the funeral arrangements, the journey passed in silence and less than an hour later through patchy traffic, they were in Barking. Zamir wasn't surprised to see the place had continued its downward spiral. He remembered being told that the town was once what Londoners described as a 'posh' place to live. It had never been that when he'd been growing up there and it was visibly worse now. Charity shops, nail bars and trashy stores were the main theme, punctuated by boarded up pubs and fried chicken shacks. It was only 11 a.m. but the dealers were already on the corners, Albos, Turks, Lithuanians – Zamir had no trouble discerning them – doing low grade coke, with a few brave Bengalis adding their 'brown' for good measure. Market stallers on the high street hawked dirt-cheap nylon clothing and stuffed toys, and at least a half a dozen religions thrust flyers at grey people emerging from the big railway station. Nobody batted an eyelid at the Lexus: it was one of many and Zamir concluded that there must have been a local dealership doing cheap finance.

'This car paid for?' His impertinence ended a particularly long silence.

'That has nothing to do with you, Zammy.' Bora's tone strongly implied that further questions would be similarly met. He was in no doubt that after the funeral he wouldn't be invited to stay for long.

There was nowhere to park outside the little terraced house and a hundred-metre walk ensued. Zamir had his bag in one hand and fiddled with a phone with the other. It was one of three he was carrying.

She was watching him. 'Please don't invite any friends, Zammy, please, you're here for dad's funeral, nothing more.'

Having set the device to UK mode, he put it back in his pocket.

His sister went on. 'Come into the house now and make your peace with Mum. Dad is in his coffin in the front room. After you've seen them both you go. I've booked a room in my name in a Travelodge in Ilford, number 18 bus, you must stay there. When you come to the funeral you keep your eyes and ears open. We have to assume the police'll be there hoping to slap you in handcuffs.'

'I look different, I've been away for three years, they won't recognise me. They won't even link me with Father.

Gozit is a common Albanian name, come on.' It was like Zamir was trying to convince himself as much as his sister. He'd been nervous at Heathrow, but kept assuring himself that his hipster beard, styled hair and fashionable western clothing put him ahead of the game.

And he needn't have worried too much anyway: international arrest warrants were rarely top of the agenda for any police force – they were always someone else's problem and more often than not just gathered dust in filing cabinets.

An hour later, having hugged his mum and shed a few crocodile tears, Zamir Gozit was in his Travelodge room sending encrypted messages from a device made of component parts of two phones that he'd brought from Tirana in his hand luggage. The assembled kit had cost him over two thousand dollars for one month's usage. He wouldn't need anywhere near that long but if he did, he could get an extension on the deal: he had vowed not to leave London until the *Hakmarrja* was satisfied and honour salvaged.

99

Freda Larssen powered her carbon fibre racing cycle up the one in ten gradients in Richmond Park with the manic dedication of a racing athlete. Of course, she had no intention of competing in any racing event: it was her own fitness she was chasing – and achieving. The ride had been preceded by a grueling workout in the gym where she paid a small fortune for the exclusive attention of a personal trainer who she treated with total disdain: 'Push me harder, you idiot!' The punishing exercise regime had been prescribed by Privette, under the heading 'anger management', presumably on the basis that energy expelled on the bike would leave less to expel on fury at others.

She got to the top of the hill, dismounted and looked at her sports watch. Not bad, but not good enough – but she knew her performances would never be good enough because they weren't fit for purpose. She had no excess weight to lose and her muscles were toned and probably too big. Her real target – to exorcise the demon of sheer hatred that raged within her – was unattainable by this method, and she was beginning to feel that the endorphins released by her intense training were doubling back on her, triggering venomous moods.

She wheeled her machine into the car park and lifted it effortlessly onto its rack atop her Audi Sports, handlebars and seat held fast by titanium clips, wheels pointing skyward. It was just after 6 a.m. and the place was almost deserted, not that the presence of others would have stopped her from stripping naked and changing from skintight nylon into a loose cotton tracksuit.

Not caring about cameras – the car was registered in the name of her company and fines were just 'litigation' overheads – she sped out of the park, through Richmond town and onto the London-bound carriageway of the A316. The traffic wasn't yet heavy and she made good time, pulling into the private office car park before 6.45. The barrier recognised her number plate and swung high enough to allow her roof-racked bike to pass under.

She kicked the cleaner out of the office showers, stripped again and slid under a powerful blast of freezing water, holding her breath, her face a mask of ferocity. She gave it a full sixty second count before hitting the lever for hot, and then relaxed a little, soaping herself thoroughly. She put on a bathrobe and padded through into her office. Her short, cropped hair would be dry within minutes. It was still only 7 a.m. and she had at least an hour to herself before what was left of her staff began their sheepish arrivals.

Despite the Stanwell Moor meltdown - word had spread quickly and many of the firm's clients had scarpered – she'd kept the company going and about half of the employees had kept their jobs, albeit under the simmering threat of instant dismissal for the slightest misfeasance. Stanwell was still top of Larssen's agenda and she was determined to defeat the Proceeds of Crime Order that the imbecilic British police had slapped on it. Once that was removed – by whichever way necessary – the property would belong to JLP Restructuring (Denmark) PLC: in another words, herself.

Would the useless bastard be at work yet? Thinking this she called Blake. He was; the fact that he'd been there all night was irrelevant. It had been a good night and the middle-aged solicitor was in considerable pain, both physical and emotional. His crashing head and chest pains vied for supremacy over the self-loathing which always followed his nocturnal debaucheries.

'I want you to make an official complaint against the police.' Her tone was flat, final.

'Ah, good morning Ms Larssen. How nice of you to call so early, and how are you on this fine day?'

What he was thinking was: *Thank you so much for this very timely hangover cure,* as he could feel the mirth rising rapidly, shoving his pains aside.

'Did you hear what I just said?'

Blake struggled to keep his voice sounding normal, 'Yes Ms Larssen, I heard you. And what would be the basis of this official complaint?'

'Corruption and gross negligence, by a useless boy named Briggs who calls himself a detective.'

The level of concentration Blake had to apply to keep his breathing steady had the side effect of focusing his thoughts, and the looming eruption of glee subsided. 'Not common bedfellows, Ms Larssen, corruption and negligence. Corrupt coppers are rarely negligent – usually the opposite, because they take great care not to get caught.' There followed a short pause before the lawyer went on. 'And the other side of the same coin, so to speak, is that negligent cops are usually too thick or lazy to be corrupt.'

'Are you trying to be clever Blake?'

He ignored the sneer. 'So, which one is it to be then? Corruption or gross negligence?'

Tension invaded very muscle in Larssen's body.

'Just get rid of that Crime Proceedings Order! If you fail you'll be putting me out of business and I'll sue you– I'll… I'll…'

She was spluttering now, through a constricted throat, and Blake started to think his client was really losing the plot. He kept calm, enjoying every delicious second. 'Proceeds of Crime Order, Ms Larssen, and I've already told you it's not something you can just get rid of, just pay to have swatted away. The police investigation could take months, years even, and the property can't be sold, assigned, or repossessed by anyone until an adjudication is made by the court. If Rankin is deemed to have profited from crime, then his property will in turn be deemed, either all or part of it, to be the proceeds of crime and then more proceedings will follow to decide how much of it can be confiscated by the Crown…'

He was about to draw breath but was distracted from this rendition of knowledgeable advice by a screeching sound. It grew in volume and developed a grating undertone and as its pitch gradually lowered, became a guttural, strangulated scream through which the words *'Shut the fuck up!'* could just about be discerned.

And then another side of Blake kicked in as his sense of mischief deserted him. 'No! You shut the fuck up! Chucking tantrums isn't going to get you anywhere, you're just making a fool of yourself. We'll discuss this further when you've fucking grown up!' Blake was spluttering now, his anger accentuating his West Midlands wail. *Fuck it,* he thought, and cut the call.

100

Another 24 hours slid by during which nothing much happened at all. Then something very big indeed occurred.

Algorithm

One of the most understated of all human weaknesses is our inability to appreciate the extent to which our existences interconnect. Even in major cities around the globe, human beings act as if they, as individuals and families, are pretty much in control of their lives, whilst still being ever ready to blame others for their misfortunes and shortcomings. It rarely if ever occurs to us that seemingly isolated events can impact enormously on us, uncontrollably and without warning. We really should appreciate an important but unpalatable fact of life: every so often, for no attributable reason, without any blame-laden chain of causality – shit happens.

The O2 Arena in Geenwich, south east London, was one of the major entertainment showpieces of the capital. With an indoor audience capacity of 15,000 it hosted some of the biggest stars in popular music. Such as Tara Breitling, an American megastar with a stupendous voice and a wild stage show featuring dozens of dancers as scantily dressed as herself. It was on this sultry Sunday evening that the final event of her UK tour was to take place, billed as the biggest show in town. Police presence was heavy, but mostly to deal with problems associated with traffic and public order logistics. Most of the attending thousands were young and middle class – tickets were expensive – and well-behaved; no real trouble of the kind expected at football matches or street carnivals was anticipated. The show was a sell-out and, had the critics ever got round to writing their reviews, would have earned adoring praise, congratulations, and awards. It ended just after 10pm, a respectable time on a school night, and thousands of satiated, smiling teenagers began filing out in a jubilant but orderly fashion, many of them young enough to be met and picked up by parents who'd waited anxiously outside in the car parks and forecourts.

So, when Ahmed Rabbani and Mohamed Khalifa detonated their suicide vests inside the main foyer, the world froze. The consequent and indescribable carnage was meant to avenge Allah for the promiscuity of the infidel, the blatant disobedience of the filthy *kafir*. Its overriding result however was to redouble the bewilderment and fear felt by the West towards a murderous culture which we are constantly told *'has nothing to do with Islam'*. The more instant outcome of the atrocity was to spark the immediate mobilisation of Her Majesty's Government's terrorism investigation task force, a coalition of MI5 and hundreds of specially trained officers from every police force in the country.

Ministers were summoned to a COBRA meeting and well-rehearsed procedures were activated. As the night wore on and the television crews besieged Greenwich, the interior halogen lighting of New Scotland Yard and Thames House blazed as brightly as those of the emergency services attending the scene of the slaughter. As the body count mounted, the decisions were rattled off, suspect lists drawn up and rapid entry police teams dispatched with understandable zeal.

Driss slept fitfully in a cannabis-induced torpor. His brother, slightly more alert but not much, followed the unfolding aftermath on Numbers' sister's phone. He wasn't particularly interested, correctly assuming that no one he knew would have been at the O2 – not their kind of music – and his selfish thoughts were limited to things like how much pain someone felt when they got their legs blown off and how much the fedz would now be distracted and too busy to be solving murders in faraway Stanwell Moor. He concluded coldly that the terrorist attack wasn't bad news for the Braganza Boys.

Then the street door of their hideout got blown off its hinges by a hydraulic blaster. The makeshift mosque that had for many months occupied the first and second floors of the building was occupied by several slumbering trainee imams who'd had nothing to do with the massacre at the pop concert, but some of their names were on the MI5 radar so the 5 a.m. visit was pretty much standard procedure.

The noise of the entry and loudhailer announcements of *'Armed police!'* had the brothers sitting upright in their tangled sleeping bags, blinking through their cannabinoid fugues.

'Fuck!' croaked Kribz. 'The place is getting hit!'

'Wha?' Driss was still trying to gather his senses as the sound of heavy boots on the carpetless wooden stairs got louder. They were still sat there, goggle eyed and mouths agape, when the door of the loft space burst open. Briefly blinded by the handheld search lights, the boys flung their hands up open palmed, squinting at the Heckler and Koch automatic weapons trained on their heads.

'Stand up and keep your hands up!' came the barked order. They did so, shakily. Driss nearly tripped on his sleeping bag and his momentary stumble drew an additional 'Slowly, you fucker, take your time!' Being told to take one's time seemed incongruous given the circumstances, and Kribz felt himself grin at the irony. 'What the fuck are you laughing at?!' The lead officer – he wore no visible badges of rank but certainly seemed in charge – was in no mood for seeing the funny side of things.

'Right, just be still, quite still, breathing is all you're allowed to do. We have emergency powers to search this building.'

The boys were in their boxers, so frisking didn't take long, they then had their hands cuffed behind their backs and were made to sit down, uncomfortably.

Driss still hadn't spoken. Kribz made the effort; it came out weak and he wished he hadn't bothered. 'Are we under arrest?'

'Not yet,' came the answer. The lead cop sounded like an automaton, running purely on adrenalin. 'The search is under the Counter-Terrorism Act. From what I can see you two don't fit the bill, but you'll understand we have to take the place apart anyway.' He wasn't really looking at either Kribz or Driss, more intent on making sure a thorough job was being done. 'Loosen those skirting boards, 572, and 192, open the cushions and check the underside of all the cupboard drawers, the dogs'll be here soon.'

Kribz began to relax, greatly relieved that he'd given Screwloose's gun to Massive and that, apart from a few small snap bags of weed and two or three blades that would get you arrested if you had them on the street, the place was clean. He watched the cops do their stuff and felt like a spectator. His brother seemed similarly calm. Then the lead cop asked for their names and proof of ID. Kribz provided the former without hesitation – quickly, before Driss started lying – and nodded to a pile of clothing in the corner of space. 'You'll find our wallets over there, there's driving licenses in them.'

Here goes, thought both young men as they heard their details being spoken into a police radio: *this is when we find out if we're wanted or not.*

101

Claude Jackson was going home, and the hospital had arranged a taxi, at his expense. It was a big people–carrier which accommodated the one-legged asset stripper, his cumbersome NHS wheelchair, an assortment of prosthetic legs, and a trainee occupational health therapist, dispatched with the patient to make sure he got home safely and that his home contained no obvious impediments to the beginnings of rehabilitation. A transparent plastic bag by his side in the vehicle contained an assortment of painkillers and sleeping tablets. A hospital psychiatrist had risk-assessed that these wouldn't be abused.

After ticking a few boxes on a clip-boarded form, the therapist left Jackson alone – all alone. He sat in his big, open-plan flat and waited for the aircon to kick in and purge the musty air of three weeks' disuse. He looked at his stump, the prosthetics and the hideous wheelchair before his tired eyes fell on the stack of files on the big glass dining table. They seemed irrelevant now and he wouldn't have known where to start, even if there'd been a need to. It was odd. Here he was, crippled for life, bereaved of so many possibilities, so much freedom now lost, beyond him. Yet somehow, he felt liberated. He had enough money in the bank to tide him over for several years, a calculation that had taken account of his projected lifestyle curtailment. He had a lot of books to read and films to watch, and now he could spend more time with his son, a visit from whom he expected that day. He wondered if perhaps this feeling of tranquility was down to the drugs that had been pumped into him over the preceding three weeks, that perhaps the morphine had taken permanent effect.

And then thoughts of Larssen and reality, as if they had followed in another taxi, were suddenly in the room with him. He put on the least uncomfortable prosthetic and, using an NHS crutch, hauled himself to his feet (he preferred to think in the plural) and looked at the laptop on the dining table. It was about four metres away and he knew that if he made the journey there would be no coming back; the promises he'd made to himself in hospital would all be broken, and he'd be back in the life that had ruined him.

Ten minutes later he was on the phone to Stuart Blake.

'So, the property still belongs to Rankin?'

'Subject to the outcome of any confiscation proceedings, yes,' replied the lawyer, sensing action in the offing. Larssen had indeed made a complaint to the Law Society about Blake's failure to get Larssen's charge slapped on the place, so she'd effectively relinquished her position as his client; he was now a free agent and could side with Jackson to his heart's content.

Blake thought it best to continue. 'When I say it belongs to him, that doesn't mean he can sell or dispose of it, the—'

Jackson wasn't going to be treated like some numpty off the street. 'Yeah, yeah, I know, the Proceeds of Crime Order freezes the asset. It remains Rankin's on paper, but the value of the asset belongs to the Crown until the Order is lifted.'

'Correct,' said the lawyer, 'and the Order won't be lifted until after criminal proceedings are complete and the court decides how much of the Rankin estate can be adjudged the proceeds of crime. When that's then subtracted, he gets to keep whatever remains.'

'Subject to any other charges on the property, of course,' finished Jackson, satisfied he was keeping up.

'Of course,' agreed Blake who then got in the finale: 'The bottom line is that the Crown gets first bite of the cherry, after which there may not be any cherry left.'

'So, Larssen's fucked then.'

'Couldn't put it more eloquently myself.'

102

Other than in the literal sense, being fucked wasn't something Freda Larssen took kindly to. Following her conversation with Blake she spent the morning going through the motions of running her company. Free of what she saw as Jackson's bovine lack of ruthlessness, she cracked her whip viciously at the staff, and at Palmer in particular. The young desker took her bullying infuriatingly well and she promised herself his days were numbered. He promised himself something similar, with the caveat that she would pay a price.

She left the office just after 1pm but didn't go to her car or bike, opting to take a walk and clear her head. It was hot and humid, threatening a downpour as dense, thunderous clouds gathered.

Her house was in the northern quarter of the village, still highly sought-after but slightly less gentrified than the Bayswater side. She kept looking at black people and thinking about the young thugs she'd seen at Rankin's place, the one that got arrested outside her office, Jackson's missing leg, *detective* fucking Briggs... round and round and round it swirled. Round and round and round.

103

Mergin Gozit, although only sixteen, was planning his next business strategy in the car wash game. The Stanwell Moor massacre was big news in the Albanian community and the now rudderless enterprise in Shepherd's Bush had become an opportunity. He knew the business like the back of his hand and the Crystal Palace outfit where he'd worked, on and off, part time, since leaving school had long since failed to give him upward mobility. He'd become respected there, granted, and his youthful looks and absence of criminal convictions kept him under the police radar when making his occasional cocaine and cannabis runs to the black clients of the south London Hellbanianz branch, of which he was a junior member. But the absence of Kemal Gozit and his lowlife mates had left a vacuum which senior Hellbanianz seemed reluctant to fill. The reason for this was little more than indolence, plus a bit of fear of the unknown. Gozit's murder was still a mystery and elder Albo gangsters were staying away from the Bush for the time being, rather than go steaming in to get heat from some unknown source. Whoever their countrymen had come up against out near the airport were obviously heavy and deserved a bit of respectful distance – for a while, at least.

So young Mergin, having spotted the gap in proceedings, was preparing himself for a trip to Shepherd's Bush. Having donned clean jeans and a new Arsenal shirt, packed his little rucksack with some sandwiches and an 'A' Level maths book he'd stolen from his sister, and put a side parting in his fashionable hairstyle, he set off for the bus stop.

Within a hundred metres he knew he was being followed and prepared his innocent student storyline for what he assumed would be a couple of bored crime squad loafers in need of something to do. But the car that slowed and stopped just ahead of him contained only the driver, who leant across the passenger seat and opened the nearside door.

'*Futu te lutem* Mergin.' (Get in please, Mergin).

Despite the polite tone the order, the boy knew better than to disobey. Without even slowing he slid into the vehicle. The conversation continued in English.

104

Old Tom Rankin doddered around his homestead slowly, wincing occasionally with pain through not taking his Co-codomol. 'It stops me shittin' properly,' he'd complain, which was perfectly true of the opioid painkiller. 'I'd rather be in feckin' agony than die of bowel cancer.'

Marlene couldn't help but agree, but she nagged him all the same. 'The wound'll not heal if you keep moving about all the time, you've to get plenty of rest.' Etc., etc.

The bits of its shattered door stacked neatly to one side, the big shed was wide open. He peered inside and got a whiff of the formaldehyde that had been used to disinfect the place after the police had done their searching. But there were still signs of blood on the breezeblock walls, and mangled bits of dog cage that featured lumps of roasted flesh and furry skin.

So, Tom stopped short of entering the shed, instead turning back towards what was left of his living animals in their kennels. There was about a dozen, including the remaining B Boys' bitch and her adolescent pups.

His thoughts turned to Kribz and Driss and the drugs they'd obviously stashed on his place, *feckin' black bastards*, but something told him to keep them on side for now, keep his powder dry, say nothing for the time being. He'd sensed that the police weren't really focused on him, nor on his dog-fighting shenanigans. It was a murder enquiry and he'd given a haphazard witness statement from his hospital bed. An afternoon of sport interrupted by a bunch of black gangsters wearing masks and gloves – must have had a beef with the Albos, he'd suggested: *Feck all to do with me, officer.*

He figured if he had to change his story later it wouldn't matter too much; any necessary variations on the original version would be down to shock. He was an old man who'd used a licensed shotgun in self defence and then taken a police bullet whilst unarmed. A lifetime of having a foot on each side of the law had made him nimble; chuck a bit of innocent Irish blarney into the mix and he reckoned he would come out of this rumpus relatively unscathed. The cocaine worried him a bit, but not much.

And of course he'd been told about the Proceeds of Crime Order and how it stopped him selling his place or, more to the point, anyone from forcing its seizure to recover outstanding debt. He hobbled back to the house with a little smirk on his face, oblivious of the Airbus that screamed overhead.

105

Doug Napper was working the Crimint system single handed – literally. Or rather single fingered. One arm still in its sling, he pecked away laboriously, seething with frustration, in the run-down dilapidation that had once been the CID office in Kennington Police Station. Opposite him sat old Macadam.

'Why aren't you off sick? You're setting an awkward precedent, fuckin' comin' in here like the walkin' wounded.'

Napper tried to ignore the retiree but had to have a dig back. 'No worse than you lot, comin' back into the job on the cheap to top up your pensions, nickin' our overtime.'

And that was that, *touché*: silence prevailed.

Napper wasn't in the mood for banter because he was worried. It was Eric's funeral the following day and he'd heard that some Trident undercover boys were going to rock up to cop some footage. He'd decided to stay away: a bit of screenwork was one thing; mingling with a volatile funeral crowd in his condition would risk raising suspicion.

He'd viewed the body worn camera footage of the stop and arrest of the suspect outside Larssen's office whilst he'd been locked up at Rankin's place. The pictures weren't clear but he was pretty sure that the it was one of the Pope brothers who got hauled in, gave a duff name and then got released pronto. There was no coverage of the other lad who'd been seen in the street at the same time.

So, Napper had little doubt that, indirectly, he'd caused Eric's murder but it consoled him a bit that the boy was himself a shooter and would've been grassing for any cop with a white envelope and a bit of smooth patter. Snouts were snouts and it wasn't for lowly PC Napper, he told himself, to worry about what befell them. The fact that he'd got to quite like Trevor Bayado aka Eric Talea aka Screwloose was neither here nor there. And he was relaxed in the knowledge that he'd done his snout's registration properly, by the book – he'd had to so as to secure the cash payments from the Informant Fund. Not to have done so would have been to risk serious comebacks if the boy himself had complained about his police handler. So, Napper expected a tug at some point – an informant registered to him had been murdered. But informants got murdered, that was a fact of life – well, death – and he was confident that the ensuing enquiry would be short, routine and without serious consequences.

There was still no forensic result on the bullet from the boy's chest and Napper wondered if Briggs had chased it up, especially regarding any match for the one that had killed Gozit. Napper suspected that Eric had been killed by a Braganza gun because he just knew how these things worked. If he'd been sussed as a snout – the best reason for being whacked – then his own gun would be the weapon of choice: it made a point. Innit. Napper smiled grimly at his internal use of the suffix.

Algorithm

He trawled Crimint, trying to stay open-minded and unfocused, but the pull of the brothers was too strong for lateral thinking. Kribz and Driss were nothing unusual. Pretty average in the scheme of things, so far. But their trajectory had all the warning signs. Kribz showed promise as a potential 'top boy'. Gang membership in the swamp was commonplace, almost mandatory. You kind of had to be in a posse so as not to get abused, excluded, or just plain ignored, and being excluded or ignored as a black kid in south London meant you were nobody, and that would inevitably lead to you being exploited, bullied, set up as a grass and then possibly murdered. The files showed the brothers to be inseparable and, as they'd got older, attractive and respected. When they'd formed Braganza they were the only two members but everyone assumed there were loads of them, and the gang seemed to exude an air of mystery because the 'members' couldn't be identified so people assumed it was secret, and power flowed from this. It wasn't planned, the Braganza USP – a secret gang, the first ever – wow, man. Then they'd recruited Screwloose with his reputation and the B Boys had muscle. Then they had their dogs – more muscle. Their highly tuned use of hire cars and well-planned, low-profile movements augmented their air of mystery and other gangs gave them more respect than they probably deserved.

Napper could see they'd played on this and their influence had grown. The intel files, when displayed as a spider graphic, showing all the connections no matter how tenuous, indicated that the B Boys were starting to exhibit signs of morphing from gang to organised crime group (OCG) to which acquisitive business was more important than petty postcode violence.

The Cornishman had no doubt that the Bs had accosted Freda Larssen outside her home address and that Kribz had led the Stanwell Moor attack, and now he strongly suspected that he'd killed Screwloose, or had got someone else to do it.

Because he now understood why Kribz had got himself nicked outside the Dane's office at 9 o'clock on a fucking Monday morning, like he'd almost wanted it to happen. The fucker had set Screwloose up, baited him, exposed him as a snitch.

Napper decided to pay someone a visit.

106

The Popes sat in separate cells at Walworth Police Station, two hundred yards from their home address in the Elephant. The police radio checks from the Arch had come back positive and the brothers had been arrested on suspicion of murder, possession of firearms with intent to endanger life, GBH, possession of explosives and a host of less serious misdemeanours. The wanted docket had been raised by Acting Detective Sergeant Aaron Briggs (yes, temporary promotion only) on the orders of his superiors on the murder team, though no one really expected the arrests and subsequent interrogations to yield any evidence. But the motions had to be gone through, and this was it.

For no particular reason, Driss was first into the interview room. Both brothers had elected to have free legal representation and the firm of solicitors next on the duty rota was called.

Katrina Swan had not long since made it as equity partner of Bache & Co, a small but well-formed outfit with offices on the first floor of a new block in the recently spruced-up Vauxhall, overlooking the river. The firm provided criminal legal aid to widen its portfolio, certainly not for the money. Swan hated going to police stations to rep sundry pond-life, but it was part of the game she was playing and needed to be done to keep the firm growing. Her career aim was intellectual property law – copyright and trademark protection stuff, a real fee earner when you got the right clients, and that, alongside medical negligence cases, was where Swan really wanted to be. As an only child from the agricultural west country, she was keen to do well, be wealthy, and pay back her parents for their love and investment. They'd worked their little farm to its – and their – limits so that she could go to a private school and then on to Cambridge. They were proud of her, but were in their seventies, exhausted and in need of retirement. Worst of all were their debts, and the bank was moving in for the kill. It was only 9.30 and she'd spoken to her worried mother twice already that morning. 'Your dad's not well again, Katty,' the old lady had whispered down the phone. 'I'm going to call the doctor to pay a visit.'

It was therefore not a cheerful Katrina who sat in the filthy interview room alongside one of her surly clients and opposite two rather tense young police officers. The lawyer had already been provided with 'advance disclosure' of the facts of the case, as known to the police so far, and had briefly raised an eyebrow at the seriousness of the allegations. This was Old Bailey stuff; QCs would need to be briefed for a long trial and some hefty fees would flow. If it went that far. She thought it ironic that it was her job to see to it that it didn't.

She'd had short private consultations with both Pope brothers separately in their cells and had given them the advice they scarcely needed: reply to each and every question with the words 'No comment'.

And that was how it went; they behaved themselves. The cops – one called Briggs and the other called Mason – were clearly out of their depth, their recorded interrogation was mostly from a pre-written crib-sheet and didn't spring any surprises. Swan was given a copy of a disc which she signed for, then left her two new clients to stew for as long as it took for the cops to run out of reasons to hold them.

She decided to walk back to the office: it would take half an hour, tops. It was hot and sticky and within minutes she'd slowed from her practised powerwalk to a measured trudge and started looking for a cab. Her business suit and high heels were attracting unwelcome attention in the Walworth Road, and she wore her leather shoulder bag crossways to make it less snatchable. She eyed the towering blocks of flats and found herself wondering how it was possible for human beings to be satisfied with living in them. No gardens, no balconies, just stifling shelter, packed in, not much better off than the battery hens on her dad's farm.

When Swan got back to the office, she was sweaty and flustered. The walk had been a bad idea, given the heat and humidity of the swamp, and the stack of emails awaiting her had travelled without discomfort.

She decided to get rid of most of them before lunch and the majority were briskly dispatched to the trash bin within sixty seconds. That left a few stickers and posers, including the dreaded one from her dad's solicitor in Bridport; the old man had given express permission for his daughter to be copied in.

She took a deep breath, opened it, and read without exhaling. It was bad: the Royal Bank had served notice that they intended to 'restructure'. Oh yeah, she thought, that old chestnut. She exhaled and felt a faint tremor in her breath.

Minus her jacket and bag, she left the office and headed at a stroll to the local Pret. Her phone buzzed, showing 'number withheld' but she hit the green button anyway.

'Is that Katrina?'

'Speaking, who is this?'

'Kribz, er, Kriss, Pope, we just seen you at the police station.' She'd given each brother a business card and remembered her sudden gut feeling that she was going to regret it.

'Oh, hi, yes, you've obviously been released then.'

'Yeah,' said Kribz. 'R.U.I. – released under investigation, they got nuthin' on us innit.'

'No Mr Pope, they haven't, and I got the impression that those two young detectives don't really believe you and your

189

brother were responsible. They're just going through the motions, but be careful, they'll be watching you and—'

Kribz hadn't called for advice. 'Listen, we'd like to meet up with you, we might be needin' your help about somethin' else, totally diff'rent, and we can pay you.'

Swan was standing waiting for pedestrian lights to go green and wanted to cut the call. 'Okay Mr Pope, call the landline number on my business card and make an appointment with my secretary.'

'Yeah, okay, cool.' And that was the end of the conversation. As Swan crossed the wide road at the end of Vauxhall Bridge she felt she'd just started walking into the beginning of something else.

107

Napper had never had any confidence in the pedestrian style of reactive crime investigation developed and used by the Met to catch murderers. His derision was self-centred and wrong. The plodding observance of procedures often uncovered evidence that the old school Jack Reagan-styled hunch followers would habitually miss; they were just eager to do little and look good. Crime investigation, as opposed to criminal investigation, was largely an uninspiring drudge through lists of actions generated by an office-based team and dished out to weary coppers who consoled themselves that it was worth it for the overtime. Door to door enquiries on sink estates where you just got told to fuck off; hundreds of hours of CCTV footage to watch and denote on endless spreadsheets; pointless written statements from liars and timewasters; laborious submissions to the Lab of debris that you just knew had nothing to do with anything. But the 99% fruitless toil was devoted to that Holy Grail that just sometimes popped up. The partial index number of a car might be mentioned, which would tally to a seemingly unrelated incident at another time and place, the logged details of which might in turn yield a nickname. Or the pestilence of repeated door knocking in a particular block might lead a petty drug dealer, weary of stymying police presence on his manor, to dial Crime Stoppers, an outfit which took anonymous calls: *'You should be looking at so-and-so for this, instead of harassing us.'*

Usually, and especially in places like the swamp, the Holy Grail never emerged, not dramatically anyway. But everything was fastidiously recorded on the lumbering Home Office Large Major Enquiry System (HOLMES) which, although a relic of the eighties, had been repeatedly upgraded and was fit for the purpose of cross referencing and plotting the results of logical and well-intentioned police labour. Well, just about, anyway.

Of course, Napper didn't think so. Or rather he kidded himself, and hopefully others, that he didn't think so. Either way it didn't really matter because PC Doug Napper, behind the affected country bumpkin, self-deprecating smoke and mirrors shit, was quite possibly an insecure loner trying to make a name for himself. The 'for himself' bit was the operative term; it was himself that he was trying to impress, and the obstacles he snuck round were made up of his own fears and forebodings. He was a misfit, always had been, so unless he did things differently, in embuggerance of the system, then in his own eyes he was a total failure.

His arm had been giving him jip so he'd taken a couple of days' leave. He lay in his dirty little flat and watched the thick cobweb on the ceiling change shape and colour. He likened it to an impenetrably intricate Venn diagram, showing all the possible logical relations between an infinite collection of different people and events. The psilocybin mushrooms he'd mixed in with his beans on toast an hour beforehand did nothing to enhance the 'logic' but did wonders for penetrability. Or so he thought. Or imagined.

Algorithm

It was all blindingly obvious, really, and all roads led to one person. The legal action to take possession of Rankin's land, the maiming of a business partner – Blake had been bang on the money – the formation of a new company to carry the deal through and the continued enlistment of the Braganza Boys to ensure an emphatic transfer of ownership on the big day of eviction, it all stacked up nicely. Kribz getting nicked outside a West End office and the little altercation on the steps of a Notting Hill townhouse were odd, admittedly, but odd things happened when you did deals with jumping jacks: they tended to be a bit demonstrative on occasions, liked to cement contractual arrangements with physical presence. The cobwebs glistened with answers, and the 'shrooms screamed that the spider was Freda Larssen.

108

Numbers wisely considered it best to stay on the right side of as many people as possible, so when he got word that Gillie and Shanker wanted a meet he set off for the Coldharbour Lane cafe pretty much right away. The terrorist attack at the O2 was still sending shock waves all over the place and rumour had it that Kribz and Driss had been swifted with a bunch of muzzies out of the Arch. But Numbers thought that one through and had come to the right conclusion: that the bros had just been unlucky – wrong place, wrong time. Anyway, they'd been released and the word was that they were back at their mum's place. He would go and see them, maybe get his and his sister's phone back, and his tablet. He had loads to catch up on and the burner he'd bought from the pawn shop on Electric Avenue didn't have social media.

The youngster walked with his head down, fists in pockets, turning things over in his mind. It occurred to him that now might be a time to get out of all this, stop skipping college and maybe do something with his life. His sister nagged him relentlessly; she was ten years older, had lost a boyfriend to knife crime and could see her brother going the same way. And then he thought of Mergin, the young Albo who'd been his ticket to acceptance by the Bs. And then he thought about money, and his sister's nagging faded away. And then he thought of Screwloose and wondered briefly why the dead boy had been last to feature. They'd known each other at school and Numbers had been scared shitless of the older kid with the mad reputation, until he'd figured out that Screw wasn't too bright and didn't deserve that much respect after all. And then Numbers had moved away with his family for more than three years, somewhere in north London, council house swap or something like that, before returning to the swamp a bigger lad. *Nah, it was Screw's own fuckin' fault he was in the morgue*, was Numbers' thinking. *Live by the sword, die by the sword, innit.* By the time he walked into the cafe he'd decided Screwy was now an irrelevance. All he'd done was intro him to the Bs, and that was only because he was a feed into Mergin. *Yeah, fuck you Screw, you 'ad it comin' bro*.

The three elders had seen him enter but their eyes were down and hooded as he took the spare seat at the table.

'You're fuckin' late,' growled Shanker, without looking up. Numbers didn't say anything.

'He said you're late, answer him,' enjoined Gillie.

Numbers still didn't reply, surprising himself with his insolence. He turned to Massive, who he was now sitting beside, as if to say 'your turn' and reasonably expected an elbow in the face. But Massive just started to laugh, a stifled wheeze at first, before the trademark grin crept across his huge black face which he slowly raised to his two henchmen across the table: 'He got balls, innit.'

'He's fuckin' dissin' us innit,' hissed Shanker, with a murderous stare at the newcomer. Then Gillie started laughing as well and Shanker thought it best to join in.

Then, still laughing, Massive put his hand behind Numbers' head, gave it a couple of gentle pats and then rammed it hard down onto the table. The boy didn't resist, just tucked his nose and chin so that his hard little brow took the impact.

'Don't be late ever again, you little cunt,' laughed Massive, before releasing the boy to let him sit upright. He did so, slowly, looking around the cafe with what he hoped was a bored expression. He considered faking a stifled yawn but didn't push his luck.

Massive got serious. 'Now listen Numbers, an' don't take this the wrong way, me an' the boys here are a bit concerned about you. We kinda need to be assured that you ain't gettin' funny ideas, if you get my meanin'.'

Numbers spoke for the first time, eloquently. 'I understand totally, I've already had the same chat off Kribz an' Driss, all you'ze brothers got nuthin' to worry 'bout, truss me, innit. I gotta business to run and I need you big men on my side.'

All three 'big men' exchanged glances, and all nodded sagely. They'd heard about Numbers' Albo coke connection, accepted that the boy would probably need muscle sooner or later, and knew he would have the money to pay for it. But this was just a bit of business logic that provided an extra layer of trust in Numbers' favour. On its own it would have been nowhere near enough. Of much greater importance was the blood bond, the ideology against co-operation with the police that was so dense, so heavy that it had its own moral gravity, bending decisions into its orbit, warping rational behaviour to such an extent that seasoned members of the black crime community guarded against too much belief in it and often, as in this case, sought additional assurances.

Massive snapped his fingers and ordered four coffees.

109

Napper sat on the Notting Hill doorstep and struggled to roll a cigarette with one hand. His trussed arm was not healing quickly and he was still on a stack of Co-codomol for the pain.

194

The opiate had the side effect of lowering his guard and he was dimly aware that his judgement was not at its best. But still, here he was, going off piste again, flouting the rules and waiting to treat a signed-up witness as some sort of suspect-stroke-potential-informant. The tactic should have been authorised by a senior investigating officer holding the rank of detective superintendent and Napper knew that, true to form, he was putting his job on the line.

He dropped the tobacco and Rizla and swore, kicking it off the step and giving up on the job.

'Pick that up and fuck off!'

His eyes started on the feet and swept up over the long naked legs, Lycra clad camel's toe, six-pack abs, crop-topped tits, slender neck and, finally, the snarling face.

'Go on, before I kick your arse.'

The cop stood up. He equalled her height, thanks only to the bottom step beneath his feet. 'I'm a police officer, Miss Larssen.' The words came out apologetically as he produced his warrant card 'I need to speak to you very privately.'

She looked him up and down.

'What the hell about?' She frowned; head tilted with the effort of trying to pigeon-hole this anomalous interruption. The scruffy beard, retro clothes and NHS arm sling made the job impossible. He didn't reply to the question. She snatched the warrant card and inspected it theatrically before handing it back to him between thumb and forefinger, like it was dirty or infected. 'Police Constable Douglas Napper, eh? What weirdo department do you belong to? Undercover clown patrol or something?'

He sensed her softening. 'No, just a street cop out on a limb,' and then he played one of his favourite cards. 'I think I've got some information for you.' It never failed: less than a minute later he was sat incongruously on a white leather sofa listening to Freda Larssen's power shower.

Algorithm

She walked into the room wearing a white towel bathrobe. She took a cigarette from a packet on the coffee table and lit it without offering him one. There'd been likewise no offer of tea or coffee.

'Right then, Police Constable Douglas Napper, give me the information.'

'I read your statement about the Stanwell Moor murders.' He watched her as he spoke. She didn't reply, just returned his gaze through a puff of uninhaled smoke.

'Seems to me like you got off lightly.' There was a pause as the limb he was out on started to bend.

'I'm waiting.'

'What for?'

'The information you say you've got for me. I didn't invite you in for your opinion.' It wasn't said irritably but rather gently, warmly, like a counsellor coaxing candour and trust.

Further out he crept. 'My opinion is expert opinion, so it counts as information. I saw you at Stanwell Moor, you might 'ave seen me on a stretcher. You was struttin' your stuff big style but I reckon you should've been nicked.'

'What?'

'Arrested, not treated as a witness.'

She stubbed out her cigarette, looked thoughtful and sat back with the tips of her fingers together, steeple-like.

'What are you hoping to provoke from me, Mr Napper? Some sort of confession to murder, an acceptance of responsibility for what happened?'

He was gaining traction; it was going better than he'd expected and he felt the limb he was out on become stronger. 'No, not exactly, but I'm getting' an interestin' reaction, that's for sure.'

An edge of impatience stole into her voice. 'I think it's time you chased the cut, Mr Napper. This is getting tiresome.'

'Cut to the chase, you mean. Okay.' He sat forward and rubbed his arm sling whilst composing his next words. 'I think that your presence on that land at the time of the murders was just too much of a coincidence, especially considerin' what you was there for. There's got to be a connection, and I reckon you know who was responsible 'cos they've had a go at you also, at least twice in the last few weeks that I know about, an' I don't think your statement goes nearly far enough if it's meant to be helpin' us.'

Larssen remained motionless, relaxed, like a grandmaster playing a novice. 'Whilst I hate to be predictable, Mr Napper, all I can say is that I've provided a full written statement and I've left nothing out. If by those responsible you mean the black thugs who accosted me outside this house, then why don't you just go and arrest them? Rankin'll know who they are, we saw them at his place and, as I've already told that idiot colleague of yours – what's his name, Briggs – the connection was something to do with dogs.' Her hands were apart now, open palms angled upwards and towards him, as if to say, *What's the problem? Do your job.*

The Cornishman felt himself retreating backwards to the trunk of his tree; it was perhaps time to climb down.

'We've already arrested a number of the suspects. We know who they are, but we haven't got the evidence to charge them.' He leant forward a bit further. 'A motive would be good.'

'A motive, what for?'

'What – or who – made them attack the place?'

She just stared at him.

'They had no beef with the Irishman, nor with the Albanians. Someone made them or paid them to go there, guns blazin', and cause total fuckin' mayhem, and that someone, I reckon, had a vested interest in scarin' the shit out of Rankin and his old missus so they would turn tail and get out of the place.'

'Hmmm.' She made the thoughtful sound with her lips pursed as she stood up, adjusting her bathrobe. She glanced at the clock. 'I think you should be going now officer, it's been an interesting little chat but I've things to do.'

Napper shrugged, got to his feet, and walked past her and out of the room. She followed. 'What are you going to do now?' There was just a tinge of trepidation in her voice.

He didn't pause or turn to face her, just kept walking to the street door. 'There's an old sayin' in my game Miss Larssen: shake any tree for long enough and somethin'll fall out – eventually.' And he was gone: out, down the stone steps, onto the pavement, gone.

Still in her hallway, Larssen just stared at the open door and felt an inexplicable unease.

110

'Where are you taking me? What's happened?' asked Mergin.

'Someone wants to see you,' said Bora Gozit, 'and you'll understand that this is going to be a very private meeting Mergin.'

'I don't want to be late for college.' The boy was feigning innocence.

'Oh, don't give me that, d'you think I don't know what you're up to? You've made what's called a *life* choice, young man, now it's time to live it.' She paused at a junction, made a left turn and continued. 'College my fucking arse.'

Mergin swiveled his eyes to look at his cousin, her drab cotton coat covering the nurse's uniform at odds with the ostentatious Lexus; how did she explain her ownership of this? he thought. He remained silent.

Bora swung into a Tesco car park, jerked her head for the boy to get out and then led him at a brisk walk through the front doors of the store. He followed her meandering route through the aisles and then out of a rear exit, down a short alleyway and into a back street. A hundred metres later they were in the receptionless foyer of an inconspicuous

Travelodge. She thumbed her phone: *I've got him, we're downstairs.*

The lock on a security door buzzed and they were allowed through into the lift lobby – she elected the stairs and they trudged up three flights. They had to pause on one of the landings to allow a man to pass on his way down. He was limping badly, with a walking stick, taking one step at a time, clearly in pain. He was also in their eyes clearly Albanian. They reached the third floor and Zamir was standing in the corridor, grinning broadly.

'Well, well, little Mergin, not so little anymore, huh?'

The boy approached his other cousin resolutely, trying to hide his nerves. He held out his hand, manlike. The gangster brushed it away and bear-hugged the boy, nearly lifting him off his feet. Bora smiled thinly.

The bad man's room had only one chair, in which Bora sat, uninvited. She looked at her fob watch. 'We need to make this quick, five minutes, no more.'

Zamir bade Mergin sit on the unmade bed. He himself then sat on the floor cross-legged, so that the boy looked down at him. 'Okay, big man, word is you've come a long way and that you have some friends in the *zezak* community, am I right?'

Mergin nodded, understanding the Albanian word for negro.

'Good, right, I want an introduction to a *zezak* called Shanker, d'you know him?'

'No.' Mergin shook his head; he wouldn't have dared lied.

'Find him for me, please, it's very important.' The last two words came out flatly, like the real person behind the bonhomie was showing a glimpse of himself, just a quick peek: *and hey, by the way, don't mistake this for a polite request.*

Mergin of course knew about his uncle Kemal's murder and guessed that his son's return to London was not unconnected. But he hadn't spoken to Numbers in weeks, didn't know that the B Boys were suspects and had never heard of anybody called 'Shanker'.

'I'll do my best, cousin Zamir.'

'I know you will, Mergin, and I'm not your cousin, I'm your brother. We are all brothers, we are Gheg, remember that Mergin, always.' The killer stood up and ruffled the boy's hair.

Bora could see it was over. 'Right, we done?' She was keen to be gone.

On their way back to the Tesco car park they saw the Albanian with the walking stick, stood glumly at a bus stop. They ignored him and drove off in the Lexus. The man was called Defrim Iseberi, had sustained his injuries at Stanwell Moor and had been advised, through the intricate London-Albo word of mouth network controlled largely by the Hellbanianz, to present himself, unaccompanied, to Zamir Gozit. He had complied, of course, and his report of having heard the name 'Shanker' on that fateful day had pleased the Travelodge guest; it was what he needed – a name, a starting point. History would be made of what followed.

111

Aaron Briggs was a busy boy. The Stanwell Moor enquiry had been handed over to Trident Reactive, a roving team of cops who spent their time and massive budget clearing up the aftermaths of gang warfare, usually with unsatisfactory results. But Briggs still had a shedful of other stuff in his bulging electronic in-tray, two of which were the shootings of Massive and Jackson. South Area Homicide were going through the motions of investigating the murder of the so-called Screwloose, and nobody expected that to conclude successfully. So, the work had been graded, commoditised, and farmed out to various units, according to their ever-changing remits and constrained resources. But Briggs was still in all the loops, cc'd into a constant blizzard of emails, many of which he deleted with barely a glance.

But the one that caught his focused attention was from the Lab: a positive comparative result on the bullets from the bodies of Kemal Gozit and Trevor Bayado – aka Screwloose – and these in turn were from the same gun as those found in the legs of Jackson and Samuka Massanga, aka Massive.

Briggs read the email attachment bearing these results several times, absorbing their consequences, assessing his reactions, the first of which being irritability that his request for the comparisons had been on Napper's suggestion. He decided it would be best to come clean, act magnanimous and write a quick report in praise of the diligent officer. *Scruffy bastard*, was his private thought. He decided to get his oar in first and called the said scruffy bastard.

'You cracked it Doug, you got a result!'

'What are you on about?' Napper sighed the words, narked by the detective's patronising tone.

'The ballistic reports came back positive. You were dead right, whoever slotted Massive and Jackson did for Gozit and Screwloose too.'

Napper managed not to be too nauseated by Briggs' contrived copspeak and took pleasure in countering with the obvious correction. 'The bullets came from the same weapon is prob'ly what you mean, unless the Lab's got a new computer with a solve button.'

It took a couple of long seconds for Briggs to absorb this, but he recovered. 'Well, yes, exactly, you know as well as I do that obviously these shooters get passed around, but it's still a good set of connections.'

Napper gritted his teeth. He was still in the street in Notting Hill and had to step into a shop doorway to continue the conversation with collected patience. 'Can you forward me the result, Aaron? I'd like to see it if that's okay.'

'Already done it mate, it's in your inbox.'

'Thanks, nice to be of assistance. Got to go!' Napper tapped the 'end call' icon.

112

Kribz and Driss sat in Katrina Swan's office, their postures respectful, their clothing clean and tidy. Swan smiled when they declined tea or coffee and then pressed a button and spoke on an intercom. 'No calls for half an hour please.' She looked up at her guests. 'Will that be long enough, gentlemen?' They both nodded.

'Right then, first of all, has this got anything to do with your arrest yesterday, or do I open a new file?'

'New file please Katrina,' said Kribz, before unhelpfully adding, 'but it's got a bit to do with yesterday.'

She looked thoughtful. 'Let's put it another way. Has what you're here for got anything to do with you being accused of multiple murder at Stanwell Moor?'

Driss was keen to contribute: 'No.' His brother agreed with a shake of his head.

'Right, next question,' said the solicitor patiently. 'Has this got anything to do with you being accused or suspected of anything else?'

'No,' they both answered together.

'Hurrah! Progress!' Swan tried to inject humour, but the brothers didn't smile. She promptly returned to being serious. 'Okay, what can I do for you, gentlemen?'

'It's about Mr Rankin. We want to help him, he's a friend of ours and the police are like targeting him and it's not right what they're doing.' Kribz spoke in his best English, going slowly, avoiding street-speak. Driss gave him a sideways glance, impressed.

'Right, so,' Swan blinked a few times, smiling, 'sounds interesting, tell me more.'

She opened a notebook but found it impossible to annotate what followed. Thirty minutes later the boys had gone, leaving her doing mental acrobatics around the concept of client confidentiality.

'Fuck, man,' said Driss back home in their mother's flat, 'you sure we can fuckin' truss' her?'

'No bruv, course not, but it's a manageable risk innit, if she grasses we'll just say we was lyin' to get her onside. Even if she recorded us in there, it ain't no proof that we was telling the truth.'

Driss wasn't buying this. 'If we was lyin' how do we know about the food, man?'

'Simple, Rankin told us innit, like he's shittin' himself and weeze offrin' to help. Don't mean to say weeze akshully fuckin' guilty bro.' Kribz watched his brother as he spoke and saw the penny dropping. 'You gettin' my drift now bro? C'mon, you agreed to this before we went to see her, weeze in it together, innit.'

Driss was now nodding emphatically with his eyes closed, 'Yeah man, sorry, jus 'ad a touch of a wobble, thass all.'

113

Although slap bang in the centre of the City of London, the office of Blake & Co, Solicitors and Commissioners of Oaths, made visitors feel they'd just walked into a Dickensian time warp. Access to the street door was via a narrow alleyway behind Bank Underground Station and, once it had been remotely opened by the lawyer on the fourth floor, the visitor was then presented with a winding staircase so steep and perilous that it consumed high levels of physical and mental energy to accomplish the climb.

Napper hated it at the best of times but the absence of the use of his left arm made the ascent on this occasion particularly difficult because he couldn't grasp the banister.

'You've really got to knock those fags on the head, me old son,' said Blake, not having to look up to hear the policeman's laboured wheezing as he stood leaning heavily against the doorframe. 'Come on in and sit yourself down. Beer? Sun must over the yardarm by now.' It was only 2pm but Blake's yardarm was notoriously flexible.

'Nah, troin' to think, mate. You'll never guess where I was half an hour ago.' Still struggling for breath, Napper moved a pile of files that occupied the visitor's chair, dumped them on the floor to join a heap of others and sat himself down, as invited.

'Go on,' said the lawyer, sensing something new on the brew.

'Been to see Freda Larssen. You were roit, she's up to her fuckin' throat in it.'

Blake waited for more; it came.

'Then I got a call, they've matched up the bullets, Brixton, Knightsbridge, Stanwell, Elephant – same Baretta, hundred per cent fit.'

Blake twisted round in his chair, opened the fridge and took out two cans of Kronenbourg, opened one, leaned across his chaotic desk to hand it to Napper, and then popped the other one, taking several gulps immediately, as if the news made it necessary. It didn't, but the excuse couldn't be wasted.

'I thought you said these lads knew Rankin anyway, independent from his dealings with Larssen and Jackson, something about him breeding dogs for them.' Blake's words were thoughtful, almost ponderous.

The cop took long pull of his beer. 'Yeah, I know, there's a long way to go—'

'And the shooting in the Elephant was your snout getting whacked. Why would Larssen have anything to do with that?'

'I know, I know.' Napper held up his beer can in surrender. 'I'm not sayin' she has sumthin' to do with ev'rythin', an' the shooting of the D7 boy in Brixton would 'ave 'ad nuthin' to do with her neither, but her business partner getting shot, then her startin' a new company, then the Rankin place getting attacked on the day she was servin' the fuckin' eviction notice, all these connections can't be just pushed under the carpet Stu. Don't you see where I'm coming from?'

'Of course, I see where you're coming *from* Doug, what I'm struggling with is where you're fucking going *to*, but knowing you, you'll be hatching some sort of weird plan.' It wasn't said with humour.

Napper chewed the words over, then washed them down with the remains of his beer. He put the empty can on the desk and stood up, a little unsteady.

'You altogether well, old chap?' Blake felt a twinge of guilt about what he'd just said. 'You look a bit pasty to me.'

'I'm foin,' replied the cop. 'Just tired, and on too many opioid painkillers. Fuckin' me head up a bit, oi think.'

114

Kribz and Driss were getting back into the swing of things. They'd attended Screwloose's funeral: churlish – not to mention highly suspicious – not to. It had gone off pretty much as expected. A half-hearted attempt at a BBQ wake followed on the estate car park, but the tweny or so attendees drifted away after the jerk chicken ran out. The Popes noticed that one of the mourners had kept her distance from the little gathering; aloof, smartly dressed, she had walked away when she'd seen the boys looking at her.

'Who was *she*?' said Driss to his brother.

'Must be Screwy's sister, or half-sister I think, I remember him mentioning that the flat was in her name but I never saw her there.' Kribz paused, frowning, and then went on. 'I remember her from school, she was a few years above us, a prefect, he was kinda embarrassed about her, they didn't have much to do wid each other, Gerry or Geraldine I think her name was, bit of a stuck-up cow.'

Algorithm

Driss had got bored with this, wanted to move on; 'Let's get out of here fam, I ain't likin' it.' Kribz agreed, and they'd walked away

The ensuing murder enquiry had gone through the motions but it was just another black-on-black job, probably Massive or his mates, the police correctly guessed, but nobody held their breath for an evidential breakthrough. There wasn't even enough intel to haul a few faces in on suspicion: it was all supposition, and arrests would only lead to accusations of racial profiling and probably civil actions against the police, funded by the rag-tag of leftist groups chasing headlines. So it was put to bed as quickly as possible. The 9mm bullet and the forensic result it yielded was interesting and could be used if anything more cropped up later to join the dots, but that was about it. Screwloose's room had been searched and dusted for prints that would come back positive matches for the Pope brothers and a raggedy list of other low lifers, but nothing to put anyone at the murder scene.

There was nothing but the fact that the bullet had come out of the same gun used on Massive, on Jackson and on Kemal Gozit. That was obviously very interesting but, again, not enough to lead to arrests: guns moved around like in a game of pass the parcel.

Anyway, this was the reasoning Kribz and Driss had settled into and, as a bed to lay in, it was doing its job. They'd come out of the police interview at Walworth totally unscathed and were confident that the 'investigation' that they'd been 'released under' would come to diddly fuckin' squat. It was highly unlikely that Shanker or Gillie would roll over and grass, and anyway, given their form, no court of law would believe a word they said. Numbers was shit-scared and would be rightly assuming that he would go Screwloose's way if he so much as thought about snitching. As for Massive – well, he would be on his own if he turned and the fedz would have to have some serious shit on him for that to happen.

Besides, there was something about the big negro that made him safe, strong, a bit of a rock.

The questions that Briggs had asked them during the interrogation – if you could call it that – had told them that the police knew about their association with Rankin and that it was something to do with dogs. They'd both stuck to 'no comment' replies, as advised by the redoubtable Miss Swan, so the information had been all one-way. So what if they were friends of Rankin? The pit bulls were a common interest and they were only trying to go legit by having a licensed breeder look after them and chip them and keep them safe from thieves.

'Did you know these dogs are illegal?' Briggs had asked.

'No comment.'

'How many times did you visit Stanwell Moor?'

'No comment.'

'Who introduced you to him?'

'No comment.'

'Did you know he was going to get evicted?'

'No comment.'

And so on.

The car of the day was a modest Ford Focus and Julie at the hire firm had been pleased to see them. The terrorist attack at the O2 had made London very nervous, on red alert, and a bit of normality was reassuring. 'Haven't seen you for a while,' she'd said.

'Ah, music business a bit slow, Julie, had a few gigs cancelled 'cos of security issues innit.'

They hadn't told Rankin they were coming and when Marlene opened the door they could see her tired face put on years in seconds. She couldn't disconnect what had happened from these black boys; their only business with her husband was bad business that didn't look like going away.

'Wait there boys, I'll tell him you're here.'

Algorithm

They shuffled about in the porch, sucking their teeth, for about thirty seconds before she returned, looking resigned and disappointed. 'He says to come in. Wipe your feet the pair of you.'

The old man was sat in his usual spot, but with his feet up and a blanket around his legs. A half-empty bottle of Black Bush was on the table within reaching distance.

'Sit yourselves down lads, I wondered when you'd pop by. Is that kettle on, Marlene?' He was facing away from them, looking out through the French windows onto his land.

The brothers sat down on the sofa, straight-backed with hands folded on their laps, like a couple of schoolboys awaiting advice from a master.

'What have you got to say for yourselves then?' He still hadn't looked at them.

'What d'you mean Mr Rankin? We did what we was told, innit.' Kribz spoke respectfully.

'You know what I'm feckin' talking about young man, don't act the innocent.' As he said this Rankin threw off the blanket and stood up with surprising agility, turning to face them. 'Was it either of you who stuffed a load of feckin' cocaine into one of the small sheds? Now that's a straight question and I'm wantin' a straight feckin' answer.'

'No Mr Rankin, it must have been one of your stupid Albo buddies, but obviously the police'll want to frame us with it, we fit the profile, innit.'

Rankin had a rough idea what Kribz was talking about and didn't seek clarification.

'That's not what they've told me. They're considering charging me with bein' a feckin' drugs dealer and then I'll lose this place for sure. D'you understand what I'm talking about?'

'Yeah, we do, confiscation of criminal property, happens to our people all the time, except that they never have much to confiscate.' Kribz spoke calmly, reasonably, letting the Irishman call the shots. Driss just sat there, stony-faced.

'What the feck were you thinkin' lads, I—'

Kribz took over. 'We've come to make a suggestion Tom, there's a way out of this, a way forward for you and for us.'

Rankin absorbed the words and leaned heavily on the table. 'Go on.'

'It's simple Tom, it's called cuckooin', you ever heard of that?'

'No, never.' the reply was emphatic and laced with frustration.

Kribz ploughed on. 'It's when somebody, er, weak, gets bullied into 'avin' their place used for drugs. It's usually a flat or a house, but you could say it 'appened right here.'

The old Irishman took his hand off the table and pulled himself to his full height. 'What?'

Driss could contain himself no longer. 'You're a victim, Mr Rankin, tell the fuckin' fedz you've been harassed by the fuckin' Albos!'

Kribz's eyes were down, embarrassed by his brother's outburst. 'Driss is right Tom, you gotta forget your pride and blame them, play the poor ol' man bit, they made you use your place for dog fightin', drugs keepin' an' any-fuckin'-thing else you can think of, an' not only that, they brought their war with a black fuckin' gang onto your place an' that would explain the shootin' and grenade attack. Put it all on them Tom, an' it gets us all off the hook.'

Rankin sat back down, heavily. 'Well, I suppose Gozit's dead so he can't talk.'

'*Egsaklee*,' soothed Driss, a bit too sarcastically.

Kribz decided it was time to move this on. 'We killed for you, Tom, we turned this place into a war zone an' 'cos of that those liquidator cunts've been sent packin'…'

'Aye, for the time bein'…'

'For the time bein' is all you need,' butted in Driss.

Kribz continued. 'Yeah, which brings me onto the next bit, you say you owe the bank fifty grand. Buy us six months an' we'll have that for you, then we can do business. Jus' hold your nerve, bro.'

All of a sudden Tom Rankin looked very tired, then Marlene came in with a tray of mugs and a teapot. Kribz changed the subject. 'Can we go out an' see our dogs please Tom?'

'Aye lads, suppose so, they're fine, and I'm not your feckin' bro.'

Marlene poured the teas and all three men carried their mugs out through the French doors, across the big patio and onwards to the kennel and pen where Lois and her now adolescent pups were being kept. Although plainly PBTs, they hadn't been seized by the RSPCA, probably on account of them not being involved in the fighting.

'Wow, they look in good form, few quid's worth there.' Driss admired the youngsters gleefully.

'Here, Tom, we owe you rent,' said Kribz, looking over his shoulder to make sure Marlene wasn't watching. He held out a hand containing £500 in used tens and twenties. Rankin took it quickly, but without snatching. 'Thanks son, that'll come in handy.'

Kribz needn't have worried about Marlene watching: she was at the front of the house answering the door again. The man on the doorstep looked like one of the beggars who occasionally pitched up looking for help from a propertied member the travelling community, but the accent of Defrim Iseberi told her otherwise.

'I have been sent to speak with Mr Rankin.'

115

It was a sunny day and Jackson was out walking. He would have been out walking whatever the weather, but the sunshine made it easier for some reason, lifted his spirits a tad. He still relied heavily on a stick and occasionally even crutches, but he was coming along and beginning to see slightly more than a glimmer of hope for the future. He was almost completely off the painkillers now, so his growing optimism was unlikely to be down to the opiates. He couldn't quite put his finger on it but, you know, he was alive – that part of it certainly could have been worse – and, although not quite alive and kicking in the literal sense, felt strongly that he'd been liberated; was now free of the crushing obligations and responsibilities that had shackled him for as long as he could remember.

A beep from his smartwatch told him that he'd clocked his first thousand steps of the day, so he sat down heavily on a park bench and allowed his eyes to settle on a pair of ducks paddling about contentedly in a manicured pond. He remembered once being told that the birds mated for life and that if one died the surviving partner would inevitably happen upon a replacement who'd suffered similar bereavement: no mad search, no panicked, grief-stricken campaign. Life could be so simple, he thought, if we could just only let it.

He loosened his prosthetic and gave his stump a gentle massage whilst trying to keep his thoughts unfocused. It was just gone 7am, his best time of the day, before he began scheming; old habits die hard. But each morning brought progress in that he was able to stave off the inevitable for an increment longer. It had not been that long since he'd dreamt of hate-filled vengeance on anything and everything that moved. Violence had been the principal theme: Larssen, the blacks, the incompetent police, Blake – yeah, he could have it too – and the Irish bastard – why not? he was surely part of it. The murderous nonsense still swept in, but later in the day now, and with decreasing debilitation.

He reflected how hatred seemed to have a half-life and began to hopefully imagine that as it followed its evaporative curve it was somehow being replaced by a sense of clarity, a feeling that, if he gave them time and space, the dots would join themselves.

He stood and set off again at his rehabilitative pace; forget speed or distance, his physio had told him, concentrate on not concentrating, make walking involuntary again, let your subconscious resume its responsibilities. A runner swept past him, then a roller skater, both keen for the office no doubt, sharpening their minds with oxygen. It was early autumn and the first leaves were falling. Soon the trees would be naked, stripped of their soft contours, exposed as their contorted, tortured selves, obliged to endure winter vulnerable and unclothed.

116

Briggs sat in front of a big, multi-coloured spreadsheet on his screen. The RILE System was an algorithm – one of many – that purported to assist investigators streamline their thinking and focus on how raw intelligence could be converted to trial-worthy evidence. In reality, it had been designed to reduce the investigative process down to a series of measurable actions, inanely attributing numerical values to the provability of suppositions. A 'score' could thus be assigned to an investigation, upon which decisions would be based: decisions on whether to progress, diminish or even discontinue lines of enquiry. Gone were the days of intuitive thinking and cops' gut feelings. Like everything else, the role of the detective had been reduced to an array of functions, commoditised, chopped up into sequentialised, bite-sized pieces to fit neatly into the Excel world of two-dimensional thinking.

Briggs loved it: it was the future and he really believed in it. Or rather he really believed that his future really depended on it. The vast, clunking mechanical beast that was the Metropolitan Police had to be fed, had to be made to look good, so those at its helm would look good and just might – might – reward those who protected them from below.

He'd already received several pats on the back for his Proceeds of Crime Act work on the Rankin assets and had put together some elegantly written arguments for CPS lawyers to plagiarise and use in their submissions to the court. He'd additionally performed well at the several policy briefings chaired by senior officers and had been given the *de facto* role of Case Lead Officer, quite a feat for an Acting Detective Sergeant. So, it was with a warm feeling in his bowels that he nourished the algorithm and served it with his incremental assessments of probabilities, witness profiles, harm to victims, suspects' profiles, etc., etc. The scores appeared instantaneously and resolved into a picture, a landscape of variously weighted possibilities that he obliged himself to progress with variously accentuated vigour.

A prominent hypothesis was that the Braganza Boys had attempted to rob Rankin, biting off more than they could chew when choosing the time and date of their raid. Had they known of the dogfight and the presence of the Albanians they would surely never have gone to Stanwell Moor. Their subsequent use of disproportionate force was explained by nothing more than their inherent predilection for violence. The algorithm liked this one, and that was good enough for Briggs. So that was the road he was on; the B Boys were the perps. He chomped on a muesli bar and scrolled across the coloured cells of his creation, pausing to add some emphasis here and there to strengthen the case, bolster the outcome, guild the lily. The 'egg on face' risk, as he privately liked to call it, was low; if it turned out wrong, he could blame the machine. If it went well, he would bask. And it couldn't really go all that wrong. The B Boys were baddies, always fair game and, given their antecedents, could not really be discounted as suspects, even though the search of their home, their arrests and interrogations, had yielded nothing. There were still plenty of unexploited avenues, not least of which being the identification of three of their members. So, Briggs kept on building the picture: the Pope brothers, and associates. Therein was a bit that the machine did not like. And associates. One of whom had inconveniently just been murdered. With one of the same guns that had been used at Stanwell Moor. Inconvenient indeed. Awkward. He called Napper.

'These shooters get pashed around all the time, Briggshy, you already know thish, we've been through thish already,' the Cornishman slurred, clearly the worse for wear. 'Washamatter, don't your fuckin' algorithm like it?'

'No, it doesn't,' said Briggs, oblivious of the sarcasm. 'It doesn't fit at all.'

'Well, besht you get off that fuckin' machine an' do some thinkin' my man, like a real copper.'

Briggs had a measure of sympathy for this line of argument but, actually, it was the ex-public schoolboy who lived in the real world, not the pissed up ex-squaddie.

'That's all very well Doug, but I've got a system to work to, a budget to bid for. If I don't present an argument in the accepted format then the money gets cut, which includes your overtime, so I've got to play the game.'

Napper was in the Coach and Horses and on his fifth pint of some particularly powerful lager. He'd been waiting for Blake for almost two hours and the lawyer's lateness was pissing him off. But Briggs' candour was impressing him and a few thoughtful seconds preceded his response. He leaned off the bar, blinking, stood up a bit straighter and concentrated on not slurring.

'Yeah, okay, see what you mean, mate, get your drift, sorry to be a bit rude there. Erm – d'you fancy a pint?'

It was Briggs' turn to be disarmed. 'What, now?'

'Yeah, c'mon, why not?'

It was only 6pm and Briggs still had work to do. It was all right for the street cops, they had no case load, no piles of emails to plough through. The likes of Napper could just get up, dress up, pretend at not giving up and then get out of their boxes after their shifts and blame the system for the shortfalls. But they didn't often invite the likes of Briggs, toe-the-company-line men, for a beer and the career detective was flattered.

'Where?'

'Coach and Horses, Greek Steet, Soho. It's a cop-free zone so don't start swingin' the blue lamp, if you get my meaning – no loud job talk.'

Briggs didn't really get Napper's meaning but didn't press lest clarity would be unpleasant. 'Yeah, okey-dokey, give me half an hour…'

Napper cut the connection and slumped back against the bar, immediately doubtful that he'd made a good move. *How was this dude in a suit going to get on with Blakey? Ah, what the hell? Be good for a laugh.*

Think of the Devil and he shall appear: in walked the tubby solicitor, red-faced and cross.

'I'm sick to death of being up to the throat in whining wankers!'

'Good evening, Stuart,' said Napper with perky sarcasm. 'Good day at the office then?'

'Shut the fuck up and get me a pint.'

'Certainly, Stuart.'

Napper downed the remains of his pint and ordered two more. Unusually, a table became vacant and the pair claimed it wordlessly. There were three chairs and they'd barely sat down before an elderly gent in white suit and fedora asked if he could have the remaining seat.

''Fraid not, friend, we're expecting someone else,' said Napper, apologetically. The man shambled off.

'Who the fuck else is coming then?' Blake was slightly concerned: solicitors weren't meant to be too cosy with police officers and he wasn't keen on the presence of an interloper.

'A colleague of mine, harmless, don't worry.'

'He'd better be. What goes on between you and me stays between you and me, mate. What's the fucking cover story?'

'Erm, jusht say we went to uni together,' said the Cornishman, slurring again.

'But you never went to fucking uni, you prat, not as a student anyway, and I went to Auriel College, so how's this cock and bull shit going to stack up?'

Napper took the point and made an amendment. 'Look, I was a gardener there, it's the truth, and we've kept in touch, and we played rugby together, and you're in the insurance game, and—'

'Good evening, gentlemen?' The inflection combined the greeting with a request to join.

'Oh, hi Aaron, sit yourself down mate, this is Stuart, an ol' mate of mine. Stuart, this is Aaron.' Napper's eyes were unfocused as he mumbled through the introduction.

'Nice to meet you, Aaron, let me get you a drink. What'll it be? This twat's been at it all fucking day but I've just got here, so you're not the only sober man in the house.'

'Yes, thankfully,' Briggs eyed Napper with a hint of disappointment. 'Cheers, I'll have a half of Guinness please.'

117

Larssen was in her power shower. She'd just cycled back from a session with Privette, so the hot jets were more to get rid of the cloying sordidness that the weekly session always left her with, rather than the sweat of the journey home. But she knew Privette was a necessary part of her life; the therapy kept her grounded; mindful of how she had to present herself to humanity.

Wrapping herself in a small white towel, she took it upon herself to check the emails, both incoming and outgoing, of every one of her staff. Like all her other administrative duties, she resented it. But ever vigilant for maneuvering assassins, she went through the ritual regularly. She sat on the vast bed, wafer thin tablet on her naked lap. After a few minutes of stroking the screen and sipping Scotch from a glass the size of her fist, she stopped and blinked. Her first thoughts were of how to deal with what was in front of her; it looked horribly like she had work to do.

She put the glass down and concentrated, without difficulty. Whatever Palmer was playing at painted a startling picture. Her muscles tensed as she read the lengthy exchange that had taken place the previous day. Palmer had entered into the preliminaries of a deal with a carefully worded email to a property finance company in the City of London. Larssen vaguely remembered Palmer mentioning this approach a few days earlier; it concerned the Stanwell Moor project in which the firm, despite the recent setbacks, had built up a residual beneficial interest, of sorts. It went something like this: Rankin was still the registered legal owner; the Royal Bank claimed equitable ownership due to it being security against the money the Irishman owed it; the Metropolitan Police had obtained a restraint order to stop it being sold or otherwise transferred pending the outcome of the ongoing investigation. But that wasn't the end of it; JLP Restructuring (Denmark) PLC also had a claim to a proportion of its value due to the fees they were owed for the work they'd purportedly done to recover the asset for the bank and Larssen had pegged that at an outrageous £100k. Palmer's job at outlining this scenario to the financiers was, Larssen had to admit to herself, attractively written. He was basically offering to sell the prospective invoice for the sum of £50k, the fifty per cent discount being to offset the risk that the oncoming Proceeds of Crime action would neither fail nor would be limited to a figure that would reflect Rankin's minimal criminal income, and that therefore the outcome would be sufficient leftovers for the residual claimants. If all went according to Palmer's plan, JLP would get the 50k up front and the City financier would collect the 100k from the bank if and after the Rankin homestead had been liquidated. Palmer had, in a separate email to Larssen, outlined the results of his research and risk assessment: a bit of dogfighting organised by a 73-year-old was never going to accumulate anything like the sort of money that the homestead was worth.

The Dane picked up her phone and called Palmer.

'What are you up to Colin? Trying to steal my company from me?'

The Cockney boy had been expecting something like this. 'Trying to earn my wages, Freda. I reckon it's a good punt, selling off this little debt that's owed to us, zero risk from our point of view.'

She couldn't disagree and had to admit that the cheeky bastard had balls.

'Yes, alright, but be careful as you go. If it progresses make sure everything is tied up in confidentiality clauses.'

'I'm not stupid Freda.'

'I know.'

She ended the call, having quite enjoyed the brief chat about some normal business for a change.

She topped up her glass, promising herself it would be the last time that evening, and lit a cigarette, making the same promise about that. Bored with checking emails, she was just about to go onto Amazon for some retail therapy when a Skype call came in. She hit accept and an image of a very bedraggled Claude Jackson filled the screen.

'Hello, Claude, are you okay?'

'As if you cared.'

The out-of-work former CEO had no intention of succumbing to pleasantries; she'd fucked him royally and he refused to pretend not to hate her. But the fetid pond of business writhed with life, of sorts, and they were part of it. The heavily polluted air they shared held them together, wrapped them up in an endless, treacherous dance routine, like combatant spiders forced to share a web.

'Of course I care, Jacko, we're whores in the same brothel, remember.'

Jackson maintained his distance, kept his cool. 'Not anymore my girl, I'm keeping well away from you. A little sparrow tells me that you're a murder suspect, seriously on the police radar for setting up a gunfight and bombing raid, right on the doorstep of Heathrow Airport. I'm surprised you're not in prison.' His tone was chirpy, gloating.

Larssen was caught off balance by this. She peered at the screen. The camera on Jackson's machine was either dirty or fogged up and the picture lacked enough resolution for her to see the detail of his face. It was like she was looking at a talking head.

'Have you been drinking?' was all she could think of.

'No, but I can see you are. How many's that you've had today? On the second bottle yet?'

She got off the ropes. 'If I was going to be arrested it would have happened weeks ago. Where are you getting this from?'

Jackson severed the link and the Skype signed off with its irritating bloop noise. He stood up, steadied himself and walked slowly across his living room to his exercise machine, five grand's worth of treadmill and multi-gym combined.

118

Blake stood at the urinal smirking. He'd just been outside to make a call and his two companions hadn't noticed his absence, too wrapped up were they in some attempt at a philosophical conversation about the application of algorithms to the investigation of crime. Pissed though he was, Napper was putting forward the interesting point of view that using algorithms was like painting by numbers and that detective work should be about creative, critical thinking, not synthesizing decisions from the application of spreadsheet formulas.

The argument was still in full flow as Blake sat back down at the table, fiddling with his flies. Napper seemed to have slowed his drinking to allow Briggs, now on red wine, to catch up. But the Cornishman had by no means sobered up, and his guard was down.

'I'm fuckin' winnin' thish, Blakey, the univershity boy is backin' down.'

'No, I'm not,' countered Briggs, 'but I freely admit that the system is there only to help us, not to dictate how to do the job.'

'Why are you letting it then? All this bollocksh about the shpades hitting Shtanwell Moor not being connected with the liquidators chucking Rankin aaf his place, your fuckin' algorithm just accepts coincidences like they 'appened all the time—'

Briggs raised his voice. 'It doesn't accept coincidences. It assesses events, profiles, sequences and times and gives them appropriately weighted scores. What comes out is proper logic which focuses the mind of the detective and prevents assumptions being made that are based on bias…'

The exchanges went on as if Blake wasn't even there. Napper was getting annoyed and starting to take it personally. 'Are you sayin' I'm biashed? You can't say that. Just 'cos I'm not rubbing Larsshen out of the picture don't make me biashed, she's up to the neck in it and your fuckin' system isn't seein' it. It's blind as a fuckin' bat, Briggsy, an' if you believe it then so are you!'

Briggs took a sip of his drink and turned to Blake. 'Sorry about this, just a little professional disagreement, old chap.'

The lawyer shrugged, 'Happens all the time, nothing like clearing the air over a drink, we do it in our game too.'

Briggs blinked. 'What, you have arguments in the insurance business? I thought that was just about assessing risk and doing cold blooded calculations about premium costs.'

Blake looked a bit miffed, but kept his mouth shut.

Napper's discretion deserted him: 'Nah, fuck this, Blakey ain't in insurance, 'eez a lawyer, mate, might as well come clean, but 'eez not a criminal lawyer, got more sense than to get involved in our kind of shit.'

Briggs regarded the scruffy solicitor in this new light. 'Oh, really? Has your detective friend told you about the case we're working on?'

Blake looked at Napper and the drunk's reaction answered the question.

119

It didn't take Katrina Swan long to track down Freda Larssen. In general terms and without incriminating themselves, the boys had alluded to the Knightsbridge shooting, saying that they'd heard that one of the dudes behind the company that was stealin' the ol' man's home took a cap in the leg, innit. Perusal of press coverage and some Googling of names had done the rest. Because of what her father was going through, Swan hated liquidators, or insolvency practitioners, as they liked to call themselves, and consequently set about what followed with careful professionalism.

'Hello Ms Larssen, my name is Katrina Swan of Bache & Co, Solicitors, I believe I may have some information you'd be interested in sharing.'

The call had been put through to the Dane as she sat in her glass reptile tank of an office. She looked up to check her door was closed, sensing that what was to follow should not be overheard.

'Go on, I'm listening.'

Swan had expected the terse response and stuck with a ponderous, almost servile tone. 'Well, erm, I'm a criminal lawyer, Ms Larssen, so I'm on unfamiliar ground here, but suffice to say this is not really for the telephone. Would it be possible for us to meet?'

Larssen swivelled her chair so that she faced the wall, ever fearful that her staff could lip read. 'I need to know what this is about Ms Swan, then I'll decide if it merits a meeting.'

Swan was not going to be drawn on detail, but helpfully elaborated. 'It's something I've coincidentally happened upon, and the source is very sensitive, but I'm sure you'll be interested, and my clients have asked me specifically to contact you about a property near Heathrow Airport.'

That did the trick of course, and the liquidator was hooked, but remained icy. 'We have many cases progressing, and several in that general location,' she lied, 'but yes, okay, let's meet. Can you come to our offices?'

No way was that happening, thought Swan, who'd prepared herself for this. 'No, that wouldn't be appropriate under the circumstances, Ms Larssen, but I'll meet you halfway, so to speak. I'll book a conference room in the Regus Centre in Fleet Street, would that be okay? If so just tell me when. We'll only need half an hour.'

Larssen wasn't unimpressed and the challenge was becoming enjoyable already.

120

'There's a man at the door for you Tom, one of your friends from Romany or Albany or whatever it is.' Marlene had come out onto the patio to relay this news and she was wringing her hands. 'Shall I tell him to come back another time?'

Kribz and Driss glanced at each other and then looked at Rankin. 'Do you want to make yourselves scarce boys?' said Rankin. 'Go into the shed if you like.'

Driss made to move, but Kribz stopped him. 'No bro, doesn't matter, we was masked up, remember, let's hear what this dude has to say.'

Driss nodded and they both turned to Rankin again. 'D'you mind if we hang around Tom, can't hurt, innit.'

'Suit yourselves, boys,' and then to Marlene, 'bring the man through my dear, and get the kettle on again.'

The three men stayed silent, watching the French doors after Marlene disappeared back through them. A few seconds later she was back and ushering Defrim Iseberi out onto the patio. He made slow progress, relying heavily on his walking stick and eyeing the two black men with open suspicion. Rankin stepped forward to offer assistance. 'Feckin' hell, Defrim, you sure you should be walking?'

'Who are these two?' said the Albanian, ignoring the question and shrugging off his host's helping hand.

'Don't worry, these are clients of mine, they had nothing to do with the rumpus.'

Iseberi didn't take his eyes off the brothers but seemed to accept the assurance. 'I need to talk with you privately, Mr Rankin.'

The old man turned to the boys and nodded in the direction of the shed. They shrugged, turned, and sauntered off towards the rear of the property. The Albanian gave them a good twenty seconds to get out of earshot before delivering his message.

'Three men dead and a lot of injuries Mr Rankin, including me.' He paused to look down at his leg which was encased in a bulky plastic cast right up to the groin. Then he returned his gaze to Rankin who was waiting for what he knew would not be good news.

It came: 'Kemal Gozit's son has come to London. He wants an explanation from you, and he wants it soon, Mr Rankin.' Another pause for emphasis. Rankin maintained steady eye contact. Albanians were like dogs: if you showed fear, they'd be onto you.

'And he wants honour for his dead father, so you must produce names, proper names and addresses, everything, otherwise you will pay personally, and he doesn't mean with money.'

Sensing the end of the message, Rankin sighed, leaned heavily on his own stick and made a show of regarding his own injured body. Then he looked back up and hard into Iseberi's eyes, 'You tell him from me, and in no uncertain feckin' terms, that I'm also a victim in this. You feckers brought your street warfare onto my feckin' property and I got caught in the feckin' crossfire, and I'm under feckin' investigation by the police. If you lot try to come after me I'll blow the feckin' lot of you to kingdom come or have you all arrested or feckin' both. Now get the feck off my premises – now, you inbred feckin' scumbag!'

The Irishman's face was puce and flecks of spittle had formed around his purple lips. He glared at his visitor with blistering contempt. Marlene had appeared at the door with another tray of teas. 'Don't bother with that, Marlene, just show this piece of shite out will you, he's done here.'

Iseberi knew Rankin and wasn't surprised by the response. He'd been insulted by the Gypsy in the past and wasn't going to take it personally, especially with a pair of *zezaks* lurking in the background. So he smiled, and said, 'Okay Mr Rankin, I will pass on your message to Zamir Gozit.' He turned around stiffly and hobbled back to the French doors where Marlene stood waiting for him. She saw him through the house and Tom Rankin heard the front door close behind the departing visitor.

The boys were back alongside him on the patio. 'Did you hear that, lads?'

'Ev'ry fuckin' word Tom, you done good,' said Kribz. Oddly, they were all standing looking at the French doors, as if the Gheg was somehow going to come back. It was Marlene who reappeared, and not looking best pleased.

'I'm not answering the door for you anymore, Thomas Rankin, I'm sick of these people you call friends coming into my house and going off in a paddy. Nothing ever ends well and one of these days somebody's gonna come here to kill you, an' prob'ly me as well!'

Kribz and Driss looked down at their feet, embarrassed. Tom laughed it off. 'Ah, away back into the house woman, an' we'll have those teas now.' Marlene shook her head and did as bid. 'Come on back inside boys, it's getting cold, let's talk some business.'

121

Uncomfortably for Swan, Larssen had got there first, located the pre-booked small conference room, and made herself comfortable in a chair facing the door.

'Hello, Katrina,' she said, standing up. 'Wow, I like the suit, you make me feel underdressed!'

The Dane's charm was disarming, as was her attire – shiny black Lycra cycling kit from head to toe.

'You're nice and early, did you cycle here?' Swan dumped her bag on the table and asked the question through a grin whilst offering her hand for Larssen to shake; the offer was accepted graciously. Larssen took an instant liking to Swan because she immediately felt superior to the younger woman who was frumpy and statuesque; someone who battled with her weight.

'Yes, sorry, I'm afraid I cycle everywhere more or less, kind of addicted to it.' Larssen feigned discomfiture, not wishing to show the dominance she felt.

They sat facing each other and Swan didn't open her bag, coming straight to the point.

'I have two clients, brothers, who are under investigation for murder. You have a client who wishes to take possession of a property near Heathrow. My clients are associated with the owner of that property.'

Larssen crossed her legs and blinked a few times, feeling her superiority ebb a little. 'Mmm, well, that's to the point, please go on.'

Swan did so. 'As I understand it – and my instructions are from lay persons with very patchy knowledge of the law – the owner of the property is also under investigation and, even more to the point, has a Proceeds of Crime Act restraint order against the property which, and you'll correct me if I'm wrong, somewhat stymies your efforts to take possession of it on behalf of your client.' She delivered the summary in a matter of fact, almost chatty tone, whilst still wearing that grin.

Larssen found herself wondering if the chirpy cadence was sarcasm, or just overdone professional pleasantness. She decided on the latter but couldn't help feeling that the woman sat opposite her had enjoyed giving her little speech.

'I of course won't ask where you got this from, Katrina,' said the Dane, returning what she hoped was a more sincere-looking smile, 'but you clearly have an idea in mind, and I'm excited to hear it.'

The solicitor continued. 'My clients have, so far, refused to co-operate with the police, as is their right, and their non-co-operation worsens your position, as I see it, regarding your seizure of the property.' She paused and allowed her smile to give way to a thoughtful pursing of her lips, as if she were giving careful consideration to her next words. Larssen waited.

'If my clients were to accept a degree of responsibility for a certain criminal act, namely a quantity of cocaine found by the police at Stanwell Moor following the firearms incident, they would expect in return to benefit, both from the police in terms of a reduction in the seriousness of the charges they may face, and from you in terms of possibly an offer of some sort of consultancy arrangement to assist them in their rehabilitation, going forward.'

The proposition was delivered in a slightly lowered tone, more quietly, conveying Swan's nervousness at the enormity of what she was suggesting. Larssen, no stranger to Machiavellian conspiracy, was slightly disarmed by the fact that this one was coming from someone whose profession demanded the highest degree of integrity. She uncrossed her legs and sat forward, placing her tanned hands on the table.

'Katrina, are you sure about this? Do you really trust these clients of yours?'

Swan shrugged and reverted to lawyerspeak. 'I'm merely acting on their instructions, conveying a request for your consideration. Whether or not I personally trust them is irrelevant. My firm is not party to the contract that may or may not transpire.'

The Dane sat back again and put the tips of her fingers together to convey contemplation. Her eyes were down as she spoke. 'So, your clients want me to pay them to take responsibility for some cocaine at Stanwell Moor so that the current owner gets off the hook and the Proceeds of Crime action disappears.' It wasn't a question, more of a summary.

'I didn't say any of that,' said Swan; caution urged her to assume a device was concealed beneath the Lycra, tight though it was. 'My clients have a sense of fairness and duty. Their consciences trouble them, but they know that if convicted of possession of that cocaine – and it would undoubtedly be a conviction for possession with intent to supply, bearing in mind the quantity – then they would face custodial sentences. They have an elderly mother and it would help if, in return for their honesty, they could be assured that she would be looked after, and that they would have something to perhaps look forward to on their release.' She paused. The Dane was nodding slowly and thoughtfully. 'Does that clarify things for you Freda?'

227

'Yes, it's an interesting proposition. I will give it consideration.' She tried not to ask the next question, but couldn't help herself: 'How much?'

Swan was prepared for this. 'That sort of detail hasn't been discussed yet, but one can only imagine that we'd be talking in six figures.'

The Dane stared at Swan whilst she got her head around this; the numerical valuation hardening her stance. 'Isn't what you're doing illegal? Selling your clients' offer to go to prison for a crime they did not commit?'

'Not if they *did* commit it,' Swan shot this back eagerly, keen to make her position clear, 'and I will of course ensure that their confession, if that's what it turns out to be, carries a hallmark of authenticity.'

'What do you mean?' asked Larssen, genuinely unsure of the terminology.

'I mean that their acceptance of responsibility will contain details that only my clients could have knowledge of.'

Larssen began nodding, slowly. 'Okay, like I say, I will consider the offer.'

'Right, I think this meeting should end now,' said Swan, breezily. She stood, shouldered her bag, and offered her hand. Larssen took it without standing; the shake was brief, perfunctory, and the lawyer turned and left the room, closing the door quietly behind her.

The Dane was motionless for several seconds, and then took her phone from its Velcro belt holster.

122

Mergin didn't like lifts at the best of times and certainly wasn't going to use either of the overworked elevators that rattled up and down the core of Slade Tower, a monument to architectural lunacy just off the Walworth Road. Numbers lived on the eighteenth floor and it was with trepidation that the young Albanian, breathing heavily after his long climb, tapped gently on the scarred and dented door of the flat. To do so he had to reach between the bars of the steel security gate, its hinges and lock bolted into the brickwork surrounding the entrance.

Mergin stared at the spyhole, willing the right person to be on the other side. The drill music thumping from inside became a whole lot louder when Numbers opened the door and set about unlocking the security grill. 'Come in and slam the gate shut after you,' yelled the young gangster over his shoulder as he retreated back into the dwelling.

Mergin stepped over the threshold and attempted to do as instructed, but a big hairy hand appeared from nowhere and pulled the grill back open. The boy froze at the sight of a big white man in a black leather jacket.

'Go on, inside,' he hissed, suddenly producing a gun from an inside pocket and pointing it at the startled youngster's forehead. Mergin held up his hands and reversed slowly. Once through the door the intruder spun the boy round and held him around the neck with his free hand, the gun at his temple.

'Shout for your buddy.' Again, the order was hissed.

'Numbers!' yelled Mergin, and then the black youth appeared at the door of the living room and gaped.

'Turn that noise off or I'll shoot this boy like a dog!' The hissing had stopped, this requirement being communicated loudly and menacingly in a powerful Albanian accent. Numbers ducked back into the living room and killed the music. 'Now come back out here where I can see you.' Numbers complied and in under three seconds he was back in the narrow hallway with his hands half raised and in full view of the gunman.

'Anybody else in here?' The gunman squeezed Mergin's neck closer to his own body and waved the pistol at the other doors.

'No, sir.' Numbers' voice came out like a squeak.

With his eyes and gun not leaving Numbers, the gunman spoke to Mergin. 'Now little man, tie your friend's hands behind his back.' He released his grip on the teenager and shoved him forward. 'Use this, here.'

Mergin straightened, turned and saw the man take a plastic cable tie from his pocket and hold out to him. He took it and turned to face Numbers.

'Turn around and put your hands behind your back.' These words to Numbers, and then to Mergin: 'Pull that thing tight around his wrists.'

Mergin's hands were shaking as he looped the tie and tugged it closed. The gunman wasn't impressed. 'Tighter.' Mergin pulled the tie a couple of clicks more and Numbers winced.

'Right, you both are coming with me, come on.'

They filed out of the flat, Mergin first, then Numbers, then the gunman, who unhooked a coat and threw it over the black boy's shoulders, so it concealed his tied hands. Out on the walkway they were met by another leather-clad Albanian who'd been waiting, standing guard.

They used the lift and were on the street within a couple of minutes. It was cold and dark and they walked the short distance in undisturbed silence. The second leatherjacket pressed a key fob and the single blink of a big Audi's indicators accompanied the clunk of its locks disengaging.

123

Briggs and Napper were in the canteen at Kennington Police Station. The place was deserted as usual and the pair were alone, staring down dubiously at the small plastic cups of grey liquid that the vending machine called tea. A pregnant silence hung; Briggs broke its waters.

'What's your relationship with this lawyer chap?'

Napper had been expecting this but his thumping headache had prevented preparation. 'Just mates, met him when I was a groundsman at Oxford University after I came out of the army. Since then he's helped me out on a discipline case, or rather the aftermath of it. He does civil actions and I wanted to sue a bloke for making false allegations against me.'

Briggs relaxed a little; this sounded a bit like the truth – which it was. 'And how did that go?'

'It didn't. Blakey advised me I didn't stand a chance; said I'd been a prat and should let the whole thing drop.' This sounded a lot like the truth.

'And did you?'

'What?'

'Let it drop.'

'Yeah, that was about two years ago, all forgotten now, moved on.'

Briggs pressed on: he needed to bottom this out. 'What have you told him about Stanwell Moor?'

'What is this, a discipline interview? I've already 'ad that, been put roight in my place.'

Briggs sat back in his chair and raised the palms of his hands, not wanting a scene. 'No, of course it's not a discipline interview Doug, I just want to know how much you trust this guy, that's all.'

Napper understood and nodded. 'Yeah, I know mate, look, Blakey's good to talk to, that's all, comes up with some good ideas. I bounce stuff off 'im from time to time when we're 'avin' a beer or three. He ain't a criminal solicitor Aaron, there's no conflict.'

Briggs regarded the man sat before him, and it all sort of stacked up. Napper was a known loner and didn't much like the company of cops, so it was logical that he would seek solace from other sources. Furthermore, he'd rather taken a liking to the similarly scruffy and unassuming Blake who, during their brief meeting, hadn't shown any signs of being a man with a mission or agenda.

'Okay mate,' said the graduate, 'I think I've got the picture – just a couple of pissheads blowing off steam occasionally, that it?'

'Spot on, Briggsy, fuck all more to it than that.'

But the detective wasn't quite finished. He sipped some of the so-called tea and grimaced. 'So, okay, and what's Mr Blake's theory about the events at Stanwell Moor?'

'Eh?' The Cornishman had thought Briggs was done.

'You heard,' chuckled Briggs. 'Don't be coy Doug, and don't tell me you've never discussed it with him.'

Napper pulled a pen from his pocket and used it to scratch beneath the plastic cast on his arm.

'You won't find the answer up there,' laughed Briggs, enjoying his colleague's discomfiture.

'The thing is,' began Napper, making more of the scratching job than was necessary, 'the thing is mate, me an' him always get shitfaced when we meet up. So it's only bollocks we talk anyway.'

Briggs sensed he was onto something. 'Well then, you're always accusing me of talking bollocks, so let's hear some from you mate.' He was still smiling, but the laughter had stopped. Napper stopped his scratching, put the pen back in his pocket, sat forward and put his elbows on the table.

'Okay, but this ain't to go any further.'

Briggs frowned and nodded. 'You can be assured of that.'

'Oh, I am assured of that Briggsy, because if it does I'll deny telling you and then you could only have got it from one place.'

'And where might that be?' asked the detective, now sensing a bit of unwelcome danger.

'DPS. I told them about my unregisterable source when they interviewed me at this very fuckin' table.'

There was a pause whilst a PCSO came in and relieved the vending machine of a Mars bar. Napper continued.

'Jackson, the one who was shot in Knightsbridge, was the business partner of the Danish woman Larssen. Blake was doing some work for them and he reckons the hatred between the pair is fuckin' white hot and that Jackson was shot in Knightsbridge on Larssen's orders.'

Briggs relaxed: this didn't add much. He allowed himself to shrug. 'I've heard all this before Doug, tell me something I don't know mate.'

Napper could have just ended it there, but he was spurred by the graduate's smuggery.

'Yeah, you've heard the general theory, but you ain't heard the detail, the fuckin' subtle bits. After Jackson was shot Larssen got Blake to make sure – an' I'm sayin' no more than that – that Jackson signed papers handin' the company over to her, that made sure that she would be able to set up a new company and take possession of old Rankin's land for 'erself.'

Briggs was beginning to see that this might be going somewhere, which worried him. 'So why did Jackson sign the company over?'

'Suffice to say, Briggsy me ol' mate, and don't ask for stuff that puts my snout away, Jackson was spaced on morphine when he signed. He made a mistake, that's all.'

Briggs shook his head, as much to clear it than to convey dismissal. 'No, doesn't stack up. Whoever shot Jackson shot Massive and Loosescrew, or whatever his name is – was – and the same bunch of nutters gave Larssen a hard time as well—'

Napper raised his good arm in exasperation, 'No, you see, there you fuckin' go again, makin' assumptions to fit your neat little picture!'

It was getting testy. 'No, I'm not, I'm dealing with the facts!' Briggs' voice went up a scale because he didn't want to shout.

Napper wasn't inhibited in that respect. 'You're fuckin' assumin' that gun 'as only been used by one fuckin' geezer!' His use of the cockney term sounded weird. 'I've told you before, those shooters are 'anded round willy fuckin' nilly. Why don't you try an' get that into your fuckin' spreadsheet algorithm?!'

This hit home and the detective blinked. The street cop held his advantage but quietened down. 'Look, Aaron, they don't all 'ave guns all the time. The attack at Stanwell was a one-off and they obviously went there prepared. They usually only carry one piece between three or four of them, so they 'ave to take turns at carryin' it. They pass the fuckin' things around like 'ot potatoes, mate. Fucksake, how many times 'ave we gotta go through this?!'

Briggs frowned, his eyes on his tea. He looked at his watch. 'I've got to go, got a meeting at Walworth. Thanks, I'll think about what you've said.' And then he was up and gone.

Napper started scratching his arm again, and his thoughts returned to Freda Larssen.

124

Kribz and Driss were at home and had just finished a chicken meal cooked by their mum, who'd then gone back out to work on her third cleaning shift of the day. They'd long since given up trying to make her take money from them.

'I don't want any of youze two's money, it ain't clean. I'm here to feed you and feed you I will with the bones of my ol' back.'

So, the stash stayed with Carly.

'You heard from Carly today?' Driss asked his brother.

'Nah,' came the reply. 'Why, you worried 'bout 'er?'

'Nah, well, she's 'oldin' a lot for us bro, need to keep 'er sweet, innit.'

A smirk invaded Kribz's face., 'You been keepin' 'er sweet, little brudda?' He'd long suspected Driss of being in some sort of relationship with the forty-something hippie woman who lived alone two floors above them. They'd cuckooed her eighteen months previously, but not in a nasty way. They provided her with food, booze, plenty puff and, if Kribz knew his brother, the occasional good seeing to. In return they got to use her flat as a storage facility for a strongbox packed with drugs and cash. It was kept under her bed and, in case she got any ideas, padlocked.

Driss changed the subject. 'Wonder when we'll hear from fuckin' what's-her-name, the solicitor.'

'Her name's Katrina Swan, you should remember it bruv, 'cos she's gonna take us to big things, innit.'

'Well, she ain't called us yet, it's been two fuckin' days bruv, an' weeze back at the fuckin' police station next week for another fuckin' quizzin'.'

'It's no sweat bro, we don' 'ave to say nuthin' innit, they got nuthin' on us. We hold all the cards, truss me, an' if our plan comes off we'll hold a whole lot more than cards, I can tell you that for sure bruv.'

Driss either didn't quite understand or did understand and wasn't convinced. 'I do trust you, course I do, but her I don't trust man, stuck up cow. Didn't you see the way she wuz lookin' at us, like we were pieces of shit man?' Driss was sat on edge of the sunken sofa, elbows on knees, looking down at his dirty chicken plate on the floor between his feet.

'Fuck man, ain't you used to that yet bro?! An' let's face it, we didn't go there looking like we'd made a fuckin' effort or nuthin', dressed up like we wuz. I reckon me an' you should take a fuckin' trip to fuckin' Burtons or some place like that, try an' look the part that ain't jus' a couple o' street fuckin' gang bangers!'

Driss raised his head slowly to look across the room at his brother. 'What the fuck are you—'

Algorithm

The younger brother was interrupted by a quiet but insistent knocking on the door. Kribz eased himself to his feet and went to investigate.

'Who is it?' Driss heard him ask.

'It's Colin, Ground Floor, gotta message,' came the hushed reply, which Driss could hear through the window behind his head. The door opened and Kribz ushered in the twelve-year-old Colin, or Ground Floor Colin as he was more accurately known. The location of the flat he lived in was prime and he was always hanging outside near the estate entrance, rarely missing a trick. He was the go-to boy for strangers looking for connections.

'There's a w-white kid out on the road, l-looking for you innit, I told 'im to w-wait and I'd speak to y-you, he's shitting 'imself.' Although black, Colin was nearly white and had ginger hair, and spoke with a stammer. He was never going to make it in a posse, but as an estate watchman and messenger he did a good job.

Two minutes later the brothers had dismissed Colin with a twenty-pound note and were bundling the white kid, who turned out to be Mergin, into a bin area at the foot of the block. 'What's going down, little man?' asked Kribz.

'They got Numbers.' The boy was hyperventilating and could hardly get the words out. 'They're looking for some guy called Shanker. If he don't give him to them, they're gonna kill him, bit by bit.' Having got the words out, Mergin sat down heavily on the dirty concrete, his back against the wall, shaking like he'd just come out of a freezer, still trying to catch some normal breath.

Standing over him, the Popes exchanged incredulous glances. Kribz asked the obvious. 'Who's fuckin' *they*, Mergin?'

'I dunno, honest, they're Albanians, but I dunno them, senior men, *Shqiptare* prob'ly, outa my league, man, way outa my fuckin' league.' The kid slipped into G boy patter, eager to be believed.

'They sent you here, do they know this is our estate boy?' Driss was worried.

'No, well I never told them anyways. They just sent me to put the word out. I already knew this was your yard, Numbers told me a coupla weeks ago, but I never told them where I wuz goin'.'

Driss's lip curled. 'You better fuckin' not 'ave man, or—'

'Yeah, okay bro, leave that for now. Where've they got Numbers?' said Kribz.

'I dunno, they just kicked me out the car, not far from Numbers' place, they followed me there, must've, they made me tie Numbers' hands, made me 'elp them man, I had no choice.'

Kribz could see that the kid was terrified. This was no act, no ruse; he wasn't capable of that.

But Driss wasn't sure. 'Outa your league my fuckin' ass, you expect us to swallow that shit?! You in on it, man, fess up!'

Kribz intervened. 'Lay off, bro, ain't no way he's comin' in 'ere wid some bullshit story.' He turned to Mergin. 'So what they expect, a fuckin' address wid a fuckin' number maybe, a fuckin' post code, like we know this Shanker dude?!'

Mergin was beginning to collect himself. He'd stopped shaking, stood up and shoved his hands in his pockets.

'All I know is that these people don't fuck about. They might be Albos like me but I'm just a turd on their boots. They won't kill me I don't think but they could make things shitty for my family an' they'll whack Numbers for fun to make an example, then they'll send me out to see you or whoever again. These guys do it for a livin', s'like normal to them, innit!' he was still trying to inject a bit of streetspeak and it sounded weird, pathetic. But the message was anything but weird or pathetic.

Kribz paced around a few times, scratching his head and rubbing his face. 'I gotta ask, d'you have any idea at all where they could be holding 'im?'

'No, Kribz, honest, they booted me outa the car and took off with him with his hands tied. There's no way they was gonna tell me where they was takin' 'im.'

Driss got his oar in. 'So how are you gonna contact them with any information 'bout Shanker?'

Kribz shot a sharp glance in his brother's direction but stopped short of a lingering glare. He could have hit him.

Mergin's face showed a flicker of insight, but he quickly moved on, trying to make out that what had just been said hadn't registered. 'I won't. They'll contact me, that's for fuckin' sure, they'll be top of the tree, man, they can find out anything about any Albo in London.'

Kribz put a touch of menace in his voice. 'We need to know how they know about your connection with us.'

The teenager started to shake again. 'Aw, come on, Kribz, I'm supplyin' you innit, ev'rybody knows you lot are under us in the food chain, man.'

'Whaddaya mean "you lot"?!' snarled Driss, always the first to take offence at racism.

'Leave it bro, the boy's right. It's easy for these dudes to figure Mergin's dealing with us, so he's their link-up guy. Don't take it personal, it's just business bro!'

Mergin watched this exchange with interest, his fear subsiding again. He was inwardly pleased with himself that he hadn't spilled the beans about the return of his uncle Zamir.

Kribz turned to Mergin: 'Go an' tell them that we'll do business, but if any harm comes to Numbers they got a fuckin' war on – they should know we'ze capable, innit.'

Mergin nodded.

'Why are they after Shanker?' This was from Driss.

Mergin shrugged, 'I dunno really, somethin' about it being the only name they had, so he would do, for honour. If they can't get Shanker they'll pick somebody else, they'll get another name, that's for sure.'

'Okay, go on, fuck off now, check in wid us tomorrow, but don't come back here,' said Kribz.

The teenager took off and the brothers climbed the stairs back to their flat, stopping at every floor to look down from the balconies to check for lurkers.

'What the fuck bro?!' said Driss as he closed the door behind them.

Kribz waved away any further protests. 'Ah, it'll buy us some time, so who gives a fuck?! Our problem is getting Numbers back, we gotta find some way of doin' a deal innit.'

Driss wasn't impressed. 'Do a fuckin' deal? With those killers, they'll prob'ly just whack Numbers now like they can't be bothered to do business so he'll fuckin' do. Like that boy just said, revenge is all they want, it's like their honour, stuff like that.'

Kribz sat down and started building a spliff, which was what he always did when he had serious thinking to do.

'I agree, my brother.' Kribz was speaking slowly now, quietly. 'They want revenge for the deaths at the Stanwell, and I think you're right, if they can't kill Shanker they'll just kill Numbers, but either way they won't stop there, they'll want more, 'specially if they find out that Shanker's only a foot soldier, then they'll come after us, an' the old man even.'

Kribz lit up, took a long pull, inhaled and sank back into the chair like he was allowing it to swallow him up. Then he added: 'I can't see how this ain't gonna be a war startin' up.'

125

Briggs had received the call twelve hours earlier and he and Mason arrived at the Rankin homestead just after 8am. They got out of the CID car and Mason opened the boot and took out a digital recording machine about the size of a small briefcase. She was tired, nervous and a bit hungover; this was the last thing she'd needed on a Saturday morning but Briggs had been insistent that the offer had to be accepted quickly, before the old man changed his mind.

Marlene opened the door and stood aside without saying a word. She was also tired, the events of recent weeks taking their toll.

The two cops mumbled their good mornings and walked quietly through to the living area. The old man was at the table and watched the pair enter from beneath his bushy eyebrows.

'Good morning, officers,' he said, almost in a whisper, 'thank you for coming at such short notice. I'm sorry to have disturbed your weekend plans, it could probably have waited till Monday, you know.'

'Not a problem, Tom, I'm sure what you have to say is important.'

Rankin nodded. 'Aye, I reckon it is that son. Take a seat, the pair of you – Marlene, is that kettle on?'

Mrs Rankin uttered something in the affirmative from the kitchen and the officers sat down at the table. Mason started preparing the machine.

'What the hell is this?' asked the old Gypsy. 'Are we going out on the radio?'

The detectives laughed politely, Mason glad of the levity; it was the first time she'd done a remote interview under caution and, despite her youth, technology flummoxed her.

Briggs sought to calm things down. 'Tom, you've indicated that you wish to put the record straight about a few things, that's what you told me on the phone last night.'

'That's right son. I've had some time to think and I suppose I must swallow my pride—'

'Okay, er, leave it there for a minute please,' interrupted Briggs. 'We need to get the recording machine set up and then I need to caution you.'

'I understand.' Rankin averted his eyes, not wishing to make Mason's fumbling more difficult. 'Come on with that tea Marlene, will you?'

'All ready,' announced Mrs Rankin as she walked in with the laden tray, pausing for Mason to move the recording machine to make way for the most important item. What's this? Radio Four?'

'I've just asked that, but I think it's private. These young officers know their job.'

Marlene shuffled off and the proceedings began; the machine was switched on, formal introductions made, caution administered.

'Okay Mr Rankin,' said Briggs, 'you've requested this interview to clear up a few matters you that your say are on your chest – er, well, please go ahead.'

126

Napper walked out of St Mary's Hospital in Paddington, wary of joining the throng of commuters down on the platform of the Underground. He'd just had his arm brace removed and felt vulnerable. The medics had told him to guard against bashing his newly healed wound against anything.

He opted to walk, before long finding himself in Notting Hill.

His thoughts had never left Larssen for long, following their meeting, and now they returned with gusto. There was no point in resisting; he knew himself better than that. Nonetheless, he decided to delay the foreseeable – stew on it, make it inevitable.

He remembered a pub in Portobello Road with mixed feelings, his memories dim and befuddled. It had changed, gastrofied now, menus on the tables, *for fuck's sake*.

He bought a pint and sat himself down, trying to look unbothered – bored, even. He was still using his right hand only, guarding its colleague, but then carefully engaging the left hand to assist in rolling a cigarette. It remembered.

'You can't smoke that in here,' warned an irritable barmaid.

'I know that love, I'm only rolling it.'

Fuckin' jobsworth, thought the cop. To keep busy and give his rested hand work, he continued rolling. After ten minutes there was a small pile of fags on the table in front of him, alongside an untouched pint. His production had speeded up to a point where he considered it best to stop, lest the vigilant barmaid decided he was a nutter and kicked him out.

He took a few gulps of lager – Berretti, not his favourite but there was little else in the regentrified joint. Looking around, he saw nothing of interest, nothing inspiring, dull as dishwater. Time to go for it – two gulps and on his feet for another one, five minutes later, same again. Then out on the street for one of his stash of roll-ups, then same again.

He thought of calling Blake; no point on two fronts: the bastard wouldn't like it in here and this was going to be a thinking session. It was mid afternoon and the pub, if that's what you'd call it, was quiet. Come around five the mushes would start piling in, he was sure, all smug from their day's fannying around on Apples and blowing smoke up each other's arses. But he had a good couple of hours before that happened, so he settled down to enjoy his own company and looked forward to seeing where what he called his mind would take him.

Napper couldn't really do structured thought; any attempt at logical problem-solving left him exhausted by failure and frustration. The years had taught him just to relax and go where his antagonism took him, his *crossness*, as he liked to call it. He had never been a bitter man and tended to see the good in people; not exactly an attribute for a cop, but situations annoyed him – malfunctioning, stupid systems that caused unfairness or injustice.

He looked up at the flat screen television suspended from the ceiling in the corner of the bar room, annoyingly showing silent golf. The background music in place was inane crap – some boy-band shit, but thankfully at low volume. He caught the barmaid glowering at him and wondered fleetingly why he made women suspicious and uneasy. He was once told: 'Don't worry, Doug, it's just the way you look and the way you sound.' *Oh, well, that's fine then.*

And then of course what he called his mind took him to Freda Larssen. He stopped, taking a long pull of his pint to savour the moment, then floated onwards. He lingered on the look on her face just before he'd left her flat two days earlier – he'd got to her, he'd hit home. Just for a moment, he'd glimpsed vulnerability and knew without doubt that he would return to continue. There was nothing to lose and hey, if it came to nothing it would still be fun and other stuff could fall out of the tree if he kept shaking it, gently.

Just over an hour later Napper was sat on some steps opposite Larssen's house bursting for a piss. He'd neglected to go before leaving the bar. His only memory of doing so was a quick look round before exiting to see the barmaid engaged in a frenzied attack on his table with a cloth and spray bottle, eager to rid it of his spillages and bits of baccy.

So now he was bursting for a piss. It was only 4.30 and he'd no idea when she'd be arriving home. The walk from Portobello Road had taken a quarter of an hour, and the nearest pub to where he sat was at least ten minutes away; he couldn't chance it. Despite his discomfort, he smiled. At least he had a pressing reason for asking to be allowed in. If she refused, he'd just let rip against her door.

He started to roll another cigarette, forgetting the dozen or so in his pocket.

'Waiting for me?'

He didn't even look up, just nodded whilst finishing the job in hand. 'You should've been a detective, Freda.'

243

'Perhaps, and it's Ms Larssen to you.'

'Ooooh, sorry.' He looked up at last with an expression of exaggerated remorse. She couldn't help but smile at his cheek.

'Come on then.'

127

Nobody bothered much about who leased what to who on the Gemini Business Park next to Beckton sewage works. The whole region, sitting between Barking and a muddy loop of the Thames, had been for years a bottomless pit for wasted regeneration money, because the only flies that get attracted to a carcass that's been decaying too long are low lifers, even by muscoidean standards, and the human equivalents who occupied the rows of run-down warehouses were there for the want of anywhere better to be. The storage units were crammed full of shit that nobody could shift, most of it way past its sell-by date, rents went unpaid and notices to quit piled up behind doors that remained locked most of the time. Popular images of dystopia usually held some degree of menacing fascination; the nonsense that any visitor to Gemini beheld was just a pile of tacky detritus, unworthy of any thoughtful description or lyrical analysis. Lorries and dirty vans rolled in and out, untimetabled and unchecked, through the oily mud of the broken roadways. Furtive men with unshaven pinched faces loaded, unloaded, transferred, hung around and smoked, muttering in guttural languages. The sound of Numbers screaming probably made them feel more at home.

The Braganza Boy's wrists were still tethered but he no longer felt the pain of the wounds the cable tie had inflicted. The terror that consumed him was that of impending death by drowning. The Albos must have had access to some old New York gangster movies and were having great fun emulating the concrete boot trick. The kid was lashed to a steel chair, itself secured to the wall behind it. His feet and lower legs were tied together with several loops of a heavy chain, attached to which were several 5kg barbell weights.

Numbers was a bright boy and what terrified him was the fact that neither Albo had worn a mask and he hadn't been blindfolded on his way to the warehouse. Logically, he was going to die whether he talked or not.

'Okay, nigger boy, we know you blackies are not good swimmers, and the weights will make sure you sink very quickly. There's a bridge along the road and you will be falling from it unless you tell us who Shanker is, simple as that.' The Gheg's English was good and the words were spoken slowly, with an almost conversational matter-of-factness.

The talking Albo put his pock-marked face close to Numbers. His breath stank. 'D'you know what? This is the first time I've done this thing. I nearly hope you don't talk so I can hear you scream as you fall.' The chatty tone had gone, replaced by sheer malevolence. Numbers turned his head away, his eyes screwed tight shut like he was trying to block out this nightmare. Then the speaker produced a phone and took some photographs. The camera flashes made Numbers open his eyes, both literally and to the possibility that there might be some hope he'd be spared, at least for as long as he could be used as a bargaining chip.

'I know a guy called Shanker, an' I know other people that knows him, but I need my phone to look through some stuff.'

The talking Gheg stood up straight, the snarl momentarily leaving his face. 'Do you think we're stupid? We ditched your phone outside. If any of your buddy boys trace it to where it is they'll get a good welcome.'

They needn't have worried, he thought – his phone was untraceable.

'My friends can't track my phone—'

'No, maybe not, but the police can, and if they turn up to where it's at they'll get some serious shit too, my little friend.'

Absurdly, Numbers considered how good the Gheg's English was. Where the hell had these bastards come from? And they were almost hoping for a showdown with the po-po. The boy's eyes were hot with the salt of his tears, his mouth parched with fear, but he was still able to marvel at the almost suicidal criminality of his captors. Although bitterly regretting his life choices at this moment, he'd always liked being a gangbanger, a street boy with credibility, earning himself bottle, respect, going up in the ranks. But these guys – wow, they were a whole new level. Outside of their own circle they respected nothing and nobody. All they did was use and abuse with unremitting ruthlessness. Numbers' sudden perception was a revelation ignited by the horror of mortality.

128

Larssen lit a cigarette whilst listening to Napper urinate thunderously; he hadn't even closed the bathroom door behind him. She turned to watch him walk into the living room, his face flushed, hair and beard dishevelled.

She held her cigarette at shoulder height and put her free hand on her hip whilst looking the copper up and down.

'What does the taxpayer think about you, officer Napper?' She was unable to stifle a giggle.

He sat down heavily without being invited, mightily relieved to have emptied his bladder. She moved closer and stood over him. 'Would you like coffee? You look like you need it.'

Napper wasn't sure he liked the way this was going. He wasn't as pissed as he probably appeared and felt both the need and the ability to take some control.

'No thank you, and don't look at me like that, I'll start thinking you fancy me.'

This took the Dane by surprise. She giggled some more and reversed a few paces but remained standing. 'Is that better?'

'Why don't you sit down?'

Playing along, she sat opposite him, crossing her endless legs slowly, provocatively. 'Do you know something, Police Constable Douglas Napper? If you weren't—'

'I know a lot of things,' interrupted the Cornishman, sensing oncoming unpleasantness.

'I hadn't finished. If you weren't such a—'

Napper was not going to be beaten. 'I know, if I wasn't such a scruffy bastard you'd lodge a complaint against me for police harassment.'

It wasn't often that Larssen was stumped and she found herself reassessing the man sat in front of her.

'Mmm, something like that, perhaps.' A chill tinged her voice, but she knew that he knew he'd parried her, and was ready for more. She decided to change tack.

'Okay, what is it you're after?' She sighed, did her usual trick with the cigarette smoke screen and tried to put on a show of being slightly bored.

Napper decided to let things flow. 'I want to know when you expect to see your black friends again.'

'I don't have any black friends, Police Constable Douglas Napper, and if I did it would be nothing to do with you.'

The cop sat up and leaned forward. 'And I want to know why you had your business partner taken out of circulation so that you could take over his company—'

This hit the spot. She hardly moved a muscle but her voice was raised and her eyes gave a telling flash. 'It was not his company! I don't know who told you that shit, it was – and is – my business. I rescued it, got all the clients, and did most of the work. Jackson just sat back and milked the money. I spent more time correcting his mistakes than—'

'And I want to know,' interrupted Napper, before pausing for a second to choose his next words, 'how you expect us to believe that it was just some kind of coincidence that old Rankin's place got attacked on the same day as you were there to serve eviction papers.'

Larssen fell silent, shrugged, puffed her fag and crushed it into a big glass ashtray that was balanced precariously on the arm of her chair.

'D'you know Douglas, I'm bored now. Game over. You turn up here drunk and harass me, I really ought to lodge that complaint with your superiors.' She stood up and took the ashtray out of the room. Napper sat still and wondered *what the fuck* he was doing there. He did a quick risk assessment and concluded that he was doing nothing wrong – Larssen wasn't officially a suspect: at most she was a witness, and not even an important one. He could cover his arse by claiming that he was just trying to jog her memory on the odd detail that may have recently occurred to her. Even assuming she'd been recording him, at worst he'd get a bollocking for being a tad unconventional in his approach. Nothing new there.

His thoughts were interrupted by the sound of her talking on the phone in what he assumed was the kitchen. He couldn't make out the words, but the tone had an urgency to it and he sensed trouble. A more cautious cop would have made excuses and legged it, but Doug Napper just settled back into the soft upholstery and lit one of his roll-ups.

129

Katrina Swan walked over Vauxhall Bridge and up into Victoria. There was no real purpose to the journey other than to clear her head. It had been two days since her meeting with Larssen and she'd heard nothing from the asset stripper. She'd suspected this would happen: the likes of the Dane played their cards close, never gave their game away until it was time to pounce.

Swan guessed that Larssen would take legal advice and would be told not to touch the offer with a barge pole. Swan also guessed that Larssen would ignore such counsel: the profit margin was way too big. Swan had done her homework, her risk management calculation meticulous.

She thought of her parents, her father's fading health, his inevitable death at the hands of Larssen's ilk. The opportunity was irresistible.

She hailed a cab on Horseferry Road and told the driver to take her to Sloane Square, not having a clue why she was going there. As the vehicle ducked and dived through the traffic she thought of those two police officers – what were their names? Briggs and Mason – and their pedestrian approach to the interrogation of two suspected murderers. They hadn't been much older than the suspects. More educated, yes, but less sophisticated. Was this the sort of police service the public deserved? She thought not; it was the police service that the liberal left had foisted on the public. She'd known a policeman once, a young Welshman she'd help represent when she'd been a trainee. He'd been charged with corruption and it was clear to her that he'd been securely stitched up by his senior officers. The lad had gone down, served two years of a four-year sentence and all he'd allegedly done was sell a few stories to the gutter press – crap about celebrities who lived on his patch. A tubby comedian had filed a report to police about her fraudulent plumber who'd fitted a bath in her Chelsea flat that was too narrow for her. It made hilarious reading in the red tops. Miffed, she moaned to her then Prime Minister pal, who'd then complained to the Commissioner of the Met about the leak, so to speak, which was traced back to Taff's computer terminal. The silly sod had got a hundred quid for his mischief. What a waste. At court he pleaded guilty. Swan had drafted the mitigation; it included his previous exemplary service – twelve commendations for bravery, tenacity, and detective ability. The judge still jailed him – *no place for you in the capital's world-renowned police service* was how it had gone.

Swan couldn't imagine Briggs being commended for bravery, tenacity or detective ability. The little prick seemed devoid of anything approaching an imagination and had been a bag of nerves when 'interrogating' the Pope brothers.

Nor could she imagine Briggs being allowed, given his junior years and lowly rank, to make a decision regarding the offer that would soon be presented to him. Swan hoped that she would shortly be talking to a more senior officer, a superintendent perhaps, or even a commander, someone with sway over the Crown Prosecution Service.

She walked aimlessly down the King's Road, pausing occasionally to peruse the odd shop window. A lull in the traffic noise allowed her to hear the insistent buzzing of her mobile, tucked deep in her bag. She fished it out. 'Hello?' She pressed the device hard to her ear.

'Hello, Katrina?'

'Yes?' She knew who it was.

'Freda Larssen. We met—'

'Oh, hi,' Swan feigned pleasant surprise, 'how are you?'

'Fine thanks. Can we meet?'

'Of course, when did you have in mind?' Swan had walked quickly into a side street so she could hear better.

There was eagerness in Larssen's voice, excitement. 'As quickly as possible, I was hoping within the next hour. I have some news for you.'

Obviously, thought Swan. 'Okay, well, I'm in Chelsea now, er…'

'That's great, I'm next door in Notting Hill, would you like to come to my place?'

Swan's warning klaxon blared, but she couldn't think of a way out. 'Er, well, I—'

'I'll text you the address. Jump in a cab, you won't regret it, I promise, Katrina.'

130

Kribz and Driss had gone out to Stanwell Moor again, more just to get clear of the swamp than anything else. They played with Lois and her pups; the family of dogs seemed contented and happy, as was Tom Rankin with the cash the brothers were bunging him.

'Can't stop thinkin' 'bout Numbers bruv,' said Driss, watching two of the pups quarrel over possession of the tennis ball he'd just thrown.

'I'm with you on that, bro,' answered Kribz quickly, having read his brother's mind, 'but we got our own probs innit. If we go round askin' questions and stirring things we'll jus' get a heap of bad attention. We gotta keep a low profile, innit.'

The winning pup lolloped up to Driss and plonked the ball at his feet. He picked it up and threw it in the direction of the other youngster, putting the odds in its favour; off they both scampered again, yelping with the delight of competition.

Kribz kept going. 'Don' forget we got gotta go back to the fuckin' po-po station next week. I'm hopin' they won't 'ave any fresh questions for us, an' I'm hopin' that our bitch Katrina's gonna pull that Briggs dude aside an' give 'im the offer.'

Driss was nodding along, bang in tune. 'Yeah, me too, but weeze doin' a bunch of hopin' bruv, we ain't got much control. If Numbers rolls over to the Albos an' then they roll over to the fedz it's anybody's guess what'll 'appen.'

Kribz was alarmed at how his brother had thought this through. He sought to calm him down. 'Nah, don' overthink things, you'll send yourself crazy. The Albanians'll never talk to the fedz, no way man, they'ze wantin' blood, an' plenty of it—'

'You don't know that for sure bro, we don't know them well enough to say that.' Driss was facing Kribz now,

251

speaking more slowly, ignoring the dogs around his feet. A Boeing screamed overhead on its descent to the runway, cutting the conversation.

Marlene Rankin called from the French doors of the house. 'Will you come in for your tea, boys, or shall I bring it out on a tray?'

Then they heard Tom answer for them. 'They'll need to come in, I want a word with them.'

131

Massive, Shanker and Gillie had arrived at the Arch separately, Massive first because he had the keys. The place was deathly quiet: the Muslims had gone and taken cover in an established mosque where they wouldn't have to worry about the police barging in.

The trio were nervous, looking around themselves. Massive took the initiative and tried to show leadership. 'Relax guys, fucksake, we'eze fine now innit, safe as 'ouses. If we get raided we just say the pieces was already here, we ain't the only ones wid keys to this place.'

Gillie agreed in principle but expressed his discomfort. 'Let's just do what we gotta do and get fucked off outa here man.' He unshouldered his sports bag, unzipped it and unceremoniously unloaded its contents onto the old sofa. Shanker followed suit. Massive didn't have a bag. They all looked down at the arsenal.

Then Shanker and Gillie both looked at Massive. Taking the hint, the big man took from his pocket the Beretta he'd used to kill Screwloose, its former owner. He didn't put it down on the sofa.

'Fuck, man, thought you'd got rid of that,' Shanker said.

Gillie regarded the weapon with envy. 'I wouldn't 'ave fuckin' dumped it, it's beautiful. Giz a look Mass.'

Massive handed the Beretta to the experienced criminal, handgrip first. Gillie took it gently and caressed it. 'Wow, it's heavy blud, I've heard of these babies, they'ze pack a punch, innit.'

Shanker intervened, spoiling the party. 'It's been used too much, anybody gettin caught wid that is gonna face some serious shit man. You need to get rid, Mass, pass it on bro. You'll get a good price, a grand at least.'

Massive took the gun back from Gillie and put it back in his pocket. 'Nah, it's got sentimental value for me innit, an' it owes me some luck, big style.'

Twenty yards away at street level Numbers was doing his best and, to be fair, he was doing pretty good. Bashed up, scared shitless and frantic with worry about where this would end, he'd still managed to even the odds in his favour, but only slightly.

Having managed to convince the Albos that he was more use to them alive and that his gang would never succumb to blackmail or kidnapping, he was now sat in the back of the big Lexus across the street from the building in the roof of which was the Arch.

Since the terrorist attack and police raid and Kribz and Driss getting nicked, the place would be 'no go,' obsolete, a thing of the past, he'd figured. As far as Kribz and Driss's use of the venue was concerned, he was right. But he'd never considered that they'd hand the keys onwards.

His hands were tied but this time more comfortably in front of him and with nylon cord to mitigate the injuries caused by the plastic pull-ties.

The Gheg called Krashjig sat alongside him; neither wore seatbelts. The Gheg called Ejdit was in the driver's seat and was worried. 'Yellow lines, we cannot be here long.'

This spurred Krashjig. 'Yeah, come on, which fucking door is it? Don't even think about fucking us about!'

'I dunno, boss, seriously, I wuz wid the others when we went in, jus' followin' 'em, innit.' His speech was slightly slurred by his slap-fattened lips. Fearing another elbow in the ribs, he gabbled on. 'It's one of them tho', definitely, one of the ones wid the intercom an' the camera above it.'

'There are three cameras,' sighed Krashjig, shaking his head. 'You know, you're not doing very well for someone with a very uncertain future.' His tone and measured English were like that of a disappointed tutor preparing a recalcitrant student for exams.

'Hey!' interrupted Ejdit. 'See now!' The driver's English wasn't so good. Teacher and pupil did so and saw Massive emerge from one of the doors, head down, hands in pockets and moving off quickly; alone.

'Go!' Krashjig's order was promptly obeyed and the Lexus auto-started and moved silently forward, accelerating effortlessly until it was alongside its unsuspecting quarry.

'Zat him?!' Krashjig's eloquence had deserted him.

'No, that's not Shanker, that's… dunno who that is,' lied Numbers, feeling the time he'd been playing for fast running out. But his protest told the Albanian that Massive would do, and he opened the nearside rear passenger door with one hand whilst pulling his gun out with the other.

'No!' Numbers tried to grab Krashjig's arm but the Albo elbowed him away and was out of the car, walking briskly between parked vehicles towards Massive. The big negro had heard Numbers' protest and was already pulling the Beretta from his inside pocket, going down into a crouch and turning to face the approaching danger. His peripheral vision had lined up the target and the Albanian didn't stand a chance. The 19mm bullet hit Krashjig in the side of the throat, severing both his aortic artery and the top of his cervical vertebrae. The crack of the gun was loud and as shocking as the plume of blood which sprayed powerfully as the dead man's legs collapsed and he went down in a heap, like a marionette that had had its strings suddenly cut.

Numbers tried to get out of the car but Ejdit hit the accelerator. The open rear door collided with a parked vehicle and slammed shut, the locking system engaging instantly. The Lexus sped off. Numbers twisted round to look through the rear windscreen. The traffic had stopped behind them and horns sounded as if the gunshot had set off anti-theft alarms. He got a glimpse of Massive crossing the road, walking briskly but calmly away from the crime scene.

Part Three:

Somersault

132

Swan stepped out of the cab, paid the fare and assessed the jaded grandeur of the terraced Georgian dwellings. *I'm in the wrong job*, she thought, allowing herself a little bitterness. Before long, her ailing father would probably see his life's labour go towards buying one of these for some bloodsucking sheeptick. She snapped out of her resentful reverie and looked for Larssen's door. Finding it, she climbed the big stone steps and pressed the intercom whilst smiling up at the camera. The lock snapped and Larssen's tinny voice invited her to push. The heavy door swung open and she stepped into spotless white opulence.

The Dane stood in the hallway, at the door of the living room. 'Hi Katrina, thank you so much for coming at such short notice. Leave the door – it will close automatically. Allow me to take your coat. Would you like tea or coffee, or something stronger?'

Swan heard the question but was preoccupied with taking in the strange atmosphere: her hostess exhibited a slight nervousness. 'Er, no thank you, I'm fine.'

She'd barely finished the sentence when Larssen said, 'I've someone here for you to meet,' in a lowered, faintly mischievous tone. She grabbed the solicitor by the arm and guided her into the living room. 'Allow me to introduce you to Police Constable Douglas Napper.' She spoke as though announcing something portentous and, Swan realised on seeing the crumpled figure in the giant armchair, with sarcasm. It was as if the hostess were demeaning her guest, that somehow this whole thing was a set up. Swan froze. The incongruity of Napper's appearance and the blank look of helplessness on his face gave the impression that he was something of a prisoner, an exhibit to be regarded with haughty amusement.

'Douglas,' went on Larssen, her tone now patronising, 'you may already know this lady, but if you don't, you should. She is Katrina Swan and she is the attorney who represents the interests of my *black friends*, as you like to call them.'

Napper's brain went into overdrive. Was this bitch trying to set him up? Or embarrass him? Possibly, but the ex-squaddie didn't do embarrassment. Was he vulnerable being here? Not really: he reminded himself that Larssen wasn't a documented suspect and her status as a witness wasn't high profile. Nah, he had fuck all to worry about, and if this tubby cow was the B Boys' brief, so what? He had nothing to say to her – but hey, he was all ears if *she* started talking. Napper detached himself from the turn of events; watched and waited for the scene to play itself out.

Simultaneously, Swan was doing her own evaluation of possible outcomes. Her clients' offer to Larssen could be suspected as an attempt to pervert the course of justice, but only if it were proven that they were lying about their responsibility for the cocaine at Rankin's place, which was highly unlikely, otherwise the communication of her clients' offer was reasonable, plausible and, more to the point, privileged: strictly confidential between the Pope brothers and their lawyer.

'Well,' said Swan, not liking the way her voice had gone a bit squeaky, 'this is a surprise.' She looked expectantly at her hostess and then at the cop, and then back at Larssen again. 'Would you mind explaining the purpose of this Freda, this, er, little rendezvous?'

The Dane was busying herself lighting a cigarette, puffing her usual camouflage around the room.

'I want you to tell this officer about the offer of assistance your clients have made, and perhaps ask him for his professional opinion as to the propriety of that offer.' There was a businesslike steeliness in Larssen's voice.

Swan's own professional persona kicked in. 'I most certainly will not, to do so would be a breach of my duty of client confidentiality.' She stood up. 'I'm leaving now. What you say to this policeman is your business, and it's not my business to witness any conversation between you – I have not been, and will not be, engaged as a mediator. I'll see myself out.'

The solicitor walked out of the room and snatched her coat from its hook. The next thing Larssen and Napper heard was the sound of the front door slamming shut.

Larssen sat down, took another puff and regarded Napper quizzically, awaiting his response. He obliged. 'What the fuck was that all about?' He sounded disinterested, as if asking the question expected of him.

'Well, Douglas, let me put it this way. I'm a great believer in seizing opportunities as and when they present themselves, and this one was just too big to pass up on.'

Napper shrugged again. 'All you've done is embarrass her. What was the point?'

She stood up and walked to the window. 'The point was to let you know that any relationship I may or may not have with these young men of colour is protected in law, a private contract, nothing to do with the police, Douglas.'

The policeman hauled himself out of the armchair, roll-up between lips, and stretched. One of his hands brushed the glass chandelier, causing it to tinkle cheerfully. Larssen had her back to him but spun round on hearing the sound. 'You needn't think you're going, we've got something to talk about and I think you'll like it.'

Napper found an ashtray and crushed out the tiny remains of his cigarette. 'Okay, I'm in no hurry, let's 'ave it, then.'

The Dane, composed again, began walking around the room as if choosing her words from various shelves and corners. 'Well, you will have gathered … that Miss Swan and I are … known to each other professionally … and that our relationship stems from her relationship with her clients who are … the men you seem to wish to implicate with me and somehow tie us up together as being jointly responsible for the armed attack at the property in Stanwell Moor.'

Napper had sat down again and was listening. The woman was struggling; she stopped talking.

'Come on then, don't stop.'

She lowered herself onto the arm of his chair. He watched her skirt ride up and couldn't help hearing – or feeling – a quiet but insistent knock of opportunity. He couldn't believe it; the crazy cow was coming on to him!

'You can fuck me if you want to, Douglas, but you cannot fuck my plan, not if you know what's incredibly good for you.'

133

Numbers was slammed face forward into the door of the warehouse. This served as a signal for those inside to open it. The boy certainly hoped that they would; Ejdit was traumatised by what had occurred half an hour earlier and the gun in Numbers' ribs was held in a hand which trembled with rage. The journey had been terrifying and the youngster spent it incapacitated by fear of what would happen if he tried to escape. The Albanian shouted and swore the whole way, his gun on his lap as he hurled the Lexus across lanes and through junctions. Numbers spent most of the trip with his eyes tight shut, praying for the nightmare to end; God only knew what awaited him now.

The door flew open and Ejdit shoved Numbers through with a loud grunt of disgust. The boy stumbled in and dropped to his knees. Tears streamed down his face and he shook like a leaf. He looked up to see two waiting figures standing ominously over him. Zamir and Bora Gozit looked down at him contemptuously, unconcerned by his plight.

'Close the fucking door,' ordered Zamir. Ejdit did so. 'Were you followed?'

'I don't think so,' replied the driver as he pocketed his gun.

'Take this piece of shit upstairs and tie him up good and tight,' growled Zamir through gritted teeth. 'I'll deal with him later—'

'No, you won't,' interrupted Bora. 'I will.' She wasn't wearing her nurse's uniform on this occasion, far from it. Leather jacket, jeans and cowboy boots turned her from a frumpy, nagging sister into a senior gang member, her hard femininity adding sinister power.

Ejdit dragged Numbers to his feet and propelled him stumbling up a steel staircase onto an open mezzanine storage floor. Numbers didn't know whether to feel relieved or disappointed that he wasn't going to get shot just yet. The change of location from his previous spot on the ground floor gave him another sliver of hope – things were perhaps going to happen down there that they didn't want him to see; an unnecessary precaution if they'd already decided to kill him. Another brutish push sent the lad headlong into a pile of wooden pallets. Ejdit secured him with cable ties to a vertical steel beam, spat in his face and left him sitting on the floor. At least the chains and weights weren't being re-applied.

He watched the Gheg descend the staircase and then tried to wipe the sputum off his face with his knee. He could hear them talking on the ground floor in their ugly language. Their hissed words were furious, murderous, but the woman sounded like she was trying to instil some sense of tactical planning.

He fought back the urge to scream, tried to internalise his anguish, the agony of which mixed with the pain of the beatings and abuse he'd already endured. His mind swirled around thoughts of his sister, his girl, college, all pleasant realities not forty hours ago, now in the distant past. He thought of the funerals he'd attended, too many in his short life – Screwloose's was the last – and found himself thinking of who'd be at his.

He heard feet on the metal stairs, his body tensed and he looked up to see the woman ascending. She approached and stood over him briefly, then did something strange; she knelt and sat back on her heels with her hands clasped together on her lap. It was a strange posture and Numbers blinked through his stinging eyes.

'Okay, listen carefully,' said Bora, not exactly pleasantly but without the homicidal tone favoured by her compatriots. 'We need to resolve this, or the killing will continue, and you will be next. I'm going to give you a phone and you're going to call your brothers and arrange for them to come and collect you. We'll hand you over in exchange for the one called Shanker because we need his blood – he has too much of ours on his hands.'

Numbers nodded, his eyes down as he considered a major problem. 'I don't know any of their numbers – you took my phone.'

The muscles in Bora's jaw worked visibly as she clenched her teeth. 'What? For fuck's sake, you don't know any numbers?'

'No, course not, why would I?' he said, almost lapsing into reasoned argument.

She closed her eyes and pursed her lips in exasperation. 'There must be someone's number you can remember. C'mon, you've got to think harder.'

A glimmer of hope flickered somewhere inside the boy's tortured mind; there was an earnestness in her voice that suggested she wanted to save him.

134

Massive jumped on a bus, went to the top deck and took out his phone. His call to Shanker to warn him and Gillie to get out of the Arch was unnecessary. They had both heard the gunshot and had quickly assumed that it and Massive's recent departure with the loaded Baretta in his pocket were not coincidental. The pair refilled their gun bags and legged it out of a rear window, across a slippery roof and down an adjoining fire escape. They'd gone into a friendly mini-cab office and were now heading south in the back of an ageing Toyota people carrier.

'Croydon, as quick as you can, brother, we've an urgent appointment.' The driver knew better than to get chatty and did as he was told.

Kribz was about to refuse yet another cup of Mrs Rankin's tea when he got the call.

'Yo,' he said, not expecting good news.

Shanker imparted the update in guarded language – the cabbie was all ears – and Kribz felt a wave of anxiety engulf him. The shit just got deeper and hotter.

'Hold on,' he told the caller, and then to Tom Rankin who sat next to him: 'Tom, can a couple of buddies of ours come out here an' meet us? Bit of business innit, no trouble, I promise.'

Marlene was out of earshot but the old man chose his words carefully anyway, sensing a lack of certainty in the assurance of 'no trouble'; these jumping jacks knew *feck all* else but trouble. 'Okay, but not for long, half an hour tops, and then you all can feck off.'

Kribz put his mouth back to the phone and gave the go ahead. 'I'll text you the address innit. Come to the front of the house, not the way you came in last fuckin' time.'

In the cab, Shanker turned to Gillie and nodded. 'We're goin' out to that place by the airport, we'll be safe there innit…'

Gillie didn't hold back. 'You're fuckin' jokin' man, the last time we wuz there we—'

'Yeah, and so that's the last place anyone'll expect to find us,' said Shanker, 'an' anyway, nobody knew it was us innit, we wuz masked up'

Gillie zipped it for a few seconds, and then went on. 'What about Massive?'

He'd read Shanker's thoughts. 'Yeah, okay, I'll give 'im a shout in a minute, but we ain't pickin' 'im up, 'e'll have shit residue on him.'

Gillie got this all right. 'Yeah, not to mention that fuckin' Beretta.'

'Jeez,' mused Shanker, 'the guy's a fuckin' liability. We gonna have some serious shit to deal wid now.' He thumbed his phone for the news, but there was no need: it had turned the hour and the driver dialled Capital Radio's volume up.

'Within the past hour a man has been shot dead in broad daylight on a busy street in south London. Early indications are that the police are treating the incident as gang related…' The urgently narrated headline was followed by a bit about how disputes between organised crime groups had escalated onto the streets at an alarming rate in recent months, etc., etc.

Then both Shanker's and Gillie's phones buzzed simultaneously as a Snapchat shout came through. Gillie was first to speak. 'Fuck, man, he needs 'elp innit, we need to dig 'im out bruv, gotta do sumtin'.'

Shanker made the call. 'Where the fuck are you Mass?'

Massive's voice was low, hushed. 'On a fuckin' bus man, in the West End, Regent Street I think…'

'Okay, get off and get underground, find the Piccadilly Line, take it out to Heathrow Airport. I'll send you a postcode or co-ordinates or sumtin' – it's the house where we done the big job but don't worry, Kribz an' Driss is there, it's safe – gizza shout when you rock up, bro.'

135
'I knew there was something real and powerful under the

scruffy exterior. Giving it all that Colombo nonsense, playing the bumbling shambles of a cop while seeing everything how it really is – you never fooled me for one second, Douglas.'

They were both on the thickly carpeted floor. Larssen lay with her head on Napper's chest. His shirt was still buttoned up and his trousers and underpants were round his ankles; he felt ridiculous. And incredulous, scarcely believing what had just taken place. *What the hell was this bitch up to?*

'You on the pill?' was all he could think of saying. She jack-knifed up and was on her feet. Naked from the waist down, she stood over him, hands on hips. 'Such a romantic, aren't you? Of course I'm on the fucking pill, as you English quaintly call it. Good God, the thought of conceiving a child to the likes of you, Douglas – well, no offence but—'

'None taken luv, but just checkin' cos oi ain't into the fatherhood shit.'

'And *oi ain't* into the motherhood shit either – and it's Ms Larssen to you!'

Napper struggled to his feet and pulled his trousers and pants up. His head was pounding and he needed a pint. 'Okay, so you're goin' to hand these fuckers a load of money if they accept responsibility for the dope found on the Rankin place?'

'No, I'm going to pay privately for the best legal representation for them, so they will be spared prison when they simply tell the truth. What's wrong with that?'

The Cornishman fished a bent little roll-up out of his pocket and lit it. 'Well, oi suppose if you put it that way it don't sound so bad, but there's one big question – why've you let me in on it?'

She made no attempt to get dressed and just sauntered over to the window. He watched the exaggerated sway of her hips. Then she turned as if an idea had just occurred to her and walked out of the room. From where he sat he could see her walk into the bathroom, then he heard the toilet roll dispenser being used, then he saw her leave the bathroom and go into the kitchen, and then he heard the fridge or freezer door being opened and closed. *What the fuck?* he thought, before making a very good guess about what she'd just done. She re-entered the living room, looking thoughtful, frowning, head slightly tilted.

'Not sure really,' she replied to the question he'd asked over a minute earlier. 'Call it instinct. It wasn't planned, but I usually fly on my autopilot and it hasn't let me down much yet.' She waved her arm at her surroundings to make the point. 'I paid a big deposit for this place, and it's fifty per cent mine. I came to London with nothing, so I'm not doing badly, but I need to pay off the balance and I've found it's always best to have an able-bodied helper along the way.'

He was beginning to get it. 'Oh, roit, and the last one ain't so able-bodied anymore, eh? 'Opping about on one leg like 'e is.'

'No,' the Dane shook her head, still looking thoughtful. 'It's got nothing to do with Jackson. I just need to cover my bases, spread the load in case anything goes wrong, and having you alongside me, so to speak, makes feel, well, you know, a bit safer.'

'How's that then?' asked Napper, even though he sort of know what she meant.

She sighed, picked up her knickers and used them, with one hand, to cover herself. 'I don't trust that Katrina, the solicitor, she's up to something, so now you have my side of the story, my motive, my, er, narrative.'

It was the second time he'd seen her vulnerability, the flesh behind the steel mask.

'Okay,' he said. And then, fag in mouth, he got to his feet and pulled up his pants.

136

Briggs walked into the shambolic office on the second floor of the run down police station. He was looking for Napper who was not returning his calls. He found no one except McAdam, sat at his usual desk reading the Daily Telegraph and drinking tea from a mug.

'Have you seen Doug Napper at all?' asked Briggs politely. He feared McAdam: an unknown entity with nothing to lose. Career cops had a distrust of contracted contingent workers: they were not subject to the police disciplinary regulations, had their pensions and were widely believed to be working – if you could call it that – for some beer money and to get away from their spouses.

'Nope, no sightings for several days… sergeant.' The pause before the title was deliberately acerbic.

'Oh, right, fine, er, he's not picking up my calls. Any idea where he might be?' Briggs really needed to speak to the elusive copper. McAdam, already wound up by an article on the falling crime detection rate, sat back and regarded the youthful CID officer with undisguised annoyance.

'D'you know what, son, not that I give a flying fuck of course, but it pains me that you're spending the taxpayer's money trying to detect the whereabouts of your own men when you should be out there nicking the scumbags what're wrecking this city…' He jerked his head in the direction of the window for emphasis.

Briggs was already making for the door, but the old retiree hadn't finished. '…which is probably what Doug Napper is busy doing right at this minute, and avoiding you to give himself a better fucking chance!'

Briggs stopped and turned to face his detractor. He'd promised himself that the next time someone was rude to him he'd deal with it head-on.

'Why are you being rude?' he asked, reasonably, his voice shrill with the fear of confrontation.

''Cos you're being fucking stupid. You should know that if Doug isn't answering his phone he's busy, and when he's less busy he just might get back to you.'

The graduate was determined not to back down. This was perfect: there were only the two of them in the room – no audience, so he could lose this fight without humiliation.

'Listen mate, it's all very well for the likes of you, sat reading the paper half the day and drinking tea and sniping. You should remember who's paying for your pensions and who's losing overtime because of you lot coming in on the cheap. Try and bear those things in mind when you're sat around telling your war stories about "when I was in the job" and "in my day we had it hard" and all that nonsense. Just show a bit of respect occasionally for the people who run this organisation and have to make the decisions.' He stopped there, levelling a practised glare at McAdam.

The pensioner blinked a few times – Briggs had won. 'Alright sarge, keep your hair on.' He leant forward and pretended to refocus on his newspaper.

Briggs walked out onto the stairwell and felt fantastic. Maybe he was a decent sergeant after all.

He wasn't too bothered that he'd been unable to speak to Napper; he'd only wanted to be sure nothing had happened to scupper his theory that the presence of the liquidators at the time of the armed attack at Rankin's was just a coincidence – as the algorithm suggested – and that there were no evidential inferences to be drawn from it.

He had no investigative input on the Knightsbridge shooting of Jackson three weeks previously and the ballistics match showing that the same weapon was used in both incidents did not trouble him. If anything, it supported his case: the B Boys were on Rankin's side and had nothing to do with Larssen.

He walked the mile or so to the busy Walworth Police Station and by the time he got there he was mentally prepared.

'Ladies and gentlemen, the Law Enforcement Risk Template, LERT in short, gives a clear indication that the perpetrators of the Stanwell Moor attack were, on the balance of probabilities, not members of the Braganza Boys. That particular urban street gang are low level street operators, connected to Rankin only in respect of their shared interest in pit bull terriers. The algorithm behind LERT is calibrated according to a system devised by the National Physical Laboratory and has been tested repeatedly by our colleagues at the National Crime Agency.'

Briggs' small audience consisted of a commander, a detective superintendent, and several detective inspectors. In the main they looked bored, but weren't hostile. His task was to persuade them that the LERT system worked in real life; they'd heard all the theory about how law enforcement decision-making could be assisted by algorithmic thinking and the efficient triaging of limited resources, blah blah. He concluded his somewhat breathless delivery, assisted by a dozen or so PowerPoint slides, and then invited questions.

The detective superintendent accepted the invitation. 'Only the one question, Aaron. You say you've applied this concept to the armed attack out near the airport – where was it, Stanwell Moor? – are we to take it that – and I'm following the case – that the firm of property developers that were trying to evict the occupant have been eliminated from the enquiry?'

'Absolutely, sir. We fed all the evidential pointers through the system and that scenario – that the liquidators were involved – came out as having a negligible risk factor.'

'So, it was just a coincidence, was it?' asked a rather sceptical DI in a crumpled grey suit.

'Not exactly sir,' said Briggs. 'The presence of the liquidators at the scene at the time of the attack was loosely linked to the attack in that the behaviour and lifestyle of Thomas Rankin, the occupier, was attracting adverse attention from various quarters, but that's not to say that the killers had any connection with the liquidators. It was just that they were all part of a bigger picture which happened to coalesce at the same time.'

'Happened to coalesce at the same time,' repeated the DI. 'Isn't that just another name for a coincidence?'

Briggs wasn't fazed by this. 'Yes sir, in the literal sense I suppose it is, but the happenstance of coincidences does not necessarily infer evidential connections and the LERT system tells us when to attach zero significance to them.' Briggs paused, perceiving that he was losing their attention, and his own credibility. 'In other words, simultaneous events can be behaviourally linked whilst being evidentially unconnected.' *That should do it*, he thought.

The silence which met this was numbed, rather than stunned. The thoughts of the attendees all ran along similar lines: *omg, more fucking newspeak buzzwords, just humour the prat and then get out of here and get back to work.*

Briggs wasn't stupid enough to think he'd made a good impression but was nonetheless pleased he'd come out of the presentation unscathed. There were no further questions and he gave way to the next speaker, a ballistics analyst from the lab. She was Chinese, young, and attractive, in that order. The assembled shuffled in their seats, looking forward to something of substance, and by God, did she deliver.

137

Screwloose's gun was no longer Screwloose's gun. It had made a name for itself and was now called Linked Series 5, having become the fifth multiple-use firearm in London that year to achieve the *linked series* status of a weapon used in more than two shootings.

The analyst had a tone that managed to be simultaneously chirpy and monotonous; it rose and fell with a synthetic rhythm that quickly became predictable, its emphasis only occasionally appropriate. She was dressed in black tee-shirt and slacks and her alabaster arms and face worked robotically beneath a bobbed helmet of pitch-black hair.

'Linked Series 5 is a Beretta 9000S Type D in 9×19 millimetre which is sometimes referred to as the 9000S D9, whereas the .40 S&W in Type F configuration would be 9000 F40. The 9000 series is available in 9×19 millimetre and .40 S&W calibres in either D or F configurations denoting traditional double-action and decocker models respectively.'

The frowning gathering looked like they were beginning to think they'd landed on another planet, what with Briggs' fucking gobbledygook and now this excursion into techspeak. A PowerPoint presentation played autonomously on the wall screen and she didn't look at it once whilst delivering her commentary.

'Discharge number 1 took place in Brixton, London SW2 on 16th July 2018. Discharge number 2 took place in Knightsbridge on 4th August 2018, discharge number 3 took place at Stanwell Moor on 16th September 2018 and discharge number 4 took place in Myatt's Fields Close on 17th September 2018.' As each location was mentioned a different street plan flashed up, the location of the "discharge" marked with a red arrow. The fifth PowerPoint slide then appeared and depicted the four locations in the wider context of a map of west and south London, the four now much smaller red arrows showing the geographical disparity of the incidents.

She went on. 'Bullets and shell casings were recovered following all four discharges and analysis shows that the rounds were from the same magazine, which can hold up to sixteen. So, unless there have been additional discharges to those we know about, the gun is still very much loaded.' This last bit of information was about the most useful so far.

'In your recent experience,' came the question from the detective super, 'how prevalent is the use of these particular guns?'

The analyst hardly drew breath before replying. 'During the past 36 months the Beretta 9000 has been used in twelve percent of all shootings in London that have come to our attention. It seems that its relative unpopularity is the consequence of its relatively high street price, as opposed to the quality of its performance.'

'So, if they were cheaper they would be in wider circulation?' persisted the super, evidently with an idea in his head.

'The indications are that the Beretta 9000 is not the sort of weapon to appear regularly in linked series, in other words it is not normally used more than once or twice before disappearing from circulation for one reason or another.'

'Such as the user being apprehended or disappearing – yes, I get your drift…'

The analyst cottoned on. 'It's a weapon that would appear to be cherished and doesn't tend to be sold on in the loose market often. It is probable that if this gun is being passed around it will be between users who are well known to each other, part of the same group or gang.'

The super was satisfied. 'Thank you,' he said, rather smugly. The others glanced at him and some nodded, sycophantically, hoping he would notice their agreement.

There were no further questions and the ballistics analyst unplugged her laptop, bobbed a formal bow of thanks and left the room silently. Following his contribution, Briggs had taken a seat at the back, directly behind the superintendent. The boss swivelled in his chair to address the graduate detective.

'Am I right in saying that your LART thing, or whatever it's called, makes absolutely no connection between the four shootings in which that gun was used?'

'No meaningful connection sir, in the evidential sense, especially given that Talea – nickname Screwloose – was a member of the Braganza gang and the probable cause of the attack at Stanwell Moor was an example of quite common disputes between black gangs and Albanian organised crime groups. The LERT algorithm, if anything, shows a disconnect between Braganza and the Stanwell attack. Any connection between them and the liquidators would probably be only tangentially coincidental in their capacity as having a business connection with Rankin. Also, whoever used the gun at Stanwell Moor was probably responsible for shooting Talea, given the proximity in time between the two incidents. Additionally, Rankin himself was a victim at Stanwell Moor.'

The superintendent, a seasoned middle-aged detective, turned away and Briggs could see him looking down and shaking his head, clearly none the wiser.

Miusze Huang had to stop on the staircase and put down her laptop to take the call on her mobile; she never failed to answer it. She identified herself and listened, frowning. 'Are you absolutely sure?' she asked, already turning to climb back up the stairs. 'Okay, they're still in the room, I'll give them the news.'

The gathering was preparing to hear from its third contributor when the analyst re-entered. She made eye contact with the detective super and walked towards him. The would-be third speaker, a uniformed sergeant from the public order planning branch, sensed he was about to be interrupted and paused his preparations.

'There's been another one,' said Huang as she drew close to the super. She was overheard and had the attention of everyone.

'D'you want to tell us about it?' asked the super.

'I think I should, it may be important.' She went to the front of the room, kept her laptop under her arm, and told of an analysis that morning which showed that Linked Series 5 had claimed its fifth victim, an armed member of the Hellbanianz organised crime network. She invited questions but there were none, and so she nodded her head and was gone again.

The super turned around to Briggs for the second time. 'Looks like we've a fucking war on our hands, son.'

Briggs was still trying to take on board this latest development, but was secure in the knowledge that Linked Series 5 had been used to kill one of the Braganza Boys, that this particular weapon did not circulate widely and it was therefore now possibly still in the hands of some other gang that, unlike the Bs, were no friends of Rankin and had attacked the Stanwell Moor homestead to get at the Albos – and this latest shooting backed up his logic.

'Yes sir,' he replied. 'I'm thinking the Church Road Soldiers need to be looked at. They're a big outfit, might fancy their chances against the Hellbanianz, and I'm convinced that this has nothing to do with the Pope brothers and their Braganza mob.'

The superintendent mumbled something about it being a job for Trident, the Met gang-busting team, and swivelled round to face the front and listen to the uniformed sergeant drone on about policing demonstrations in Trafalgar Square.

Briggs took out his phone and thumbed a text to Napper.

138

Krashjig had been pronounced dead at the scene. A HAT (Homicide Assessment Team) car had been there within minutes and, following a quick in-situ photo session, the body had been searched and removed to the mortuary at Guy's Hospital to await a postmortem examination. The bullet and casing had quickly been recovered and fast tracked through the lab, and its origins recognised – hence the efficiently timed call to Huang. In addition to his gun, wallet and a couple of wraps of coke, Krashjig's phone had been seized and rushed off for analysis. Technicians had unlocked it, but its encryption software was state of the art Encrochat and it gave up nothing.

And that was about all Zamir Gozit was worried about. 'Did he have anything else in his pockets? Any other phone? Was his gun clean of serial numbers?' He fired these questions at Ejdit who, credit to him, gave stoic assurances all the way. Not because he was sure of the facts, though: he just knew that if Gozit got any more stressed or angry than he already was then he, the lowly driver, would be the messenger who got shot – literally.

Although not understanding a word, Numbers could hear Gozit's ranting from where he sat on the mezzanine storage floor and it didn't bode well. Bora had left the building, presumably to fetch a phone for him to use to summon his friends – yeah, right, fat chance of that. But then he thought again. He had to buy more time, had to think fast. The only number he knew by rote was his sister's.

He listened to Gozit bollocking Ejdit some more and then make a phone call in a different tone. He heard a number and the name Gemini. The Albo boss was giving instructions for someone – or some others – to join the party.

Then the warehouse door opened and closed and Numbers heard Bora's voice. An exchange took place and Numbers picked up the subtext that she had some sway with the boss man, like she was telling him to calm down, urging patience. Numbers sensed he had a little more time; surely somebody, somewhere, was missing him.

139

Tom Rankin sent Marlene upstairs to watch some TV in the bedroom. He opened a side gate so that the new visitors wouldn't have to walk through the house. Kribz had asked him to expect three in total, first two and then one on his own.

'We're gonna really appreciate this Tom, you're diggin' us out big style man an' we'll make it worth your while.' Kribz got a sideways glance from Driss as he said this: business had not been good and the safe under Carly's bed was far from full.

'Never mind that, I want you lot out of here as soon as you like. Mrs Rankin isn't too happy about our place being used as a rendezvous point for you lot, and the police could pay me a visit any time, as you well know, boys—'

Kribz's phone buzzed – Shanker and Gillie were out front, and Massive had just joined them.

Rankin limped round the side of the house – he'd discarded his crutch against medical advice – and brought the latest guests through. 'Come on boys, join the feckin' party – more's the merrier.' Then he recognised Massive: 'Oh, it's you! Here's me thinkin'…' He stopped there.

Massive said; 'What was you thinkin'?'

Rankin was leading the trio to the rear of the house, so had to speak over his shoulder; 'Nothin', it doesn't matter now.' The old man chose to assume, correctly, that any dog-related dispute between the brothers and this big fella had been resolved.

Kribz and Driss, standing on the raised area between the paving and the kennels, burst out laughing together at the sight of three violent drug-dealing gangsters looking as nervous and wary as children on their first day at a new school.

'Yo bluds!' exclaimed Kribz. 'Welcome to da new hood, innit!

Rankin didn't like that one bit. 'It's not your feckin' new feckin' hood, it's my home! Now I'll make you all a mug of tea and then you get yourselves fecked off out of it, d'you hear?!'

'Yeah, yeah, sure Tom, it's jus' their faces, man.' Kribz was still creased up, as was Driss, who couldn't have spoken if he'd wanted to. Even the dogs started barking, sensing fun and mischief.

The old man turned to the latest visitors. 'Don't take any notice of these two, they're gettin' too damn familiar with me. Now then, do you want a mug of tea each?'

Shanker declined: tea wasn't his favourite beverage – it reminded him of Wormwood Scrubs – but Massive and Gillie accepted the offer, nodding and muttering 'Yes please' and 'No sugar', a bit tersely, like they were in a cafe.

'Right, sit yourselves down over there,' said Rankin, pointing to an old pub garden table with its integral bench seats. 'I'll get the tea, you'll drink it and then be off.'

Four of them did as they were told and squeezed onto the benches. Massive stayed standing, fidgeting, moving his weight from one leg to the other. He looked terrible, exhausted.

'Come an' sit down, Mass, an' tell us what 'appened,' insisted Kribz.

'I can't fuckin' sit down, man, I jus' shot a guy. I'ze buzzin' innit.'

Kribz stood up, extracted himself from the bench seat and took hold of the big guy by the shoulders. He could feel him shaking. 'It's gonna be okay bruv, we'ze safe here—'

'I tink I killed 'im, the blood spewed out all over the place.'

He obviously hadn't heard. Kribz brought him up to date. 'You did kill him man, stone fuckin' dead. Now come an' sit down an' tell us what 'appened before the Gypsy comes back out, quick, an' then we'll work sumtin' out, innit.'

140

In a tiny south London flat a telephone was ringing. Sharon Brade could hear it as she struggled with the key to open the door; the police never fixed the locks properly after they'd broken in with a search warrant. Once in she threw her bag of college books onto the floor and picked up the landline receiver, not expecting much more than some nuisance call from India about her involvement in a non-existent road accident.

'Hello?'

'Shaz, it's me. You gotta listen carefully an' take sumtin down in writin', sis. Get a pen an' paper.'

She'd been beginning to worry about her brother, but then a few days' absence wasn't that unusual. It was just that this latest spell had come a bit too soon after they'd got raided by cops asking him if he'd been on some job near the airport.

She grabbed a biro and an unopened junk mail envelope. 'Go on then, I'm ready, but where are you?'

'Don't matter where I am, I need you to get hold of Kribz or Driss. Their numbers are your old phone I borrowed, it's in my room. Give either one of them this number – 07866 097906. Tell them to call me urgent, you got that?'

'No, you said it too quick,' scolded Numbers' sister. 'Say it again, slowly.' He did as he was told and the number got written.

'What d'you want me to tell them? Where are you?' But Numbers had cut the call and was handing the burner phone back to Bora Gozit.

Sharon was older than her sixteen years and rightly sensed her brother was not in police custody, but that he wasn't in control of his current situation either: the fear in his voice was palpable. She found the old iPhone that Numbers had been using for the past few days and, sure enough, both Kribz and Driss had been added to the contacts list; she'd never met either of them but had heard lots about the Pope brothers and knew that Kribz was the one to speak to.

Kribz was still counselling the shell-shocked Massive, Rankin still out of earshot, when he picked up the call.

'Is that Kribz?'

'Yeah, who's this?'

'It's Sharon Brade, Numbers' sister. He's in some kind of big trouble and he needs you to call him urgently. I'm going to text you the number.'

'Where is he?'

'I dunno, I'm going to text you the number, just call him please. Will you do that?'

'Yeah, sure.'

Sharon cut the call and texted the burner number her brother had given her.

'Who was that?' asked Driss. The other three shuffled uncomfortably on the bench seats, awaiting the next development which they knew wouldn't be good.

Kribz was thumbing the phone onto private mode so the recipient of his next call wouldn't see its source.

'Numbers' sister, she's sent me a number for him. I'm gonna call him.'

Thirty miles to the east, on the other side of London, the burner phone warbled its factory set tone. It was in Bora's hand and she gave it to Numbers. 'Keep to the script, or they'll hear you scream.' Her words needed no emphasis with Zamir and Ejdit stood menacingly behind her.

Numbers tapped the green icon on the unregistered device. 'Hello?' he said, unnecessarily.

'Is that you, Numbers?'

'Yeh, who's that?'

'It's Kribz bruv, are you okay?'

'No bruv, anything but, you gotta come an' get me an' you gotta bring Shanker wid you, or they'ze gonna kill me for sure.'

'What they wantin' Shanker for?'

'Dunno, bruv—' Numbers was interrupted by Bora snatching the phone from him.

'Right, my friend,' – she spoke calmly, clearly – 'I will now send you a text with the address and postcode of where we are. If you do not arrive here within three hours from now, bringing with you the one called Shanker, this little boy of yours goes in the river with a big weight on his feet, and then we'll visit your Irish friend near the airport to exact our taxation on him instead. I will send you a photograph.' And then she hit the 'end call' icon.

Kribz was on his feet by then, turning away from the table to concentrate. He took the phone from his ear and looked down at it. Sure enough a pic appeared: Numbers' bruised, tear-streaked face with an address and postcode as the accompanying text.

141

'You be fucking careful mate,' said Blake to Napper, the exhausted looking cop having arrived at the lawyer's office just before he closed shop for the day to disembark to the nearest pub. What they were discussing was not to be overheard.

'I've thought it through, Stu, I ain't doin' anything wrong, not criminal anyway—'

'No, but they'll fuck you over on discipline code charges. You'll lose your job, your career.'

Napper had considered this as well. 'I'm sick of the job, and as for a fuckin' career, well, that's a joke anyway...'

Blake was getting cross. 'I thought you wanted some advice, so you're getting it. I'm not just going to agree with everything you say and tell you that you've got fuck all to worry about when you've clearly got a lot to worry about if you do what you've obviously made up your mind to do.'

And of course Napper had made up his mind: he was going to keep schtum about the offer that had been made to Larssen and her intended acceptance of it when, according to the police disciplinary regulations, it was his duty to report this new intelligence to his superiors and have it recorded as an indication of an intention by Larssen, the Pope bothers and, by association, their own solicitor, to pervert the course of justice. But that intention existed only if the brothers were not in fact responsible for the presence of the cocaine stash on Rankin's land, a scenario which flew in the face of reason.

Napper had gone over this with Blake and, to be fair, the experienced solicitor had been impressed by the policeman's legal logic, but still, he would get roasted alive if the plan went wrong. Napper went over it again, as if thinking aloud.

'There's no real evidence to prove the Braganza Boys done the attack on Rankin's place. They wore masks and gloves and then disappeared without trace – a proper pro job. I'm surprised the B Boys were up to it to be honest, didn't think they 'ad it in 'em.'

'So why are you so sure it was them?' Blake was puzzled by his friend's unswerving belief.

Napper sighed, rubbed his arm and moved his weight from one buttock to the other. 'Oi just *know*, Stu. There's not another black gang in the whole of London what even knows where Stanwell Moor is, for fuck's sake. It couldn't ''ave been anyone else, an' the B Boys 'ave no previous connections with Albanians. Rankin 'imself provides that connection.'

Blake followed the train of thought. 'So, you think Rankin set the whole thing up, had the black gang rock up to see off the Albos?'

'Yeah mate,' said Napper, unconvincingly, 'somethin' like that.'

Blake sensed that his pal had had some sort of interesting afternoon, that his evident tiredness and sensitivity were not entirely work related. A smirk appeared on his chubby, badly shaven face. 'You altogether well mate, not been up to naughties have you?' He was already reaching for the fridge door and two cans of Kronenbourg appeared.

Napper's eyes were down as he allowed himself a smug little smile. Nodding, he confessed. 'Yeah, mate, rumped 'er this afternoon, didn't I, on the floor in 'er 'ouse, got the carpet burns on me knees to prove it.'

'I knew it! Good on you, son! Fucking best traditions of the Metrophallopian fucking Police Farce!' Blake's voice broke into falsetto; he was delighted.

Napper grinned and they cracked their tinnies. Blake took a long pull, or tried to; his swallowing was interrupted by the beginnings of seismic activity. The tremors started in the stomach region and quickly spread, engulfing his entirety. The shuddering grew rapidly more violent, and he just managed to place his beer on the desk before the mouthful he'd just taken erupted from his contorted countenance.

'Aahh! For fuck's sake!' The cop was unable to dodge the spray. Blake managed a strangled enunciation. 'Talk about being in too deep! You don't fuck about do you...' he was now helpless but managed to shriek the punchline: '...or rather, you fucking *do*!'

Then, quite suddenly, Blake recovered his composure. So suddenly in fact that Napper was unnerved by the lawyer's transformation from a giggling, overgrown schoolboy to a steely-eyed schemer.

'*Noli defacare in dorsum tuum hortum,*' said Blake in a flat, advisory tone.

'Oh, don't start the Latin shit Blakey, what the fuck are you talking about?'

'Don't shit in your own back garden,' came the translation.

It took the cop a few seconds to digest this. 'I'm kinda just doing my job.' The words came out lamely; lacked conviction.

'Well don't then, stop rocking the boat, think about it, if I can get Jackson legal ownership of the Rankin property I'll hit him with a twenty percent fee, and after that you won't find me ungenerous – if you get my meaning.' The tone had become creamy, conspiratorial in a pleasant sort of way.

Another few digestive seconds preceded Napper's response. 'What are we talking about?'

The use of the 'we' was a green light to Blake. Napper was the brief's best friend and the pair had known each other a long time, but he was still a copper, so caution was often built into Blake's approach when grey areas were being navigated.

'Do your sums, son. Jackson could cream off three hundred grand if he gets that place back for the bank. That'll be sixty grand for yours truly and then a nice little thankyou drink for his nameless introducer.'

'How much is a nice little drink?' The cop mumbled the words, like his lips could hardly bear to speak them.

Blake answered matter-of-factly, enjoying his friend's discomfort.

'Put it this way mate, I'm a great believer in equality, so go careful, don't fuck things up, any more than you have already.'

The lawyer drained his can in several loud gulps and reached backwards for the fridge door again.

142

'We got a fuckin' war on our hands, bruvs, and it starts fuckin' now!'

They all looked up at Kribz; he'd assumed the generalissimo role they'd last seen him perform three weeks previously in the big shed less than fifty metres from where they now sat.

'What the fuck?' moaned Massive, still traumatised by the murder he'd just committed; any more action and he'd be in serious risk of battle fatigue.

'Who says, bro?' The question was from Gillie, clearly in no mood to be taking orders from anyone.

'Yeah, who fuckin' says?' backed up Shanker.

Kribz stood firm and puffed out his chest. 'We got a brother bein' 'eld hostage out east. We gotta be there in three hours from now or he's gettin' wasted, ain't no doubt about it.' The gang leader was already eyeing the two bags Gillie and Shanker had brought with them and had no doubt Massive was still toting the Beretta.

They were interrupted by old Tom Rankin, limping from the patio towards them. 'You boys about ready to leave yet? Don't be getting too comfortable now,' he said, trying to keep it light. When he focused on the looks he was getting he stopped his limping and just stood there. 'Aw feckin' hell, what the feck's 'appened now?!'

Kribz stepped forward. 'We got to get to the East End, Tom, and fast. We ain't using the trains and the car we've got ain't big enough and it's got too much camera footage on it, tyin' it up to your place. You got some transport you can lend us?'

It was a long way off being the first time that the old Gypsy had regretted getting involved with the maelstrom of trouble that called itself the Braganza Boys.

143

Palmer always got into the office early, usually first. He liked to monitor his colleagues' start-of-day moods, before their guards went up, before they'd properly donned their little corporate masks. As usual however, he hadn't beaten Larssen. She was at her desk, unshowered and still gleaming in her sweat-soaked cycling gear. He tapped on the door of her soundproof glass office, holding up his offering of a Costa Americano. She had to rise from her desk to open up and did so with a smile – but more at the coffee than at its bearer, who she trusted like a hole in the head.

'Thank you, Colin, you're a star.' She took the drink from his hand. Before she managed to close the door he asked her if she had a minute.

'Yes, sure, *entre,*' She tried to sound friendly, accommodating. Palmer gauged her mood: not bad, still a bit high on cycling endorphins.

He closed the door behind him. She put down her coffee and threw herself back into her big white fake leather chair and swivelled on it, legs provocatively akimbo. 'Let me guess – Stanwell Moor.'

'Correct,' replied Palmer, putting his hands in his pockets to appear relaxed – he'd not been invited to sit.

Larssen picked up the Costa cup and started prising the lid off. 'Right, I've been thinking about that.' (She hadn't.) 'Hold fire on that deal please, there've been developments.'

She took a tentative sip, inwardly scolding herself for not having thought of this earlier: too much whisky inside her when she'd read Palmer's email.

Palmer looked disappointed. 'What kind of developments? Have we lost our interests in the place?' He was referring to the equitable interest in the land that accrued from it being security on their fee payment.

The Dane heard the faint tinkle of a warning bell; why was this pushy little spiv taking such an interest? She crossed her legs and regarded him balefully. 'That would not be your problem, Colin. It's enough for you to know that I'm not doing any deals regarding that property until the police investigation is complete. Thank you for the coffee.'

Hands still in pockets, Palmer shrugged. 'Fine, I was just wondering, that's all. I'll tell the interested party to shelve it for the time being.' He turned and sauntered out, closing the door behind him again, not as quietly as politeness would have required.

Half an hour later he was out on the pavement having a smoke and calling Jackson.

'She's fucking up to something.'

144

Briggs found it extra tough working with the Trident team. They were a bunch of hard-headed coppers with countless years of combined experience in dealing with inter-gang violence in the metropolis and beyond, much of it bloody and fatal. The young graduate sat in a corner of the huge squadroom. It was in a converted warehouse on an industrial estate between Croydon and Streatham, one of those parts of south London that was neither inner city nor suburban, neither rough nor regentrified, just a nondescript, in-between area that attracted little attention but had good transit infrastructure and low rents.

The real cops weren't unaccustomed to visiting personnel and afforded Briggs a modicum of courtesy, coffee and stale biscuits, and a dirty desk with a docking station for his laptop. He'd been granted a three-day attachment to provide background briefings on what had gone down at Stanwell Moor and how the gun called 'Linked Series 5' kept cropping up, its latest cameo having been right outside where the Pope brothers had been nicked in the mosque raid following the O2 terrorist attack.

The Trident operation was focused on the murder of Krashjig, and the investigation encompassed the recent behaviour of anyone they suspected. The emerging picture was slanted by the Trident approach towards all things gang and drug related. These cops rarely if ever thought outside that box, but it was a big box and usually did the trick. Their scorched earth approach – to search as many premises and arrest as many suspects as quickly as possible – almost always yielded results and caused a lot of damage to London's criminal classes in the process.

But it was expensive and the overtime budget was already rocketing; the squad of three detective sergeants and twenty detective constables had been given one week to clean up the mess, after which the job would be wound down and they'd be moved onto the next outbreak of warfare – there was always plenty.

Briggs was taking special interest in the work of a young DC sat at a nearby workstation. She was attractive, in her thirties and concentrating grimly on the task before her: viewing the recorded CCTV footage of Hampton Street and its junction with Walworth Road where the Krashjig murder had occurred. The footage had been collected from Southwark Council and, on pain of legal action for non-co-operation, local businesses. The owner of the cameras above the door of the building which housed the B Boys' hideout could not be located and they appeared defunct anyway. But the cop still had plenty of material to work through and it wasn't long before she identified several vehicles worthy of further research. One was a big black Lexus 570.

It is a historical fact that black criminals liked to drive flash motor cars, but two generations of being persistently stopped by police had instilled the professional practice of using nondescript hired vehicles when on business. This never stopped them being pulled over more than they'd like, but the odds of them getting nicked by vehicle identification went down, especially when their hire cars got passed around during leasehold periods: *'dunno who was driving it on this day or that,'* or *'it got thieved from us, innit.'*

Albanian criminals hadn't quite got there yet. Sure, highly organised groups at the top of the Albo hierarchy have a pool of high-end cars that they pass around between them continuously, but their arrogance and a lower susceptibility to police harassment combined to render them less disciplined when it came to keeping their wheels under the radar.

Zamir had told Bora to give the Lexus keys to Krashjig and Ejdit. She'd protested but they were low on time and their taking of Numbers as hostage made the schedule even tighter. Kidnapping was a high-risk activity with a narrow window of opportunity; it was never long before it got very heavy police attention.

The DC doing the research called her superior over to look at one of the three screens on her desk. Then he called over his superior, and a small crowd of them gathered. And then a meeting was called and everyone shifted their attention to the front of the squadroom.

Awestruck, Briggs watched the real-time investigation unfold, and listened as the groundbreaking development was communicated to the team by the superintendent in an understated, almost anodyne tone. It was all just another day in the office for these guys, thought Briggs; they were probably just wondering if they were going to get home that evening, it being a Friday. The superintendent looked weary, no doubt worried about the overtime bill.

The detective responsible for this untimely breakthrough had checked out the vehicle and found it to be registered to a limited company with an accommodation address in Barking. Further checks revealed the company to be nothing more than a shell with nominee directors, and the address to be a multi-occupancy affair with a nail bar on the ground floor below several conversion flats with various intelligence reports indicating their use as brothels. Krashjig's body had been identified from its fingerprints – an Albanian wanted on warrants by the Greek National Police and the UK Border Force – and the gun recovered from near his body was a Heckler and Koch with Lithuanian Army markings, another tell-tale sign, as Albo gangsters habitually used these weapons. Overall, the emerging picture had Shqiptare written all over it, the name given to the Albanian mafia, an organised crime network way above the Hellbanianz and with its fingers in every pie on every continent on the planet.

The Trident detective superintendent briefed the room on the latest finding like he was reciting blank verse; there was nothing unexpected here, including the zero prospect of a weekend off. The one slightly unusual aspect to this was that it seemed like the Albos had come off second best in this latest little tiff: they didn't often fight amongst themselves at street level and when they fought with others they rarely lost. The CCTV footage had captured a fleeting image of what looked like an IC3 – police code for Afro-Caribbean – leaving the scene on foot, but where he'd come from or had gone to wasn't clear.

Briggs took avid notes and, once the meeting was over, set about contriving an email to his own command unit, taking care to weave in a proprietary take on the proceedings, like he'd been a contributor.

Busy trying to shine, he missed the activity at another desk, one with an ANPR terminal. A DC was tracking the points across London at which the Lexus had been spotted by the cameras, and the conclusion was soon drawn that it had been driven home to 'Little Tirana' – Barking.

145

It had struck Tom Rankin that the only way he was going to get these five mad bastards off his premises was to take them himself, and fast. They'd told him about the looming trouble – and it was big trouble – with the Albos, and the last thing he wanted was a rematch kicking off on his land, which seemed the odds-on outcome if the B Boys hung around much longer.

He had grunted agreement – he knew there'd be money in it – and was now leading the five fully armed young men through his house and out onto the front drive, with its mishmash of parked vehicles and various garages. One of the garages, the biggest, rarely seen open, contained the old Gypsy's pride and joy: a 1955 Albion Chieftain FT37 diesel six-wheeled dropside lorry. Rankin undid the padlock and swung open the double doors. The sun was positioned just right and illuminated the magnificent vehicle in all its green and yellow liveried glory. The proud owner turned to face the young men. They regarded the unveiled spectre; Kribz and Driss managed uncertain smiles, Shanker and Gillie exchanged glances, and Massive's face burst forth with his huge trademark grin. 'Jeez, boss, it's fuckin' awesome!' The big negro stepped forward into the garage, sucking his lips and caressing the lorry's spotless bodywork.

'Is she not beautiful?' beamed Rankin, thankful for the admiration and interest. Massive didn't look like he did much polite, so his appreciation of the vintage motor seemed all the more genuine.

'Right lads, let's get this lovely lady started and get ourselves on the road.' And with that Rankin climbed up into the cab.

The boys stood back and watched. 'Fuck,' said Driss, 'we goin' to east London in that thing?'

'Looks like it,' said Kribz, dubiously.

Then Rankin turned the key and the diesel engine roared into life like an awaking tiger, eager for action. The spectators were impressed, but taken aback; they'd never heard anything like it and instinctively backed away as the lorry moved out onto the forecourt.

The Gypsy opened the door and climbed back down onto the muddy, broken tarmac, wincing with pain; he'd momentarily forgotten to guard his injury. The engine was still running.

'I'm just going for a word with the wife, I'll leave her to warm up.' He disappeared into the house, leaving the gang to assess their new transport, wondering how they were going to spend the journey. There was barely enough room for one passenger in the cab and the payload area, its dropdown sides rising not three feet from the floor, was concealed by a tubular steel frame over which was slung a mouldy green tarpaulin 'roof' which provided just about enough headroom for passengers to sit on the floor beneath it.

Driss approached the lorry tentatively, put his foot on the rear mudguard and hauled himself up to peer through a tear in the tarp into the load space.

'It's clean anyways, and dry.'

Massive didn't need the help of the mudguard; he stood on his toes and looked through a different tear. 'Fuck, man, ain't gonna be comfortable.'

Kribz had sidled away a few yards. Having fished a business card out of his pocket, he was tapping out Katrina Swan's number.

146

Numbers was trying to remember how to pray. A couple of additional Ghegs had turned up at the warehouse and he could hear them getting instructions from Zamir Gozit, with Bora interrupting and contradicting him continuously. He couldn't actually see what was going on from his enforced seat on the mezzanine floor, but it was obvious that if his posse turned up – and he'd convinced himself they would – then they'd be well advised to be armed to the teeth: he could hear magazines being slammed into the stocks of pistols.

At least they hadn't started up the barbell weights and chains trick again and he took some encouragement from thinking that if he was going to be rescued then he wouldn't have to be carried out of this place with half a ton of metal wrapped round his legs. *Fuckin' embarrassin', man.*

The shit was going to hit the fan, of that Numbers was sure: there was no way the Bs were going to hand over Shanker in some sort of exchange and he didn't for one second believe that the Albos expected them to. They wanted a battle and they were up for it, as long as it was on their home turf; no way would they risk going to Rankin's place – their threats to do so were empty, for the time being – to them it would be cursed and probably under some kind of police control or surveillance.

The steel stairs were rattling again and Numbers waited to see who would emerge onto the mezzanine. It was Bora, alone. She looked concerned, had on her nursey face. Neither spoke as she drew near and regarded the prisoner professionally, stooping and going behind him to inspect his tied wrists.

'How are you feeling?' she asked, tersely.

'Oh, fuckin' great, never better, just love bein' fuckin' kidnapped an' threatened wid' bein' drowned, excitin' innit.' Numbers felt he could take the piss like this, not fearing the woman, so was shocked when she slapped him hard across the face with the back of her gloved hand. 'What the fuck did you do that for? I wasn't bein' insultin'.'

She hissed at him. 'Don't get clever. You're not out of trouble yet, a long way off it.'

He nodded, looking up at her like a scolded schoolboy. She softened a little, stooping again, this time in front of him, to put her hands on his knees; her breath smelled of garlic.

'Listen,' her tone was urgent – sincere, even, 'there will soon be some major trouble happening. You'll be better off up here – that way you stand a chance. If you try to interfere or help your friends my brother will kill you, that is for sure. Do you understand?'

Numbers hadn't stopped nodding and held eye contact with the woman, whilst wondering how he would have a chance of interfering or helping friends trussed up like he was. But she was right that he was safe up on the mezzanine with a steel floor under his arse. If the action stayed at ground level he would just stay put and keep trying to remember how to pray.

147

Briggs left the squadroom in search of coffee. He tried to call Napper again – still on voicemail so he left yet another message: 'Doug, call me, you need to know what's happening.' Then he pocketed his phone and no sooner than he'd started grappling with the vending machine, it buzzed. He answered without looking at the screen. 'Doug, where the fuck have you been?'

A short silence preceded the reply. 'Mr Briggs?' said a female voice.

'Yes, er, sorry, I thought…'

'Mr Briggs, it's Katrina Swan. You'll remember I represent the Pope brothers. I have something to tell you.'

'Really? And what might that be? They're due back at the police station next week.' Briggs did not need any whinging excuse-laden request for a bail period extension.

'Yes, I know that, but this is urgent, very urgent. Is this line secure?'

Briggs forgot about coffee: why would a solicitor want a secure line?

'It is at this end.' He looked at his phone screen; she was calling from a land line. 'Go on, what's happened?'

'Right, first of all, Mr Briggs, this is being recorded so you don't have to take notes. I'll supply you with a copy in due course.' In other words, *this is being recorded so don't try to put words in my mouth.* 'My clients intend to prepare written statements in which they will accept responsibility for the quantity of cocaine found during your search of the Rankin property at Stanwell Moor and state that Mr Rankin had no knowledge of its presence there.' She stopped, awaiting a response; there was none – Briggs was lost for words. 'Did you hear me, Mr Briggs?'

'Yes, er, yes I heard you. Have these statements been made in writing?'

The question irritated Swan, but she decided to be patient. 'No, not yet, but I must assume until I'm told otherwise that they will be. The important thing at the present time is that my clients have instructed me to pass this information to you, so that you know their position in advance of their attendance at the police station next week.'

The graduate detective had by now sidled into an empty office for more privacy, wishing that he also could record the conversation. 'Okay Ms Swan, I'll make a note of your call and look forward to seeing you and your clients next week—'

She interrupted. 'There's more. My clients have instructed me to tell you that they, as we speak, are on their way to an address in east London in anticipation of being violently engaged whilst they attempt to secure the release of one of their friends who's been kidnapped and held against his will. They want you to meet them there.'

Briggs tried and failed to make the connection between the first bulletin and the second bombshell which totally eclipsed it. He knew the procedure for kidnappings and a list of chronological actions scrolled involuntarily across his mind's eye.

'Right, Ms Swan, I need to know the name of the kidnapped victim and the address of the stronghold.' He pulled out a pen, sat down at a vacant desk and grabbed a notepad.

Swan was keen to commit in writing. 'I'll email it to you presently, will you—'

It was Briggs' turn to interrupt. 'No, I'm not at my terminal. Email it by all means but also give it to me now, please.'

And twenty seconds later the location of the kidnap stronghold at the Gemini warehouse was known to the Metropolitan Police.

148

Mergin felt wretched. No matter what happened now he was more or less done for. He'd been propelled in an instant from a promising career as a networking street dealer to a slot at the bottom of Hellbanianz food chain with a great big target on his back; the black gangs would be looking out for him with plenty kudos to the *gangsta* who capped him.

He decided to act. He set off on his mountain bike and headed south from Barking, towards the river. He'd heard various stories and rumours about the Gemini warehouse and figured that was where he needed to be. Not that he had a clue what he was going to do there.

He bounced across wasteland, past recycling plants and abandoned building sites, the bumpy ride doing nothing for his concentration. His mind was enduring a similarly turbulent journey, dodging this way and that, unfocused on anything but the general direction: he had to make a difference, do something, otherwise he would be a nothing for the rest of his life. It was like he was a nothing now, so, from nothing to something, he urged himself on through the dirty puddles of broken detritus that comprised his London, his nearly-new bike filthy, the thick tread of its tyres clogged with greasy mud.

As he approached the Gemini Business Park the body heat he'd generated beneath his woollen hoody seemed to escape, to be replaced by the chill of apprehension. *What the fuck was he doing?*

Riding more slowly, he headed for the rough end of the park, where the new, quite recently erected warehouses petered out, leaving the ramshackle remnants of the old site in which anything and everything went unnoticed.

His hood was up and over his baseball cap, his hands were cold on the handlebars and he wished he had gloves on. The small rucksack on his back contained only a few items, one of which was his phone which he could hear buzzing every so often; he'd decided to ignore it – whatever plan he was about to produce wasn't going to be interfered with.

149

Tom Rankin was in the house for about three minutes, and when he emerged he went straight to the driver's door of the lorry. The boys didn't notice that he was carrying something wrapped in a plastic Lidl shopping bag. He shoved this behind the driver's seat and climbed into the cab. He loved driving his Albion and, when the big diesel engine roared the vintage truck sounded like it loved being driven. 'Come on then, you feckers, all aboard!' he shouted above the din.

Kribz climbed up into the passenger seat, and the other three clambered awkwardly over the tailgate, grumbling about the absence of furnishings in the cargo space. 'Fuck, man, this ain't fuckin' luxury!' etc. Despite the stressful circumstances, Kribz couldn't wipe the grin off his face as he sat next to the chuckling Irish driver.

'Come on, my lovely lady, let's show these bastards what you can do!' In under a minute they were thundering out of Stanwell Moor village and Kribz was enjoying the view; he felt safe in the accurate assumption that he was so far out of context that even his own mother wouldn't recognise him sat up high in the passenger seat of the vintage Gypsymobile.

The four passengers in the back were not enjoying the ride at all. Sat with their backs against the trailer sides and under the canvas tarpaulin, they were in for a bruising journey.

'Fuck's sake!' bawled Shanker, 'this is like the fuckin' army!'

'What the fuck do you know 'bout the fuckin' army?' sneered Gillie.

'I done three months in the cadets, man, when I wuz in Feltham YOI, they gave us the choice, 23-7 lockdown or three months on the moors in Scotland. I done it, man, an' it was like fuckin' this, rough as shit, man…'

Gillie was impressed. 'Wow, dude, I never knew this, did you get a gun?'

Shanker wasn't sure if Gillie was taking the piss or not, but decided to play along. 'Yeah, course, bro, but only wid blanks, no real bullets, they didn't truss us, innit.'

Massive roared with laughter, his gleaming teeth nearly lighting up the gloom beneath the tarp. 'Like you're fuckin' surprised?!'

Driss was laughing too. 'Hey bro, you sounded like you enjoyed it tho', why didn't you join up full time? I heard of some boys doin' that sometimes, like after they done their sentences.'

Shanker was the only one not laughing. 'Yeah, I wuz thinkin' of applyin' but they told me not to fuckin' bother.'

'Why wuz that, man?' asked Driss, forcing a straight face.

Shanker knew he was getting fucked about, but still played along because this was no time to fall out with his comrades in arms. 'They said I wuz too violent, innit.'

Massive rolled over into the foetal position, helpless with laughter.

'Too violent, ain't that the point of bein' in the fuckin' army? You can't really go about killing people without being fuckin' violent,' pressed Driss, keen to get to the bottom of this.

'Yeah, I know, but they said I wuz bad at decidin' who to be violent with, man, like it didn't really matter to me if the other guy was on my side or not. They said I couldn't pay attention to orders and I wuz 'in-dis-crim-inut', whatever that means.'

This did it: Driss lost his composure and joined Gillie and Massive in their uncontrolled hilarity. Thankfully, Shanker saw the funny side of it and laughed along, without once even looking at the holdall by his side.

Save for regular *Shits* and *Fucks* when the wagon hit a bump or braked suddenly, the journey took on a silent and pensive mood. None of the young men were sure how this was going to end, other than badly. Gillie was still recovering from his shotgun pellet wounds and kept having to take painkillers because his injury had left him with a trapped nerve. Out of the blue, he made an impromptu declaration. 'I owe these fuckers some serious shit. I wuz nearly killed fuckin' tree weeks ago, today is payback time an' if they'ze harmed Numbers they'ze getting paid back wid a fuckin' load of interest.'

'What are you ramblin' on about?' laughed Driss, trying to hide his apprehension.

Massive was toying with the Beretta, caressing it, frowning at it like he was amazed by the feeling of power it gave him. 'He's right, bro, we need to let these fuckin' illegal

297

immigrants know whose town this is. I don't mind doing business wid them, but it's our back yard innit.'

Shanker stayed silent. He kept thinking about the way Kribz had avoided his eye contact when they were boarding the truck; something was a little bit wrong.

Half an hour later the young men under the tarp felt the wagon slow down, take a couple of sharp turns and then proceed at a more leisurely pace. Driss peeled back a section of the tarp to peer out. 'What the fuck? We ain't nowhere near east London. Where the fuck is this?'

150

Ever the frustrated detective, Blake had decided to stir things up a bit. He assumed Napper hadn't met Jackson, and had convinced himself that an introduction, properly managed, could do no harm; the police investigation needed sexing up a tad and, having met Briggs, he'd decided that the boy with a degree from some former polytechnic was nowhere near to providing the boost that the taxpayer deserved.

The lawyer chose neutral ground and had booked a table in the steakhouse above the Hippodrome Casino, just off Leicester Square. It was quiet – three in the afternoon – and the place was big and spacious.

He arrived first and a waiter showed him to an alcove table. 'Would you like to see the menu and the wine list, sir?'

'No, I'll wait until my friends get here, just get me a pint of Peroni, please.' And off went the waiter whose journey to the bar was interrupted by the arrival of Claude Jackson asking for directions to the appropriate table. As he was being steered across the large dining room Blake noted how his limp was barely noticeable.

'Hey, Jacko, you look fucking great, fella!' The lawyer rose and offered a podgy hand which Jackson regarded dubiously before giving it the flimsiest of shakes.

'Would you like the wine list and menu now, sir?' enquired the waiter, sensing a change in mood.

'Yeah, okay then,' chuckled Blake, 'but I still want that pint of Peroni.'

Jackson sat down heavily and rubbed his thigh – the one without the natural lower leg attached to it.

'Still giving you jip, mate?' observed Blake, effecting sympathy.

'A bit, old chap. Those fucking stairs didn't help.'

'Mmm,' mused the lawyer, 'but you haven't got a crutch or a stick, you're doing well, buddy – top man!'

'What's this all about, Stuart?' Jackson wasn't in the mood for small talk.

'Ah, right, I want you to meet someone, a police officer, mate of mine, he'll be here in a—'

'What, are you serious?!'

'Yup, deadly,' replied Blake without hesitation. 'This guy is a close friend of mine and has an interesting way of looking at things.' Then, in a quieter, more conspiratorial tone: 'You've got fuck all to lose, mate, and maybe quite a lot to gain.'

As he spoke, Blake spotted Napper entering the room and making a beeline for the table, ignoring the welcoming but rather startled waiter. The cop was dressed, as usual, like a New Age traveller. The round table was set for three and Napper plonked himself down on the vacant chair.

'Claude, Douglas – Douglas, Claude,' introduced Blake, suppressing the urge to giggle triggered by the expression on Jackson's face.

Napper held out his hand. 'Pleased to meet you, Claude.'

For the second time within five minutes, Jackson regarded a human hand with apprehension, and the shake he gave Napper's was equally uneasy.

'Doug, I've told Claude what you do for a living,' chortled Blake, 'and, to be fair, I think he's a bit nervous. Perhaps you'd like to allay his anxieties.'

The cop and the lawyer had rehearsed this, although not in great detail, and Napper was taken slightly aback. 'Oh, right, okay, erm,' he pursed his lips, eyes darting around the table in search of words. He found them: 'I'm involved in the investigation of a gang of south London criminals who I believe were responsible for your, er, injury.'

Jackson continued to regard the policeman with undisguised aversion and, by way of response, just shrugged. Napper felt his hackles begin to rise. He scratched his scruffy beard. 'Okay, I'll come to the point…'

'Please do,' muttered the spiv, his rubbery lip curling.

'I reckon, and it's a theory backed up by some recent intelligence, that your business partner had something to do—'

'Oh, for fuck's sake, not that shit again!' Jackson directed this at Blake, as if holding him responsible for the words just spoken.

'Hear him out, Jacko,' urged Blake, suddenly not finding this funny any longer. 'He's got a fucking bombshell for you, more than one in fact.'

Jackson sighed and turned back to Napper, a look of irritated resignation on his oval, clean-shaven face.

'Right, bombshell number one,' said Napper, almost patronisingly, 'the bullet what took your leg off came from the same gun that was used in a shoot-out near the airport, on the property that you and Freda Larssen was tryin' to seize, and Larssen was present at the scene.' He stopped for effect. The oval face was gaining length. 'Bombshell number two – the scumbags I suspect of doin' both shootings are, er, bein' financially supported by Freda Larssen.'

Oval no longer, Jackson's expression was now one of incredulity. 'Can you prove this?' was all he could think of to say.

'Of course – well, the bullets 'ave been forensically linked, the other bit isn't evidential yet, but it will be soon.'

The asset stripper was all ears now, although still regarding the cop like he'd just crawled out of a hedge, which to be fair was how he looked.

'What sort of financial support? How much?'

Napper shook his head at this question. 'Not sure yet, but what you should be askin' is "why", and the answer to that is that she's paying them to get old Tom Rankin out of the shit so he don't get POCA'd.'

Jackson blinked a couple of times before turning to Blake for help.

'Proceeds of Crime Act, mate—'

'Yes Stuart, I know what bloody POCA stands for. What I want to know is why I'm being told this. What the fuck has it to do with me?'

'Oh, come on Jacko, stop playing the innocence shit.' Blake was overdoing his annoyance, but it wasn't totally fake. 'If the POCA action evaporates then the equity in the property is retained by the Irish guy who you've – or rather now Larssen's got her claws into – and then you – or rather she – can proceed with the repossession.' He sat back, palms outwards.

'Exactly, *she*. I'm not a partner in her new company. She stole it…' Jackson's line of argument was reasonable. Napper looked from one to the other like he was watching a game of tennis.

'Ah, but that's where it could get interesting. If this fine upstanding officer of the law here,' – the lawyer plonked his hand on Napper's khaki-clad shoulder – 'can prove that she's paying those thugs to take the blame for the two kilos of coke found on the property, and as far as I know there's no independent evidence to link them to it, then that's perverting the course of justice and could fuck Larssen right up the arse on several fronts!' Spluttering and flushed, Blake took a long pull of the Peroni that had just arrived.

Jackson chuckled for the first time in a long time. 'Anatomically interesting, Stuart,' but his smile faded as his quick brain caught up: 'but I see what you mean. If she got convicted of something like that then it would be a lot easier for me to sue her for the return of my half of the company.'

'Exactly. Spot-fucking-on! Except that with exemplary damaged chucked in it could be the lot, not just your half.'

Jackson was still thinking, staring at the table. This fitted in squarely with what Palmer had recently told him about Larssen shelving a plan to sell the debt owed by Rankin to some bunch of collectors in the rough end of the City. The asset stripper's mood lightened a little, his thigh had stopped aching and – again for the first time in a long time – he had an appetite. He grabbed the menu from the loitering waiter.

151

Numbers hadn't been given a menu or any choice of food. Instead, Bora was spoon-feeding him with cold vegetable soup from a can. He felt stupid and humiliated, his body ached, his trussed wrists burned and his bruised face hurt as he gulped down the ghastly mess. But he took solace from the fact that he'd seen her open the ring-pull tin and that consequently the shit he was ingesting wasn't laced with – well – shit. He also forgave himself for accepting sustenance from his captors, on the basis that it would give him strength to fight, run or both if his B Boys intervened. No way would they attend expecting a civilised negotiation; it was going to be a gunfight and the Albos were up for it.

He could hear the preparations being made on the ground floor beneath him, the guttural swearing and nervous laughter. More men had arrived and they were psyching themselves up.

Numbers estimated that an hour had passed since Bora had snatched the phone from him to issue Kribz with the chilling demand. So, two hours to go before the weights and chains went back on his legs and then a short trip to the nearest bridge. Surely his gang, his family – his brothers! – would not let that happen – surely not. No, they would be on their way.

And he was right. Kribz had maintained a respectful silence as Rankin had driven the Albion down off the Western Avenue and onto the travellers' site that had, for the best part of half a century, occupied the wasteland beneath this tangle of elevated motorway intersections. He'd glanced at the old man a couple of times and could tell that whatever was about to happen would be somehow beneficial. The Gypsy had a plan and it obviously involved some kindred spirits.

There was a rap on the cab rear window that separated it from the payload rear under the tarp. 'What the fuck?' was Driss's muffled question. Kribz swivelled round and gave his brother a thumbs-up sign with one hand whilst putting the forefinger of the other to his lips. *Shush, wait, it's fine.*

'Here we are,' said Rankin as he pulled on the handbrake, its ratchet engaging loudly. Then he switched off the engine and suddenly the only sound was the whooshing of fast traffic over the huge structures thirty feet above their heads.

'You and your boys make sure you stay on board. This won't take long and then we'll be on our way again.' And the old man opened the driver's door and disappeared down onto the ground to face the small crowd that was already gathering.

Kribz watched and listened as best he could. There were five of them, one man in his sixties, the rest boys in their late teens or early twenties. Rankin spoke to the elder.

'*Kushti divvus,*' said Rankin.

'*Kushti divvus Tamas, sashin?*' said the elder, his little band of helpers now walking around the Albion, inspecting and admiring.

Kribz strained to make out what was being said and although he didn't understand a word of Romany, he was happy that the tone of the conversation was cordial, that Rankin was asking for something and that the travelling elder seemed to be in ready agreement. After less than a minute the two old men spat on their palms and shook hands.

Kribz had never dealt with travellers but had heard that they weren't racist and occasionally helped county line drug runners with a bit of transport now and again. Sitting up in the Albion's cab he was able to look down on the youngsters and this made him feel uncomfortable, like he was being undeservedly aloof. Whenever one of them looked up at him he smiled, pleasantly, and nodded a greeting, keen to show a bit of kinship.

He looked around at the neat rows of dwellings, trying to work out whether they were caravans or bungalows. The site was like a miniature village with numerous contradictions: drab but colourful, chaotic but orderly, scruffy but clean. Women were hanging out washing and tending to tomato plants growing from rusty oil cans, toddlers with grazed knees and runny noses played with communally owned Tonka toys on the grimy broken tarmac driveway. And even the most garishly painted semi-permanent buildings and outhouses were dulled, sullied by a shadowy film of pollution deposited from the motorways overhead.

Kribz watched as Rankin and the old traveller sauntered off towards a nearby mobile home that looked uninhabited. They paused and something changed hands: money no doubt, cash readies, *vonga*. Then the elder turned to the group of youngsters, jerked his head a few times and barked some orders. Immediately, two of the older boys stepped up for instructions, leaving the others to eye them jealously. The two recruits were then dispatched into the unattributable caravan and emerged a minute later wearing unseasonally heavy Crombie coats, the purpose of which was obviously to conceal something. Kribz tensed, not liking the look of where this was going.

Rankin walked back to the Albion with the pair of young Gypsies in his wake. He opened the driver's door and leaned in. 'These two boys are comin' along for the ride. They're handy feckin' lads, you might like to tell your friends to trust them.'

152

The remit of the Metropolitan Police Flying Squad was, historically, to catch armed robbers who hit banks and cash-in- transit vans daily across London. But that was then, a long time ago, before ATMs and when online banking had never been thought of. To survive evolution, the modern Flying Squad, whilst still dealing with the odd cash-in-transit blag and commercial knock-over, spent most of its time combatting the rampant problem of kidnapping in the capital. Several times a week a hostage is taken and a ransom demanded, usually money or drugs, but sometimes the perps ask for more elaborate dividends.

Briggs had done a good job on the activation procedure; the correct calls had been made and emails sent, the well rehearsed command system had kicked in and three Flying Squad cars were on route to Beckton from their base in Putney. Coming from another direction was a pair of Trojan Units; big white troop carriers crewed by cops armed to the teeth with the latest Heckler and Koch hardware. For the time being, the Flying Squad had primacy; it was their job to take control of the situation. Trojan was to be nearby and on standby, for when the shit hit the fan.

Kribz could only imagine the chain of command he'd sparked off, but his imagination was insightful: he'd been on the receiving end of a good few police operations during his short career and his awareness, enhanced by countless hours of Netflix action and CGI game interaction, informed him that if he didn't make some sort of decision pretty soon the unfolding drama would get messy.

The Albion was roaring over the Paddington flyover, Rankin having worked his way up through the gears whilst wrestling with the shuddering wheel. The noise and vibration inside the cab did nothing for Kribz's concentration and added a hellish backdrop to the turmoil and stress he was grappling with. He had to keep forcing himself to think of Numbers to stay focused on the job ahead; they were on a life-saving mission, nothing less.

The travelling conditions were far worse out back under the tarp, but the noise and bone-jarring turbulence being endured by the rear passengers were helpful; created a level playing field – stopped ice from forming so there was none to break. The two Gypsy boys in the big overcoats had clambered over the tailgate while the B Boys shuffled round to make room, acknowledging the newcomers with suspicious grunts but privately glad of the extra muscle, along with whatever was under those coats.

As the Albion rumbled loudly along, Driss ventured the question: 'What's your names?' He tried to say it pleasantly, but the noise and vibration caused him to shout.

'Michael,' shouted one.

'Michael,' shouted the other.

'We're both called Michael,' they shouted, in unison.

Gillie and Shanker looked at each other. Massive lit up the gloom with his grin.

Not only did the Gypsy boys have the same name – Michael O'Donnell – they were first cousins and looked like identical twins, from their greasy black hair down to their tackety dealer boots. Their Irish accents were those of youngsters who'd had no formal schooling among the *gorga*.

'How's it goin' anyways fellas?' shouted one Michael above the din, addressing the four black guys who were now sitting on the opposite side of the lorry floor.

'We'ze good, how are you?' replied Driss, keen to be the spokesman.

'We're good an' all,' yelled the other Michael.

The B Boys were all grinning now. Massive decided to lower the tone – focus proceedings – by taking the Beretta from his pocket, purporting to check it over. The Michaels looked at the gun, and then briefly at each other. In perfect synch, they reached beneath their coats to each produce a sawn-off shotgun. The weapons were about a eighteen inches in length, their truncated stocks giving them the appearance of huge, double barrelled duelling pistols. The B Boys stopped grinning. Shanker tensed, his hand moving instinctively towards the holdall on the floor between his legs. One of the Michaels broke his gun and peered down the barrels; his cousin followed suit, showing they were ready and fully briefed.

'Don't worry about us, fellas, we're on your side, we feckin' hate feckin' Albanians,' shouted one Michael.

The other one pitched in. 'Aye, they're feckin' cunts, we'll get your man outa there, no feckin' problem.'

Then they both fished cartridges from their pockets and loaded the sawn-offs, snapping them shut, loudly and in unison, like it was a practised drill to emphasise commitment.

The B Boys just stared, to a man not sure what the fuck they'd been teamed up with.

153

'Jesus Christ, Doug, you need to switch on your phone occasionally… are you okay?'

Briggs added the question to temper what he thought might be taken as criticism: although outranking Napper, he didn't have the bottle to admonish him.

'Yeah, I'm fine, what you been after me about?'

'Your friends the Braganza Boys are this minute on their way for a shoot-out with the fucking Hellbanianz.' The expletive wasn't for effect: Briggs was stressed, unsure how the emerging conflict was going to impact on his career. He'd done everything by the book, obviously, but knew that if anything went wrong in Beckton – and the mounting shitstorm had all the ingredients of a recipe for disaster – he'd have to be pretty nifty to dodge the morning-after bullets.

Napper was in a cafe at the back of Waterloo, awaiting the arrival of a plate of liver and bacon. It was a noisy place and he had to press his phone hard to his ear. 'How d'you know this? What the fuck's 'appened?' He didn't even notice when the waitress plonked his food on the table.

Briggs got a brief shot of enjoyment from being in front for once. 'Doesn't matter right now, but I reckon you should make yourself available, mate. The Flying Squad are running the show from Putney, best you put a call into them – or I'll do it for you – let them know you know how these lunatics operate, you've seen them performing—'

There was no way the street cop was having Briggs do his bidding. 'Okay, right, text me the squadroom number, I'm on it!'

'Will do,' said Briggs. 'Call me with any news, please.' Napper grunted, ended the call and waited for the SMS message. It came within seconds and his liver and bacon got cold as he tapped in the number and waited to be patched through to the Flying Squad control car.

154

The Albion was stuck in slow traffic on the eastbound carriageway of the Euston Road when Kribz started thumbing through his call log. He'd had an idea. There was a slim chance he could do something to gain advantage, somehow tip the odds in favour of saving Numbers' skin without taking too many hits.

Mergin had spotted the black Lexus and was circling the Gemini estate hopelessly, at a total loss as to what to do next.

Then his phone buzzed. Skidding to a halt, he put his foot down into a muddy puddle. He expected the call to be from a family member, bearing warnings or reprimands, but he didn't recognise the number and felt instant excitement.

'Hello?' he squeaked.

'Is that Mergin?' asked Kribz, for once not having to shout as the Albion was idling.

'Yeah, who's this?' Mergin was pretty sure he knew the answer to his own question.

'It's Kribz. Mergin, d'you know what's 'appened?'

'Wasn't my fault Kribz, I swear, they followed me, I—'

'Okay, okay, that's fine Mergin, I believe you, bro, but we need your help—' The gang leader felt a rush of hope, but was interrupted.

'I dunno how I can help you man, it's family, innit, but that won't stop them cappin' me,' Mergin had picked up a bit of G boy lingo and was doing his best to sound appealing, because appealing was what he was doing, trying to cover his arse and hedge his bets at the same time – he knew that if Numbers got killed every black gang in London would be after the price on his head; those boys stopped fighting amongst themselves whenever some whitey got their blood boiling.

'Don't worry, Mergin, I just need you to put me in touch wid them, tha'sall. There's a woman been callin' me, but she come in on a hidden number innit an' I can't get back to her. Can you deliver a message Mergin?' Rankin was moving the old wagon up through its gears and Kribz had to raise his voice for the request, giving it an appropriate urgency.

The young Albo was up for this, seeing an opportunity to make a low risk, positive contribution. 'Yeah, sure, Kribz, I think so, I'll do my best, what do you want me to tell her?'

'Just tell her to call me man, asap, the po-po's got wind of what's 'appenin', man, we need to do this thing somewhere else!' shouted Kribz.

'Okay, I'll do—'

'Is Numbers okay?!' interrupted the stressed-out gang leader.

'Dunno.' The boy's answer was the truth. 'I ain't seen him since they took him, but he won't be havin' a good time, that's for sure, they've got him in the warehouse I think—'

'I know, an' the police are on their way now, or so I've heard, I got a tip-off.' Kribz was trying to cover his tracks: he could see Rankin giving him a sideways look. Then the lorry went into an underpass and the signal was lost.

'What's going on, son? What's this about the feckin' police!?' yelled Rankin.

Kribz reassured the old man. 'Don't worry, I'm lyin' to them, there's no fuckin' police, not what I know of anyway, I'm tryin' get onside wid them innit, or there's gonna be a fuckin' bloodbath Tom!' He was looking at Rankin and found himself unsettled by the gleam in the old Gypsy's eye and his grin of determination which was going to take a lot of wiping off.

'I thought that's what we're going for, lad, am I not right? Eh? Why d'you think we picked up the feckin' O'Donnell boys?' Rankin was looking at Kribz as he shouted, eyes not on the road.

'Watch out – fuck – eyes front bro!' The traffic had slowed up ahead of them and Rankin's excitement had distracted him. Just in time he slammed on the anchors, nearly putting Kribz through the windscreen as the old lorry went from twenty miles an hour to zero in about ten yards, ending up less than a foot behind the vehicle in front.

Immediately there was a loud thumping of protest on the rear window of the cab. Kribz twisted round to see Driss's face, wide eyed, mouthing *What the fuck?!!*

155

Napper was sat in the rear of a Flying Squad armed response

vehicle making its way steadily along the embankment south of the river towards the east. The driver and fellow back seat passenger, having grunted greetings to the new passenger, had fallen silent and the talking was being done by the cop in the front, an athletic looking detective sergeant in his mid thirties called John Sawyer. Napper had met him before, on a boring IT course at one of the Met's training establishments and knew him enough to have confidence in his abilities.

'Right, Doug, I'm told you can fill us in on a few gaps in the intel, is that right?'

Napper had mentally prepared for this and thought he knew what was required: no-nonsense risk management stuff, subject profiles, capabilities.

'I know nothing about the kidnappers that nobody else knows, 'cept that they're Albos, prob'ly Hellbanianz—'

'Yeah, we know that,' Sawyer chivvied, interrupting. 'Go on.'

'The Braganza Boys gang, if it's them we're up against, seem to 'ave joined up with another bunch called D7, and they're the ones with the firepower, and plenty of it – I've seen that first hand – put together they've got brains and muscle, and stacks of bottle, they'll go in guns blazin' and enjoy it.'

'Right.' Napper watched the back of Sawyer's head as it nodded. 'You on speaking terms with any of these nutters?'

Napper could see where this was headed for. 'Not directly, but there might be a route into them.'

'The thing is, Doug,' said Sawyer, irritation in his cockney voice, 'we've got a major problem – and don't get me wrong, it's not with you – we don't have a normal sort of victim for this kidnapping.'

The driver gave a snort of derision. 'You can fuckin' say that again!' – another cockney voice.

'Shut it, Brownie, just drive, and slow down a bit for fuck's sake, we ain't in a hurry.'

Napper was confused: the journey seemed to lack the urgency he might have expected and the Flying Squad boys were less than keen.

'Sorry, not sure what you mean,' apologised the Cornishman, trying to curtail his own accent, for fear of getting any of the usual 'carrot-cruncher' comments from these natives of London.

'What I mean, Doug, is that we've been sent on a kidnapping job and all we're heading for is a fuckin' gun battle where we're piggy in the fuckin' middle. We've got no control. Normally we have the victim on-side, that's the person who receives the ransom demand, d'you get what I mean? We need you to get alongside him, or her or them, who whoever the fuck it is. All we've got so far is a dodgy solicitor givin' us a postcode and a load of fuckin' hysterics!'

Napper got where Sawyer was coming from; it was the job of the Squad to moderate communications between the abductor and the would-be ransom payer, play for time, surround the stronghold and then hit it. This operation was going nowhere until they had the B Boys under control and compliant.

No pressure then, thought Napper. 'Well, the intel as I have it is that the Albos are holding a B Boy younger, threatening to kill him unless his mates hand over one of their members, a maniac called Shanker, and there's no way that'll fuckin' 'appen.' He paused to think and they waited. 'Let me call Briggs, see if he can get me connected, that's all I can do.'

Sawyer opened the window and lit a cigarette. The smoke blew back and hit Napper in the face. 'Best crack on then, mate, otherwise this job's goin' dahn the toilet.' He took a drag of his fag. 'You've got ten minutes mate, or I'm calling in to request Trojan units take primacy, then we pull out of the picture.'

'Good idea, sarge,' said the driver.

'Shut the fuck up,' exhaled Sawyer. Napper took out his phone and hit Briggs' name on the contact list.

156

Swan was in a quandary: she had no doubt she'd sparked off some sort of law enforcement chain reaction – even these days the police would have to do something on receipt of a tip-off about a kidnapping and imminent gun battle – and her problem was whether or not to inform Larssen who was, after all, a paying client with a strong interest in the Pope brothers' case. She made the call.

On seeing Swan's name on her phone screen, Larssen hesitated for a second. Had that fucking idiot policeman talked? Reported his misdemeanour to cover his arse, snitched on her for trying to corrupt him? These doubts had riven the Dane's thinking almost continuously since her last bout of impetuousness; acting on instinct usually paid dividends but on this occasion she was fretting that she'd gone too far.

'Hello Katrina.' She was unable to hide the trepidation in her own voice.

'Hi Freda. I'll come straight to the point - my clients are being very co-operative. They've instructed me to inform the police that one of their gang has been kidnapped and that they are, as I speak, on their way to free him.'

The lawyer paused, allowing Larssen a few seconds to absorb this, and it certainly took several very long ones.

'And have you done so?'

'Yes, about forty minutes ago. I've no choice – as a member of the legal—'

'Yes, yes, I'm aware of your duty of care rules,' said Larssen, taking control. 'Where does this put me?'

Typical, thought Swan: number one first. 'Nowhere, really. I just thought you should be aware that my clients, to whom you've become inextricably linked, seem willing to work with the police to some extent, actually almost alongside them, further mitigating any criticism you or I may face regarding the brokerage of deals.'

Larssen didn't even bother trying to pretend to understand this gobbledygook; she was too busy thinking. 'Does this latest turn of events jeopardise Rankin in any way?'

Swan thought for a second, assessing the question. 'No reason to suppose that it does. I can't see how he would be involved, unless there was something in it for him.'

The Dane was mollified. 'Okay, fine, thanks for letting me know. So long as there's no shit taking place on my land, I need the Irishman to stay squawky clean.'

'Squeaky clean,' corrected the solicitor.

'Whatever,' said the Dane, and cut the call.

157

Mergin had banged on the door of the warehouse until he'd been let in by a furious Zamir Gozit. 'What the fuck are you doing here, you little cunt?' had been the greeting.

But things had soon settled down after Mergin delivered the message to Bora.

'The only way the police could know about anything is if the blackies told them. I say we just kill the boy upstairs and be done with it – game over, we'll have had our blood then!' hissed Bora.

'No!' Zamir wasn't having it. 'That boy is not enough, he's only a piece of shit. You insult our father if you say by killing him we'll have had our blood. I need to see them all dead, all of them!'

Bora closed her eyes and nodded, frantically reconsidering, then she spoke with quiet determination. 'Right, we'll arrange for me to meet them, draw them out, but we have to assume that the police are on their way here now. We've got to get out of this place, go somewhere else, some other place—'

'Where?! What other fucking place?' shouted Zamir.

'If you kill him, they'll kill *me*.' Mergin tried to control his voice and sound mature, but it came out as a desperate plea.

Bora and Zamir broke off their heated exchange and turned to face the youngster. Ejdit and the other Ghegs were also looking at him. They were all speechless because Mergin was right, dead right. He had the floor so he seized the moment.

'It's okay for you guys, you've got protected lives, I gotta live on the streets if I want to be any use. I'm telling you, if you kill Numbers then I'll have to disappear or get capped, there's no two ways about it, Bora. I won't even be able to go to college, I won't be able to leave the house.'

Bora took a deep breath and turned away to walk across the concrete floor to the other side of the warehouse. All eyes were on her as she took out the burner phone.

Kribz's phone vibrated: withheld number – he knew it was her. 'Yeah.' He said the word flatly, and as loud as he could without shouting: the Albion was out of the underpass and roaring eastwards along the City Road.

'Fuck you,' Bora's voice was steady, almost academic, as if she was ordering a takeaway meal, 'get your black arses here or you'll never see your boy alive again, and if the police turn up it'll be the same result.'

And that was it. She turned to Mergin. 'And you stop your fucking whining. Nobody asked you to get involved in the drugs business. I did everything I could to keep you out of it.' She paused whilst pocketing the burner before adding, almost as an afterthought, 'You can go and live in Liverpool for a while, run some county lines, keep out of the way.'

Thus Mergin's concerns for his own safety were summarily shelved as a minor distraction.

Bora walked back across the floor to face Zamir. 'Right, you heard that, now we leave that boy upstairs and we get out of here.' She spoke resolutely – Zamir had no choice but to agree; he was, after all, a wanted man and had to avoid police contact at any cost.

'Where the fuck to, Bora?' Zamir was getting worried, and it was the second time in two minutes he'd asked what other venue his sister had in mind.

'Round the corner. Ejdit knows another place near here. We need to hide that fucking car and disappear – live to fight another day, Zamir, it's an English saying used by English cowards who often run away. But like I say, they live to fight another day.'

Ejdit had stepped forward, the other two Ghegs behind him. 'Yes, Zamir, come on, need to lay low, you cannot afford—'

'Yes, alright!' spat Zamir, furious that he was having to retreat. 'But tomorrow we go to the farm near the airport. I want those blackies crawling on their knees in their own blood less than twenty-four hours from now!'

Numbers was listening intently from upstairs on the mezzanine floor. He'd heard Bora speaking on the phone in English and worked out that she'd been talking to Kribz. What he'd heard had turned his stomach: the B Boys were trying to cut some sort of deal – they may not be coming – and what was this about the police? If his crew had called them then the Albos would be certain to cap him, just to make a point. You never snitch to the po-po, never, or threats get carried out.

And then he heard the warehouse door being opened; seconds later he was alone in the building.

158

Kribz had given up hope that his crazy plan would work. The Albion was in the east end of London now and the traffic on the Whitechapel Road had slowed it down to a stop-start progress through junctions and snarl-ups. The gang leader kept looking down at his phone, even though he'd turned up the ringtone volume. Surely, soon, contact would be made.

Rankin missed nothing. 'You expectin' a call, son?' he asked with a sly glance across the cab.

'Maybe. I'm hopin' we can do a deal wid' them, innit. You don't want to get shot again, do you?'

'I've no feckin' intention of getting shot, son, I'm not leaving this feckin' wagon. I'll drop you mad bastards off and that's all I'm doin'.' Rankin had obviously given this some thought and Kribz couldn't blame him for his reluctance: the old man was still limping badly and was no way fit enough for a walk-on part in a shootout.

'Don't blame you man,' he said. And then his phone rang.

'Hello, who's this?' He didn't recognise the number.

'Is that Kribz?' said a weird accent.

'Yeah, who's this?'

'My name's Doug Napper, Kribz. I'm a police officer and I have some information for you. It's urgent.'

'What information might that be?' Kribz tried to hide his relief and keep his distance.

Napper tried to keep his voice calm, businesslike. 'You've reported a kidnapping and I've been given the job of meeting you. I'm your liaison officer.'

'Why've you got to meet me? I've given you the address innit, ain't you even there yet?' Kribz was choosing his words carefully: no mention of the 'P' word.

Napper was ready for this. 'You gave us the postcode, Kribz, that just takes us to the Gemini Business Park. There's hundreds of warehouses on that place. We need you alongside us, talking to the kidnappers so they guide us in without knowing it.'

Kribz sounded like he knew the cop had a point, but he had his own agenda also. 'Okay, but this better be fast, we got less than an hour before our boy gets fuckin' whacked. Where've you got in mind?'

Flying Squad control had already sorted what they called a 'safe house', a disused office block in a place called Galleons Reach, about a mile from the Gemini Business Park.

Napper began to explain this location to Kribz, but didn't get finished.

'That's no fuckin' good, man, these dudes ain't arksin' for a ransom. Well, they are but they ain't getting' it, it's a bloodbath they'ze wantin', nuttin' less innit.'

Despite the background traffic noise at both ends of the line, Napper was pretty sure he was talking to the masked commander of the Stanwell Moor incursion. He'd thought through this probability and the consequences of the Braganza Boys recognising him and then assuming that he was hand in glove with Rankin, thereby giving the old man the unenviable title of 'snitch'. That would certainly put the cat among the pigeons and they would walk away from their deal to save his skin from the POCA action.

Oh well, shit happens. The stroke Larssen was trying to pull wasn't something he was keen to have anything to do with, but he *was* keen on continuing to have plenty more to do with Larssen. The lonely Cornishman had been relying too long on drugs and booze for gratification and the Dane had come at him out of the blue. He was honest with himself about his intentions: play her along for more carpet burns, then be ready to duck when she lashed out for payback.

He persisted professionally. 'Listen, Kribz, if you want us on side you're gonna have to play the game. Be at Galleons Reach in thirty minutes and we'll have the stronghold surrounded whilst you engage with the kidnappers.' Napper's phraseology was intended to be formal. He assumed the conversation was being recorded and had to be heard to be following procedure.

'Whad'ya mean "stronghold"? What fuckin' stronghold, man?' This wasn't for effect; the B Boy leader was genuinely confused – and getting agitated.

'That's where they're holdin' your boy, that's what we call it, the stronghold, and we need you under our control to tell you how to negotiate—'

Then Kribz had it. 'Okay, send me the address… and the co-ordinates, not just the postcode, innit. Okay, you gettin' this?'

'Okay, sendin' it now, call me on this number if anything changes.' Napper's voice went a bit shrill with sudden apprehension – there was going to be a shed load of unknowables coming his way, but – he thought it again – shit happens.

159

He wasn't the only one assessing possible repercussions. Larssen was drinking and smoking and trying to figure out why she'd had sex with a smelly policeman; it certainly wasn't physical attraction. She'd always trusted her feline instincts – they'd never failed to open new and interesting vistas – but this occasion had her thinking she'd got her wires crossed. What if Napper tried to spoil her plan by arresting her for that perverting the course of justice thing that Swan had warned about? Well, it was his word against hers and she was confident that the wad of tissue paper in her freezer would swing things her way if needed. Even in liberal Denmark cops weren't allowed to fuck witnesses and some nice DNA would scupper any denials.

But she wasn't happy; she didn't have enough control. She poured her drink down the kitchen sink and refilled the glass with water, drank it and put the kettle on. Time to think hard, and fast.

She was on her second strong coffee before the fog lifted and some clarity emerged. There was another way to make sure that old Irish Gypsy could avoid having his land – *her* land – confiscated by the police or the Crown Persecution Service or whatever it was.

Sober and invigorated by inspiration, she stripped and donned her cycling gear. A few minutes later she was on

Ladbroke Grove, thighs pumping, oxygen and adrenaline intoxicating her venomous thoughts.

160

Six miles across London, someone else was in a toxic mood. Claude Jackson had not appreciated being set up by Blake to meet the copper called Napper. In his view, lawyers were there to be instructed, paid, harried, and then put back in their box until needed again. Blake was a mischievous bastard who seemed to take delight in inventing his own ditties and making others dance to them.

So, it was with more than a little resentment that Jackson found himself dancing – metaphorically speaking of course, given his anatomical deficit – to an off-beat melody that kept encroaching on his thoughts. Did they have a point after all? Was Larssen behind the Knightsbridge attack? Nah, he very much doubted it and neither the cop nor the brief had come up with anything even remotely resembling evidence.

But he could see where they were coming from. Herein lay an opportunity for him to discredit Larssen – in itself attractive, for obvious reasons – and thereby open up a clear path to sue her for the return of his company and, by extension, the proceeds of the Stanwell Moor repossession. Two million quid would pay for his retirement with the best prosthetics thrown in.

He fished out the copy of his statement to Briggs about the fateful evening at the Knightsbridge restaurant. He snorted a line of the best Bolivian Gold, poured himself a glass of malt, propped his stump on a beanbag and started reading.

After the first half dozen sentences he was irritated by the pedestrian grammar that sullied his account of events, but forgave himself for not insisting on improvement, given his state of mind at the time of dictation. He'd signed it as being truthful which, as far as it went, it was. It was only four pages in length and, aside from a few preliminaries about the occupation of the witness and purpose of his visit to the restaurant, centred on the actual shooting, the descriptions of the assailants – ski masks, gloves and dark clothing with the odd glimpse of brown skin – and his escape in the cab to hospital. The only reason why it went to four pages was that Briggs had laboured detail. *Was it the right or left hand that held the gun? Did you see any name tags on the clothing? The skin tone around the eyes, was it dark, medium or light?* The prompting questions were, he supposed, quite reasonable.

Jackson was aware that the other diners had been approached for their own accounts and Briggs had said something to the effect that they had had nothing of any substance to add. Again, perfectly reasonable – on the face of it. On the face of it: therein lay the hazy point that Blake and Napper had been making. The police investigation had been based from the outset on the shooting being a botched robbery and, for the third time, Jackson could see no reason to criticise that perspective; he himself had formed the same conclusion.

But the emerging connections were piling up and Napper, who seemed to be some sort of rogue or corrupt officer, was on a quest for a missing link, the final piece in the jigsaw that would provide a causal connection between Larssen and the gang of thugs called the Braganza Boys.

The cocaine propelled his consciousness into a wildly elliptical orbit, its trajectory flashing past unearthly scenarios which normally would not merit even the most perfunctory consideration. But coke doesn't do merit, doesn't discriminate against the undeserving. Nor is it bothered by that sentimental concept known as the truth.

He lay back on the sofa and stretched, breathing deeply, his thoughts soaring with lacerating acerbity, examining detail with nuclear exactitude.

There had been a leakage during his meeting with Blake and Napper, a leakage which told him that they weren't telling him everything. They were holding back on him whilst asking for his help. They were prompting him to reveal something they already knew, like they needed to hear it from him as evidence from a private witness to corroborate their intelligence.

He'd seen it in the glare the cop flashed at the lawyer about halfway through the meeting. It lasted an instant and was a warning: *Don't go there, don't mention that*. The trace of a smirk on Blake's face at the time had then promptly disappeared.

Why was Napper so keen to implicate Larssen? Put her in bed with the black gang? No jury would ever believe such an outlandish assertion. He kept breathing deeply and told his brain to think more laterally.

And a few minutes later he had it – it was so simple.

The police needed a causal link between the attack on him and the attack on Rankin's property. The forensic evidence provided by the serial use of the same gun wasn't enough; they needed a motive, and the implication of Larssen would provide that, so they needed him to beef up the evidence to put Larssen in the picture!

He was on a roll, and the more he allowed his mind to wander, the better it got. He was sufficiently knowledgeable on the law to know that there were two general strands of litigation: criminal, where the state prosecuted and punished the citizen; and civil, where citizens went against each other for restitution and damages. Generally, the twain never met. But there was no law against evidence arising out of one strand being used in the other, subject to certain rules and constraints. As far as he could make out, the evidence to put Larssen in the criminal dock alongside the black gang was circumstantial at best, a vague motive and few coincidences, but not much else. What Blake and Napper were after was for him to sue Larssen in the civil courts where the standard of evidence was much lower. That way they could flush out all manner of shit about the Dane's psychopathic business practices.

He liked it and could understand why the unlikely duo had not been specific about what they wanted: it had to come from him; he had to be the instigator of the civil action, he had to be the one to call Larssen to account. Yes, it was all falling into place; he could get compensated, Napper would get his fucking criminal convictions or whatever the hell he was looking for, and Blake would earn a tidy fee out of representing him in the civil proceedings.

161

The Albion pulled into the near-empty car park of Galleons Reach. The barrier seemed to have been opened specially for the occasion, otherwise the dozens of bays would have been loaded with vehicles. The office block itself was an eighties folly that had never been used, or possibly for a short time by some now defunct telesales outfit. It was five storeys high with whitewashed windows and not a sign of life. Except for a solitary figure, hooded and wearing an army surplus anorak, standing just inside the open door, a figure which receded into the shadows on the noisy arrival of the gleaming ancient lorry.

Rankin switched off the Albion's engine and the sudden silence was deafening.

'Stay here, I won't be long. I'll call if I need you,' said Kribz, sounding anything but convincing. He opened the door and slid down onto the tarmac. As he walked around the back of the wagon Driss popped his head out through a flap in the tarpaulin.

'Wassamatter bro, why we stopped? Where the fuck is this?' Blinking and squinting, he looked all around.

'I gotta meet someone. All of you stay put, bro, this won't take long and could save Numbers without us gettin' fuckin' shot at.' Kribz spoke with the tone he used when making it clear to his younger brother that his course of action was not up for debate.

But Driss tried anyway. 'Man, we ain't got long, those fuckin' Albos mean business, innit!'

Kribz took a deep breath and showed his gritted teeth. 'My brother, I'm fuckin' telling you, stay put an' truss me.' He hissed as if struggling to keep his temper. He wasn't, of course; the demeanour was just a bit of theatre for the benefit of the other occupants of the wagon's payload area who were sure to be listening. Driss got the message and winked at his sibling. Not returning the wink, Kribz turned and started walking towards the office block.

'Wha' the feck's goin' oan?' said one of the Michaels to Driss when he ducked back in under the canopy.

'S'all unner control, man,' was the reply.

'I don't like this, bro,' moaned Shanker. 'We can't even see nuthin, could be some sorta ambush, blud.'

'Yeah, best we get fuckin' ready then,' said Massive, who then started to peel back sections of the tarp, enough to afford them at least some vision. 'Sittin' here blind is freakin' me out.'

Over a hundred metres away, at the far end of the car park, the Flying Squad officers sat watching.

'Jesus,' said Sawyer, 'there's quite a little army of them, probably tooled up to the fucking teeth.'

'Why don't we get Trojan in to deal with them? They're like sitting ducks there, it'd be a doddle,' said the driver.

'Yeah, right, and then negotiations get stopped and the hostage gets slotted. Be sensible Brownie, there's a procedure to follow.' The DS saw his driver's point, but he was used to sticking to the containment tactic, as crazy as it often seemed.

Kribz walked slowly towards the building, hands in full view. He'd left his piece in the Albion's glove compartment, knowing that Rankin wouldn't touch it. 'If this wagon gets feckin' searched that thing's got feck all to do with me,' the old man had grumbled.

There was an awkward scraping noise as the steel framed glass door was pushed open, like it hadn't been used in a very long time, and the hooded figure stepped out into the low sunshine. And then the hood came off and Kribz stopped walking. It took him a good three seconds to compute what he saw before him, and then his mind reeled: *What the fuck was going on? What sort of set-up was this?* His first reaction was to glance back at the Albion in search of signs of complicity. The sun was glancing off the wagon's windscreen in a way that blocked his vision of its driver.

He looked back at the cop who had by now produced his badge. 'You... you was at...,' was all the gang leader said before he nearly bit his own tongue off.

Napper couldn't see who was behind the wheel of the Albion. He'd never clapped eyes on the vehicle before and had no logical reason to make a connection – but black urban street gangs don't usually rock up in vintage traveller's wagons...

'Come in, Kribz, you're the victim here, remember. We need you to help with the hostage negotiation.' Having seen the consternation on the gang leader's face, the hesitancy, the looking around for an explanation, Napper felt he had the upper hand; had the guy flat-footed in no-man's land.

Kribz wasn't the only man with a reeling mind. With the sun behind him Tom Rankin had had no difficulty recognising Napper as he emerged from the office block. His first reaction was to start the Albion and go for the gate, but he had a wagon load of armed men on board which he wasn't confident of being able to jettison at short notice. Being barely able to walk, never mind run, he figured he was pretty much stuck with one big shitty situation. 'Mary mother of Jesus,' he growled through his teeth. 'What the feck have I got meself into?'

162

Jackson had gathered his thoughts, or rather the phantasmagoria of notions his turbo-charged brain had manufactured. He now imagined he was able to mentally list and categorise them into a hierarchy of probabilities and was confident that, with further 'thought', he would reach a resolution, a silver bullet which he would straddle and ride into a blissful heaven of riches and revenge.

163

Kribz immediately regretted looking around at the Albion on recognising the man in the doorway. He'd been masked up at Stanwell Moor, he'd fuck all to worry about; *stay cool,* he told himself, *you're the fucking victim*, remember.

But it was too late. Napper had seen the hesitation, the tell-tale glance round at the wagon – when you're in trouble you always turn to check for back-up, was how the copper had seen it, and he knew he had his man.

'Come in, please, follow me.' Napper's voice was steady, authoritative. The gang leader complied.

A makeshift control room had been set up in the defunct building: two laptops and a radio base, and a coffee urn with a stack of plastic cups.

'Coffee?' offered the cop.

'No. Thank you.' Kribz's head was still spinning – who the fuck *was* this freakshow?

'Okay, sit down. The number they're using has been traced to the location they've given you, but it's not exact, so we need your help—'

'But we're satisfied it's a genuine job.' The interjection came from a fat man sat at a table with one of the laptops in front of him.

'Thanks,' said Napper, not knowing the techie's name. 'This is one of our comms technicians, Mr Pope, he'll make sure we have a clear voice to the kidnappers.'

Kribz blinked. *Mr Pope* now was it, he thought, his guts churning with shock and unease.

Then they were joined by another: Detective Inspector Geraldine Lashford seemed to appear from nowhere. Dressed in what looked like some sort of uniform – black trousers tucked into black boots, black tunic and a black baseball cap with a chequered black and white band around it – she radiated a cheerful authority. She regarded Napper for a couple of seconds, rather too thoughtfully for his liking, like she was putting a face to name. Then her eyes met those of *Mr* Christopher Pope and her demeanour changed.

'Oh my God, I don't believe it... it's you,' she said coldly, the smile suddenly gone from her face.

'What the fuck,' was all Kribz could muster, glad he was seated and able to appear relaxed. Napper found himself trying to compute the ramifications of this mutual recognition, unsuccessfully.

'No introductions needed here, then,' he surmised.

'No,' confirmed Lashford, her eyes still on Kribz, a blizzard of possible connections confounding her own thought processes. She mustered some focus; 'Mr Pope and I went to school together, that's all,' – a brief pause – 'isn't that right, Chris?'

'Yeah, Gerry, that's right.'

She was keen to maintain a semblance of authority. 'Right, Chris, this is how it goes: we establish contact with the kidnappers – with your full co-operation – and then we set about achieving an outcome that will avoid violence to either the hostage or anyone else.' She paused again, both to assess his demeanour and control her boggling mind – *he'd seen her at Michael's wake, would he say anything?* She was slightly reassured by his slow, sagacious nodding; the rest of his body remained motionlessly slouched in the metal chair, arms folded across his chest. She went on; 'First question, Chris—'

'Kribz.'

'First question, Kribz,' she had also by now sat down, 'are the kidnappers personally known to you?'

'No.'

'Do you know the individual called Shanker?'

'Yes, he's sat in the wagon outside.'

Lashford was surprised. 'Were you on your way to deliver him to them, to pay the ransom?'

'No, Gerry,' Kribz sat up straight for this one. 'We wuz on our way to fuckin' shoot our way in there an' rescue our man, the one you'ze call the hostage.'

They were sat less than ten feet apart and Lashford regarded the gang leader carefully, thoughtfully. 'So why the change of heart? What made you change tactics and come over to us?'

Kribz leaned forward for emphasis. 'Cos I'm sick of all this, Gerry, I ain't seen you since school, you've obviously taken a hard route to get where you are, but mine's been harder, I'll tell you that for nuthin', an' it's kinda weird that you should be here, sort of fate innit, like evrytin's come full circle, you get my meanin'?'

Napper had perched himself on the edge of the desk and shifted uncomfortably, embarrassed to be witnessing this nonsense masquerading as a wistful exchange. These two were using the shared past as a convenient vehicle, a bed to share, so as to take the edge off things. Fair enough – if it helped oil the wheels.

'Yes, I do get your meaning.' This came out too conversationally even for her own liking so, with a sharp intake of breath, she stood, turned and issued some acronymical instructions to the comms man.

Outside, the Albion's cargo was getting restless.

'What the fuck?!' snarled Shanker, unaware that he'd just been mentioned by a police hostage negotiator. 'Who the fuck is he meetin' in there?'

Driss was likewise agitated. Massive and Gillie were exchanging worried glances and the two Michaels sat in their big Crombies like coiled springs, fingers on shotgun triggers.

Up front behind the wheel, Rankin had had enough. It had taken him a good five minutes to absorbe what he'd seen and although he couldn't work it out for sure, one thing was for certain: these black bastards weren't being straight with him.

'Feck this for a game of soldiers!' he shouted, bringing himself to his senses. He started up and revved the Albion's engine, then reached down to a lever that wasn't the gear stick. Somewhere beneath and to the rear of the cab a set of ancient but well-maintained hydraulic pipes jerked into action and two pistons beneath the payload section of the wagon moved slowly, for the first time in a long time.

The two Michaels knew about wagons and were the first to realise what was happening. 'Feck's sake,' said one to the other. 'We're gettin' feckin' dumped!'

Within seconds it was plain to all: the wagon was tipping. Driss tried to bang on the rear windscreen of the cab but it was rapidly disappearing below his reach. The rickety frame supporting the tarpaulin started to slide first, not being properly secured to the base of the truck.

'Fuckin' hell!' shouted Gillie.

'Dis some kinda set-up?!' was all Shanker could think of saying.

Massive wasn't grinning.

Thirty seconds later the rear of the Albion had reach forty-five degrees from the horizontal and Rankin stamped on the clutch and engaged first gear. The six young men, having slid up against the inside of the tailgate, were preparing to jump and when the wagon lurched forward, they had no choice. Rankin was laughing; he couldn't see enough through his wing mirrors but knew what would be happening. With the truck's rear section almost fully raised he had to drive slowly, but he wasn't about to stop; those feckers had guns and he wanted to go home – alone.

Kribz had been given a script and was going through the motions of preparing to talk to the kidnappers. He was rapidly beginning to regret his decision to follow police procedure – it was going to take too much time. Then he heard the noise of the Albion and the shouted protests out in the car park. He stood up and rushed across to a gap in the whitewash on one of the windows. Seeing what was happening, he made for the door.

'What d'you think you're doing?!' Lashford exclaimed, realising that her flimsy control of the situation had suddenly evaporated.

'Change of plan, Gerry, gotta go babes.' And Kribz marched out of the building.

The sight of his troops jumping and tumbling out of the wagon's now nearly vertical tail end made Kribz sprint, and within seconds he'd caught up with the Albion, overtaken it and was standing facing it with one hand raised like a policeman on point duty. Rankin was having none of it and swerved the chugging machine to get past. Kribz jumped onto the running board, opened the driver's door and took Rankin by the throat.

'What's your fuckin' game, you cunt?!' screamed the gang leader as the wagon stalled and halted.

Rankin sprayed spit. 'Yez talkin' to the feckin' police an' I'm not goin' to feckin' jail for yuh! Not for feckin' nuthin'!'

There then followed a ridiculous struggle during which Kribz managed to launch himself over the old Gypsy to get his hand onto the passenger side parcel shelf beneath the dashboard. Realising what was happening, Rankin tried but failed to block him and the next thing he knew was that Kribz had the barrel of his gun hard into his neck.

The old Irishman couldn't move but laughed out loud. 'Ha ha, what yah gonna do now then, tough guy? Shoot an ol' man when you're surrounded by your rozzer mates, eh?'

This was indeed a very good point, but Kribz was in no mood for logical argument. 'Right, you'ze gonna put the back of this truck down now an' then drive us to Beckton, otherwise I'm gonna say this gun wuz yours an' I took it off you.'

Rankin was still laughing, mainly because he knew Kribz couldn't see what he was looking at. Lashford and Napper had left the building and were walking cautiously towards the Albion – and Lashford had a gun in her hand.

'Do it, Tom, or the deal's fuckin' off, bro!'

It then hit Rankin that he couldn't be falling out with these guys if he wanted to keep his home and stay out of prison. The whole idea was that they would get in bed with the police and he reminded himself that he had no choice but to play along; their use of his homestead fitted in nicely with a story he could give later, if need be, about them making him drive them to the east end of London at gunpoint. 'Okay, get off me, they'll tink we're havin' a feckin' cuddle!'

Kribz chucked the gun back under the dashboard and slid backwards and out of the cab. He didn't take his eyes off Rankin as his feet hit the deck and couldn't help but smile at what he heard next: 'And I'm not your feckin' brother!'

Across the car park, about the length of a football pitch away, the Flying Squad men had been watching these recent events from their car with mounting frustration.

'If that wagon takes off I'm giving Trojan the green light. They'll take it out before it gets to Beckton and then they can hit the stronghold. I'm fucking sick of this pussyfooting about.'

'Shouldn't we have them hit now? Look at the fuckin' lucky bags those fuckers are carryin'.'

'Tooled up to the fuckin' teeth, sarge.'

'Shut the fuck up. We have to take our orders from that bitch Lashford, after she's done with her touchy-feely negotiating shit. Chain of command – we break it and we're all back in fucking uniform.'

164

Kribz was about to walk back into the building with Lashford when his phone buzzed.

'Are you coming or do we kill him? Might as well let me know, it'll save time.'

Bora didn't try to sound clever or clinical and Kribz could hear the dread in her voice, like she knew this was going to end badly whatever happened.

'Yeah, ten minutes, fifteen tops, and I'll tell you sumtin' else wot might save fuckin' time; if you harm that boy – my brother – I'll fuckin' die to kill you.'

And Kribz did sound both clever and clinical as he turned and got back into the Albion, this time through the passenger door. Rankin had lowered the back of the wagon and the boys had scrambled back on board, keen to get moving as they'd seen the squad car and figured they were under surveillance.

'C'mon Tom,' Rankin thought, 'let's go into feckin' battle, remember you don't even have to get out of this sharabang of yours!'

He gunned the big engine, crashed it into gear and let out the clutch. Feck it! he thought, nothing like some real action. I'm feckin' seventy-three, it'll do me no feckin' harm!

Lashford and Napper walked quickly back into the office building. The DI leaned over the comms man, pushing him aside, and spoke into the radio set. 'All units from Eagle Five One, victim no longer compliant, engage overt surveillance on vehicle reg number MST 511, haulage vehicle, believed now on route to vicinity of stronghold.'

Listening cars, including the Trojan units, knew this to mean that the Albion was now to be followed but not engaged until such time as its location identified that of the stronghold, and the hostage.

'You heard her, let's go. But give it some distance – we don't want those fuckers taking shots at us from the back of that fuckin' pikey wagon.' Sawyer spoke wearily as he fastened his seat belt; he'd been hoping for a tidy resolution and things now looked like they were going to be anything but. Being led into a shoot-out by one of the armed factions wasn't a scenario they covered on the hostage recovery course.

Inside the building Lashford was on the phone to her superintendent who'd heard the overt surveillance order go out. 'We've got no choice, sir. If we disrupt Pope's gang we'll lose the hostage and we can't force Pope to give us the exact stronghold location. It's like he's recruited us to help him take on the Albanians.'

The superintendent was stumped by this, his risk management algorithms in total meltdown. But he did what he could to retain control.

'Right, there's a black Lexus MPV to be found, but there's no ANPR in that general area of Beckton, just a load of industrial estates and waste disposal units. The stronghold could be anywhere, but if we locate the Lexus then—'

Lashford wanted to be encouraging but couldn't see where this was leading. 'Sir, with respect, we can't rely on the perps parking their car outside the stronghold. We have to play ball with Pope, we've no choice.'

'Okay, er, just be careful then. I want constant updates. Trojan are alongside you.' Lashford was about to reason that giving Trojan high visibility would only exacerbate the situation, but the superintendent had cut the call.

'Wait!' Kribz was looking down at his phone as he shouted this to Rankin. The Albion was about ten metres from the gates of the car park and the Irishman was eager to be back out on the open road. Gypsies didn't like being inside fences.

'Wait, stop the fuckin' wagon, Tom!' Kribz now had the phone to his ear and the exasperated Rankin throttled back and applied the brakes.

'Ah, what the feck now! Make your feckin' mind up!'

'Mergin. Yeah, I can hear you but only just bro, speak more slowly, an' louder.' Kribz's face was screwed up, trying to concentrate above the Albion's engine. 'Cut the fuckin' engine!' he yelled at Rankin, who did so promptly. He listened to Kribz's end of the conversation.

'Fuck, you sure, bro? …Okay, wait, I got an idea…. No, listen Mergin, this is what we'ze gonna do….'. Then Rankin's attention was grabbed by the sight of Lashford striding back towards the wagon; *fearsome looking bitch*, he thought, not catching the rest of Kribz's side of the conversation.

Kribz finished his call with Mergin as Lashford reached up and opened the Albion's passenger door. 'Having a touch of the seconds, Chris? Very wise, mate, because what you were thinking wouldn't be good, so come and do it my way, and that way I don't have to fucking nick you!'

She was preaching to the converted and Kribz alighted from the cab of the Albion and once again rendered himself available for deployment as 'victim communicator'.

165

Except there wasn't anyone to communicate with. The comms man reported that the location of the stronghold phone, never reliably pinpointed at the best of times, appeared to keep changing, and there seemed to be sporadic encryption going on, just to make things worse. And now there was nothing, like the device had been deactivated altogether.

His opinion was asked for. 'The only time this ever happens, guv,' he told Lashford, 'is when the 'nappers are on the move, like they're spooked or something, decided to leg it, that's all I can think of.'

Lashford and Kribz had only just walked back into the block and neither were seated. The DI looked at the gang leader. 'What d'you think's happened, Chris? Have they said anything about moving the hostage if you didn't show?'

Kribz felt lightheaded. The adrenaline pumped through his body like a natural amphetamine and he struggled to keep his thoughts focused. He saw Napper looking at him, regarding him carefully from where he stood leaning a bit too nonchalantly against the wall.

'Er, no, they never said nuthin' to me 'bout nuthin,' it was just like get to this fuckin' Gemini place and they'd direct me in—'

'Stop holdin' back on us, Pope!' Napper had walked quickly across the room and was in Kribz's face. He turned to Lashford. 'He's up to something, knows more than he's lettin' on,' then back to Kribz: 'Come on, give us the full fuckin' story or we'll have that fuckin' wagon out there turned over and you'll be responsible for everything we find in it!'

'Hey hey hey, steady on, PC Napper,' interrupted Lashford. 'You have no authority here. This is a Flying Squad operation, you're here as an advisor, nothing more—'

'Look, ma'am, I know that, but this man and his little outfit ain't here for no reason, they're not innocents and—'

'PC Napper!' Lashford had had enough. 'Go over there and sit down. I'll call you over if I need you.' The Cornishman's involvement had rattled her and she'd resolved to sideline him as much as possible; she'd deal with him on another day – if another day ever happened.

Napper did as he was told, smirking like he'd been sent to sit on the naughty step. That would do, he thought.

Kribz and Lashford pulled up seats next to the comms man; he was awaiting instructions, his two screens showing live maps with locations of Trojan and Flying Squad units dotted around the Beckton area, also awaiting instructions. All roads led to Kribz.

'Are you going to call them, Chris? What are you waiting for?' There was urgency in Lashford's voice: she was expected to be in control and wasn't living up to it.

'I'm waiting for them to call me, they said they wuz gonna lead me in—'

'Can't you call them and ask what's happening?'

Kribz thumbed his phone. The comms man interjected. 'Do it from this, please, so I can get a grip. We need to record it.'

'Yeah, come on, Chris, you have to play it our way, please,' enjoined Lashford.

Kribz ignored them, putting his own phone to his ear. 'Nah, it's gone onto voice mail—'

Then Lashford lost it, 'What the fuck are you playing at Pope!? Give that phone to him.' She tried to snatch Kribz's phone but the gang leader held it back, out of her reach. He had his eyes on the floor, determined and pensive. Napper watched from where he sat five yards away, still smirking.

'They said they'll call me. If they hear any of your fuckin' clickin' 'n' whirrin' noises they'll get spooked an' shoot our brother.' Then he looked up and straight at Lashford. 'And don't call me Pope, or I'll call you Lashford. You wuz a bitch an' a bully at school, just coz you wuz a fuckin' prefect an' up the teachers' arses!'

Napper's smirk turned into a grin; the comms man just gaped.

'Head girl, actually, and you were a little git in the second grade, bragging about being in a gang even then. Now you're a gang leader, or supposed to be, so show some leadership and be responsible—'

And then Kribz's phone buzzed.

166
At the same time, so did Napper's; it was Larssen.

She didn't mess about with preliminaries. 'I sincerely hope you have control of the situation, PC Douglas Napper.' The words were hissed.

Napper was unimpressed. He turned away to reply. 'Hello dear, no problems here, everything under control. I'll try not to be late. Okay, bye!' He cut the call – it had attracted no attention; all eyes were on Kribz who had his phone to his ear.

Then he lowered it and looked at Lashford. 'They're changin' location. We're supposed to be makin' our way over there, we can't hang about here much longer.' His tone was calm, factual.

'Jesus Christ! Give me that!' Lashford snatched Kribz's phone from him and looked at the screen – number withheld. She handed it to the comms man, expecting him to have the kit to trace incoming calls.

'That's no good, guv'nor. I need to be on it for at least thirty seconds, and this set-up only narrows down to two hundred metres.'

Kribz retrieved his phone and pocketed it.

Napper sent a text.

167

It took Mergin less than ten minutes to cycle the two miles between Gemini and Galleons Reach. With legs on fire and gasping for breath he raced into the car park, bouncing through puddles, head swivelling in search of Kribz. The gang leader saw him through the office window, stood up and made for the door.

'Where are you going? You've got to stay here!' shouted Lashford. He ignored her and stepped out to make himself visible to the young Albanian.

'Mergin!' he shouted, waving unnecessarily; the kid had seen him and dismounted, threw down his bike and walked towards him, a look of wide-eyed desperation on his young face.

'Do they know you've come here?' asked Kribz, confident no-one else could hear him; the pair had met halfway between the office block and the troop-laden Albion, a good 30 yards from each.

'No, I just went for it.' The boy was still breathless. 'Your plan better be good, Kribz, or Numbers is a gonner!'

Mergin was still looking all around the car park. He spotted the Flying Squad car, parked a hundred yards away, just inside the perimeter fence opposite the gate.

'Who's in that car?' he asked, panic in his voice.

'Po-po prob'ly, don't worry 'bout them, I've got the situation unner control innit. Come wid me.'

Kribz held the youngster's arm, firmly but gently, and walked him to the office block, talking to him, imparting instructions. Not hearing what was being said, Lashford was waiting at the door, expecting an explanation.

'This is Mergin,' said Kribz matter-of-factly as he pushed the boy past the DI and into the building.

She followed, eyes blazing. 'What the hell's going on? Who *is* this young man!?'

Kribz turned to face her, grinning and putting his arm around Mergin's shoulder.

'I've just told you, officer. This is Mergin, and he's *our* hostage.'

Lashford stared at Kribz. Mergin stared at the floor.

'So what do you hope to achieve by this Chris, and what do you expect *us* to do *now*?!' Lashford's palms were open, as was her mouth. She turned quickly back to the comms terminal and picked up a secure handset.

Kribz took out his own phone and speed-dialed Rankin. 'Bring the wagon over here, Tom, please.'

The old Gypsy was angry and suspicious. 'What the feck's goin' on? And who was that boy you've just taken in there? He looks like a feckin' Albo to me—'

'Just bring the wagon over Tom, please, you don't have to get out of the drivin' seat, just bring it over. I want my posse nearer me.'

Rankin threw down his phone and started the big engine. Driss, Massive and Shanker all exchanged glances in the back, as did the two Michaels. At least something was happening; it had been ten long minutes since they'd been unceremoniously unloaded and reloaded by the unpredictable Irishman.

'Wha' the fuck's 'appnin' now?!' Shanker exclaimed, steadying himself against Massive, who just grinned menacingly and reached for the Beretta.

'Fuck knows, bro, but I'm 'appy for some fuckin' action.'

Driss's face was up against the rear windscreen of the cab, looking at where the truck was heading. 'We're movin' towards them offices, where Kribz is,' was the news he relayed. The two Michaels pulled out their sawn-offs, synchronised, and checked they were loaded.

'Steady, boys,' cautioned Driss. 'Wait for orders, keep those things outa sight.' He was worried; the two young Gypsies were near the tailgate and would be first out if there was trouble.

Rankin let the Albion lumber forward in low gear, slowly, his eyes glued on the building. His phone, face up on the passenger seat, was still connected to Kribz. He picked it up. 'What d'you want me to do? Come through the feckin' window?'

'Bring it up to the side. I want to be able to see outa the window, make sure the back is facin' the gate.' Kribz's voice was composed; he'd donned his commander persona, the one Rankin remembered from the big shed at Stanwell Moor.

'You better know what you're feckin' doin',' he muttered.

168

'Where is that little cunt?!' screamed Zamir. The Albanians

had been busy relocating to another building fifty or sixty yards away, arguing about whether to enlist more men and what to do with their hostage, when Mergin had slipped away.

Bora was both pleased and worried. 'He's probably just gone home, scared shitless,' she said, but the doubt could be heard in her voice.

'I'll have the skin off his fucking back,' seethed Zamir as he shouldered an AR-15 assault rifle and picked up a box of ammunition with his free hand. 'Right, come on, those blackies could be here any time, we gotta be ready, for them or the fucking police. You stay with that boy upstairs,' he ordered Ejdit, 'and if I give the word, kill him.' The Gheg nodded glumly; he'd known that was coming.

Then the burner phone vibrated in Bora's breast pocket. She dropped her bag and took out the phone, her eyes widening as she looked at the screen. It was live video of Mergin, boggle-eyed with a gun in his mouth. Kribz's face came into view. 'Ones a-piece now, bitch. We got your boy, now wee'ze even. You ready for a deal?'

169

'Heyup, we're on the move,' announced Sawyer on seeing the Albion edging forward to the office block.

Brownie started the engine.

'Not so fast,' said Sawyer. 'They're not goin' nowhere, just takin' up position.' He pressed his radio button. 'Eagle to Gold, have you got sight of that wagon? It's heading for the control base.'

Lashford responded. 'Gold to Eagle, yeah, affirmative, all under control, stand by until further notice.' If there was panic in her voice, Sawyer didn't detect it. Lashford was right, in a sense: the situation was under control – but not hers.

A career of unopposed promotions – she'd played the politics with aplomb – state-of-the-art courses and sheltered assignments had seen her rise to her rank with relative ease.

Upon taking up her Flying Squad posting she'd been told it wouldn't be for long and she'd soon be away from the sharp end and back to the safety of an admin role. Hostage negotiator was a box she had to tick and, when all was said and done, it wasn't as risky as the title implied. The procedures were designed to be totally regulated; career-damaging decisions were kept to a minimum and carefully managed with several layers of accountability so the buck could always be passed. But the planners had never bargained for a scenario like this. She sat down when Kribz produced the gun, not because she wanted to – her knees gave way, as quickly as her mouth went dry.

'Don't worry, Gerry,' laughed Kribz, as he pushed Mergin gently backward onto a chair, 'it's all in the script.'

What script? thought Lashford, not at all reassured and very worried indeed.

The tubby comms man had frozen, a sheen of sweat appearing on his brow.

Napper stayed still, taking stock, his mind dancing through alternatives, possibilities. Kribz was watching him. 'Don't do anything silly, Mr Napper, come and sit down over here. If this goes wrong it'll be down to the lot of you, and if it goes right we'll all be winners.' Napper moved slowly and did as he was told, keeping his hands visible.

Holding the gun to Mergin's head – the boy looked terrified, as briefed – Kribz took out his phone again, glancing down briefly to thumb Driss's number. 'Get in here, bro, bring Massive wid you,' was all he said.

'Wha's 'appenin'?' was his brother's annoying response.

'Jus' fuckin' get in here, but don't run, walk casual or you'll spook those fedz in the car.'

Napper thought about making a lunge for Kribz, but then thought better of it: the man was clearly a nutter, holding a gun to a kid's head in front of three police officers, at least one of them armed. And Lashford knew that going for her own weapon just wasn't an option.

Driss and Massive walked into the room, quietly, unhurried, as instructed. The younger Pope's eyes widened as he took in the scene. Massive just grinned, for want of a better reaction.

'What the—?' exclaimed Driss.

'Just give some cover Massive, ev'rything's fine,' said Kribz, with his gun in Mergin's face and his eyes on the three cops.

It was then that he made the fateful transmission, sent that game-changing video to kick off a small war.

170

Exasperated by the constantly changing orders, Ejdit unfastened Numbers and dragged him down the steel stairs from the mezzanine floor. The boy hadn't understood a word of the fury that had erupted when the Albos saw what was on Bora's burner phone but feared the absolute worst and was limp with terror; this was it; the river or a quick bullet, was all he could think.

Getting bundled into the back of a big Lexus – there were now two parked outside the warehouse – didn't help at all. His hands were still tied behind his back and the cable tie was cutting into his wrists. His head pounded with stress and his guts were on fire. Then, suddenly, he was calm – *hey, death'll be better than this; just make it quick*. He actually smiled; so this was what growing up was like, becoming a man – a bit late, but at least he'd made it.

171

'How d'you think you're going to get away with this, Chris? You'll get fifteen years if you don't stop this madness!' Lashford's voice was raised, but she wasn't shouting: the truth was volume enough. She was right and Kribz knew it. He'd crossed one great big red line, but there was no going back.

'This is the only way, Gerry. Those nutters are after blood. This ain't just one of your normal hostage gigs, like "pay up and you get your man back". They'ze wantin' a fight to the death innit, all your fuckin' negotiation bullshit don't mean nuthin' to them. This is all they unnerstand!' He nodded down at Mergin, who sat staring at the gun in his face, not totally convinced he was safe.

Napper decided he'd been quiet too long. 'You're chuckin' everything away, Kribz, what about the deal you—'

The gang leader had been ready for this. 'Shut the fuck up, you weirdo cunt!' He spat it out without taking his eyes off his "hostage". 'Don't fuckin' wind me up!' This was for effect – well, sort of – he *was* wound up, but wanted to make himself look desperate. 'The deal's still on, we can take anything after this.'

Driss and Massive were still just standing there, neither having fully got to grips with events. Kribz sensed their discomfort. 'Right brothers, the Albos'll be on their way, we've got about five minutes. Gerry, start getting some firepower called up but keep them back out of sight. Massive, sit down bro, relax.'

And all the while Kribz's gun was on Mergin, he made his hand shake a little, deliberately, and put stress in his voice he didn't feel.

'What deal's this?' asked Lashford, her training kicking in as best it could; keep people talking, distracted, unfocused.

Napper stayed quiet; he'd said his bit.

'We'll talk about that later,' muttered Kribz, aware of the ploy. 'More urgent stuff to see to right now. Get on that radio and get your fuckin' armed respondin' men here, or whatever they're called. Do as I say, if this goes wrong there'll be a bullet festival, I promise you'ze.'

Lashford swivelled her chair round to face the workstation. The comms man threw a switch for her.

'All units from Gold, we've got a major redeployment…'

172

'What have you been doing, you fucking little trickster?'

Not usually bothered by this kind of question – it was one he faced often, albeit usually more politely – Blake was slightly taken aback; something told him that this time she was ahead of the game.

'Ah, good afternoon Ms Larssen, nice of you to call. I was only just thinking of you—' went the crap before the inevitable interruption.

'Stop your stupid nonsense. You've been talking to Jackson, betraying confidence against your code of conduct. What's going on!?' Her raised voice had a calming effect on the lawyer. He sat back, rearranging his desk with his feet.

'Nothing that you need to know about, Ms Larssen, as you're no longer my client. Try to keep up.' He looked at the fridge as he spoke, and then the clock: too early.

'Is *Jackson* your client?' she asked, her voice losing power.

'You'll know that's none of your business, Ms Larssen.' He paused and she fell silent. He went on. 'Suffice to say there may be some realignments in the air, consequent to certain intelligence coming my way,' Blake felt it coming, the first twinge, the slight tightening of his copious stomach, 'certain facts…' his nostrils were widening, 'liaison related, the sort of stuff that's usually quite private…' his face was reddening, 'but far be it from me—'

That had her. 'What the fuck are you talking about? Are you drunk!?'

Glad that he wasn't, Blake fought like hell for control and would have loosened his tie if he'd been wearing one. He tried to breathe deeply. 'No, Ms Larssen, I'm perfectly sober, as it happens. What concerns me is your present state of mind. You're clearly worried about something. D'you need any help?'

'Why would I need help?' She was back peddling.

'That's why you usually call, when you're angry or embarrassed.' He circled – the kill was in sight.

'I'm not embarrassed…'

'Of course not, Ms Larssen,' Blake was struggling again, fighting off images of Napper bonking this crazy bitch.

She thought of asking him why she should be embarrassed but decided that would be pushing her luck. She was still in her office and pacing about. Most of the staff – what remained of them – had left for the day.

'After all, why should you be?' teased Blake. Almost giving up the fight against the mounting tremors, he could discern the pitch of his own voice rising as his throat tightened with the effort of suppression.

'Look,' she went for it, 'I'm neither embarrassed nor concerned. I just always know when I'm being talked about and it's always bad for business. Now please advise me what you know and I'll pay you for your trouble.'

Blake's buttocks slipped down off the edge of his chair, leaving him pivoted on the small of his back, his heels on the desk preventing further subsidence. He was quivering quite violently now; this would have to end soon.

'No no no,' his voice now a falsetto, 'couldn't possibly divulge intimate details. Client confidentiality aside, it would be most vulgar to do so.' He barely got the words out when his legs gave way and his arse hit the floor. His chair scooted backwards, hitting the fridge with a bang.

Larssen's mind went crazy, trying vainly to join the dots and make sense of this madness. Blake relieved her, the impact with the floor instilling a moment of coherence. 'Put it this way, Freda (formality forgotten), I'm on friendly terms with a certain police officer. Let's leave it at that, shall we?'

The Dane gaped at her phone, holding it away from her face like it had suddenly become infected. She ended the call and left Blake to roll around on the floor of his office, holding his guts and roaring with joy. He knew he'd probably regret what he'd just done, but what the fuck; shit happens.

173

Two Trojan carriers were parked up within two hundred yards of the Gemini Business Park, well out of sight to avoid causing alarm.

They were twelve-seater personnel wagons, but only had six or seven cops in each, to make room for the hardware. The officers were accustomed to the boredom of waiting for events that, fifty percent of the time, never occurred. Some played cards, others read, one or two slept. There were ten constables, two sergeants and an inspector, all in combat gear, very fit, and heavily armed.

The inspector groaned when the order came out from Lashford. 'Fucking hell, always the same, another hour and we'd have been off.' He was in the shit again – it was his wedding anniversary. 'What the fuck am I gonna tell her this time?'

'Sounds tasty though guv, by the sound of her voice – like somethin' big's gonna go off,' said the sergeant who sat alongside him.

'Yeah, wake this lot up, they could do with some action.'

The sergeant engaged the rest of the troops on the operational channel, leaving the inspector to talk to Lashford on the encrypted Flying Squad line.

'Gold from Trojan Eight Zero, we're getting your co-ordinates fine. Do we just steam in there, or do we stay with containment?'

'Trojan Eight Zero from Gold, stay with containment for the time being, but make yourselves known. Stay back but be visible. You'll come to a fenced off car park with an old lorry in it. There's a building inside the perimeter, that's where we are. You receiving this?' There was a lot of static and Lashford wasn't sure.

'No,' interrupted Kribz, 'keep them outa sight, Gerry, or those Hellbanianz won't come anywhere near that gate, never mind drive through it. Get them into the car park, then you can be as visible as you fuckin' like!'

Lashford glared at Kribz, like they were back at school and she as Head girl was taking shit from a junior – but she knew he was right, and turned back to the radio. 'Correction, Trojan Eight Zero from Gold, stay out of the three hundred metre perimeter zone until further notice. We want them to come all the way to us, then we'll hand over to you when they're inside the fenced area.'

'All received, Gold, you're loud and clear,' assured the Trojan inspector.

Lashford went on. 'We've got a hostage exchange unfolding between two armed gangs. The group in your current area should be moving now. If you see them don't engage, let them come. Have you got that?'

'Yes, got that. What's happening after the exchange? Are we just letting them all go, guns and all?' The inspector was having problems with the aftermath plan.

'Await further orders on that one, Gold out.' And that was all Lashford could cope with for the time being. She looked around at the absurd situation: an operational control room with a hostage held at gunpoint in it. She swung round to face Kribz. 'Is this going in accordance with your plan, Mr Pope?' She was pleased with the hint of sarcasm she managed to inject, noting that at least her voice was steady, belying the turmoil she felt, the possible outcomes that took turns to scream within her, not least the hideous scenario that she, as police Gold control, was handing over law enforcement supremacy to an armed criminal gang – career-damaging stuff in the extreme.

Kribz jerked his head at Massive, who obediently stepped forward. 'Keep watch over him, free me up a bit bro,' he said, quietly, nodding at Mergin who sat back straight, hands on knees. Massive took out the Beretta – Linked Series 5 – and made a show of checking the magazine. Kribz kept his gun in his hand, gesticulating with it as he spoke.

'Right,' he announced with obvious reference to Massive. 'This man won't worry about killing that boy if he has to. Don't make any mistake, we're all fucked now and we knows it. All we can hope for is that this goes off without bloodshed, and that's what'll happen if we're left alone to deal with it, but you'ze lot interfere you'll 'ave blood on your hands too.' He addressed both Lashford and Napper as he said this; the comms man was irrelevant and just sat there sweating profusely.

'Gold from Eagle One, are you receiving me?' An authoritative male voice boomed over the central channel.

'I need to get that,' said Lashford to Kribz, like she was asking permission. The gang leader nodded.

'Eagle One from Gold, yes, I'm receiving you, we've got a major situation here—'

'I gathered that much,' responded the voice of the Flying Squad commander. 'Are you able to talk freely?'

'Negative, I'm—'

But Kribz interrupted. 'Yes you are! Talk real freely, Gerry, it don't fuckin' worry me, no secrets!' He walked up to where she sat, glaring at her.

'As you can hear sir, we're not quite in total control,' said Lashford loudly so the microphone on the desk could pick up. She held eye contact with Kribz, feeling reassured by her near absence of fear.

'Put that fuckin' phone on the floor!' shouted Driss at Napper who he'd seen texting; the Cornishman complied and Driss kicked the device away, out of reach.

The commander spoke again. 'Okay Gold, the Trojan units are in position as you've requested, ready but unengaged. Ask your hostage taker if we can send a drone over—'

'No!' shouted Kribz. 'You'll panic them, remember they've—'

'I'm not talking to you, Mr Pope, I'm talking to DI Lashford. I communicate only with *her.*' The commander's voice was firm: he was a man used to being in charge.

Kribz backed down and fell into line, despite himself. 'Tell him no, Gerry, those Albos are mad as fuck, they'll kill—'

'What?' she laughed, humourlessly. 'And you're totally sane, are you?!'

Kribz couldn't help but smile. 'Well,' he conceded, 'I suppose it don't look like it jus' now, Gerry, but at least we're reducin' the chances of getting' your buddies blown away. We'ze handlin' it, innit, you've gotta jus' give us space an' keep out the way.'

174

Bora let Zamir drive the Lexus. She gave him directions from the co-ordinates on her phone. She'd done the research and knew where they were heading; they'd be there in five minutes according to the satnav app.

Ejdit and Numbers sat in the back, the B boy less terrified now that he'd cottoned on to what was happening. He was getting exchanged for Mergin. Fuckin' hell, he thought, what a turn-around – if things went well.

Zamir kept looking in the mirror to check their other car was following – and that no-one else was on their tail. 'This could be an ambush. How can we trust these blackies?' he seethed.

'We've no choice. They've got our little brother. We've got to do the deal. If the police try to hit us we'll fight our way out. We've still got our own hostage.' She swivelled round to face Numbers. 'You're not safe yet, you little shit, so don't do anything fucking stupid, do you hear me?'

Numbers nodded frantically and, just for good measure, received a hard dig from Ejdit's elbow. 'She fucking means it. I nearly hope it goes wrong so I can kill you,' spat the Gheg.

'Shut the fuck up, you Dulles pig!' yelled Zamir, mounting the kerb to undertake a bus.

'Alright, just cool it, both of you!' said Bora, trying to control herself and everything else. 'Take the next right. Come on, move over to the centre of the fucking road, have you forgotten how to drive in this fucking country?!'

Zamir pulled hard down on the wheel and cut across oncoming traffic. Horns blared but he got the car off the main road and headed towards Galleons Reach. The backup vehicle had managed to stay behind him, full of gun-toting, coked-up Ghegs.

175

Rankin drummed his fingers on the steering wheel, still having to remind himself what he was doing there. He knew the whole thing was damned perilous; he didn't like being so far away from home, didn't really like having to trust a bunch of darkies and didn't like being responsible for the two Michaels sat in the back of his wagon; they were mere boys, probably related to him. But his instinct told him that things had to be met head-on, that to hide away in his Stanwell Moor hacienda would just delay the inevitable – these Albanian scum would come for him, and he had his missus to worry about. At least this way he was taking the fight to them, or at any rate helping to. Albanians were a bit like Gypsies, he reckoned: if you show no fear, if you come back at them, they'll most likely leave you be.

In the back of the wagon Gillie sucked his chops and shook his head. 'What the fuck is happenin' bro? We could get hit any minute, an' I hate bein' kept waitin'.'

Shanker nodded agreement but stayed silent. The pair were sat opposite each other, near the front of the payload area. The two Michaels were still at the rear near the tailgate. The tarp had become partially dislodged during the tipping incident and they had sight out of the back, across the expanse of the near deserted car park.

'Is that car still there, Michael?' asked Gillie, politely, not worrying which Michael chose to answer.

'Aye,' said one of them, 'still there, bro, but I can't see if there's anybody in it.'

Shanker laughed. 'I like the "bro" bit. Where'd you get that talk, man? You one of us or sumthin'?'

Both Michaels looked at him. He couldn't see their faces because they were silhouetted by the setting sun, and that was probably for the best.

'No,' said the other one, 'we're not the same as you, but we work with you boys a lot so we pick up some lingo. That's all, d'you hear?' A hint of a warning came through the Irish brogue: *'Don't get too familiar, we just work together. We're not friends – or brothers, to be sure.'*

'Yeah, okay bro, we get your drift, I wuz only jokin'.'

One hundred and fifty yards away the three Flying Squad men peered across the car park, watching both the building and the Albion.

'What a fuckin' crazy situation,' said Brownie. For once he wasn't told to shut the fuck up – well, not exactly. 'You can say that again,' said Sawyer, 'but don't fuckin' bother, it's obvious.'

The detective in the back seat pitched in. 'We ain't got an escape strategy, that gate where the wagon is the only way out—'

'And that's fuckin' obvious as well! For fuck's sake, what am I working with? Cut your crap, the pair of you, we do fuck all till we get orders, and even then we'll do fuck all if we risk gettin' shot. The way I'm reading this is that command's lost control. If there's a rumpus we just sit back and watch and then pick up the fuckin' pieces.'

The car fell silent.

176

Larssen was back home in her flat, pacing about, brimming with frustration and rage. Numerous scenarios flashed through her mind, the worst being that that fucking stupid policeman had turned against her, not worried about his jizz in the freezer, not worried about the money she could give him... Jesus, what a mess! If he disrupted the deal she had with the Pope brothers – or at least with their solicitor – she could forget Stanwell Moor and the £2m deal, it would be gone, out of fucking sight!

At that moment there was nothing further from Napper's mind. He sat quite relaxed, though, stretched back in the office chair where he'd been told to sit, his legs crossed and extended, his hands clasped behind his head, like he was watching the telly, or had a front seat at Lords. He knew the DI couldn't take any chances, had to let Kribz keep control; the situation was very volatile and there was the small matter of the other Pope brother and the one he knew to be Massive, standing there armed, like they were hoping for action, and whatever else was in the back of that wagon – Napper had seen first-hand what these boys were capable of, only this time it was worse. Back in the shed at Stanwell Moor they were masked up with an exit plan. This time they had little to lose – their plan had to work or they were going away for a long time. He couldn't help but admire the audacity of it: if the hostage exchange went off without violence the Met hierarchy would no doubt report the facts to the CPS, who would then have to decide if prosecuting the Pope brothers was not altogether in the public interest, given that they, or at least Kribz, would have had probably saved the life of a hostage and averted a major gun battle. On the other hand, if it went wrong and the opposite happened, then the Braganza gang would be banged up for most of the rest of their lives. Napper reckoned it was fifty-fifty.

Kribz gazed intensely through the window; he could see the gate – it wouldn't be long now. In his right hand was his gun, in the other his phone. It buzzed.

'One minute and we'll be there. How are we going to do this?' Bora's voice rasped.

'You'll see a big car park with a high fence round it. Drive in and park up in the middle of it, away from the building and the wagon that's in there, we need to see you. Then call me back and we'll do the swap.' He awaited a response, but the line went dead. After less than two seconds the phone buzzed again. Kribz answered without looking at the screen.

'Yeah?'

'Mr Pope, it's Katrina Swan. Are you able to speak to me?'

The last thing he needed was to talk to a solicitor – not yet anyway. 'Not really, Katrina, kind of busy at the mo.' His eyes didn't leave the gate.

'So I gather. Listen, Mr Pope, I'll be brief. If you persist with what you're doing I won't be able to represent you in your dealings with Freda Larssen. If what I'm being told is correct and you're committing serious organised crime with the Stanwell Moor property owner, then your claim to sole responsibility for the cocaine found on his place won't cut any ice. They'll know he's in bed with you, so to speak, and the POCA action against him will stand.'

As preoccupied as he was, Kribz got the drift of this, and found himself regretting bringing Tom Rankin out on this gig. 'I ain't got time for this now,' was all he could think to say, 'but don't worry, there's gonna be plenty work comin' your way tomorrow, so best you get some sleep tonight.'

Napper listened to this and allowed himself a smile; the ball was rolling.

177

'There it is, over there. I don't like this, slow down.' Bora's voice was tight, controlled. Zamir shared her concern and followed instructions. She called Kribz's number. 'We're nearly there, this better not be a trick, we still have—'

But Kribz had rung off.

'Right, they're comin' in,' he announced, unnecessarily; Lashford was already giving an update.

'All units from Gold, location car park about to be entered by primary abductors. Stand by and maintain positions.'

Bora twisted round to check that their support car was behind them – it was – and then turned to Zamir. 'Come on, then, let's do this.' And the cars pulled forward, slowly covering the final fifty metres to the gate before turning into the car park.

Bora's burner buzzed again. 'Stop in the middle, between the wagon and the office building. None of you need get out of the cars.' Kribz's voice was cool, clinical. Bora had the phone on speaker and Zamir nodded acknowledgement of the instruction.

'Okay, this is simple.' Kribz was still in control. 'We send your boy out and you send our boy in, they cross halfway, our boy comes to us and your boy goes to you and then you just fuck off outa here, you gettin' this?'

'Yes, we're getting it,' said Bora, slowly and clearly, her eyes on her elder brother's face in search of tacit agreement; there was none – his jaw just tightened and his knuckles whitened on the steering wheel as he edged the Lexus forward into position. He looked in the rear view mirror; their backup car was right behind them, its four occupants looking like they'd just been sprung from a gulag; there was no way anyone would dare an ambush, not even the police.

'Fuck me,' said Sawyer as he peered through a pair of binocs. 'They've brought a fuckin' small army.'

The trio in the Flying Squad car had been listening to the updates Lashford had been permitted by Kribz to give over the operational channel, the most recent one being 'Hostage exchange imminent, all units continue to stand by.'

Rankin sat motionless in the cab of the Albion, trying to work out if he would be able to get the wagon past those two cars and out of that feckin' gate if it all kicked off. He figured if either car tried to block him, he'd just take out the fence; it didn't look that strong and his old beauty, even unladen, would pack a punch, to be sure.

Behind his left ear Gillie and Shanker stared wide-eyed at the new arrivals. 'Fuck, bro,' said Gillie. 'No way we can take that lot on, there's one fuckin' big posse there!'

'D'you's two mind feckin' tellin' us what the feck's goin' on?' shouted one of the Michaels, who were both getting seriously agitated.

Then Shanker got a call from Kribz. 'Hey bro, just sit tight, in case you ain't been watchin', we got one of their youngers in here an' we'ze swappin' him for Numbers, then the two cars should just go. So stay outa sight, you hear me?'

'Yes bro, fuckin' loud an' clear, we'ze fuckin' outgunned anyways, by the looks of things,' replied the jailbird, relieved, then announcing to Gillie and the Michaels: 'Jus' cool it now, it's gonna be okay, they'ze doin' a swap an' it'll all be done and over with.'

Over in the office block Kribz was preparing Mergin for his walk-on part. 'Right, Mergin, it's showtime, let me tie your hands. You heard what I said to your people. Just walk out there nice and slow, no runnin', an' when you pass Numbers don't speak to him, just keep your eyes forward, you got that?'

Mergin nodded and Kribz used a length of spare computer cable to tie the boy's hands so that they were in front of him and visible, before Mergin began shakily making for the door. Kribz walked close behind him and jerked his head at Massive to follow. There was a short lobby between the office entrance and the external door which gave Kribz enough cover to do what he did next. He nudged Massive, motioning for him to do something. The big negro's eyes widened, but Kribz was having no protest.

'Trus' me, it's for the best, bro,' he whispered. Massive relented and followed orders. Now out of Lashford's sight and just inside the external door, Kribz deftly dropped something into an open compartment of Mergin's little backpack which he'd been wearing throughout. If the boy noticed the additional weight on his shoulders, he didn't say anything, probably too concerned about what lay ahead. Although they were out of sight of Lashford and the comms man, the transaction wasn't missed by the forgotten Napper who still sat quietly at the rear wall of the office.

Kribz had his hand on the kid's shoulder, pushing him gently but firmly forward out of the door; the low sun was right in their eyes now, but they could see movement at the Lexus.

178

Briggs had wheeled his way into the Flying Squad ops room in Putney and was keeping up with events, or at least as much as anyone else was able to do, given Lashford's embarrassing loss of primacy in the Galleons Reach makeshift control site. He overheard the Flying Squad Commander, a man called Musker, trying to fend off some very serious phone calls, most probably from the office of the Commissioner herself at Scotland Yard, at the same time as standing almost on top of the comms staff who manned the consoles.

'Gold from Eagle One, situation update please,' demanded Musker.

'Eagle One from Gold,' responded Lashford, as professionally as her now vaporising career prospects would allow. 'All under control sir, hostage exchange about to take place. If we continue with a non-confrontational strategy we should have a peaceful outcome.'

Musker walked away from the console shaking his head and mumbling 'Yeah, right, peaceful so long as we let two bunches of armed thugs just walk away with fucking impunity!' He was a big, bluff man in his fifties, used to getting his own way. Having spent a successful career bullying his way through the ranks it rankled him that his forthcoming retirement would leave him remembered as the Flying Squad Commander who handed over control of a kidnapping operation to an urban street gang. He strode across the room and addressed a couple of uniformed superintendents, whom he outranked.

'Right, get your Trojan units ready for action. As soon as the Albanians leave that controlled zone, I want them engaged.'

The subordinate pair exchanged glances but nodded their *Yes sirs*.

Musker did a distracted lap of the room, frowning and stressed to the eyeballs; he still wasn't happy. He turned back to the control desk. 'Right, I want SO19 snipers on the roof of the nearest building outside that perimeter fence with a clear line of sight. I want it fully covered.' There was a sheen of sweat on his forehead and his words were accompanied by flecks of spittle as they left his mouth. The comms sergeant gleefully set about formulating the encrypted order to the specialist firearms unit. This was more like it.

'And,' continued Musker, 'I want drone coverage, got it?'

'Already done, sir. Skyranger unit deployed three hundred metres south of controlled zone.'

'Good, get it airborne, now.'

The comms sergeant nodded.

179

'Go on then, you've heard what's happening, take a nice

steady walk across to that building – and don't speak to Mergin.' Bora twisted round in her seat to say this.

Numbers had tears rolling down his face. He tried to open the rear passenger door with his tied hands, but it was locked.

'Let him out, Zamir,' said Bora. Her brother disengaged the locking system and Ejdit leaned across the prisoner to open the door for him.

Numbers eased himself out of the big car, his watery eyes on the office block. He could see Mergin taking his first steps out onto the tarmac; all he had to do now was walk towards and past him and into the building.

The sun in his eyes, Mergin had to squint to achieve the corresponding opposite perspective, but he could see the two vehicles and the silhouette of Numbers slowly approaching. The two youngsters did exactly as they were told, eyes glued to their respective destinations. They crossed paths in silence, without exchanging eye contact.

The grenade stunt the B Boys had pulled at Stanwell was still prominent in Albanian shared consciousness, and one of the occupants of their backup car spotted Mergin's backpack. The Gheg called Zamir. 'He's wearing a bag on his back, I think we should be careful – there might be a bomb in it.'

Zamir didn't even bother talking to the caller. He leaned out of the car window and shouted at Mergin, still 30 yards away. 'Take that bag off your back and drop it on the ground!' He shouted in English. Bora hadn't heard what the Gheg in the backup car had said but figured it out instantly.

Mergin heard the order but couldn't comply. Instead he made some shrugging motions to indicate that his tied hands made him incapable of getting the bag off his back. He kept walking towards the car.

Zamir got out of the vehicle and drew his gun. 'Stop there!' he barked, levelling his weapon at the boy's head. Mergin halted, terrified. He was streetwise enough to realise what Zamir was worried about.

'It's okay, Zammy, there's nothing in my bag, just books an' shit!' Mergin almost shrieked the plea, but he knew it wouldn't do any good – he was stuck in no-man's land.

Bora got out of the car too and, fearful of her brother's capabilities, walked round to put herself between Zamir and Mergin. 'Put the gun away, Zammy'.

Bora tapped her phone. Kribz picked up. 'What's the problem?'

'What's in the bag is the fucking problem you idiot! How can you expect us to let that boy anywhere near us when he could have a bomb on him?'

'Okay,' conceded Kribz, 'send him back and I'll take the bag off him.' Getting this done was worth the back-down, he figured.

'There's no way that's happening – you come out here and take the bag from him, or untie his hands, but if he tries to get back inside that building, we'll attack it!'

Kribz knew he had no option if this was going to work, but he also knew that it only took one of those mad Albos to lose it and he'd get whacked as a parting shot.

'Would you mind telling me what the fuck is going on?' Lashford voice was strained with exhaustion; she didn't expect an answer but just felt she had to ask anyway.

Kribz ignored her. He was staring through the glass door at the approaching Numbers, willing the boy to make the remaining thirty or so yards of his journey. He suddenly felt compelled to make a move; if he didn't the kid would take a bullet in the back. He walked out of the building with hands visible.

'Hurry up and fuckin' get inside,' he snarled at Numbers as the pair crossed. And then he was relieved to be between the kid and the Albanians, blocking their line of fire. He kept walking, but slowly, mind racing to come up with an idea; it didn't.

Mergin was stood stock still, shaking like a leaf. He tried to get his hands free, but they were tied too tightly. He tried vainly to shrug off the rucksack, tears streaming down his face.

'Don't do anything stupid,' hissed Bora to Zamir. She could see him shaking with rage, and the fact that he was a wanted murderer was foremost in her mind. 'You of all people have to get out of here.'

If this was meant to make Zamir Gozit see sense, it failed. If anything, it had the opposite effect. He just stared across the tarmac, breathing heavily through his nose, flicking the safety catch of his weapon – on and off, on and off.

'Take it easy, Zammy, listen to your sister, boss,' urged Ejdit now also out of the car, 'Let's just get the boy—'

'Stop fucking talking to me! Both of you!' snarled Zamir, watching as Kribz unfastened Mergin's hands. The boy wriggled free of the rucksack and it dropped to the ground. Kribz turned to walk back to the building.

Zamir got two shots off before his sister and Ejdit knocked him off balance, Bora managing to wrench the pistol out of his grasp. The struggle didn't stop them all looking at Kribz, forty yards away and limping; one of the bullets had found his left leg.

180

Rankin had sat in his wagon watching this drama, long since having given up trying to work out what was going on. As far as he was concerned he was just the driver of a troop carrier, and as soon as it went tits up he would be out of it, even if he had to leave the O'Donnell boys behind; they would just have to fend for themselves; he'd had enough of these feckin' shenanigans.

The old Irishman had watched as Kribz had got Mergin's hands free before turning and commencing his walk back to the building. He'd found himself holding his breath, sensing something was about to happen.

He saw Kribz fall a millisecond before the crack of Zamir Gozit's weapon reached his ears. The decision he'd made a few minutes earlier went out of the window and the Albion roared into life like an angry tiger.

Kribz was in agony – the bullet had grazed his thigh, enough to tear muscle but not cause serious injury. He twisted round as he hit the deck, in time to see Mergin sprinting for the Lexus and Zamir still pointing his gun at him; he decided to play dead.

'Fuck!' bellowed Massive from where he stood, still just inside the doorway of the building. Driss gaped out of the window, as did Lashford. The comms man blurted a situation report over the radio. 'Shot fired in car park, man down, repeat… wait… HGV approaching suspect vehicles at speed… second suspect vehicle now moving…'

Rankin didn't watch a lot of television, but he'd recently seen a program about drones and the damage they could do, especially against personnel carriers. He watched the Skyranger move across above the car park and stop, hovering at about 200 feet. He was in no doubt that it was lining up the Albion for imminent attack. He slammed on the brakes.

'Yer feckin' hoverin' bastard,' he growled, reaching behind the driver's seat and opening the door of the wagon in one coordinated movement. All the while he didn't take his eyes off the sinister little robot that hung in the air above, about 50 yards away.

Both barrels of the Purdy were loaded, but he had no spare cartridges; his aim would have to be true. Rankin didn't know that not only was the drone unarmed and harmless, it was also looking the other way. He rushed the first shot and missed the machine, but he saw how it seemed to flinch to the left due to the draft of the passing pellets, and re-aimed accordingly. The second blast did the job and the lightweight flying eye in the air, no bigger than a tonka toy with propellers, exploded into a thousand pieces. 'Take that, yer feckin' little piece 'o' shite!' roared the Irishman triumphantly, before climbing back into the cab and stowing the now redundant weapon.

Ignoring Driss's orders to stay where she was, Lashford lunged over to the console, desperate to show control. 'Eagle One from Gold, strongly urge Trojan deployment, the drone's been shot down and a gun battle is imminent.' Her eyes were out of the window and across the car park as she spoke, her voice strained and screechy.

Zamir hadn't been aware of the silent drone but had been momentarily distracted by the double blasts of Rankin's shotgun. He was about to take another shot at Kribz but Bora managed to get between him and his target and was screaming at him. 'No, Zammy, get back in the car! We gotta get out of here fast. Come on!'

Ejdit was at her side. 'Yeah, boss, come on, let's go!'

Bora had hold of Zamir's gun arm, trying to drag it down. Something made her look round to see what her brother was aiming at – his target seemed to have changed. She saw Driss, gun in hand, sprinting towards his brother.

The Ghegs in the backup car were emerging from their vehicle slowly, unsure, guns at the ready, unsure what to do.

Ever the tactician, Rankin was focused on the secondary threat, and the big old wagon was thundering towards the Albanian mobsters spilling out of the Audi. It had more than seventy yards to cover and the first volley of shots from one of the Scorpion machine pistols went high, but Rankin felt several of the bullets skid over the roof of his cab. His foot was hard down so he couldn't go faster, but he kept his head low, determined to have a big say in *whatever the feck was happening*.

The boys in the payload area had all been flung against the tailgate by the acceleration. One of the Michaels tore off the tarp and managed to stand up, steadying himself against the supporting crossbars. His cousin followed suit and both aimed their sawn-offs at the target vehicle. Another rake of Scorpion fire had them ducking and blasting one barrel each in quick succession. The range was too far for the shotguns to be lethal, but the crashing blasts spooked the Ghegs and they started to scramble back into their car. The Albion got to just thirty yards from the Audi when the Michaels emptied their second barrels, simultaneously. The pellets found their target this time and one Albo caught a swarm of lead in the back of his neck. Another, already halfway back into the car, let off a Scorpion strafe at the Albion's windscreen; it imploded and Rankin took two bullets in his shoulder. Screaming, he kept his foot hard down and the wagon hit the car broadside.

Gillie and Shanker were out of the truck and joining the re-loading Michaels, surrounding the wrecked Audi and pumping shots at the three Ghegs. The one with the Scorpion died first, shot by Shanker. The one with the neck full of shotgun pellets was screaming on the ground and the driver was unconscious over the steering wheel, the impact of the collision having knocked him out cold.

Then Gillie, Shanker and the two Michaels all turned to face the next approaching challenge; the Flying Squad car was racing across the tarmac, announcing its purpose with blaring two-tones and flashing blue sidelights.

'Steady Brownie, take it easy!' cautioned Sawyer as he clicked off his Glock's safety catch. The cop in the back seat did the same. Brownie took the car to just over fifty yards from the Audi and Sawyer turned on the PA system. 'Armed police, throw down your weapons!'

'I don't see any fuckin' guns,' snarled Shanker, raising his weapon to point it at the car, 'an' I 'ain't gettin' fuckin' nicked by no po-po cunts in a little toy motor car!'

Gillie was about to present the counter-argument that perhaps it was time to calm down a bit, that there was still time and circumstances to run some kind of 'self-defence' shit, that it had been a 'them or us' kind of thing, but he had no need.

The sound of the first Trojan wagon crashing through the peripheral chain mesh fencing a hundred yards behind them did all the talking. It was followed by a second, and then a third; they hadn't bothered with the gate: the route they'd chosen was quicker and a lot more persuasive. The three big, modified Ford Transits charged towards the Audi, fanning out expertly around it before halting and discharging over two dozen armed, black-clad cops who took cover behind their vehicles and aimed their weapons menacingly at the wide-eyed B Boys and their Irish helpers. The Trojan inspector repeated the order just given by Sawyer, only this time it was louder and a whole lot more convincing than the Flying Squad effort. The B Boys complied and the Michaels did likewise.

'Now walk away from the car, and stay away from that wagon, and stay away from each other.' The foursome did precisely that. 'Now all of you kneel down and put your hands behind your heads.' Again, speechless obedience. As he dropped his gun, Gillie could taste the prison tea.

The Trojan cops were edging forward, looking very mean with their MP5s and crouching approach. Their inspector gave a curt instruction to Sawyer over the operational channel: 'CID unit in the grey Vauxhall – vacate and stay out of the way!' Brownie was already reversing at speed.

Two officers 'helped' Rankin out of the Albion. 'I can't lift my feckin' arms up, I've been feckin' shot!' yelled the Irishman as he was manhandled onto the tarmac. The Gheg with the neck wound and the unconscious driver of the Audi were similarly dealt with, dragged into starfish positions on the ground. The dead Albanian was clearly in no such need but the Scorpion was kicked away from his body just in case.

Bora and Zamir had just frozen, as had Mergin and Ejdit in the back seat of the Lexus, which was about twenty yards from the Audi.

'Hey, you lot, do the same! Get out of the vehicle, put your guns on the ground, hands behind your heads and kneel down!' shouted a sergeant, concerned that those in and around the Lexus were looking worryingly uncooperative.

Bora looked at Zamir, reading his mind as she threw her gun down and started walking backwards, away from the car. 'Do as he says, Zammy, or they'll shoot us for sure.'

But it was all very well for Bora. She hadn't just shot a fleeing man in broad daylight, nor was she wanted for murder by the British police.

Ejdit opened the rear passenger door, threw his weapon onto the ground and got out of the car slowly, with his hands held high. Mergin emerged from the other side of vehicle, also with his hands up. The cops crept closer, peering through their gunsights at the remaining danger that was Zamir Gozit.

Driss was crouching over Kribz. 'You a'right, bro?' Kribz was twisted round in a prone position, watching the drama.

Lashford and Napper gped in silence through the window of the improvised control room, its designation now obsolete. Massive stood behind them, not knowing what the fuck to do. The comms man turned on speaker mode to provide an audible soundtrack. 'Trojan have control,' had been the most recent update.

But Trojan did not have control. Neither Bora nor Ejdit tried to stop him, both knowing it was pointless – their best and only course of action was to keep themselves and Mergin out of the way as Zamir leapt back into the driver's seat of the Lexus and started the engine. The cops crouched low, guns trained on the vehicle as it roared off across the car park, its momentum slamming the rear doors shut. Brownie was still reversing the Flying Squad Vauxhall towards the western-most periphery. It looked like Zamir was going after it so Brownie took what he judged was evasive action, yanking the car hard round so that it ended up alongside the Lexus and pointing in the same direction.

'For fuck's sake!' roared Sawyer. 'Get away from him you cunt!' Brownie put his foot down and steered the Vauxhall clear of the bandit vehicle, which then reached the perimeter and started doing a lap of the car park at breakneck speed. Zamir was making a desperate dash for the hole that the Trojan wagons had just punched through the fence.

'Right, now chase the fucker, try and stay with him but keep—'

'Alright Sawyer! I know what I'm fuckin' doin'!' Brownie shouted back for once, sick of always taking the brunt from the DS. The two tones on the Vauxhall were blaring again and they could see what the Lexus driver was heading for. They could also see a Trojan wagon tearing across the open space, its driver intent on heading off the escapee.

Zamir had the car at full throttle but calculated that he wasn't going to make the hole before the Trojan unit. He steered hard away from the periphery and pointed the roaring Lexus back towards the centre of the car park, as if aiming for the other two Trojan carriers, the Audi and the Albion, with their surrounding assortments of armed cops and incapacitated suspects.

Thinking the Lexus was about to be used as a lethal weapon, the Trojan inspector put his MP5 to his shoulder and fired three shots in quick succession at the windscreen of the car. It was still over fifty yards away but the cop was a good shot and tore off Zamir Gozit's left ear. The Gheg was instantly unconscious, his foot slipped off the accelerator and the car slewed to a halt. The inspector dispatched two of his men to attend to it and Zamir's limp body was dragged out into a puddle of water in the broken tarmac and briskly handcuffed.

The blaring of additional two-tones heralded the arrival of more police and numerous ambulances; within minutes the car park was buzzing with controlled chaos. Napper walked casually across to where Driss was attending to his bleeding brother.

'He needs to go to fuckin' 'ospital, man,' urged the younger Pope.

Napper stood looking down at them thoughtfully. 'And you two need to chuck your guns and give yourselves up,' he said, before being distracted by the sudden intervention of two paramedics who set to work on Kribz. Napper then continued walking across the tarmac towards Mergin's rucksack which lay where the boy had dropped it, for a moment attracting zero attention. Without stopping, he stooped, picked it up and looped one of the straps over his shoulder and continuing his casual walk towards the Flying Squad car. Neither Sawyer nor his two men had noticed, their attention being on the Trojan containment theatre.

'Alroight lads?' said the Cornishman chirpily, as he opened the door and slid onto the rear seat.

'Well, yeah, the circus merry-go-round is done and fuckin' dusted,' replied Sawyer. 'Is Lashford coming out of that building at all, or has she fuckin' fainted in there?'

'Not sure sarge, but somethin' needs to be done about them Braganza Boys, they're armed and had us at gunpoint, I suggest you don't just let them walk off like fuck all's happened, even though they woz the so-called victims at the start of all this.'

'I doubt if they'll do that, not with one of them obviously goin' into hospital now.' Sawyer was watching as an ambulance trundled across to where the paramedic was still tending to Kribz, with Driss standing watching like a spare prick at a wedding.

'Good point,' agreed Napper, 'specially as the one on the deck is their leader.'

Then they saw Lashford emerge from the office block with Massive right behind her.

367

'Fuck me, speak of the devil, an' who's the big spade with her? He was in the wagon, wasn't he?' said Brownie, keen to get his oar in.

'Yeah, one of the B Boys,' grinned Napper. 'Don't worry, he ain't armed.'

181

Dumbstruck was how Briggs felt in the Flying Squad control room. The blizzard of radio traffic had been thick, fast and chaotic and he'd not been alone in struggling to keep up. The bodycam footage from the Trojan units had been streamed live, but it was so voluminous and multi-sourced to be of little use unedited. Uniformed Trojan units had disrupted the war, but it would be down to CID detectives to assemble the five-hundred-piece evidential jigsaw puzzle.

As the day wore on and night fell on London, the decision makers worked late on their contingencies. Tasks were drawn up and allocated according to the inevitable damage-limitation strategy; the investigation was named Operation Convolute. To prevent it becoming a stamping ground for comedians, operational nomenclature was performed by a random name-generating computer programme, but nobody failed to notice that the machine had developed a sense of humour on this one.

For her sins, and possibly for the box-ticking purpose of giving her a chance to atone for those sins, DI Geraldine Lashford was given a job on it. Briggs was seconded as her helper.

Police eye-witness accounts, backed up by police body-worn video footage, put Gillie, Shanker and the Michaels in serious evidential shit. They couldn't quite make out whose bullet had killed the dead Gheg but, viewed as a joint enterprise, all four looked like facing murder and attempted murder charges. They'd all been armed and very ready for action, so claims of self-defence wouldn't cut any ice at all.

Segregated and locked up in separate custody facilities, they were attended upon by different teams of detectives who got '*no comment*' responses to all questions.

Kribz, Rankin, Zamir Gozit and the Gheg with the neck full of lead all took up valuable NHS private rooms at the London Hospital in Whitechapel, all guarded by equally valuable armed officers. They were all suspected organised criminals and all under investigation; high-risk detainees regardless of injuries.

A meeting of very senior officers took place at New Scotland Yard and Lashford made her way there on the underground in a trance of concentration, mentally mapping out defences to hypothetical charges of criminal negligence, misfeasance in public office, and aiding and assisting offenders; her paranoia in orbit, she battled hard to maintain emotional control. All she could do was focus on the events of that day at Galleons Reach as she'd perceived them, and the decisions she'd made to manage the blizzard of risks she'd encountered.

She alighted Westminster Station and walked to the grey building on the Thames embankment. It was after three in the afternoon. The events at Galleons Reach were now being lauded as one of the most serious major incidents to have occurred in London that year. The postmortem examination of the dead Gheg was in progress, but the biggest inquest had not yet begun. The blame game would, as always, be an exercise in damage control. Senior officers' career damage, that is, and of course reputational damage to the Metropolitan Police.

And the media were over it like a bad rash. A Sky OB rig, fitted out with the best police radio trackers, no doubt, had turned up at the scene for the aftermath; short shrift had been given. The Met Press Bureau was enduring an onslaught; word had got out about the somewhat unusual circumstances of the hostage negotiation. With so many big-mouthed coppers involved, such a leak was inevitable.

The question was: How did a one-way, run-of-the-mill hostage release negotiation descend into something out of a Mortal Kombat video game?! And Lashford didn't have anything even approaching an answer. She dabbed her pass through the electronic security gates and shuffled into one of the four lifts on the ground floor. The elevator swept her upwards and less than forty seconds later she was walking along what was known as the 'corridor of a thousand cuts' on the fourth floor of NSY.

She took a deep breath before entering the funereal atmosphere of the room. The adrenaline kicked in, enabling her to stride with apparent confidence to what she correctly assumed was her assigned seat midway along the long boardroom table; a dozen pairs of eyes pretended not to be watching her. She shuffled some papers for something to do and waited for those who'd been standing to take their seats. They were still waiting; the chair at the head of the table was still unoccupied.

No sooner had the assemblage sat down when a diminutive middle-aged woman entered and they all stood up again. The Commissioner of Police for the Metropolis wore her uniform and a very thin smile. She took her seat and invited all to do likewise.

'Well,' she sighed, 'never a dull moment, is there?'

Silence; just shaking of a few glum heads in agreement.

'Detective Inspector Lashford?' cued the country's most senior cop.

Lashford raised her arm. 'Yes, ma'am.'

'Perhaps you'd like to open. We've all read Commander Musker's report but let's have a blow-by-blow account from you, please, from the front line, so we're all on the same page.'

Lashford was fully prepared and became suddenly calm. Her report was factual, dispassionate, and confined to what she had witnessed. It did not include the irrelevance that she had gone to school with two of the main protagonists. The professionalism of her delivery satisfied the Commissioner: 'Thank you DI Lashford, I have no questions, does anyone here need to ask DI Lashford any questions?'

More silence, the solemn heads shaking again.

'Very well, this is what I propose we do.' The Commissioner then proceeded, without notes, to issue a stream of unambiguous instructions, the following of which would navigate her enormous lumbering vessel through the perilous political waters that undoubtedly lay ahead.

182

The Flying Squad car took the south-of-the-river route from Galleons Reach back to its base in Putney, dropping Napper off at Kennington nick on the way. Sawyer grunted at the Cornishman as he got out of the car. The journey had taken place in silence, the Squad cops in their own mental spaces, getting their shit together for the inevitable debriefing questions. Neither watched Napper walk unhurriedly from the vehicle to the steps of the police station, and even if they had they'd not have noticed the little rucksack under his arm.

Napper trudged up to the second floor. He had to force himself not to rush, to stick with his dopey, indolent style; the internal CCTV was probably inactive in the semi-defunct building, but you could never be sure. He opened his bashed-up locker in the PCs' changing room and stuffed Mergin's rucksack in amongst a pile of soiled uniform garments. He quietly closed the door and locked it, before walking casually out of the room, across the narrow corridor and into the cold, damp-smelling office.

As per usual, McAdam was sat at his desk. 'Fuck me, it's the Pirate of Penzance,' he mumbled, barely looking up from

371

his newspaper. Napper ignored the greeting, took a seat and started logging on at one of the ancient workstations.

'You heard what's happened?' asked McAdam, a bit more politely.

'No, oi 'aven't, wha's 'appened, then?' said Napper, tiredness exacerbating his accent.

'Those Flying Squad wankers've fucked up again, had to hand over a kidnapping job to Trojan. One of the DIs got held fuckin' hostage, you couldn't fuckin' make it up.'

Napper focused on his screen, which was still blank as the old computer struggled to power up. He decided to feign engrossment and dismissed McAdam with 'I'll 'ave a look at that in a minute, gotta input a Crimint while it's still fresh in me moind.'

Having coaxed the outdated machine into life, Napper set about deleting the reams of meaningless emails that crowded his account, until he found the ones he was looking for. It had originally been sent by the lab to Briggs, who had then forwarded it to him. It summarised the analysis of the item known as Linked Series Five, a PowerPoint attachment mapping the weapon's geographical progress with theories in accompanying narrative naming possible suspects. He gave it a quick peruse and, satisfied that his theory faced no immediate danger, moved on to checking how the Galleons Reach debacle was being spun by the Press Bureau.

"A gun battle in east London has left one man dead and four with gunshot wounds. An otherwise successful resolution to a gang-related kidnapping was marred when the warring factions exchanged shots in full view of police. Several arrests have been made. Commander Colin Musker has insisted that the situation is now under control and under full investigation. The Independent Police Complaints Commission has been consulted."

Par for the course, thought Napper, wondering what passed for something being under control. He fished out his tobacco and started rolling a cigarette. His arm still hurt from the Stanwell Moor injury, reminding him that he had an appointment with the force physiotherapist the next day. He found it odd that there was nothing in his inbox inviting him to a debrief, or at least some sort of consolation meeting, but the dust was still settling; the lull before the storm.

He took a stroll out into the back yard of the station and lit his fag, exhausted. Looking around at the decommissioned police vehicles and piles of discarded office furniture, he reflected on how the Metropolitan Police seemed to be in the throes of devouring itself and shitting out its own body. He was darkly reminded of how, as a boy growing up in a Cornish farming community, he'd watched a sow eat her own piglets, whilst giving birth to them. He remembered thinking that she had either not been properly fed or had gone stark staring mad. Having to work hard to make the analogy fit, the nicotine hit helped him come up with the theory that, to survive this latest drama, the Met would feed on its own little ones.

He flicked his fag onto a rain-soaked stack of obsolete computer carcasses, yawned, and smiled. Whatever happened next, he was going to be one step ahead.

Part Four:

Broth

183

Kribz writhed on the sweaty polythene mattress cover. The painful bruising caused by the bullet wound to his thigh had spread throughout his entire leg and buttock. 'Jeezus lady, those paracetamols ain't hittin' the spot. Got anything stronger?'

It was 2.30 a.m. and the diminutive Filipino nurse couldn't help having sympathy for the not unpleasant young man with a policeman at his bedside. She wheeled in a saline drip feeder – a plastic bag suspended from a stick – and plumbed it into the cannula poking out of the back of the patient's hand.

'Press that little button when the pain gets too bad, sir,' she said, smiling, then silently disappeared. Kribz reached for the button and gave it a vigorous stab with his forefinger, the exertion making him wince. In less than a minute he was floating on a feather bed of morphine. Thus relieved of the constant moaning and groaning, the cop concentrated on his paperback.

Two rooms along the corridor, Marlene Rankin, never interested in reading anything more challenging than a price tag, sat pensively at her husband's bedside. His head was turned away from her; he couldn't look her in the eye.

'I'm waiting,' she said flatly.

'What for? A grovellin' apology?' he muttered, exhausted by his now mounting injuries and the blistering volley of scorn he'd just received.

'No, Tom, more than that, I want to know why you're trying to get yourself killed, it's like you're determined!' Her voice was on the cusp between anger and frustration. 'I just don't understand it.'

The old Gypsy turned his head painfully to face his wife. 'It's all part of a plan, Marlene, you've just got to—'

'All part of a plan?! Are you a feckin' madman? Why the hell did you ever get yourself involved with this lot?'

375

He turned away again, thankful for the presence of the armed policeman in the small room – a good reason to stay silent.

Driss and Massive were being held in a Met Custody Centre in Croydon. Gillie, Shanker and the two Michaels were in a similar establishment in Stratford. A strategy had been drawn up by which they would be in police custody for 72 hours, charged with 'holding' offences such as possession of firearms and rioting, for which there was overwhelming evidence, and then remanded in custody by a magistrate over a series of video link appearances. None of them were going anywhere whilst the investigation progressed and additional charges formulated, if appropriate. Likewise with the Albanians, all of whom – except for Mergin and the dead one – had been shipped out to county police stations in Kent and Surrey, the Met having simply run out of safe space.

Checks on Zamir Gozit had revealed that he was wanted on warrant for murder. The ambulance he was in had been consequently diverted to the hospital wing of Brixton Prison.

'I hope your mothers die of fucking cancer, you British pigs!' was one of the many pleasantries dished out to paramedics, police and prison officers as they played their respective parts in his care and detention. His name was at the top of the list on the whiteboard on the wall of the makeshift major incident room at Barking Police Station. The Flying Squad had handed over the investigation to the North Area Major Investigation Team, which had hastily assembled a group of cops and analysts – a 'murder squad' - and housed them in one of the many cold offices of the partially decommissioned Victorian building in the London suburb known as Little Tirana.

The Flying Squad had been glad to get shot of the job and had sent Briggs packing back to Walworth, from where he'd been turned around on a sixpence and dispatched to Barking.

Mason had been assigned to accompany him, and she wasn't too pleased about it.

'I don't see what this has to do with us. We're Walworth officers, and how the fuck are we supposed to keep travelling back and forward to Barking every day? I live in fucking Streatham!' It was a familiar moan and Briggs could only empathise; he lived in Balham, also south of the river. Barking was ninety minutes each way for both, on a good day.

They were sat side by side on an underground train; the rattler jerked and shuddered from stop to stop as it made its unhurried way to the northeast frontier of the capital. The carriage was almost empty, but the pair still exchanged comments out of the sides of their mouths, wary of being overheard or lipread.

'Are the Braganza lot fucking suspects or victims or fucking what?' seethed Mason.

'Wish I knew,' said Briggs, his pained expression more about the woman's language than the question itself, difficult though it was. As much as he tried to pull off a bit of police vernacular occasionally, public school and uni hadn't prepared him for women who talked like fishwives.

Their journey ended and they walked out of the rail terminus. Barking High Street was, as usual, buzzing with hostility. It was a Saturday morning and the street market was preparing itself for a day of what passed for legitimate activity. Stalls hawking cheap nylon clothing and cheaper plastic toys were staffed by sullen, resentful eastern Europeans and south Asians whose idea of a good day was ripping off the public and spiting their competitors. Most of them would rather make a bent pound than an honest fiver, such was the business ethic in the lawless town.

Walking through the bitter, hateful atmosphere, the two officers kept their heads down, feeling exposed and vulnerable. Briggs took off his tie and stuffed it in his pocket. Mason kept a tight grip of her leatherette shoulder bag.

Broth

Barking Police Station was another sclerotic organ of the Met body corporate. It had been closed for two years, condemned as unfit for purpose – the listed hulk was useless as a working building, but valuable as a commodity for conversion to luxury flats. But then someone asked the planners if they knew who would want a so-called luxury flat in the middle of one of London's third world satellites. So the project was shelved and the building re-opened as another 'non-public access policing base'.

To gain access, Briggs had to make a call from the street. He and Mason then stood and waited for more than five minutes before a tired-looking PC in a dirty uniform opened the big, reinforced door and let them in, barely bothering to glance at their IDs. 'Back office on the third floor,' mumbled the dirty uniform, before disappearing off into what had once been the front office of the station, now just a tearoom strewn with old newspapers and ruined furniture.

When they walked into the incident room, Briggs and Mason both cheered up a bit. It was like a little oasis of sanity, even though it existed because of something approaching the opposite.

'Hey, the Walworth contingent, welcome aboard!' DI Geraldine Lashford had been given the role of assistant Senior Investigating Officer and was putting on a brave face, despite it having enough egg on it to make a dozen omelettes. Her grin was far too wide to be sincere as she marched across the room to greet the secondees. 'Gerry Lashford. I'm a Flying Squad DI but I'm on this because of my knowledge of the suspects.' She vigorously pumped the limp hands of Briggs and Mason, in that order.

No, you're not, thought Briggs. *You've been offloaded here so you can carry the can for the Flying Squad fuck-up.* 'Pleased to meet you, ma'am,' he said, hoping to sound enthusiastic. Mason stayed silent.

'Okay,' breezed Lashford, 'there's a briefing in half an hour. Help yourselves to tea or coffee, and we've got chocolate biscuits – but no Jaffa Cakes.' She was trying to be funny, light, as if this were just the commencement of another murder enquiry, with its usual banter about overtime, work distribution and dress code piss-takes. Murder squads were invariably hastily convened outfits, the core Major Investigation Teams being quickly augmented with the most available officers and civilian analysts, and then housed in the nearest available premises. The mood was usually buoyant with expectation and lively chatter between cops getting to know each other or catching up after lengthy postings apart. But the cloud enveloping Operation Convolute was dark and glowering. Everyone knew that, waiting in the wings, was the Independent Office for Police Conduct; its humourless staff would be setting up their own incident room in a comfortable office at New Scotland Yard. And they would have Jaffa Cakes. So, the mood at Barking had an underbelly of dread; this ooperation would end with blood on the walls and the assembling individuals were preparing to watch their backs.

The whiteboard on the wall bore only the name of Zamir Gozit, printed in black felt tip, along with the suspect's date of birth. Stuck beside it was a small mugshot dating back to a time when the man was merely a young Hellbanian, before he'd become a Shqiptare graduate, committed at least one murder and scarpered back to his homeland. There wasn't the usual accompanying spider's web of associates, no pins with coloured threads depicting links and associations, no photographs of weapons or scenes to focus the staff and keep the job in their frontal lobes. For the objectives and strategies of the operation had yet to emerge; the policy file which logged the decisions of the Senior Investigating Officer lay open on a desk at the end of the room, behind which sat a man wearing an expensive suit and a haunted expression.

379

Broth

Detective Superintendent Duncan Passey stared down at the thin manila folder and wondered where to start.

The senior command course he'd just completed at the College of Policing had not come anywhere near preparing him for this; the murder of Jakib Stellic was the easy bit and the suspect, Leroy Gillison, was in custody and would probably be charged – once the CPS got their arses into gear and made a decision. It was the maelstrom of precipitating events, surrounding circumstances and sheer volume of impending work that had Passey wishing he was elsewhere.

He opened his rough book and started making notes for the briefing he was due to deliver. That was the way to do it: start writing and something would come. Begin with lists. Victims, suspects, victim-stroke-suspects. Cops. Victim-stroke-cops. Cop-stroke-suspects. But he didn't write down the last category – couldn't bear to. Ten minutes till briefing, till all eyes would be on him. He looked along the length of the room, tried to gauge the heavy atmosphere. Just upwards of twenty staff were present, still arranging desks and plugging in terminals. He watched the two that had just entered being greeted by Lashford; the young DI was overdoing the brave face. He recognised Briggs from some course or seminar on the Proceeds of Crime Act, remembered thinking that the young detective was probably a bit like himself – a career cop, always on the lookout for opportunities. And now here they were, standing on the same wobbly tightrope.

He watched as Lashford, having welcomed the newcomers, set about supervising the whiteboard, pointing to where she wanted to add the pictures of subjects with the nicknames 'Gillie' and 'Shanker' positioned together but significantly distant from that of Gozit. Likewise with the two boys who'd given the surname O'Donnell: they were to be together in their own corner of the board. 'Massive' and Rankin were destined to be floaters, alone and occupying random positions, likewise with the two hostages with the names 'Mergin' and 'Numbers'. Then Lashford appeared to make a show of aplomb, theatrically gesturing to the top of the board where she wanted the Pope brothers stuck. 'Kribz' and 'Driss' were up there, alongside Zamir Gozit. *What utter nonsense,* thought Passey. He'd worked hard all night to make sense of the incoming deluge of hastily written notes, intel reports and body worn video summaries and, from where he sat, it looked like Lashford had been digesting a different meal altogether – and she'd been at the high table!

Passey stood, shoved his hands in his pockets and sauntered as casually as he could over to where Lashford was posturing. 'Nice work, Gerry, picture taking shape I see,' said the young Super, smiling pleasantly.

Lashford wasn't stupid and knew immediately that this was leading to something. 'Thank you, sir,' she said, doubtfully.

'Got a minute?' asked Passey, his eyes still on the whiteboard, the tone of the question slightly lowered.

'Sure boss, d'you want to go somewhere?' Lashford sensed embarrassment in the offing, so the question was rhetorical.

'Yeah, let's take a walk and have a pre-briefing briefing.' Passey was already making for the door. They got out of the office and as far as the dirty stairwell before the Super stopped, satisfied they were out of earshot.

'Right, Gerry, let's start again. This isn't a standard murder enquiry, it's a postmortem examination masquerading as a murder enquiry, do you—'

The DI always took comfort from the fact that people couldn't see her blush and she interrupted with practised confidence. 'Of course I see that, boss, and, with respect, you should see that I have to go through the motions—'

'And it's too obvious that that's what you're doing. You allowed the kidnap victim to take control, you witnessed the shootings. You shouldn't even be on the job – but I know why you are and you'll know if you stop to think about it. So please just stick to the admin role and stay off the detective work. I don't want to show you up, Gerry, but you need to take a back seat—'

'But I—' She thought she knew what was coming.

'But nothing. Never stop assuming for one second that we're being watched very closely, and clear that whiteboard before some clown snaps it with an iPhone and leaks it to the press.'

She hadn't thought that was coming.

He went on. 'From now on just keep your head down, read the incoming material from the witnesses and detainees – if any of them choose to speak – and don't make notes that can be later disclosed. Just keep a watching brief and keep me informed, constantly.'

He paused and she waited, watching his jaw flex as he thought on his feet. 'That's all. Come on, briefing time.' He turned on his heel and walked briskly back along the corridor and into the big room. She followed, again feeling thankful she blushed invisibly.

Passey called the office to order, introduced himself and did the usual trotting out of the MIT procedures which everybody knew anyway. He came across as capable and confident, polite and unemotional. There was not a trace of familiarity, no cosy jokes or swearwords, nothing to tempt interpretation. Duncan Passey was a consummate politician.

184

Bora Gozit rolled over and spilled her guts. Having been reassured that Mergin was safely in protective custody, she decided she had nothing to worry about. Zamir had been the cause of all this and there was no way she was taking any of the blame. She adopted the stance that she had been acting under her elder brother's murderous influence and had gone along with Numbers' kidnapping whilst in fear for own life.

She was given the benefit of the doubt and the assignation of 'witness under investigation'. She'd abandoned loyalty to Zamir, disassociating herself from him at the same time she'd disassociated herself from the loaded 9mm Glock she'd thrown on the back seat of the Lexus just before being arrested. Her fingerprints were explained by her claim that she'd been coerced into carrying it.

She was an NHS nurse, had no previous convictions, had just lost her father to a murderer who had not yet been caught and could now also be classified as a kidnapping victim who had watched whilst the Metropolitan Police appeared to acquiesce in the abduction of her teenage brother. To treat Bora Gozit as a suspect and hold her in custody would not be in the best interests of the investigation.

She was interviewed under caution in the presence of a solicitor, gave a good account of herself and was released with Mergin on the undertaking that she would make herself available to due course to provide a detailed witness statement. She politely assured the officers that their protective support was not needed unless she was called upon to give evidence against Zamir or any of his friends, warning them chillingly that if she did so the necessary protection would be beyond the resources of the Metropolitan Police.

The Michaels were charged with GBH; Gillie and Shanker were charged with murder. They were all remanded into the custody of HMP Belmarsh in south east London

Ejdit and the other Ghegs, including the one with the neck full of shotgun pellets, were charged with a medley of firearm-related offences and remanded in custody also. Two of them, including the dead one, were already wanted for historical offences and – apart from the dead one – faced deportation.

Kribz, Driss and Massive were being detained on suspicion of firearms possession and unlawful imprisonment, but had not been charged. It was the elder Pope who was causing the splitting headaches at New Scotland Yard. Passey had made the policy decision to delay charging him for as long as possible – and not at all if the CPS agreed - given his original occupancy of the role of kidnapping 'victim', along with that of arguably making some attempt to assist police resolve the impossible situation at Galleons Reach. Following his discharge from hospital, he would be held at an 'unspecified police location' pending a decision from the CPS as to what the hell to do with him.

185

Katrina Swan had spent most of the morning on a train from Exeter to London. She'd had three days of unmitigated hell with her parents and was relieved to be returning to work for a well-earned rest. Her father's Alzheimer's was worsening exponentially, and her mother was exhausted. Katrina had salved her conscience by providing some respite: cleaning, cooking and attending to the pile of urgent correspondence that teetered on the old man's chaotic desk in one of the damp spare rooms of the farmhouse. The noose was tightening, and the only options were either to sell up totally or negotiate a reversion of the equity on the farm by which her parents would lose freehold ownership but at least keep their home for the duration of the life of the last survivor. The second plan had its obvious merits but given the old man's rate of deterioration would leave Mary Swan with many lonely years trying vainly to run a failing business.

With the nightmare 150 miles behind her, Swan felt herself relaxing as the train pulled into Waterloo. She took out her phone and thumbed her emails, diary, texts, voicemails. Emails: nothing that couldn't wait; diary: no major changes; texts: mostly garbage; voicemail: only one, but it wiped her mind clean of her father's farm. She had to listen to it three times, frowning as she concentrated on the rambling message. Kribz's phone had been confiscated for police analysis and the message was from the withheld number of a police issue device. But she recognised the voice, and that her client was drugged, or in shock, or ill.

She called her office and told her secretary she was on her way directly to Charing Cross Police Station. Having emerged from Waterloo she lugged her overnight bag over Hungerford footbridge and across the Strand. The public waiting area of the huge central London police station was busy with tourists asking directions, people reporting thefts, and others complaining about anything they could think of. Swan had to wait over a quarter of an hour to get to the head of the queue.

'I've come to see my client, Mr Christopher Pope. You have him in custody and I'm his solicitor.'

The civilian desk clerk consulted a terminal and frowned. 'We don't have anyone by that name in custody at this present time.' The clipped Polish accent aggravated the smug tone.

'But I have a message from him, instructing me to attend here. Could he have been transferred to another station?'

Swan wasn't familiar with police bureaucracy and naively expected enthusiastic assistance. The clerk didn't even put on a show of concern. 'Nothing at this present time, madam.' Her voice trailed off as her eyes refocused on the queue behind the lawyer.

Swan hauled her bag back out onto the street and tried Kribz's number – unobtainable. Then she tried Driss's – same. She hailed a cab and went back south of the river to her office in Vauxhall, her mind already on the stack of work that awaited, regretting the forty billable minutes she'd just wasted.

186

There are over forty cells under Charing Cross Police Station, serviced by a full-time, 24/7 staff of detention officers. Driss occupied a cell in the sub-basement. Kribz, having just been transferred there from hospital despite the agony he was in, was on the floor above, nearer to the medical room with its team of custody nurses. His leg was heavily bandaged and the pain it gave him was only just slightly dulled by co-codamol tablets. The hospital staff had removed his canular prior to his transfer, so there was no more morphine for him to float on. Dressed in a white paper boiler suit, he lay on the hard mattress with his hands clasped behind his head, the remains of a microwaved meal on the floor beside the bench-bed. Through the waves of pain he sluggishly tried to assemble the shards of memory that floated about randomly in his head. He speculated on how long it would take Swan to visit him, factoring in their incommunicado status and the possibility that the lawyer was probably not up to the job any longer, given the slight upturn in complications. He thought of Driss whom he'd seen being taken away from the scene; separation from his brother was always painful.

187

The remoteness of the Galleons Reach car park, the impending tsunami of internal scrutiny and the coincidence of an Extinction Rebellion demo causing havoc on the same day all combined to make efforts to keep the media at bay remarkably successful. There was the usual dribble of leaks, of course, but press coverage was brief and anodyne, with no mention of the fatality or injuries.

Consequently, Napper was thoroughly enjoying the experience of relating the incident, or his version of it, to an astonished Freda Larssen. She sat on the edge of the white leather sofa, elbows on knees, legs akimbo, mouth agape. The cigarette in the ashtray burned unattended.

'Please tell me you are fucking joking, Police Constable Napper.'

'I would if I was, but I'm not. Rankin drove them there in his lorry. He was in it with them up to his neck, shot down a police drone and took two bullets for his trouble.'

'Has he been arrested?'

'I don't think so, not yet, he's probably still in hospital, but he'll be questioned, that's for sure, and I 'aven't a clue what he'll say.'

The Dane slid herself back into the sofa and ran her hands through her short hair. The plan to disassociate Rankin from the Braganza gang, and thereby defend him against the POCA proceedings, was rapidly turning to *rottelort*, and Larssen could see a lot of money slipping from her grasp.

She let her hands drop to her sides and Napper noticed her face take on a pinched look: unattractive, bitter. *What a horrible fucking woman,* he thought. Despite her hard-earned muscularity, her body seemed to give up, sagging in the sudden absence of the arrogance and determination that had just deserted its owner.

Then he remembered he was there to do a job.

'Don't let it bother you too much, Freda. You've still got me and we've still got a deal – 'aven't we?' He made it sound like he cared about her and their little arrangement.

'Yes, I suppose so, if you think it'll help, but I'm not sure how. If Rankin is proved to be involved with the black boys then the police will seize everything he owns, especially fucking now!' and she was suddenly on her feet, reinflated with rage. 'Right, I need you to sort this out. Get that fucking solicitor, what's her name, Katrina Swallow—'

'Swan.'

'Whatever, get her to—'

'I don't have any influence over her. She has to take instructions from her clients, I can't interfere—'

'You said you would—'

'I said I would keep you informed of stuff, an' tha's what I'm doin', I'm takin' a big enough chance jus' bein' ere!'

Napper knew that his west country accent became broader when he got agitated, and he knew how to affect this when the agitation was fake. He looked her up and down as he spoke, her frame once again lithesome. She got the wrong end of the stick. 'Don't even think about it,' she sneered down her flared nostrils at him.

'All oim thinkin' about is how oim goin' to get things back on track for you, tha's all.' The cop stood up wearily and started walking towards the door of the living room.

'Where are you going? Don't think—'

'I'm goin' to the fuckin' toilet, is tha' alroit?'

'Yes, but don't piss on the seat. And don't take too long, I need a shower.'

The last sentence was music to Napper's ears as he unzipped his fly and took careful aim.

188

Jackson struggled up the narrow wooden staircase that led to the office of Blake and Co, Solicitors and Commissioners for Oaths. Office singular, because the tatty door bearing the title led into only one room which, although reasonably sizeable, only just about had the capacity to accommodate the tubby lawyer's utter incapacity to achieve anything like orderly administration. And it smelled – stank, even.

Upon knocking and hearing a loud 'Come!' the visitor pushed open the door and put his prosthetic leg first. He blinked two or three times to take in the squalor, before focussing on the grinning bulk that lay almost horizontally behind a small mountain of papers, takeaway food cartons and tattered books; it had to be assumed there was a desk under there somewhere.

'Welcome to my centre of operations, Mr Jackson,' greeted Blake, making no attempt to either rise or hide the pleasure he took from his visitor's dismay. 'Don't mind the mess. I operate the deep litter system. When it gets to the top of the pile I shovel it around and maybe even do a bit.' He chortled the quip; it came out practiced, a bit hackneyed.

'Chuck that shit on the floor and sit yourself down,' he continued, referring to the stack of files occupying the chair on the other side of the small mountain. Jackson was using a walking stick, an elegant accessory from Swaine & Adeney in Piccadilly. He leaned it against the wall, but it fell as if fainting at the clammy stench of stale beer and body odour. He picked up the stack of files and did his best to place, rather than 'chuck', them onto the stained carpet, but his inability to stoop necessitated a compromise.

'Anyway, thanks for popping in. You'll understand that as a one-man band I can't do home visits, Claude.' Blake was suddenly more serious and hauled himself into a sitting position as he spoke, his voice momentarily peaking to falsetto with the exertion of movement. Jackson had not said a word, having yet to summon the capacity to do anything but acclimatise himself to the stifling environment. There was no offer of tea or coffee.

'Right, heard what's happened?' There was a twinkle in Blake's eye.

'No, pray tell.' Jackson braced himself for the inevitable cliché-laced monologue. It didn't come. He was treated instead to a detailed account, gleaned and recalled in totality from numerous scanty snatches of media coverage of the events at Galleons Reach – and of course a one-way telephone conversation with a certain member of London's finest. The expert narration was punctuated with informed opinion and educated guesswork, and the cloying atmosphere of the seedy little room rapidly evaporated.

'Fuck me, where did you get this from?' Jackson was blinking again; he'd perused the news feeds that morning but the desultory reportage had done little to enlighten him.

'It's called joining the dots, Claude, and I've made a couple of calls. You develop a nose for stuff after twenty years being a frustrated detective. I've got antennae that twitch, know what I mean?'

'So where does this put me?'

'That all depends on a lot of things. Depends on who's all been arrested and what the charges are, but if what I'm told is correct and old Tom Rankin was involved, it puts you pretty much out of the picture as far as getting your company back's concerned. The Gypsy'll find it hard to make out he's peripheral to the Braganza men or boys or whatever they fucking call themselves and the POCA action'll stick like shit to a blanket. He'll be marked up as a serious organised criminal and the Crown'll swipe the Stanwell Moor place lock stock and fucking barrel.' Blake's delivery was thoughtful, serious. Jackson waited for more, expecting some sort of solution perhaps. None came.

'Have you dragged me over here just to tell me this? You could have done it over the phone.'

'True, very true, but I want to know if you've given any thought to what we discussed over that nice bit of grub in the Hippodrome. And now this has happened I want to know if it's going to concentrate your mind a bit more, instead of you just lolling around feeling sorry for yourself and hoping for something to drop in your lap.'

And then Jackson got it: Blake wanted him to come up with the silver bullet that would put Larssen in the frame for conniving with the black gang. There was a pause before Blake added, 'Come on son, you need to think of something before it all slips away from you.'

'Have you been talking to your pet policeman lately?' asked Jackson, keen to deflect the pressure from himself.

'No,' lied the brief, 'and it's got fuck all to do with you if I have. Suffice to say we're waiting for you. We have to. Whatever I do has to be on your instructions. You've got to give me something to work with mate.'

'Okay, let me think about it. I've got a man back at the firm with his ear to the ground, I'll give him a call later.'

'Good, that's more like it, but… hey, d'you know what?' Blake looked theatrically at his watch. 'Somebody's moved the fucking yardarm.' He sniggered, leaning backwards to reach for the door of the fridge.

Jackson sighed and shook his head; it was barely 11 a.m.

'No Stuart, it's too early, and—'

A can of Kronenbourg hit him squarely in the chest.

'Shut the fuck up Jacko, we'll have a couple here then I'll buy you lunch. I need to show some client care hospitality on the accounts.' Blake tugged the ring-pull and beer froth spurted onto his belly. 'Fuck.'

189

As the day wore on Kribz began to think that Swan hadn't received his voicemail, or that if she had she'd chosen to ignore it. The cops in whose care he languished had all the information about his and Driss's forthcoming appointment with Briggs and Mason at Walworth, but that was four days away and they seemed in no rush to start arranging the meeting.

'Has my solicitor been in touch yet?'

'Not that I know of, mate,' replied the sergeant standing over Kribz with a clipboard, making notes as the custody nurse changed the several layers of dressing around his leg. 'Do you want to make another call?'

'Yeah, I'm worried, innit, she should've come by now.'

The sergeant scribbled some more then, tapping his biro on the clipboard to punctuate a decision, slouched off to fetch a Met issue mobile.

'By the way,' mentioned the sergeant as he handed over the device, you're here under a false name we've given you: Lander, Stephen Lander.'

'You're fuckin' jokin', man, why didn't you tell me this before?!' The protest was reasonable; Kribz now knew a hazard of incognito detention: no fucker could find you, even when you wanted them to.

The detainee had to Google Swan's number again, before hitting the hyperlink. The lawyer picked up almost immediately.

'Katrina Swan.'

Kribz made it quick, succinct. 'Katrina, it's Chris Pope, I'm being held at Charing Cross Police Station under the name of Stephen Lander. They don't want anybody to know I'm here is why, innit.'

'That would explain why they didn't know you at the reception desk when I attended this morning.' She got this in quickly to let him know she was on-side. 'What are they holding you for?'

'Ain't you heard? There was a shoot-up over the east end innit, I took a cap in my fuckin' leg. Sorry to swear, I was only tryin' to help them sort it out—'

'What, the police shot you?'

'No, it was…'

The sergeant tapped with his biro again, this time on his watch, causing Kribz to trail off and then resume. '…Look, I need you to come, I ain't seen Driss and—'

'Who? Sorry, it's a bad line—'

'My bruv, Derek. Look, can you get here, Katrina? They'll have to let me see you—'

'Okay, I'll be there in an hour.'

'Fine, can you bring some—' Kribz had been going to ask her to bring some fags, but the lawyer had cut the call.

Alone in her small, brightly lit office, Swan gazed out of the window for a long twenty seconds, mentally reconnecting the sequence of events preceding her involvement with the Popes. The logic still stacked up.

190

Briggs and Mason were actioned to visit Rankin, and the duo

made the shortish journey from Barking to Whitechapel in a tatty murder squad pool car. They'd ID'd themselves to the armed cop who sat outside in the corridor and were now at the Gypsy's bedside waiting for a nurse to finish attending to his medication and the sticking plaster over his cannula that had become loose. Briggs couldn't help thinking she was making a meal of it, just because they were there. Rankin was thinking she could take as long as she liked, not looking forward to what he thought would was going to be some *feckin' awkward questions.*

'Are you comfortable now, Tom?' asked Briggs, once the nurse had finally disappeared.

'Yes, son. Come on then, crack on, but I'm warning the pair of you, I'm feckin' knackered, so don't expect too much in the way of sensibleness,' was all the old man could think of saying.

'Don't worry,' chipped in Mason. 'This is just a chat. If it gets to be a bit much just say so and we'll leave it till tomorrow.' It was gone five and she was keen to make tracks.

'But you'll understand that we need to get your side of the story. This won't be used against you. You're not under caution and it'll not take too long.' Briggs got this in quickly, concerned that the patient would snap up his colleague's offer too readily.

He needn't have worried. 'Like I just said, crack on.' Rankin hadn't given either officer more than a second's eye contact; his head was twisted round, and he seemed to be focused on some imaginary dot on the wall.

'Okay, let's cut to the chase. What were you doing at Galleons Reach the day before yesterday, Tom?' Briggs' voice was flat, monotonous; he'd mentally prepared the opening question. Mason's pen was poised.

'What, apart from getting shot?'

'Yes, Tom. Before you got shot, what led to you being there in your wagon?'

'That's an interesting question, son.' The old man was still staring at the wall. 'I suppose you could put it down to me havin' the fighting Irish in me, only this time I might have taken it a bit far.' His voice weakened as the image of Marlene's face, etched with exhaustion and worry, invaded his mind.

'Carry on,' said Briggs when the pause that followed passed the ten second mark.

'Eh?'

'Carry on Tom, just give us a picture of what you were thinking when you decided to go there.'

Mason couldn't help being a little impressed by Briggs tack: some sort of open-ended approach, probably learned on a course.

'I was prob'ly thinking if I didn't do something to help the blackies fight the Albanians then the Albanians would be comin' after me – and they still feckin' might do.'

'What d'you mean "probably", Tom?'

'What I say, probably, ev'rything's only probably, son, nothin's definite, it's all about takin' risks and cuttin' odds – you should know that in your business.' Rankin was still looking away, up at the wall.

'Do you think the Albanians wanted to get back at you anyway, before Galleons Reach?'

'Quite feckin' possibly. The shenanigans back at my place wouldn't have helped. They're prob'ly thinkin' I set them up, and then Kemal Gozit gets killed. Those Albos don't forget that sort of thing, so I suppose I was takin' the war to them before they came to me—'

'And did you set up the attack at your place?'

'You've already asked me that and the answer's still the same – no.' The old man turned his head painfully and faced Briggs, looking him square in the eye.

'Did Kribz or Driss or any of their mates put you under any pressure to take them to Galleons Reach?' came the next logical question.

Rankin turned away again and spoke to the wall. 'No son, they had no need to. It's my own fault I was there, but I have to say that if they hadn't got there in good time those feckin' Albos would have murdered their young fella—'

'We were organising—'

'You lot couldn't organise feck all, from what I could see those boys saved the day for you, even if it did get a bit messy, and you might like it to cross your minds that I'm a feckin' victim again here. How many times have I got to be shot before you—'

'I hear what you say, Tom, but you were armed, you shot down a police drone—'

'Right, that's your lot. I'm tired now, time you were off, the pair of you.' This time the Gypsy closed his eyes for emphasis. The two cops looked at each other, just as another nurse walked in with a tray of meds.

'Okay officers, time's up I'm afraid. Mr Rankin needs his medication,' she announced, breezily.

They stood. Briggs looked down at the patient. 'We'll pop in again soon, Tom.' The Gypsy opened his eyes but didn't reply. The cops shuffled out, mumbling their thank-yous to the nurse who had her back to them, fussing over the drip feed and monitors at the bedside.

Even if they'd seen her face they would never have put a name to it, then or thereafter. Nobody ever recognised Bora Gozit when she was in uniform.

191

Napper could move quickly when it suited him. Having waited until the gushing shower was in full flow, he slid silently into the kitchen. The door of the big Smeg freezer put up a bit of a fight before the suction lock relented to his second pull. The thing was crammed full and he had to work fast, almost having empty it and then neatly replace its entire contents to accomplish his mission. Less than a minute later he collapsed back into the living room chair at the same instant as Larssen turned off the shower. He listened, imagining her towelling herself down, then he heard the hairdryer – that wouldn't take long. And it didn't; suddenly she was padding across the floor in front of him, looking for her cigarettes, stark naked.

'Like I said, don't even think about it. My dressing gown is in the washing.'

He wasn't thinking about 'it' at all. He was rolling a fag to give himself something to do, heart rate still elevated following his incursion. He was pleased with what he'd just accomplished.

'I suppose it was just a one-off last week was it, so you could get me under your control?' His eyes were still hooded as he lifted the roll-up tonguewards to moisten the paper.

'I don't know what I was thinking, but yes, I suppose fucking you has had that effect.' She lit up and slunk closer to stand over him. He lifted his eyelids and found himself gazing at her bush. Then she turned on her heel and walked away with no hint of a 'come hither' buttock sway. She sat down and crossed her legs, took a puff and blew smoke towards the ceiling.

'What've you got for me, then?'

'What d'you mean? I've told you ev'rythin' I know, you're bang up to date.'

'Bang up to date perhaps on what's happened. What I want to know is what you're going to do about it.' She uncrossed her legs and recrossed them.

'I can't do nothin' about anythin', and as for makin' any kind of contact with that solicitor, the one called Swan, forget it, that would drap me roight in the shit.'

Larssen put on a bored expression, like she was finding this tedious.

'I could "drap" you "roight" in the shit anytime I want to, Police Constable Napper, you can be very sure of that.' Her smug tone was that of a person used to being in total control, and Napper had no doubt as to the source of her confidence, which he'd just neatly eliminated.

It was the cop's turn to pretend; he put on a worried, vulnerable expression, taking care not to overdo it.

'Yeah, I get that, and my career would be in tatters if they found out about me shaggin' a witness, but I still can't do much more than I'm doin'. Reporting back to you, keepin' you informed and in the loop, what more can I do?' He wanted to hear it from her, and he couldn't be sure this wasn't being recorded. A sexual relationship with an important and volatile witness was career-damaging, true, but conspiring to pervert the course of justice was on a different level altogether.

'What if I told you that Claude Jackson was planning to have me killed?'

'I wouldn't believe you.'

'Why not? He's got plenty reason to.'

'I would need evidence, cos you've got plenty reason to make wild allegations against him, stitch 'im up for somethin' he hasn't done.'

'I'm not trying to stitch anyone up, as you put it. I have a genuine fear that my former business partner is planning to have me murdered, and it's a fear based on what I've heard from a trusted friend.' Her voice was flat, like she was going through the motions, thinking aloud. The conversation was chess-like, the players exchanging slow, reptilian moves.

'Okay, if you're insisting that I take this forward, I'll need a written statement from you, signed.'

'Fine, let's do it now.'

'I 'aven't got any statement forms with me. I'll 'ave to come back tomorrow.'

'Go on then, fuck off, be back here tomorrow, 9 a.m.'

Napper stood up, brushed fag ash off his cargo pants and treated himself to a nice lingering look at her endless legs.

'See you then, I'll let myself out.' He couldn't help smirking as he walked past her to the door. She didn't get up.

Out on the street, he hurried around the nearest corner and pulled out his phone.

'Speak of the fucking devil,' answered Blake. 'I was just going to call you, you cunt.'

'Why were you going to call me a cunt?'

'No, I was just going… never fucking mind, can you get to the Coach, pronto, like now?'

'Yeah, twenty minutes I suppose, why?'

'Suffice to say there's been a bit of progress. Come on, there's a pint waiting for you!'

Napper ducked down onto the Central Line, pausing momentarily to take something from his pocket and drop it in a waste bin. He made his way to Soho, hardly daring to think about what he'd just pulled off.

192

Swan endured another fifteen minutes in the public waiting area of Charing Cross Police Station. Her feet and legs ached as she killed the time Googling weight loss programmes on her iPhone.

When she got to the head of the queue the Polish desk clerk called her forward and the glass security door opened with a loud click. 'Hello again,' said Swan cheerfully. The look she got in return was vacant, bordering on surly. 'I'm a solicitor and I'm here to see my client, Mr Stephen Lander.'

The clerk did her usual thing with her terminal, glanced at the visitor's ID – nothing more than a driver's licence – and pressed a button to deactivate the lock on a side door leading to another, smaller waiting area, at which she jerked her head.

Swan's polite smile almost turned into a chuckle at the woman's rudeness.

Five minutes later she was being shown into an interview room where Kribz already sat. Had it not been for the circumstances, she wouldn't have recognised him. The confident, almost urbane young man she was expecting was a crumpled wreck of a boy, his face riven with pain and anxiety.

'Hi Katrina.' The voice was flat, bereft of the bounce she remembered.

'Hi Chris, how are you?' was all she could think of to ask as she sat down to face him across the small table bolted to floor. There was a recording machine on the wall, but it was switched off; the meeting was for private consultation only, not an interview under caution. The sergeant who'd shown Swan in slid out, saying, 'Just knock when you're finished, please.'

'You heard what 'appened?' Still the flat, resigned voice.

'Not really, they haven't told me much, only that you're being held on suspicion of firearms offences and that I, in your interests, must not divulge details of your detention to third parties. I'll be told more before they interview you, I suppose—'

'When's that gonna be? I've been here nearly 48 hours and they've just reviewed it and said they've got a court to agree to three fuckin' days – 'scuse the language.' He stopped, eyes on the table, mouth open, shaking his head slowly as if trying to string together the chain of events that had landed him in such deep, deep trouble.

'Do you want to give me your account of what happened?' She took a notebook from her shoulder bag. 'At least then I'll have an idea what to expect.'

Swan had always been good at taking fast, succinct and salient attendance notes: it was stock-in-trade stuff. But the story that Mr Christopher Pope relayed beggared her writing skills as well as her belief. She attempted to interrupt him a few times but gave up and just let him jabber.

After ten intense minutes she was seriously wishing she was elsewhere, like in the middle of a complex property transaction, or up to the neck in insolvency papers.

Kribz's account had been meandering and was peppered with the usual expletives and *innit*s, but it was largely coherent, ending with, 'and the rest is 'istory, innit.'

Swan cleared her throat and shifted her buttocks on the hard plastic seat.

'Well, even on what you've told me just now, I don't see how the police cannot charge you with firearms and hostage-taking offences. The CPS would give them no choice, regardless of how you saved the day in that car park, and my guess would be that, assuming you were convicted, a judge would have little choice but to hand you and your brother custodial sentences.'

'You haven't got a fuckin' clue, have you!'

'What?'

'One of our younger brothers had been kidnapped – I've just told you that – and we wuz 'elpin' the police to get 'im free, but they wasn't doin' enough, fuckin' around, and then Mergin called me, an' then there was an opportunity.'

Swan was getting it. 'To use a counter hostage, for an exchange? But why wave your gun around, scaring the—'

Kribz pressed on. 'I know enough about the po-po to know that they wouldn't have agreed to us usin' the Albanian kid as a hostage to get our hostage back, so I, we, had to put an act on innit, look tough, so that stupid cow Gerry Lashford, the DI, wouldn't get in the way an' fuck it up, that's all.'

'Okay, okay, let me think about what you've said and contact the investigating officer – whoever that might be – no doubt they'll be wanting to interview you soon, so we'll have more time to talk before they do that.' She stood up and put her notebook and pen in her bag.

Kribz took her offered hand and shook it firmly, trying to stand as he did so. The adrenaline rush had made him forget his injury and what was meant to be a polite smile quickly became a grimace. 'Ah! Shit, sorry.' He dropped back onto the chair.

'That's okay. Careful – get some rest and see you soon,' said the lawyer; she couldn't wait to get out of the room. She knocked on the door and a custody officer opened up and escorted her from the building, wordlessly.

193

Napper walked into the Coach and Horses to find Blake holding Jackson playfully but firmly by the lapels of his Saville Row jacket. The asset stripper was leaning with his back against the bar and his face turned painfully away from the spluttering solicitor.

'You've got to come up with something, Jacko. Napper needs—'

'What?' said the cop, from less than two yards behind.

Blake swung round, releasing his captive.

'What do I need, Blakey?' Napper smiled reassuringly at Jackson as he spoke.

'You know what you need, so now that you're here you can tell him yourself, you scruffy cunt!' laughed Blake as he handed Napper the full pint of Stella that had been waiting, as promised.

The Cornishman looked around the pub. Lunchtime was warming up and it was getting busy. 'Let's just 'ave this one then fuck off somewhere else, eh?'

'What a good idea,' agreed Jackson, uncomfortable both physically and otherwise. He needed to sit down, preferably with a table between himself and Blake whose verbosity was now accompanied by generous salvos of spittle.

'Let's go for a chinky, then, a cheap one. I don't want to be seen bein' woined and doined in some posh joint again by members of so-called respectable professions. It's bad for my street cred.'

'Ooooo,' falsettoed Blake, 'get the people's copper, eh? Alright then, Eddie fucking Shoestring, down your pint and lead the way.'

Out of politeness, Blake and Napper pretended to dawdle so that Jackson could keep up as the trio made their way down Shaftesbury Avenue and into Chinatown. In spite of what he'd just said to Napper, Blake chose the venue, a place called Plum City where the food was plentiful but the wine tasted like Doctor Pepper's latest button polish.

They'd only been seated a couple of minutes before Jackson got a call and had to hobble back out into the street, frowning at the name of the caller on his screen.

'He still ain't on board, is he?' said Napper as he perused the dim sum menu.

'Don't worry—'

'This is goin' nowhere fuckin' fast, Blakey. The guy's just expecting us to do it all for him.'

'No he's not. He's thinking hard, I can tell. You having wine or sticking to the beer? I think it's that Tsing Tao shit in here.'

'I'm not 'avin' any more to drink, got a lot on my moind and I wish this so-called buddy of yours would shape up otherwise we're pretty much stuffed.'

'Give him time, Doug, he's not fucking stupid. He knows this is his window of opportunity and that it'll pass – he'll come good, I betcha.'

'I fuckin' 'ope you 'aven't told him about me and—'

'No, course I fucking haven't, you dick. That's going no further, and I still think you're mad going anywhere near the psycho bitch, the—' Blake saw their companion making his way back from the door and zipped his lip.

'Sorry about that,' puffed Jackson as he sat back down, trying and failing to lean his Swain Adeney stick against the table; it clattered onto the slate tile floor. 'Oh, fucking thing.'

The cop and the brief watched Jackson pick up the menu.

'That was one of my boys on the phone. Well, one of Larssen's boys now, but still one of my boys.' He was staring at the menu as he spoke, not wishing to look excited, not giving anything away.

'And?' said Blake.

'Could be something interesting. Apparently she's just got into the office, ranting and raving about the rumpus in the East End. My man's saying that she seems to have a lot more details than what's been reported by the press.' Then he looked up and across the table, engaging eye contact with Napper. 'Maybe she's got a friend in the police. Wouldn't put it past her to have a copper in her pocket – what do you think, Doug?'

Napper didn't flinch, meeting Jackson's pointed gaze head-on. 'Quite possibly, but she probably won't need to have anyone "in her pocket" as you put it. She's in contact with my colleagues on the Stanwell Moor job. Nuthin' to stop one of them from givin' 'er the heads-up on recent events, she 'as a right to be kept informed, to some extent anyway, if she's a witness in any sort of danger.' The cop stopped there, shrugged, and went back to the menu. 'What the fuck is Char Siu?'

'Barbecued pig,' said Blake, with just the hint of a smirk.

194

The cop on duty outside Rankin's room cursed his luck when the nurse gave him the news. There had been a burst of activity after an orderly had gone in with a tray of food and then come out again in a fluster to alert the medical staff. After a frenetic fifteen minutes a doctor emerged and told the officer that the patient had sadly died of a heart attack, that they had done everything they could but he had succumbed to a combination of his age, possible pre-existing conditions and of course his injuries. The officer dutifully made notes and radioed in the development.

When the news hit the incident room in Barking, Passey called the squad to order.

'Okay, the old guy called Tom Rankin, the one with the wagon, has just died in hospital. As far as we know at the moment this doesn't really change much. We have body-worn video footage and other police evidence to the effect that the bullets that hit him came from one of the Albanian guns. Forensics will do the rest but at least we know we're not looking for any new suspects as they're all in custody.' He looked round the room as he spoke; the expressions of the two dozen or so faces ranged from bored to politely grim. It wasn't bad news to them: another murder to process equalled more overtime.

The development presented Briggs with a bit of a problem however.

'Does this fuck up the POCA thing?' Mason whispered to him through a smile.

He turned to face her. 'Not really. Makes it a bit more difficult, but the criminal property becomes part of his estate, so the POCA action will be against the beneficiaries of his will.' That shut her up, and the smile faded. Briggs watched Mason turn away and wondered how such a bright, attractive girl could be so bitter and nasty. He stood up, made a show of stretching languidly and walked unhurriedly to the door, down the stairs and out into the enclosed back yard of the building. It was cluttered with awkwardly parked police vehicles and a few cops standing in groups of twos and threes, chatting and smoking.

He found a patch of private space and called Napper. 'No doubt you've heard, then?'

'Heard what?' The Cornishman had just extricated himself from his luncheon buddies and was about to descend into the underground station in Leicester Square.

'Rankin's dead – heart attack in hospital.'

It took a couple of seconds for Napper to compute the ramifications; the old man's demise did him no harm at all.

'Doesn't surprise me really. There's only so much shit an' bullets an ol' geezer can take.' He heard a tinge of sadness creep into his own voice, suddenly realising he'd got to quite like the old Gypsy.

Napper was glad he'd had that seemingly pointless lunch with Blake and Jackson. He would have to put the decision down to impeccable gut instinct but in truth he'd been catapulted onto cloud nine by the visit to Larssen's place and had needed the grounding. He got off the Tube at Lambeth North and did the five-minute walk to Kennington nick at what he figured was a normal pace; it was all he could do not to sprint. Returning McAdam's grunted greeting with a cheerful 'Hi, mate,' he sat down and logged on to the Crimint system from his usual terminal.

Napper was good at writing Crimint entries, and this one was going to be top-dollar stuff. Not too much detail, spot-on keywords and, most importantly, enough gaps and omissions to help smokescreen any personal interest. It took him less than five minutes and he was gone, out of the building and back onto the Tube. One more little job to do and then home to get – and keep – his head down.

195

Colin Palmer had received a text message from Jackson to give his former boss a call, and had done so whilst watching the incandescent Larssen through the soundproofed glass wall that encased her workspace. He'd managed to keep a straight face as he reported the ongoing histrionics.

'I can't hear what she's saying now but she marched in a few minutes ago screaming about that Rankin bloke being a fucking gang member and shooting at coppers over in the fucking East End, something to do with a kidnapping. Have you heard about this? There's been nothing on the news so I don't know where she's been getting it from…'

'Wait, who's she talking to now?' Jackson was standing on the pavement outside the Plum City restaurant, phone pressed hard to his ear against the traffic noise and leaning heavily on his stick.

'I don't know, she's in her office with the door closed, but some poor cunt's getting a right flea in his ear.' Palmer could barely conceal his glee and almost chuckled as he spoke.

'Okay Colin, thanks for calling me back with this, er, interesting news. Catch you later.' Jackson had then cut the call to go back into the restaurant.

The ear getting the flea had belonged to Katrina Swan who had not long left Charing Cross Police Station. She was professionally prevented from either confirming or denying the accuracy of what Larssen had told her, but she'd made a very educated guess as to the source of the Dane's information.

'I've no idea where you've got this from,' she'd lied, 'but I will take instructions from my clients in due course, as and when the need arises.' She'd then excused herself on account of having to descend onto the underground system and ended the conversation before hailing a taxi back to her office.

196

It was probably too early to be making this call, thought Napper, given that not an hour earlier he'd created the Crimint entry which was unerasable and immediately traceable to himself, but things were coming to the boil and the planets were aligned. Those planets being a full-scale murder enquiry that followed a fucked-up hostage negotiation, an embarrassed police force desperately looking for headline-grabbing results and a sociopathic insolvency practitioner badly needing a serious downfall.

He stood at the battered payphone in Ozman's Cafe in the Holloway Road – no CCTV in there, for sure – and shoved two pound coins in the slot. He'd just visited the evil little toilet and unravelled the loo roll. The Crimestoppers recorded message sounded tinny and tired, and seemed to go on forever. When he got to speak he did so in his best south London G-boy accent, with the inside of the toilet roll between his mouth and the receiver for added obfuscation.

'There's a woman that lives near Ladbroke Grove, she's got a gun in her place, she's from Sweden or somewhere, innit, an' she's gonna kill some dude in the next cuppla days, the address is 16 Stanley Mews and the woman goes by the name of Freda, is all I'm sayin'.'

He replaced the receiver and pocketed the loo-roll core as he listened to his coins clatter down into the cashbox. He felt the Turk behind the counter looking at him, so he ordered a black coffee and took a seat away from the window, thinking about how long it would take for the dots to join up.

It took longer than he would have liked, but it happened all the same and within two hours the words 'Freda', 'Stanley Mews' and 'gun' were linking up in the Boolean search fields on a researcher's screen in the Barking incident room. The young civilian investigator at the terminal logged the hit but wasn't sufficiently experienced or motivated to think anything more of it; the flagging protocol would bring it to the SIO's attention in due course. Fortunately, 'due course' was very much due and Passey was urging the collating officer, a middle-aged DS with a beer belly and a modicum of professionalism, to tell him about anything and everything before the end of the shift.

'There's the usual dross, guv'nor, but there's one little snippet you might like to know about. A Crimint entry and an anonymous Crimestoppers report make it double-stranded, so it could be something.'

Passey, roving the room with his hands in his pockets, walked over and stooped to look at the collator's screen. What he saw made him straighten, scanning the office for a free pair of hands. 'DS Briggs, can you come over here please? Looks like we've got a job for you.'

197

Exhaustion and whisky had gifted no more than an hour's sleep to Larssen. She lay tangled in the silk duvet and glared at the ceiling, which seemed a long way off being hers to call her own any time soon. Those idiot black bastards were going to be made to take the blame for this, totally, and exonerate the Irishman; tell the police they made him do whatever he'd done, forced him at gunpoint, threatened to kill his stupid wife, whatever – that POCA shit would be going nowhere and that land at Heathrow would be hers. She rolled off the bed and stretched, thinking about hitting the road on her Boardman. Richmond Park and back, that would help clear the thing she called her mind.

She charged up the espresso pot, put it on the gas and stepped into the shower with the dial turned to cold. The freezing jets shocked her system out of self pity, focusing her, concentrating her venom. She kept the water on cold for as long as she could stand it, then hit the control for ten seconds of hot, then back to cold again. She stepped out, wrapped a towel around herself and padded back into the kitchen to find the stovetop bubbling.

She lit a cigarette, letting it dangle her mouth sluttishly as she poured the thick black liquid into a tiny cup. She cursed and squinted as a wisp of smoke laced her eye. She picked up the espresso cup and made to head for the living room. She was in the hallway when the hydraulic breacher blew her front door open.

'Armed police!' screamed the lead officer, a female inspector wearing a little number that looked like it had been designed by H.R. Giger. Larssen stood quite still, one eye closed against the smoke from her cigarette, espresso cup in hand. The team of ninja cops stormed in, occupying the apartment like a deluge of floodwater.

'Freda Larssen?' gasped the inspector, clearly quite excited.

'Correct.'

'How many people are in here?'

Larssen removed the cigarette from her mouth and looked around at the sudden occupation. 'Oh, I see, a guessing game. Okay, I give up. You tell me, how many people are in here?'

'I mean before we arrived,' said the inspector, the wind suddenly out of her sails.

'Oh, that's easy, just one, just me, how may I help—'

'We have a warrant to search this property for firearms. Do you have any firearms in here?' The inspector was nervous, hyperventilating almost, the pitch of her voice too high to be even remotely authoritative.

'Not that I'm aware of, officer.' Larssen still hadn't moved, other than to raise her cup and take a sip of espresso.

'Go in there and sit down, please.' The inspector pointed through the door of the lounge.

'Am I under arrest?' asked Larssen, complying.

'No. Well, er, not yet anyway, depends if we find anything.' The inspector was calming down a bit now, relieved at how this was going.

'Am I allowed to get dressed? You have a lot of men in here and I've only—'

'They won't touch you, don't worry—'

'I'm not worried, not one bit—'

'You fucking should be, love.' The voice was that of a burly male sergeant who appeared through the lounge door, his gloved hand holding something which he showed to the inspector.

'Where was it?'

'In the freezer.'

'Show it to her – but don't let her touch it.'

The sergeant had to stoop slightly to bring what he held down to Larssen's eye level. The Dane looked at the Beretta 9000S and, for the first time in her life, thought she was going to faint.

'Where the fuck did you find that?' Her words were malformed through rubbery lips.

'Like I just said, in your freezer,' said the sergeant.

'Freda Larssen, I'm arresting you for possession of a class one firearm. You do not have to say anything—'

'Fuck off! You fucking pigs, you fucking planted that!'

Larssen threw her cigarette and coffee cup onto the floor and shot to her feet. The towel that had been covering her fell away – just as Aaron Briggs walked into the room.

'Well, well, well, *Detective* Briggs, come to see what your fucking thugs are doing to me, eh?' Larssen screeched, as the sergeant picked up the towel and attempted to throw it over her; she swiped it away, preferring the show of naked vulnerability. 'No, I'm fine like this, what you see is what you fucking get!' She spat the words at Briggs, then turned briefly to the female inspector. 'Go on, you have a good look also, I've no doubt you're a lesbian!'

'Get dressed, Freda, and calm down, you're doing yourself no favours.' Briggs spoke calmly, eyes fixed on the Dane's face.

'Oh, "Freda" now, is it? Now that you've planted evidence on me you're trying to be nice! Hah!'

The inspector issued a short order over her radio and two more female officers appeared, one with a pair of handcuffs at the ready.

'Miss Larssen,' announced the inspector, 'if you don't get a grip of yourself we'll handcuff you and forcibly wrap you in a constraining blanket. Now cover yourself up and let these officers take you to find some clothes.'

Larssen ignored her. 'You're going to regret this, Briggs, I'll fucking *kill you!*' Her voice started low but the last words were shrieked and punctuated by a lunge at Briggs that took both female PCs and the male sergeant to suppress. The naked woman, glistening wet from her recent shower and a sheen of sweat brought on by her rage, writhed on the floor like a snake in its death throes as cuffs and leg braces were applied and a police issue blue blanket wrapped around her.

'Go on, that's it!' gasped the now crimson-faced Dane. 'Fucking kill me, spray CS gas at me, stop me from breathing – you'll fucking pay for this, Briggs.'

Briggs would later feel proud of his facade of professionalism; he just stood there, looking down at the panting woman.

'No, Freda, you're the one who's going to pay.'

198

Napper had accrued a lot of annual leave and thought it a good idea to take a few days off. He knew his sudden absence would do nothing to detract from the suspicion that was about to fall on him, but figured he would need to be at his best to face the imminent barrage of scrutiny, so he needed a rest. He lay on his back and waited for the ceiling of his tiny room to start moving, for the colours to appear on his walls and move to the music that belted out from his ancient hi-fi system. The mushrooms always did their job.

Katrina Swan sat in the interview room for a full five minutes before Kribz shuffled in, followed by two officers who, having nodded subdued *good morning*s before sitting down and activating the recording machine, formally introduced themselves as Detective Sergeant Aaron Briggs and Detective Constable Rebecca Mason. Upon invitation, the suspect and his legal representative, in their positions on the other side of the table, did likewise.

'Okay, Mr Pope, we meet again rather sooner than expected,' said Briggs with a smile. 'Do you need to have some time with your solicitor before we start?'

'No thanks,' replied Kribz, 'we 'ad a good chat yesterday.'

Briggs looked at Swan who nodded confirmation.

Then Mason delivered the caution, all about warning the suspect that it may harm his defence if he failed to mention now something which he might like to later rely on in court.

'Who says I'm goin' to court?' Kribz sounded tired but reasonable, not combative; the question was accompanied by a show of his palms.

'Well,' began Briggs, 'nobody, yet, but as you know you've been arrested for possession of firearms and unlawful imprisonment, so we're just going to, er—'

'Gonna what? If you got the evidence, why don't you jus' charge me, innit?' Kribz kept up the conversational tone.

'That's not my decision,' said Briggs, 'what I want to do now is ask some questions relating to the alleged offences and the events that led up to them. As my colleague has made clear, you don't have to say a thing unless you want to, but you'll understand that we have to put the questions to you – and you'd be well advised to listen because you'll probably learn a lot, Mr Pope.'

Kribz nodded, frowning, eyes flicking from one officer to the other. 'Okay, carry on then.'

'Thank you.' Briggs opened a notebook and looked down at a handwritten list.

'Do you know a woman called Freda Larssen?'

'No.'

'Have you ever met a woman called Freda Larssen?'

'No.'

'Do you know a man called Claude Jackson?'

'No.'

'Have you ever met a man called Claude Jackson?'

'No.'

'You were seen at Galleons Reach associating with a man called Thomas Rankin. How long have you known him?'

'Few months.'

'How did you come to know him?'

'Business.'

'What kind of business?'

'He's a dog breeder, has kennels. He was looking after two dogs for us, and some pups.'

'Do you know a youth nicknamed Numbers?'

'Yeah, course I know Numbers.'

'Is he a member of your gang, the Braganza Boys?'

Swan wasn't having this. 'That's a leading question, officer, you're assuming my client—'

'Yes,' interrupted Kribz. Swan looked at him, shrugged and made a note, just for something to do to cover her embarrassment at being overruled.

'Are you the leader of the gang called the Braganza Boys?' continued Briggs.

'Suppose.'

'Do you know a man called Douglas Napper?'

'No. Er, yeah, he's that undercover cop, innit.'

'Okay, let's turn to the events at Galleons Reach. It's a matter of record that you went there to assist police to negotiate the release of the hostage you know by the nickname Numbers. Did you, either before going there or whilst you were there, cause a youth called Mergin Gozit to attend that venue?'

'Eh?'

'I'll put it another way: did you procure the arrival of Mergin Gozit at Galleons Reach so that you could then take him hostage at gunpoint?'

413

'Sort of, yeah.'

'What d'you mean, "sort of"?'

'He's a mate of Numbers, innit, he kind of volunteered himself so we could use 'im as a bargaining chip 'cos you'ze lot were fuckin' the job up.' Kribz spoke as though what he was saying was obvious and reasonable.

'What, volunteered himself to get tied up and threatened with a gun?' Briggs heard his own voice rise. Mason had to stop herself from smiling.

Kribz didn't bother stopping himself from grinning. 'Made it look good innit, kept Gerry in her place. She was shittin' 'erself.'

'By "Gerry", do you mean Detective Inspector Lashford?'

'Yeah, went to school wid 'er. We go back a long, long time, Mr Briggs.'

Briggs hadn't been ready for this. 'What? You're... you're saying that you...'

'Yeah, I know her an' she'd knows me, knows what I'ze capable of, innit.' Kribz was still grinning.

'We all know what you're capable of, Mr Pope, we have your previous convictions—'

'Yeah, but she's seen it for herself innit, back in the day.'

'I see.' Briggs looked down at his crib sheet to press on. 'When you were arrested at Galleons Reach you had in your possession a Glock automatic—'

'No comment.'

'What? I haven't finished the question yet—'

'I'm not answering any more questions, Mr Briggs, with respect. I want a chat with my solicitor now, please.'

Briggs inhaled deeply, nodding. 'Okay, no problem. For the benefit of the recording, this interview will now be suspended whilst Mr Pope has a private consultation with his legal representative.' He looked at his watch, announced the exact time and switched the machine off.

199

Three miles to the west, another police detainee sat in her cell. Now unshackled, Larssen wore nothing but a white paper custody overall and soft canvas slippers. A police nurse had needed to treat one of her ankles for a superficial injury caused by the leg brace. The prisoner had adopted a strange, trance-like manner, refusing to answer questions or engage with the custody officers regarding meal choices or possible pharmaceutical requirements. The only time she spoke was when the duty sergeant asked a question.

'Do you wish anyone to be informed of your arrest and detention?'

'Yes, my solicitor.'

'And who might that be?'

Larssen gave the name of a lawyer who was not on the list of those who attended police stations at public expense.

'Er, that solicitor doesn't appear to do legal aid work,' said the duty sergeant through the six-by-nine-inch slit in the cell door, having briefly consulted his electronic clipboard.

'What do you mean?' snapped Larssen, staring at the floor.

'I mean that that solicitor doesn't provide free legal advice to criminal suspects, is there any—'

'I'll pay.'

200

Miusze Huang stared at the weapon that lay on her spotless work surface. It had been fast-tracked for her specific attention by an enthusiastic Detective Sergeant Briggs. Not that the identity of the submitting officer was of any interest whatsoever to the firearms analyst; she was simply fascinated by the science. She looked up at her triple screens, checking the results for the umpteenth time, just to make sure. Incontestable.

'Linked Series 5,' she murmured, expressionless, 'at last, you've come home to Mummy.'

201

Gerry Lashford was making the most of what she knew was the lull before the storm – if you could call a full-scale murder enquiry a "lull", even when the suspects were already banged up. She knew that the powers above had made her deputy senior investigating officer for a reason – to keep her busy and out of harm's way. She also knew that as soon as the workload calmed down she was in for a miserable time, notwithstanding her recent passable performance at the Commissioner's meeting. Getting held hostage whilst in charge of a hostage situation isn't a good career move and her future postings would reflect that.

The team was dissipating at the end of the shift on the second day. Things had settled into the standard major incident routine and Passey seemed satisfied that everything was under control.

'Fancy a drink, Gerry?' he asked.

'Well, yeah, sure,' Lashford was keen to stay on-side, 'but not round here boss.' She giggled nervously. 'Barking's well, you know—'

'No, I didn't mean in Barking, I can't wait to get out of the place. What about we get over to the Hill, civilisation?'

'What, Notting Hill?'

'Yeah, I want to pop into the nick to check something out. It'll only take ten minutes and then we could have a couple of swift ones round the corner in the Ladbroke Arms.'

'Okay boss, I'll drive.' She kept smiling to hide her concern: Passey was either hitting on her – unlikely, given his career aspirations, or this was leading to some political stunt – highly likely, given his career aspirations.

The journey across the capital was easy in terms of traffic but a palpable tension accompanied the pair like a passenger on the back seat. Little was said, save for the odd generic copspeak exchange about pensions, the Commissioner (who they both agreed was great) and overtime funding. Lashford pulled the pool car into the back yard of the beautifully manicured Victorian cop shop on Ladbroke Grove. The Met had tried to close it down, but the wealthy residents of the regentrified village had objected, and got their way.

'Okay, you go and set them up and I'll be ten minutes, tops,' said Passey.

That was a worry: what was Passey going to do that he didn't want her to know about? But she pulled herself together and shook off her paranoia.

'Okay boss, what's your—'

'Guinness please, extra cold.' And he was off and in through the back door of the police station. Lashford locked the car and walked in the opposite direction, out of the back gates, across the road and into the Ladbroke Arms.

202

Blake had not represented anyone in police custody since his trainee days, and even then his jobs had been confined to miscreant cops, locked up by their own kind for all kinds of weird and wonderful stuff: corruption, sexual assaults, domestic violence allegations. When he'd set up his own firm he'd decided that criminal legal aid was not going to feature on his menu and didn't bother applying to be included in the scheme that would have put him on a duty rota, to be called upon to sit in dirty interview rooms to hold the equally grubby hands of the great unwashed for the pittance the legal aid authorities paid, when they got round to it.

So, when he got the call from the Notting Hill custody sergeant to say that a detained person had requested his services he was understandably surprised and about to curtly decline – until he heard the name.

'Oh, er, okay, but I'm not in the legal aid scheme,' he spluttered, alarm klaxons raging in his ears about conflicts of interest and certain stuff being a bit close for comfort.

'She's prepared to pay privately, Mr Blake,' announced the sergeant.

The klaxons fell silent.

203

The Ladbroke Arms was quiet, subdued – a picture of midweek urbanity. Lashford had only seven years' service under her belt, but even she could remember when the place would have been full of drunken off-duty coppers and sundry pond life from the local sink estates. Not anymore, though. The place had been bistrofied; menus adorned every table and unwelcome kitchen odours put paid to what should have been the nice hoppy smell of beer.

He was standing at the bar fingering his phone, a half-drunk pint of cider at his elbow. For a second, Lashford considered turning tail and walking out; she was instinctively averse to coincidences, and this was just too much of one.

But then he looked up and smiled. She walked forward boldly, hoping he hadn't spotted her fleeting hesitancy.

'This is too much of one,' she said, verbalising her thoughts for authenticity.

'Too much of one what?' asked Napper, knowing exactly what she'd meant.

'A coincidence of course. What are you doing here?' She rummaged in her handbag as she spoke, affecting distraction. 'Tch, where's my fucking purse?'

'On me, what'll you have?'

'Vodka and tonic please, small one, I'm driving.'

Napper turned to attract some attention from the bar staff. Lashford checked her phone: SMS from Passey: *Delayed, be there in 30.* She decided to stay *schtum*, say nothing to Napper, see how things panned out.

'Let's go outside, I need a fag,' said Napper, handing Lashford her drink. The pair sat down in the beer garden and the Cornishman got out his tobacco. Lashford waited.

'Mmm, coincidences,' mused Napper, just before he licked his Rizla and looked Lashford full in the eye.

'My guess is that Passey told you to be here,' said the DI, not flinching from the eye contact.

'Who?'

'Passey, the SIO on the Galleons Reach job. Don't you know him?'

'Never heard of him.' Napper was being truthful.

Lashford decided the change the subject.

'Look, er, I need to thank you for your support the other day. You were calm and collected, you knew how to handle those guys. I was shitting myself, to be honest.'

'What makes you think I wasn't, and—'

'How well did you know the Pope brothers, before all this happened?'

'Not personally at all, but well enough from an intel point of view.' He paused and made a little show of glancing around to make sure no one was listening. 'Not like you,' he then added, with a sinister inflection.

'What d'you mean?' Lashford sensed trouble.

'You went to school with one of them, didn't you?'

'Yes, but so what? I'm three years older than him and he was a little fucker then. What are you suggesting?' She felt fear - and Napper smelt it.

'Hmm, nothin' really, it just seemed that you were a bit familiar out there at Galleons Reach.' He took a puff of his fag. 'That you was frightened of him, maybe, or a bit too familiar, like.'

'Of course I was frightened, he was waving a fucking gun around. I had to manage the situation!' Lashford could scarcely believe she was hearing this. 'I think I managed the situation well!' she added, feeling her face heat up and the tears begin to well. *What was this crazy bastard up to?!*

'Well, sort of,' said the Cornishman. 'I watched every little exchange between you and Pope and it looked to me like he

419

had somethin' over you. I don't want to add petrol to the flames you're already fightin', Gerry, but it might be an idea to think about us two lookin' after each other, know what I mean?'

Lashford was aghast; this lunatic was trying to blackmail her, make sure she gave a good account of his actions at Galleons Reach.

'Oh, fuck off, Napper!' she hissed. 'And you know that's not true! The comms man was there, he'll vouch—'

'The comms man was busy with his own shit, he didn't see what I saw—'

Lashford had had enough and sprung to her feet. 'You saw fuck all and you fucking know it, Napper. You're a fucking idiot and I'm going to report this conversation, I—'

'I wouldn't do that if I was you,' came the calm but firm interruption. 'If you flag up that I'm insinuatin' sumthin' it'll have to be followed through and it'll add to your troubles – think about it.'

Napper wasn't enjoying this; bullying by nuance wasn't his style, but he had odds to stack in his favour and opportunities couldn't be missed. It was a tried and tested method: when you're in the shit, kick up a dust-storm and besmirch the senior ranks. Do it with subtlety and it may just blunt the sword that's hanging over your head, was what he told himself.

Lashford stared at him for a full five seconds and then sat down again, slowly.

'D'you know what Douglas, I just might have something to contribute to this conversation.' Her demeanour had changed dramatically, she faced him squarely, her hands on the table, fingers splayed.

'Go on,' said Napper, feeling himself tense, ready for escalation.

'You had an informant who you registered in the name Eric Talea, am I right?'

'Yeah, correct.' Napper took a gulp of cider; his mouth had suddenly gone dry.

'Well, Douglas, I'm going to tell you a secret which, if you've got any sense, you'll keep.' She was no longer angry or irritated, but appeared thoughtful, resigned.

'Go on.'

'He was my brother.'

Napper response was fast, automatic: 'Was?'

'Yes, *was* – he's dead, and I'm certain you know that, the same as I'm certain you know his real name was Michael Brooker and I'm equally certain you know his streetname was Screwloose.'

Napper's neck had thickened, but there was an unsureness, a vulnerability in Lashford's voice that sustained him.

'You can be as certain as you like Gerry, but all this is fuckin' news to me.' It would have passed for convincing, but he spoiled it by too quickly taking another gulp of cider.

'Whatever, I don't expect you to admit anything, and none of this would do me any good either, being the sister of a gang member and not reporting the fact for remedial supervision, but if things get to a point where I've got nothing to lose I'll turn myself over to Professional Standards and take you with me.'

Napper didn't move and remained silent, but his eyes dropped to his pint glass and she knew she'd hit the target.

She went on in the same quiet, reasonable tone: 'My brother told me you'd given him the name Eric Talea, and that you're asks of him were getting bigger all the time, and that you'd handed him money in envelopes inside old books, including one about British slavery in the Victorian era. A book answering that description was found when they searched Michael's home address after he was murdered. You knew he was a convicted criminal and a Braganza member, and you didn't come clean about it, you didn't increase his status to that of participating informant and put the risk control procedures in place, therefore you put him in mortal danger – and he got murdered as a direct consequence of your willful negligence.'

She rose and walked off into the fading light, towards the Tube station, in no mood to wait for Passey. She would text him later with an excuse about feeling unwell, which was true.

Napper had intended to wait for Blake who he knew by that time would be in the nick over the road – the lawyer had called him earlier with a breathless newsflash of his latest assignment – but he decided that he'd had just about enough for one day and the brief's update on Larssen would have to wait, so off he went home to mull over this latest development.

204

'I often wondered what you looked like,' lied Larssen. She'd refused to be moved to an interview room when told of the arrival of her chosen lawyer, so the private consultation was taking place in her cell.

'Didn't want to overdress, Miss Larssen,' said Blake as he looked his client up and down. 'Wouldn't have liked to make you feel underdressed.' Blake was in his usual rugby shirt, cargo trousers and trainers, topped off with three days' growth on his face and a self-inflicted crewcut with tufts where he'd missed bits. Larssen was sat on the blue plastic mattress that covered the bench-bed. Blake walked across the cell and sat down beside her. She stood up and turned to face him. He looked around himself. 'Always wondered what it was like to lay on one of these.'

'Be my guest,' sneered the Dane. Blake took up the invitation, swivelling round to put his feet up and lie back, hands behind his head on the pillow that was also made of blue plastic but encased in a white paper pillowcase.

'Mmm, not too bad,' he smirked.

She glared down at him.

422

'They've just told me they're not ready to interview you yet,' said the supine solicitor.

'I've no intention of being *interviewed*,' said the detainee, her emphasis to ridicule the polite English colloquialism for interrogation.

'So why call me here, then?' Blake frowned at the white tiled ceiling.

'So that I can interview *you*.'

Blake's horizontality had had the convenient effect of raising his already high blood pressure and consequently reddening his face, so an additional uptick in floridity would, he hoped, go unnoticed. 'Oh, right, you going to caution me then?' he said to the ceiling.

Larssen took to walking slowly around the cell, her hands stuffed way down into the vents at the sides of her paper overall. They weren't pockets as such, but the effect was the same in that the pose prevented gesticulation or spontaneous assault.

'Actually, yes, you should be very *cautious* to tell me the truth about what you and Jackson have been up to.' She stopped walking to stare down at her interviewee's face. It registered not even a flicker of concern.

'No comment.'

'Have you been talking to Thomas Rankin?'

'No comment.'

'Have you been talking to any of those young black men who seem to be set on ruining my life?'

'No comment.'

'Have you—'

'You're wasting your time, Freda.' the words came out with a strangulated wheeze as the solicitor exerted himself to swing his legs off the bench and haul himself to his feet. 'I'm here to represent you in your capacity as a detained suspect. My dealings with or knowledge of other people has nothing to do with you. I'm leaving now.'

Larssen stepped forward, placing herself between the lawyer and the cell door. 'No, you're fucking not!' she snarled. 'Not until you've answered me!'

Blake attempted to push past her, but the Dane, taller and fitter, grabbed his rugby shirt and pushed him back onto the bench. To describe his reaction as 'bouncing back' would be an exaggeration of Blake's athleticism, but it certainly looked like that on the CCTV screen the duty sergeant and his assistant were watching from the nearby custody processing room.

'Fucking hell, what the… let's get down there Frankie, it's fucking kickin' off!'

By the time the two officers barged into the cell Larssen, naked from the waist up, had hold of the puce-faced Blake around his thick neck in something akin to a half-Nelson wrestling hold. 'He has just fucking assaulted me! I want the dirty bastard arrested and I'll press charges!'

Blake's flailing arms were totally ineffective, his hands nowhere near his captor's body – subsequent review of the CCTV record would show that she herself had ripped down the upper part of her paper overall whilst simultaneously immobilising her legal representative.

The cop called Frankie, a butch lass with close cropped hair, got in between the combatants and prized Blake free of Larssen's grip, before expertly spinning the Dane around, putting her on the floor and applying a pair of handcuffs with a vigour that would have been even more forceful had it not been for the presence of both the sergeant and the camera in the corner of the ceiling.

'You fucking lesbian bitch!' screamed Larssen, the veins on her neck protruding like cables. 'I'll sue the fucking lot of you!'

Frankie controlled the prisoner, using the knee-in-the-small-of-the-back technique.

'Right, Frankie, okay, just leave her and let's get the fuck out of here,' shouted the sergeant, who had just pushed Blake out into the passageway. Frankie did a silent count to three and sprung up and away from the writhing woman, only just managing to join her supervisor as he slammed the door shut before Larssen hit it with the full force of her half-naked body.

The two cops and Blake stood in the passageway by the heavy steel door, its eye-level service hatch thankfully closed. The banshee-like din coming from the other side worried the sergeant. 'Fuckin' hell, I'm getting the inspector to section her, get her out of here and into a secure mental unit. She's a liability!' Turning to Blake, he dealt with his next priority. 'Are you alright, sir?'

The solicitor was rubbing his neck with one hand and doing strange exercises with his other arm, as if gauging its mobility following a sporting injury.

'Yes, I'll be fine. Did you catch all that on camera? There was no way I assaulted her. I was trying to leave and she stopped me.'

'Don't worry, sir,' assured the sergeant, I'm sure the footage'll bear you out.'

'Cunts! Cunts! Cunts!' came the muffled scream from behind the door, followed by a dull, repetitive thudding as the deranged prisoner vented her fury against the reinforced steel.

205

Briggs was becoming accustomed to being out of his depth. He was growing gills, or an aqualung, or some other breathing apparatus that extracted oxygen from the toxic darkness he found himself swimming through wherever he went. The preceding few months had been a dispiriting series of alien situations for the young graduate detective; nothing on his Portsmouth University course had prepared him for the mental acrobatics he was having to perform whilst ricocheting around like a pinball in a dysfunctional arcade machine. But it felt like he was getting better, hardening up, growing into the job, surviving.

Having been told he wasn't needed at Barking, he'd gone into the CID office at Walworth to prep for the Larssen interview. It was nearer to Notting Hill and he needed some peace and quiet. Had it only been a matter of the finding of a firearm at the suspect's home, things would have been fine, but it was a Beretta – *the* Beretta – and that made everything a tad more difficult.

The email from Miusze Huang was massive. The gun had been identified as Linked Series 5 – the fifth on a list of firearms that year with multiple shootings to their names. LS5, as he shorthanded it in his notes, had been used in Knightsbridge (Jackson), Stanwell Moor (Kemal Gozit), Myatt's Fields (Brooker, aka Talea, nickname Screwloose) and Elephant and Castle (Krashjig). So, it seemed like Napper had been right all along – she was complicit and the gun being found at her home was compelling, as was her offer of legal funding to the Pope brothers, but… something wasn't right.

Briggs' copper's instincts were nowhere near up to developing even a flaccid indication as to where he should have been pointing his thoughts, so all he could think of doing was a through-the-motions textbook interview plan, a cribsheet for banality, a tickybox gameshow quiz, more likely to brief the suspect on police knowledge than to elicit any sort of confession or co-operation. Knowing Larssen as he did, the woman would probably just yawn disdainfully and answer 'no comment' to each predictable question.

He read through the notes of his previous meetings with the arrogant bitch, remembering how he'd found himself trying to decide whether she was a sociopath, psychopath, narcissist, or at the point on the psychologists' Dark Triad diagram where all three converged.

He wondered why he kept being given tasks that were above his pay grade; surely a DI or at least a more experienced

DS than himself – he was still only 'acting' in the rank – should have been on the search in Notting Hill and conducting the interview of someone found in possession of a linked series firearm with one maiming and three murders on its scoresheet. It would later dawn on him that it was because he was dispensable. He was not being handed opportunities to gain experience and progress his career, far from it; these hazardous jobs exposed him, whilst shielding those above him.

He'd been informed of Larssen's current demeanour, that she was refusing to leave her cell and had made allegations that her solicitor had helped himself to a feel-up during a private consultation. This was a welcome development to Briggs: with a bit of luck she'd be deemed unfit to interview. His thoughts were interrupted by the appearance of Mason, suddenly at his side, excited, gleeful.

'Have you heard?' she said, grinning.

'Heard what?'

'PSD've nicked Doug Napper. Larssen's alleged that he's been fuckin' giving her one and planted that gun in her place while he was at it.'

Briggs did the usual filtration exercise on Mason's language and diction – he always had to work out whether she was being deliberately rude to him – but the enormity of the news almost immediately assumed prominence. And, to him, it wasn't bad news. Interviewing Larssen was now off limits to him: she was PSD property, and they were welcome to her.

He feigned frustration and disappointment. 'Oh, for Christ's sake, PSD'll have first pickings then, we won't get anywhere near her until they've finished. They'll spend ages mollycoddling her, taking her statement and—'

'They're already on it mate, turned up at the Hill half an hour ago, the same ones what interviewed Napper after the shit at Stanwell Moor.' Through her smirk, Mason was giving her colleague a perceptive look, head tilted slightly to one side.

'I know what you're thinking, Rebecca,' sighed Briggs as he sat back in his chair, chucking his pen onto the desk in front of him.

'What?'

'That I'm relieved to be getting off the hook, that I don't have to do the interview now—'

'Yeah, and I don't fucking blame you, mate. You've been slung in at the fuckin' deep end on this, and if it's any consolation we all think you've done fucking well!' Standing over him, she reached forward and put her hand on his shoulder.

Briggs had to stop himself from getting up and hugging the girl. The angst and pressure he'd felt building up over the summer, the constant self-doubt and insecurity, the sleep-interrupting fear, all coalesced to force tears to well up. He looked down, feeling his face beginning to burn. He allowed himself to think he'd been interpreting her coarseness wrongly, that she really was on his side after all.

'Hey, come on, fucking chill.' The hand was still on his shoulder. 'Let's go for a coffee, on me.'

'Thanks Rebecca, but I've got some serious thinking to do.'

Mason shrugged. 'Okay, give me a bell if you change your mind, I'll be in the caff over the road.'

Briggs watched his colleague walk breezily out of the office before turning back to his notes, frowning. Yes, he probably had had some breathing space now; PSD would hog the job and milk it for all it was worth. If he was still allocated the interview of Larssen in respect of the firearm find it would probably be squeezed in at the end of her detention period, by which time God only knew what developments would have occurred.

206

Following the private consultation, Kribz had declined to be interviewed any further. Swan had advised that it was probably in his best interests to be co-operative, given the irrefutable evidence of his actions at Galleons Reach, not to even mention his possession of a loaded firearm, but the gang leader rightly suspected she lacked the street-wisdom of an experienced criminal brief. 'Are you sure, Katrina?' he'd asked.

'No, Mr Pope, as a matter of fact I'm not sure. I'm going to have to take some advice myself. Even to an experienced criminal lawyer – which I must confess I'm not – this is an unusual case. You're already under investigation for being involved in one shooting incident—'

'They can't prove that I was even there,' Kribz interrupted, referring to the Stanwell Moor rumpus, 'so they can't bring that into—'

'I know, well, you're right but it doesn't help, and anyway, they've got you red-handed on this one—'

'So fucking what? I'm admitting to it, innit. I went there to help 'em, they was fuckin' useless, had to do it our way innit, before they fucked the whole thing up an' Numbers got fuckin' wasted!' He'd been getting angrier as each minute passed, and the co-codamol was wearing off; his leg was throbbing with the sort of deep, relentless pain that could stop the toughest man thinking straight.

'But—'

'No buts, Katrina, if you was in the pain I'm in you'd see where I'm comin' from. I'm lucky to be fuckin' alive, innit!'

'Okay, okay, I'll make my representations to the officers, tell them you're in too much pain to be interviewed. But there's just one more thing I need to clarify.'

'Whass that then?' Kribz was wincing now, his face twisted with discomfort and exhaustion.

'The cocaine at Stanwell Moor. Do you still intend to co-operate with the police regarding that?'

'Fuck, I dunno, 'ave you spoke to that Larssen woman lately?'

'No.'

'Let me think about it – an' please get the nurse to come in here now, I need some more of those pills before I fuckin' die.'

Swan stood up, walked to the door and tapped on it loudly. Once again, she couldn't wait to get out of there.

'All done? Ready to continue?' said Briggs as he and Mason had re-entered.

'No, officer, my client is in considerable pain. I really think he's in need of urgent medical attention.'

The interview had then been formally terminated and the custody nurse called in to examine the detainee. In turn, she'd called the police doctor, who had then advised that the prisoner be returned to hospital; the pain had become unmanageable, rendering further interrogation totally inappropriate; any evidence gleaned from an agonised suspect would be inadmissible in court.

207

It never crossed Napper's mind to deny he'd been visiting Larssen 'off grid', so to speak. So what? he'd thought. The worst that can happen is that I'll get disciplined for making undocumented visits to a witness. Stupid, fine. Reckless, maybe. But not a criminal offence. His considerable antecedents for being stupid and reckless wouldn't do him any harm at all; he was a maverick, always off piste – known for it, so they couldn't be surprised. As for having sex with the woman, well, he could deny that now.

And they weren't surprised. 'Well, here we are again then, Doug,' said DI Colin Reeve with a big smile. Sat next to him was DS Gill Durman, also smiling. But there was something about the smiles that Napper didn't find reassuring. And this time round the meeting was not in the dilapidated canteen at Kennington Police Station.

Napper had received orders to attend New Scotland Yard, and he'd done so, on time and reasonably smartly dressed in an ill-fitting sports jacket, chino trousers, a white shirt and a tie with a curry stain on it. He'd trimmed his beard, albeit unevenly, and plastered his hair down with cheap shampoo. It didn't occur to him that the smiles worn by the two PSD officers were more mirthful than friendly.

And when the smiles faded, which they did quite quickly, the Cornishman knew he was in bother.

The room was white walled with the standard table, four chairs and a recording machine which was switched on without further ado. Napper was cautioned and asked if he wanted a solicitor or federation representative; he was entitled to either. He'd already decided to decline and did so with a shrug and an explanation: 'No need, I'm foin, I know what I've done and I'm bang to roights.'

Durman kicked off. 'Okay, Doug, let's start by asking – do you know Freda Larssen?'

'Yes.'

'How long have you known her for?'

'Two or three weeks, erm, no, maybe longer, a month or so.'

'How would you describe your relationship with her?'

'Professional.'

The smiles returned, but only briefly.

'She alleges that you planted criminal evidence – a Beretta handgun – in the freezer of her home address.' Durman then produced a photograph of the weapon and pushed it across the table at the interviewee. 'For the benefit of the recording,' said Reeve, 'DS Durman has just presented PC Napper with a photograph of the said firearm.'

Napper looked at the picture. 'I've never seen that gun before in my life.' His comment was meant to sound helpful but came out too eager.

'Do you deny planting the gun in Freda Larssen's home?' asked Durman, getting to the point.

'Yes, as I've just said, I've never seen that gun before, let alone handled it or planted it.'

Durman regarded him for a couple of seconds, then:

'Okay, going back to Larssen, when did you first meet her?'

'Stanwell Moor was when I first saw her, but I wouldn't call that a meeting, I was getting carted away on a stretcher, just got sight of 'er.'

'Okay, when did you first meet her to speak to her?'

'I went to her place in Notting Hill. I was – an' I still am – convinced she 'as something to do with all this. She's behind the Braganza Boys, and I'll stand by my word on that.'

This was what Reeve and Durman had expected. Reeve intervened. 'Right, if your visit – or visits, because there's presumably been several – were in the course of your duties, why can't we find any mention of them in your duty records?'

Napper answered this one quickly. 'You'll 'ave noticed that there's not much mention of anything in my duty records. It's the way I like it. The less you put in writing the less you can get picked up on. But what you will 'ave found is my entries on the Crimint system. I'm conscientious about my intel contributions.'

Neither PSD officer was going to be drawn on this; the frequency and content of Napper's Crimint entries were still being gone through and no doubt they would throw up more questions than answers about the Cornishman's activities.

Durman moved on. 'Did your relationship with Larssen become intimate?'

'No, definitely not,'

'She said it did Doug,' said Reeve.

'She's lyin' then.'

'Why would she do that?'

Napper snorted. 'I dunno, she's a nutter, obviously.'

'She's claims to have evidence, forensic evidence,' said Durman.

'What sort of forensic evidence?'

'Well,' said Reeve, keen to draw this aspect of the enquiry to a close, 'we haven't actually found any yet but—'

Napper decided to get on the front foot: 'What this boils down to, how I see it, you've got a nutter of a woman who'll do anything to get her hands on that place at Stanwell an' for a long time I've been convinced that she's got the Braganza Boys on side to help her, whether they knew it or not. They was either plottin' with her or she was manipulatin' them—'

'And so convinced were you of your theory that you planted evidence in her house to prove it. That's how it could look from where we're sitting, Doug.' Reeve delivered this with an air of concern, like it worried him that this misfit of a copper was making such a bad show of it. Napper just shrugged.

'You see… you know… this is what's worrying me, Doug.' Reeve's concern gave way to frustration. 'You don't even seem bothered. You're already under investigation for trespass at Stanwell Moor, and now this. It's like you've got a professional death wish – don't you want to keep your job?'

This was a very good question which Napper had been asking himself quite a lot recently. He took a deep breath and let it out as a weary sigh. 'If the force wants to get rid of me then it will. In the meantime I just do the job my way. If that's not good enough then so be it, sack me, but don't try to fit me up with criminal charges.'

'We're not trying to fit you or anyone else up,' cut in Durman, 'but the IPOC are all over us like a rash and whenever there's police contact deaths, they want scapegoats, blood on the walls, Doug, and your relentless nonsense puts you on offer. Anybody would think you're deliberately trying to fit *yourself* up!'

Napper just shrugged again.

'Right. DS Durman, show the officer the video,' said Reeve, wearily.

Durman took out a tablet from her briefcase, powered it up and positioned the screen so that it was facing the suspected officer. She then introduced it into the interview. 'For the benefit of the recording, I am now about to show PC Napper video footage captured by a Metropolitan Police surveillance drone deployed above the Galleons Reach location at the time of the armed incident and the events which followed it.'

It had occurred to Napper that something like this was in store for him and he'd tried to be mentally prepared for it. Tried and failed. The preceding ten minutes had lulled him into thinking that anything caught on the body worn cameras or overhead drones hadn't featured his actions, and had been hoping that the drone that Rankin had shot down had been the only one – but it hadn't, it had been swiftly replaced. His doubling heart rate didn't prevent the blood draining from his face. He managed to lean forward to look at the screen; it showed him walking across the Galleons Reach car park, stopping to pick up Mergin's little rucksack, looping one strap over his shoulder and then continuing towards the Flying Squad car. It was as if the drone camera was focusing on him and him alone, despite other ongoing events being more deserving of attention.

'Do you recognise yourself there, Doug?' asked Durman.

'Yeah, 'course, that's me.'

'Do you agree that you are the individual picking up the rucksack and putting it on your shoulder before proceeding to get into the police vehicle?'

'Yeah.'

'What did you do with that rucksack?'

'Shit, I'm sorry, I put it in my locker at Kennington.'

'Where is it now?'

'Still there. I know, I'm sorry, I just forgot about it. I should have got it to the exhibits store, sorry.'

'What was inside the bag?'

'A few schoolbooks an' some sort of little computer game, nothin' important.'

'Did you remove anything from the bag, PC Napper?' This question came from Reeve.

'No, I just had a look inside an' zipped it up again and shoved it in my locker. It must still be there.'

'No it isn't', corrected Durman. 'We searched your locker and retrieved it, and you're right, there was nothing of any significance in the bag. But what we want to know is why you didn't put it into the exhibits system as per regulations. Can you tell us?'

Napper shrugged yet again. 'I was just knackered, just wanted to get off duty an' go 'ome. I fully intended to do it the next day, just forgot, tha's all.'

It was Reeve's turn. 'Okay, moving on to your Crimint entry about the firearm being at Larssen's place, where did you get that intel?'

'Christopher Pope told me, when we was together in the car park at Galleons Reach—'

'Oh, come on, Doug, you cannot expect us to accept that! You're acting as the main liaison link on a live hostage job and you just happen to get information from the victim about the location of a firearm – a linked series firearm at that – and all you do is make a Crimint entry more than twenty-four hours later! Is that really what happened?'

'Yes sir, that's really what 'appened. Kribz – that's Pope – seemed keen to get it off 'is chest, but I didn't see it as bein' important, under the circumstances, like. We was in the middle of something big an' the important thing as I saw it was that the gun he was talking about wasn't puttin' anyone in immediate danger, so I just dealt with the intel later, in the normal way.'

Reeve regarded Napper with a mixture of disbelief and resignation. By having no good explanations, Napper had all the explanations. Standard logic didn't apply. He was sailing close to the wind but there was no hard evidence that he'd crossed any serious criminal line. The PSD man decided not to even bother asking the Cornishman if he knew anything about an anonymous Crimestoppers call made from a north London cafe on the same day as the Crimint entry had been logged; any such question would just be met with another shrug of the shoulders, so why bother.

'Alright, Doug, let's leave it there. Well, unless there's anything you wish to add, of course. You know what's been alleged against you and you've denied the allegation, so I take it you'll just want to leave it at that—'

'No, I need to tell you about something else, just in case you don't already know. Larssen's got the Popes to put their hands up to the cocaine found at the Stanwell Moor place, so Tom Rankin gets off the hook and doesn't get POCA'd.'

Reeve and Durman exchanged glances.

'Where did you get this from?' asked Durman.

'My confi source at first, that's why it's not on Crimint. I was still tryin' to verify it when Galleons Reach kicked off, but the more I think about it, the more it fits, specially now the gun's been found at her place.'

'Is this intel recorded anywhere at all?' asked Reeve, primarily for the want of something better to say.

'Not as far as I know. The Popes was due to be interviewed next week, by Briggsy prob'ly, but events 'ave sort of overtaken ev'rythin' else—'

'Yes, yes, we know all that, and we're aware of the Popes' offer to admit responsibility for the cocaine found after the attack on the Rankin property.' Reeve paused for a couple of seconds, then: 'What I want to know is how you've come up with Larssen being behind this offer, if that's what you're saying—'

'Yes, it's exactly what I'm sayin', and she's more than capable of it, she's a fuckin' psycho, trust me on that one, I promise you.'

Durman's turn: 'Did Larssen herself tell you about this? Did she admit to you that this is what she was doing?'

'Yeah, she confirmed it, and there's a solicitor involved an' all, the one that's representin' the Popes. Swan's 'er name, Katalina Swan, or sumthin' like that, she's in on it an' all.'

That was it, thought Napper. He'd said more than he'd intended to, put his involvement with Larssen slap-bang in the evidential chain, but what the fuck? It was evidence, and him being the source would save his skin – for a while, anyway.

Again, the PSD cops were caught slightly off balance. Reeve sought to regain control. 'Right, Doug, we're going to end this interview here and, right now, you're going to sit in this room and write a full statement about what you've just told us, every detail, including hearsay. Do you understand?'

'Yessir.'

'Do you want us to retrieve any notes you may have tucked away anywhere?'

'No sir, none of this is written down anywhere—'

'Why aren't I surprised?' sighed Reeve, rising wearily from the table. Smirking, Durman packed away her tablet and notebook and switched off the recording machine.

208

Despite there being no evidential link between the Beretta and Galleons Reach, and nothing to put Larssen in the frame as having any direct involvement in the incident, Passey was intrigued by the emerging history. The gun was linked to just about everything else the so-called Braganza Boys were suspected of, and now the linkage was operating in reverse; wherever that weapon popped up you'd find a connection –

albeit tangential – with the B Boys or their associates.

Napper's full statement reached the SIO by email late that evening, less than half an hour after Passey had received notification that the CPS wanted Larssen to be charged with possession of an unlicensed Section 1 firearm. The prosecutor intended to object to bail on the first court appearance the following morning so that the woman would be remanded in custody, pending further investigation into her suspected involvement in forensically linked criminality.

Passey hadn't witnessed Larssen's behaviour in her cell at Notting Hill but, having attended the station to find out firsthand more about her, he'd been on hand to see the video recording of the darkly comical incident. It had reassured him. He'd been worried that the woman was going to be an unwanted complication in Operation Convolute, but now he was satisfied that she could be placed firmly in the wildcard category; irritating but not a major problem, given her obvious irrationality. The CPS were recommending that a psychiatric examination be undertaken to assess her fitness to stand trial. This didn't bother Passey; the prisons were chock-a-block with nutcases – being a psychopath was no defence in criminal proceedings as the condition didn't amount to legally defined insanity.

Back in Barking incident room that night, he called the Notting Hill custody inspector.

'Hello, Detective Superintendent Duncan Passey here. To whom do I speak, please?'

'Good evening, sir, we met earlier, Inspector Wade, I showed you our latest video nasty, how can I help you?'

'Yes, Mr Wade, what's the latest on our lady friend, has she been charged yet?'

'Yes sir, unlawful possession of a Section 1 firearm. She'll be transferred to Westminster Magistrates' Court first thing tomorrow morning and I'll be glad to be shot of her.'

'I take it she won't be wanting that solicitor to represent her, the one she's alleging indecently assaulted her.'

'No,' laughed the inspector, 'she sacked him. Er, it seems she never really wanted him to represent her, she just wanted to have a pop at him. Now he's out of the picture she's wanting another brief be present in court tomorrow, a woman called Swan from a firm on the legal aid list—'

Passey wasn't really interested in this. 'Yeah, okay, that's fine Mr Wade, we'll leave it to the CPS now. Have a good day.'

The call thus ended, the SIO sat back, stretched and rubbed his eyes with his fists. He was alone and took a few seconds to relax and survey the deserted incident room, the last of the staff having finished their shift and gone over an hour previously. He donned his jacket and prepared to follow suit, then his mobile buzzed. Tutting, he picked up. 'Duncan Passey.'

'Duncan, long time. Colin Reeve, how's it going?'

Passey and Reeve knew each other: their paths had occasionally crossed. They disliked each other for no reason, just that healthy professional tension which often existed between competitive, ambitious men.

'Hi Colin, what can I do for you at this ungodly time of day?'

'Nothing really, mate, just tipping you the wink about a certain officer you might like to keep an eye on, just in case you don't already know about him,' said Reeve in the spirit of professional good intentions.

'Oh, okay, and which officer might that be, Colin?'

'Napper, Douglas Napper, a PC the squad used as their intel link on your job—'

'Yeah, yeah, I've just read his statement, bit of a bloody eccentric I would say, what—'

'Yup, and you can say that again, Duncan. I'm working at Professional Standards now and he made that statement after we'd finished interviewing him. The Larssen woman's alleging he planted the gun at her place while he was visiting her.' Reeve delivered this with pleasure, knowing it would needle the SIO.

'Good for him. Sounds like my kind of copper,' lied Passey, sensing the need to take the wind out of his opponent's sails.

'Just thought I'd let you know, mate, in case you were going to give him anything important to do,' replied Reeve, retreating somewhat.

'So you haven't suspended him, then?'

'No, no reason to, the woman's in custody, out of the picture, and he's admitted to being a prat but unsurprisingly denies having anything to do with the gun being at her address. He'll have to be redeployed, that's all. We've stuck him back in uniform and put him on restricted duties, for his own sake if nothing else.'

'Okay, Colin, thanks for letting me know.' The call did not end unpleasantly and Passey finally got out of Barking Police Station and made his way home for the night.

209

Blake was in his office and was quite relaxed. Apart from a fading red weal on his neck where Larssen had grabbed him, and a small tear to the collar of his rugby shirt, he was intact. The custody sergeant had apologised profusely, assuring him that the video footage from the cell camera showed nothing to support the crazy woman's claim that the solicitor had molested her, and Blake had even been asked if he himself wished to make a complaint. He'd declined, of course: churlish not to.

It was gone midnight, but he wanted to get the call in, be the first to impart the news.

'Jacko, me old mate, have I got news for you!'

Jackson had paused his Netflix binge session to answer the phone. 'Good evening Stuart, I'm all ears,' he said, wearily.

'Larssen got arrested yesterday. Possession of a firearm. She's in custody and going fucking nowhere fast.' He had to make an effort not to sound excited.

Jackson took a couple of seconds to absorb this, then: 'How d'you know this?'

'Went to see her, didn't I? She nominated me as her legal representative, or at least pretended to, then fucking bashed me up in her cell and alleged I'd grabbed her tits!' The lawyer had given up on his attempt at professional calm and his voice was ascending the octaval scale.

'Jesus Christ, I can't believe it! She had a gun?!'

'Yes mate, in her flat, and she's saying Doug Napper planted it there!' He was saving the best bit for last.

'And what do *you* think, Stuart?'

'What do you mean, what do *I* think? What I think's got fuck all—'

'Did Napper plant the gun?'

'Course he fucking didn't, the woman's stark staring mad – you of all people should know that. D'you want to know the best bit?'

'What?'

'The gun's the one used on you!' Blake was shrieking now.

'Oh for fuck's sake, Stuart, this has got to be some sort of fucking stitch up! Napper's been determined to implicate Larssen in all this and now it just so happens the gun gets found in her place and she's blaming him for it being there! It bloody stinks to high heaven!'

'I know it does,' said Blake, at a more moderate pitch, 'but it can stink all it likes, because there's other evidence that she was doing business with the B Boys…'

'The what?'

'The Braganza Boys, who've all been nicked after a shoot-out over in the East End the other day.'

Jackson was slumped in one of his big easy chairs, his stump elevated on a coffee table. He sighed and rubbed his forehead.

'Does this mean she'll be charged with being involved in shooting me?'

'No, not as far as I can see just now, these guns get passed around a bit. But it's certainly a Braganza gun, and what's more it was used at Stanwell Moor as well, to kill one of the Albanians, and Larssen was actually fucking there at the time!' Blake's voice was rising again. He was thinking aloud, the ramifications hitting him one by one.

Jackson had a reasonable knowledge of the law. 'I'm getting you, I think. So, apart from possible evidence of conspiracy and unless more proof comes to light, the only offence they've got her for is possession of the gun.'

'Spot on, Jacko, at the very least. She can scream all she likes about the police planting it on her, but that's a standard defence when you've been caught bang to rights in possession of a fucking murder weapon.' Impressed by Jackson's lucidity, the lawyer had managed to re-moderate his tone to befit the gravity of the subject; it occurred to him to remember that he wanted Jackson to retain him as a lawyer, not a jokey pal.

Jackson had by this time struggled to his foot and had crutched himself across the room to the drinks cabinet. His phone was on speaker and he lay it down so he could pour himself a large Scotch.

Blake heard the clinking. 'Er, don't go on a bender, mate. I was just about to suggest we had a meeting tomorrow, here at my office.'

'You mean later today, Stuart.' Jackson had looked at his Rolex.

'Yeah, right, be here by ten. I'll have coffee ready.'

210

Katrina Swan was trying to work out why she'd got involved in this mess, and how she'd prepared her exit strategy. The more she thought about it, the better she felt. Her initial dealings with the Pope brothers had been strictly above board: attending the police station to represent them during interview under caution, as per her duty as a legal aid lawyer. What had happened subsequently was obviously more contentious: brokering a deal to come clean on drugs possession in return for financial support. She'd approached Larssen at the Popes' behest; they wanted financial support in return for owning up and going to prison, probably for several years.

No! That was ridiculous; she was worldly enough to know that boys like the Popes valued their freedom more than anything else. There was no way they intended to go through with the plan and Swan inwardly chided herself for even briefly entertaining the possibility. The most likely outcome would be that the brothers would play a long game – run the clock down and, at the last possible moment, pull out of the deal and swear blind that they'd had nothing to do with the stash and that Larssen had bribed them to keep Rankin off the hook and thereby scupper the POCA order.

Swan turned this over in her head a few times and really couldn't see anything terribly wrong with the arrangement – provided of course that it was based on a semblance of the truth, a believable scenario. Otherwise the deal would amount to perverting the course of justice. But surely that was absurd, and who else would have stored that cocaine in the shed at Stanwell Moor? Nah, she was fine. It had the Popes written all over it: they'd been cuckooing the old Irishman so the narrative was solid enough. She'd done her homework and cuckooing – the use of a vulnerable person's home as a venue for illicit behaviour – was a standard strategy amongst urban street gangs. The only question was: to what extent was this

Tom Rankin guy vulnerable? But that was for others to worry about. She'd only been the messenger, the linkage between the Popes and Larssen, and she'd merely been acting on her client's instructions.

Round and round went the reasoning behind the frown on her worried face. So fixated was she that Notting Hill Tube Station almost eluded her; she had to leap from her seat and virtually dive out onto the platform. Gathering herself, she ascended the escalator and walked out onto the pavement, briskly covering the two hundred yards to the police station in the bright morning sunshine. It was 7.30 and she'd been called by the custody officer as detainee Freda Larssen had demanded to see her before being taken in the custody van to Westminster Magistrates' Court.

'She's refusing to leave her cell as usual,' said the custody officer. 'We're going to have to drag her out to get her to court.'

'But she still wants to see me first?' asked Swan, confused.

'Yeah, but you're not going in there alone. Me and a detention officer'll have to accompany you. She assaulted the last solicitor and I'm not risking that happening again.'

'The *last* solicitor?'

'Yeah,' replied the weary sergeant, 'but I'm not going into detail about that. Come on, I've got a lot to do.'

The sergeant opened the door and the detention officer led Swan into the cell. Larssen was sitting on the bench-bed with knees pulled up under her chin and her arms wrapped around her legs. She looked small, vulnerable.

'Hello Freda, how are you?' said Swan, professionally.

'You have a talent for stupid questions, Miss Swan.'

Swan didn't think she deserved that. 'What do you mean? I think that's the first question I've ever really asked you. Up till now it's just been you telling me what to do.' The custody sergeant and the detention officer exchanged glances.

'Yes,' croaked Larssen, 'and there's more to come right now. Tell your fucking black gangster clients I want nothing more to do with them. They're working with the police to incriminate me – and you can make a note of that, officer, just in case we're not being recorded.' The last bit was directed at the custody sergeant.

'Right, fine, will that be all? Do you want me to attend court this morning?'

'Yes, I want bail, and I'll pay.'

'I don't think it'll be as simple as that, Freda. The Crown Prosecution Service will ask for a remand in custody and, given the circumstances, I won't have a cat in hell's chance of stopping them getting it.'

'Just try, please.' Larssen's voice had a slight tremble to it. She was fearful.

'Of course I will. Okay, see you in court, Freda.' Swan spoke with finality: she was keen to finish this before the woman made any more mention of the Popes within police earshot. She turned and walked out of the cell, and then out of the building, with a spring in her step. She looked at her watch – still early, time for a coffee before her next little Underground journey: Charing Cross Police Station and the illustrious Pope brothers for *their* pre-court chat. Very handy, she thought, very handy indeed. She could now impart news of the latest development and prepare for the other bail application, which she thought she might have a chance of winning.

The morning was wearing on and the Tube was busy; she had to stand and hang on to the handrail, her free arm wrapped tightly around her briefcase. Conflict of interest, perverting the course of justice, aiding and abetting offenders: these topics and other aspects of jurisprudence kept popping up in her mind.

She was sailing close to the wind, that was for sure, but her curiosity had not got the better of her to an extent that would

Broth

lead to criminal charges, or even Law Society disciplinary proceedings. She'd always been acting on clients' instructions. As regards conflict of interest, she considered the possibility of having to recuse herself from one of the parties because before long they would probably start making allegations against each other and if co-defendants fell out they had to be separately represented. If she dumped Larssen her firm would lose litigation work on the Rankin property. If she dumped the Popes she would lose a big payout from the legal aid fund. One or the other would have to go; not quite yet though, she thought, deciding to see how things panned out on the bail applications first.

211

Larssen was first up. The court scheduling officer had been told that the Dane was a security risk and liable to misbehave at the slightest provocation, so it was decided to get her dealt with and out of the way. The district judge, a relative youngster in his forties, had been likewise tipped off and regarded the defendant with interest as she was led up the stairs from the court holding cells and into the dock.

Swan, having arrived in good time to prepare her application, sat facing the bench. She stood up when Larssen's name was announced. 'I represent this defendant, sir,' she managed, before the prosecutor, also facing the bench alongside her, stood to open the case.

'Your Worship, you will see that this defendant appears before you on an indictable-only charge. Her transfer to the Crown Court will therefore be automatic.'

'Yes, Mr Openshaw, I'm aware of that,' said the magistrate. 'What's the position regarding bail?'

'The Crown objects to bail in the strongest possible terms, sir.' The prosecutor went on to list several reasons why Larssen's release on bail would, given the seriousness of the offence, risk her absconding, interfering with witnesses and

446

committing further offences whilst awaiting trial by jury. The magistrate remained impassive, then invited the defence advocate to speak.

'Miss Swan?'

'Your Worship, my client will be contesting the charge and my instructions are that her defence will be based on her own allegations against the police—'

The district judge interrupted. 'Miss Swan, it is not the purpose of this hearing to air the essence of your client's defence. Please confine yourself to the matter of bail by addressing the prosecution's objections.'

'Your Worship, yes, I understand, and my instructions are to ask that you grant bail so that my client may prepare her defence.' Swan found herself gabbling, struggling to piece together a cogent argument. 'She has several avenues of enquiry to pursue in order to obtain evidence to prove that she is the victim of a conspiracy—'

'But surely that's *your* job, Miss Swan, and she can instruct you to carry out these enquiries on her behalf. The court has just heard that the prosecution fears she will interfere with witnesses should she be granted bail. No, I'm sorry, Miss Swan, but on this occasion your application for bail has failed. The defendant will be remanded in custody for seven days.'

Swan had never really thought she'd had a chance, but the brutal put-down was worse than she'd expected. 'Very well sir, but I—'

'You're useless!' came the hiss from the dock. Swan swivelled round to see the livid Larssen being shepherded back down the stairs to the holding cells. Turned back to face the bench she sat and shuffled her papers with her head down, face burning.

The dock officer began to introduce the next case. 'Case number two on your list, sir—'

He was interrupted by clearly audible shouting from the basement. 'What are *you* doing here!? Have you done a deal with them?!'

'… Christopher and Derek Pope.'

The Popes were both looking down and behind them as they climbed the last wooden steps from the cell area into the dock. Driss was grinning; Larssen's shouting had become muffled and unintelligible, but she could still be heard.

Swan glanced around to see her next two clients standing side by side. Kribz leant heavily on the brass rail which topped off the wooden dock.

'Yes, Mr Openshaw?'

'Sir, as you will see from the charge sheet, these two defendants are accused of false imprisonment and possession of firearms. The case is an unusual one—'

'Yes, most unusual. The brief facts – as I have them – are very interesting, Mr Openshaw.' Some district judges could not stop interrupting.

'Indeed, sir, the Crown objects to bail on the grounds that the defendants are members of what is known as an urban street gang and have in the past demonstrated their ability to influence others and interfere with witnesses. Their capacity to commit crime whilst on bail is equally demonstrated by the fact that the offences for which they are before you today were allegedly committed whilst they were on police bail pending an investigation into an earlier incident—'

'Mr Openshaw, I've read the case summary as it stands, thank you. Miss Swan, I take it you have an application?'

'Your Worship, yes. At the time of the alleged offences these defendants were assisting police to resolve a hostage-taking incident, and their assistance helped ensure that the hostage was successfully released. Had it not been for their intervention the outcome would in all probability have been most unsuccessful. I ask that you grant bail, albeit with conditions, so that the prosecution may review the case in the light of proper consultation with the police as regards a possible reduction in the seriousness of the charges.' Swan found herself babbling again and braced herself for another knockback.

The district judge was nodding before she'd even finished. 'Yes, Miss Swan, as I've just indicated, I'm familiar with some of the important details of the case and, subject to conditions, I'm minded to grant bail to these two defendants.' He then turned to the prosecutor. 'Mr Openshaw, perhaps you could make an offer as to the conditions which the Crown would be prepared to accept. Will you do that, please?'

Openshaw was prepared. 'Sir, yes, the Crown accepts that the risks raised by allowing these men to be remanded on bail would be mitigated by the conditions that they observe a strict curfew, refrain from contacting any witnesses, attend Walworth Police Station twice daily and,' – and then came the hard one – 'provide a surety of five thousand pounds each which would be forfeited in the event of their failing to appear at the next and subsequent hearings or their breaking any one of the aforementioned conditions.'

Swan, in any event uncomfortable in a criminal court setting, was completely at a loss as to what was supposed to happen next. As a primarily civil lawyer, she was totally flummoxed. 'Your Worship, whilst I have no doubt that my clients will in principle accept these conditions on their bail, I have not had the opportunity to take instructions from them as regards the availability of a suitable person prepared to stand surety for the not inconsiderable sums stipulated. I would therefore—'

Her flow was stopped by a gesture from the district judge; he was pointing, for Swan's benefit, at someone at the back of the courtroom. She swung round to see an overweight but very smartly dressed man nodding at her, his hand raised unobtrusively to shoulder height, like a cautious bidder at an auction.

'I think the gentleman at the back of the court wishes to be of assistance, Miss Swan. Perhaps you'd like to have a few seconds with him.' Swan stepped out from behind the advocates' bench and made her way to the rear of the room.

The Popes' eyes followed her and they slowly turned to get a look at the volunteer.

'Fuck me,' whispered Driss.

'Shut the fuck up,' murmured Kribz.

They had both immediately recognised Claude Jackson.

The hushed courtroom waited whilst a brief and inaudible conversation took place. Swan was seen to nod in agreement to something before returning to her place. 'Sir, the gentleman is a business associate of the defendants and is happy to offer his recognisance and stand surety for the sum you have specified.'

'Mr Openshaw?'

'Sir, erm, this is somewhat unexpected. I will need to take instructions from the officer in the case and, erm, possibly, if it would assist the court, ask a few questions of the gentleman himself, if that would—'

'Yes, yes. Miss Swan, ask the surety if he would be prepared to answer questions as to his suitability, please.'

Swan had no need; Jackson, dressed in a smoke blue linen suit and pink, open-necked shirt was already making his respectful way towards the witness box. He stepped into the oak wood structure and waited to be questioned.

'What is your name, sir?' asked the judge, smiling pleasantly.

'Claude Jackson.'

'And your profession?' The judge was making notes.

'I'm a property developer, Your Honour.'

'You've no need to address me as "Your Honour", Mr Jackson, this is not the Crown Court. Please relax. What is your relationship with the two defendants?'

'We have a mutual business interest, sir, and it's important that they're at liberty to conduct some tasks on my behalf, sir.'

The judge frowned, his reassuring smile fading. 'Okay, Mr Jackson, the mind boggles somewhat, I have to say. These young men don't strike me as being typical of the, er, property developing community, if I can put it that way.' The judge was regarding the Popes with open incredulity. He refocused on his notes. 'Very well, do you fully appreciate that if either of them even in the slightest way fails to meet the bail conditions I'm about to impose, you will lose ten thousand pounds?'

'Yes, sir.'

'And are you able to lodge the full amount with the court today?'

'Yes sir, I am.'

The brothers in the dock sat stony-faced, hardly daring to look at Jackson. Driss could hear Kribz controlling his breathing and endeavoured to do likewise. The custody officer stood beside them, awaiting instructions.

'Very well,' said the judge again. 'Do you have any questions or observations, Mr Openshaw?'

The Crown prosecutor stood up, looked at Jackson and then at the judge. 'Sir, obviously this gentleman will have to complete a few formalities and the officer in the case will need to conduct checks on his probity and, er, solvency, and then, if all's well, I see no reason why the defendants should not be granted bail.'

Hence, the judge wrapped it up: 'Derek and Christopher Pope, you've heard what's been said and your legal representative will explain things more fully. You'll be taken back down into the holding cells for the time being pending the completion of the paperwork. Should your surety come up to proof then you'll be released on bail with the following conditions attached.' The judge went on to itemise a series of strict terms about reporting to Walworth Police Station, surrendering their passports and not interfering with witnesses, and then the brothers were led back down the stairs.

'Next case, please,' sighed the district judge.

212

'Next case, please,' said another judge, an hour later and about two miles away in the City of London, in which there was no defendant as it was the Mayor's and City of London Court of the civil jurisdiction.

This was the natural habitat of Stuart Blake. Having little in the way of the advocacy skills needed in the criminal courts, he was more at home arguing the finer points of property and contract law and presenting paperwork which, surprisingly for a man with such a chaotic lifestyle, invariably approached perfection.

'Sir,' opened Blake, dressed in what passed as a suit and tie, just, 'I appear on behalf of the applicant in this matter to request that a previous order to transfer the assets of an incorporated company be nullified—'

'Yes, Mr Blake,' interjected the judge, 'I've actually had a chance this morning to peruse the papers and I have to say that this is a rather unusual application.' The judge was frowning down at the scruffy lawyer before him, clearly unimpressed.

'I couldn't agree more, sir,' said Blake, cheerfully. 'It's actually quite bizarre, and there've been developments since the papers were prepared, sir.' Blake was enjoying this immensely and waited for the inevitable question.

'Go on, Mr Blake,' said the judge, still frowning.

'Less than an hour ago, sir, at Westminster Magistrates' Court, the person most likely to attempt to resist the application was remanded in custody on firearms charges, and I am reliably informed that she faces the possibility of further charges in respect of her conduct of the company of which she, three months ago, became sole director.'

The frown disappeared. 'I see, and your client, er, Mr…'

'Jackson, sir, Claude Jackson.'

'Yes, thank you.' The judge was leafing through papers as he spoke. 'Erm, right, Mr Jackson wishes to resume his directorship of the company, is that correct?'

'Yes sir. If you were to grant my application this morning the company and its assets, which include ongoing business transactions, would revert to him automatically.'

'But wouldn't the other party, er, someone called Larssen, is it?'

'Yes sir, Freda Larssen.'

'Would she not remain a co-director?'

'On paper for the time being sir, yes. Her removal from the register as such will be dealt with through a separate application to Companies House, I—'

'Very well, Mr Blake. In the absence of Freda Larssen or anyone to speak on her behalf, I hereby make an interim suspension of the original order. It will be nullified for thirty days, and if there is no counter-application to reverse the nullification within that time it will become permanent.'

'Thank you, sir.'

Blake left the building, pleased with himself. Jackson was waiting, stationed in a nearby Costa, as arranged.

'Fucking doddle,' beamed the lawyer as he walked in. 'Give me another twenty-four hours and JLP Restructuring PLC, or JLP Restructuring *Denmark* PLC as it's now called, will be back in your podgy little hands, Jacko me ol' son. Can we go somewhere else? I need a fucking pint.'

213

Bora dressed down for the occasion. Hair tied back, loosely, not scraped; no earrings; no lipstick. White blouse, beige pullover, brown slacks and a waxed Barbour. She looked more like a social worker than an OCG senior.

Broth

The slap-crashing of the electromagnetic door locks resonated with the curt instructions of the staff: 'This way please,' 'Contents of your pockets and bags on the tray please,' 'Wait here please,' 'Wait there please, have your Visiting Order ready please.' Etc.

She had to go through the procedure twice: Zamir Gozit was in the Secure Unit, Belmarsh's prison within a prison. So, after two X-ray arches and two frisks by surprisingly attractive female prison officers, she sat across a small table from her brother. One side of his head had a large pink sticking plaster over it, covering the gash wound that had, courtesy of a police bullet, replaced his left ear. Bora thought it best not to mention this; her brother had always been known for his vanity.

'You have *kanun*, Zammy, the old man is dead. It's over, our father is honoured, I—' She spoke quietly in the broadest Gheg dialect she could muster.

'No!' he interrupted through clenched teeth, his jaw muscles working. 'Nowhere fucking near it. I'm going to pay heavily soon, very heavily. An old man having a heart attack in hospital doesn't do it, Bora.'

They were both very conscious of cameras and the prowling prison officers in the visiting area, not to mention hidden listening devices. Enough had been said – she wanted to get out of the place. 'I'm going now.'

'You've only just got here. You have twenty minutes. Stay, or you'll arouse suspicion.' His expression had softened. Bora relaxed a little.

'I'm surprised they didn't hold you, lock you up, just for being with me in, what they call it? Joint enterprise?'

'I'm released. They think I was acting under duress – your duress.' She looked down as she said this: she was on thin ice.

'Is that what you told them, that I forced you to be in that car with me, and have a fucking gun in your hand?'

'They never saw me with the gun. I said I was just along for the ride.' She paused. 'But I'm not out of the woods yet. They could still change their minds, decide to charge me, but at least I'm out and about, Zammy—'

'How is Mergin?' interrupted Zamir, keen to move on, not trusting himself to address the hurtful possibility that his sister was helping the police.

'He's fine, they asked him a lot of questions but he gave them nothing, pretended to be stupid.'

'Not too difficult for him,' said the prisoner, grinning, and they both laughed a little. She looked down again, nervous, fidgety.

'Okay, I'll let you go,' said Zamir. 'But remember, Bora, *kanun* isn't done yet. I need more.'

She nodded, almost imperceptibly, and rose. He did likewise. They knew not to try to embrace – strictly against the rules. 'When is your trial?'

'Sentencing, you mean. I'm pleading guilty.'

'What?!'

'Yes, to manslaughter, I'm hoping for ten years at worst, and maybe a transfer to Durres Prison in the old country, then I'll get open conditions. It's my best option, Bora. If I plead *not* guilty they'll stick with murder and I'll probably get convicted and get life with a minimum of twenty and have to serve it all in this country.' He was referring to the gangland murder for which he'd been wanted for several years. Most of the witnesses had disappeared and he'd been advised that the CPS would be very happy not to have to prepare for a full-blown murder trial that a guilty plea to manslaughter would obviate. He'd also been advised that he would probably serve any sentence for the most recent misdemeanours concurrently, meaning that the predicted ten years for manslaughter would be the end of it.

She stared at him, open mouthed. For the first time ever, her brother looked defeated, and accepting of defeat. She'd expected him to be angry, defiant. No, *kanun* was all he was after and he'd face the consequences. A real Gheg: she was proud of him, which made her one as well.

She nodded deeply, almost a bow, turned, and allowed herself to be escorted out of the room.

214

'I was temporarily incapacitated, Mr Tremayne, out of the picture for several months, unfortunately. But I'm back now and my friend Freda Larssen is now out of the picture – permanently.'

Jackson had spent hours preparing for this. He was back in his office and looking good. Apart from his elegant walking stick and a steadily growing midriff, there wasn't a lot of difference. The staff – those that were still there – were all genuinely pleased to see him back at the helm, particularly Palmer, who reckoned his loyalty would soon be repaid by way of a remunerative hike.

The man on the other end of the line was ponderous. 'I read, or heard – can't remember which, possibly both – that you were shot, Mr Jackson. You sure you're okay now? Our clients are nervous about adverse publicity, I'm sure you understand that—'

'Yes, of course, Mr Tremayne, and it's a nervousness that's well justified and usually rewarded, but I can assure you that the root of the problem has been thoroughly exorcised. You'll see the word "Denmark" has been removed from our company name, and—'

'That's only the name, though, Mr Jackson. What my clients are concerned about is the interest the police have in the property. Some sort of Proceeds of Crime Act confiscation order was looming, was it not?'

'It was, you're right, but we think we have that under control now, being that the person at whom the POCA application was directed has sadly died—'

456

'Yes, we know that, but we're advised that the confiscation could now be made against the estate of the deceased, which means that Mr Rankin's death has no effect on the proposed confiscation.'

Jackson had been worried about this, and Tremayne was right; anyone with a legal or beneficial interest in the Rankin estate, including the Royal Bank and its handsomely paid agents and consultants, would almost certainly lose out if the CPS decided to forge ahead with the POCA action.

'Technically, Mr Tremayne, you're right, of course, but it's a matter for the CPS and the courts. It's not set in stone that they'll go ahead with the confiscatory action. There have been other developments which muddy the waters, so to speak, and I'm hopeful that they'll back off and leave the estate alone.'

Jackson spoke fluently and with authority; he'd done his homework – and had his fingers crossed. Blake had told him that, given the indications from the Pope brothers that they'd been responsible for the presence of the cocaine on the Rankin property, and given the mounting evidence that Rankin had been arguably more of a victim than a perpetrator of the criminal mischiefs pertaining to Stanwell Moor, then it was very possible that the CPS, not known for its boldness at the best of times, would simply chuck the towel in and move on to something easier. Particularly as they would also face legal resistance and counter claims from both Jackson and Tremayne who'd want to demonstrate that Stanwell Moor was not solely the proceeds of crime, but also the proceeds of indebtedness to the powerful Royal Bank which wanted the property sold so it could get its money back. Add to that the fact that the ultimate buyer was an American conglomerate with tentacles slithering around in influential governmental nooks and crannies, and the odds that the CPS would find a reason to fade out of the picture looked good.

215

The defendant wore a grey tracksuit zipped up to her throat. Had her hair been longer it would have been noticeably greasy. Her eyes had dark circles beneath them and there was no make-up to cover the abscess on her top lip.

As a person facing almost certain imprisonment if convicted, Larssen qualified for publicly funded legal representation. Consequently, Swan had instructed a competent barrister to represent the Dane at the Old Bailey. His name was Andrew Ballantyne and he sat on the advocates' bench in front of his instructing solicitor, wearing a very perplexed expression; he'd just spent almost an hour with the defendant in one of the many holding cells beneath this vast building, the cornerstone of English criminal justice, where her case had been transferred for this unusual pre-trial application.

Carl Openshaw, appearing for the prosecution, was a 'solicitor advocate' and, as such, had rights of audience at the Crown Court. He stood.

'My Lord,' he addressed the red-robed senior judge appropriately, 'I have just had the benefit of an informal conference with my learned friend Mr Ballantyne, and based on what we have discussed I believe that he has an application to make.' He sat.

'Yes, otherwise we wouldn't be here,' said the judge, irritably. 'Mr Ballantyne?'

Ballantyne stood. 'My Lord, I thank my learned friend for according me precedence.' He paused to collect himself; this wasn't going to be easy.

'My Lord, prior to meeting my learned friend this morning, I spent about forty-five minutes with the defendant. I hereby report to the court that, before I consider myself competent to represent her, I must respectfully apply to your Lordship that she be made the subject of a psychiatric examination to assess her fitness to stand trial—'

'What?!' screeched Larssen from the dock.

Ballantyne continued. 'Aside from continually insisting that the firearm to which the principal charge on the indictment refers was planted by the police, her demeanour can only be described as incoherent—'

'Rubbish! It's you who's incompetent, you couldn't—'

The judge intervened. 'Miss Larssen, allow your barrister to present his argument, or you will be taken down to the cells and these proceedings will continue in your absence.'

'Fine then, put me back down there. You're all totally corrupt. This country is a shithole!'

Ballantyne persevered. 'My Lord, I submit that—'

His Lordship had heard enough. 'Yes, Mr Ballantyne, I am minded already to adjourn this case to enable a psychiatric report on the defendant to be prepared. Do you have any observations, Mr Openshaw?'

Ballantyne sat down and Openshaw bobbed up. 'Only to acquiesce with my learned friend's application, My Lord. I am informed that the police have been unable to illicit any cogent or intelligible response from the defendant as she has steadfastly refused to be interviewed under caution, and had it not been for my learned friend's pre-emptive application I myself may have had no option but to make an identical request.'

'Very well,' said the judge, 'case adjourned for twenty-eight days for psychiatric reports. The defendant will remain in custody.'

'Ha, now there's a fucking surprise,' sneered Larssen, as she was led away by two burly female prison officers.

Ballantyne swivelled round to consult his instructing solicitor. 'Was that okay?' he whispered.

'That was fine Andrew, thank you. I suppose I'll have to go down to the cells now for another volley of abuse.' Swan sighed, whilst standing and gathering up her papers.

'Do you want me to come with you?'

'No, don't bother. I'm not going to be down there long and there's no point in giving her two targets to shoot at.'

Ballantyne nodded. 'Okay, Katrina, I'll have my clerk submit my fee note to your office, no rush for payment.' They shook hands and Swan left the courtroom, bowing briefly to the bench before she did so. The judge didn't notice; the next case was already being called.

She stepped out into the cool autumn afternoon and decided she needed a drink. The bars around the Old Bailey were not unaccustomed to lone females and she felt quite at ease walking into the Magpie and Stump, especially as she knew she wouldn't be unaccompanied for long.

The pub was busy and she didn't see them at first, so she just headed straight for the bar.

'Gin and tonic, please.' She had to almost shout at the barman.

'I'll get that,' came the voice from behind.

216

Miusze Huang's report landed in Briggs' inbox within twenty-four hours of his submission of the Beretta to the firearms forensic lab. The Chinawoman had done a thoroughly professional job, as would be expected, and the linked series analysis was comprehensive and very clearly presented.

217

The entity responsible for the distribution of fortune has a strange way of doing things. We bemoan bad luck with practiced vehemence, but we rarely thank our gods for the good stuff – unless we are Marlene Rankin.

'Oh, blessed Mother of Jesus, thank you with all my heart,' she muttered, having just heard the news on BBC Radio 2. It had been announced that, due to baggage handlers' industrial action – the lazy bastards were striking again – passenger flights in and out of Heathrow had been rerouted through Gatwick and Luton. Marlene's Catholicism bordered on the fanatically superstitious; she had no doubt whatsoever that the hand of the Holy Mother had intervened to lay on a quiet day for the occasion of her husband's funeral.

A hearse drawn by black horses had been arranged and the organisers, the O'Donnell family from Shepherd's Bush, were busying themselves on the Rankin estate to ensure the event would be a fine occasion. They were Tom's nearest relatives east of the Irish Sea and were all in attendance – apart from the two Michaels, of course, who were in prison awaiting trial.

Tom's death had changed Marlene overnight; it was like his spirit had just upped sticks and transferred itself into the old girl's body. She'd never been a shrinking violet, and now she was in full bloom, a serious force to be reckoned with.

And Marlene had her own family; her sister lived in nearby Staines, where the descendants of many travelling families had relented, dropped roots and adopted the housebound style of the *gorja*. The childless Marlene doted on her sister's three adult daughters and the four fussed about like hens, chiding and scolding the menfolk.

'Not there, there, yeh feckin' eedjut!'

'Eh?'

'I told you to put all the meat on that table and the drinks on the other one, yuz can't be mixing the two up!'

Some of the Shepherd's Bush men had rarely set foot inside of a house and could remember when funerals consisted of a piss-up on a riverbank with a burning coffin on a boat floating past. The niceties of food and drink on tables were alien to them. Their wives were still shopping and the stuff was coming in through the front in waves.

'I think that's about the lot, Marlene,' said one huge babushka of a Gypsy woman, as she dumped three bulging Lidl bags in the hallway.

461

'Good, fine, thanks Mary,' said the Rankin widow, but she wasn't looking at her volunteer; her distracted attention focused on the big BMW that had just pulled slowly into the driveway.

She recognised the driver as Driss. The rear passengers were less visible but she assumed by their colour they were Kribz and one of their mates. It was the front seat passenger who had her hackles rising.

'Mary mother of God, what is that fecker doin' here? And what's he doin' comin' with them boys?'

Her helper turned in the doorway, so that both formidable women were staring at the car as its occupants tentatively stepped out of the vehicle.

Jackson, dressed in a grey suit and determined to be crutchless, had to steady himself against the Beemer whilst finding his feet on the uneven ground. The boys attended to him like a small army of minders. They were all wearing white shirts and black ties.

'Feck me,' exclaimed the big woman at Marlene's side, 'it's like the feckin' mafia's turned up!'

'I wish to feck it was the mafia,' said Marlene, quietly.

'Good morning, Mrs Rankin.' Jackson's voice was raised, but not rudely; his tone was respectful, almost plaintive. 'I tried to call, but your number is constantly engaged.'

This was true; Marlene was sick of the thing and had left it off the hook. She didn't reply to the asset stripper, just stood there, regarding him balefully.

'We've come to show our respects, Mrs Rankin. May we come in?'

The widow was about to answer in the very firm negative when the windscreenless Albion roared onto the driveway with a grinning Massive at the wheel. Following the mandatory forensic examination, the wagon had been released from the police car pound and the big African had eagerly volunteered to retrieve it.

Kribz, Driss and Numbers turned briefly to acknowledge the latest arrival, then back to see Marlene's reaction. She wasn't impressed. 'What've you brought that thing back here for? My husband died in it!'

Jackson was walking slowly towards her. 'No, he didn't, Mrs Rankin, he died in hospital, of a heart attack—'

'Aye, after these boys had got him in a gunfight what put him in hospital in the first place!'

'We need to talk, Mrs Rankin, with respect. I've got some good news for you. I've persuaded the bank to leave you alone. You can live here for the rest of your life.' Jackson was still walking, now only about four yards from Marlene, his approach open, conciliatory.

The widow softened a little; this was indeed good news. Although distracted by the funeral arranging, she'd been worried sick about what would happen to her if the foreclosure had gone ahead.

'What's the catch?' she said, raising her hand to halt Jackson's progress.

'There's no catch, Mrs Rankin. I've negotiated a reversion. That means the bank takes legal ownership of the property but doesn't take possession until you pass away, which I hope will be a long time in the future.'

'Aye, I bet you feckin' do,' sneered Marlene, remembering to be highly suspicious of anything coming from the lips of this soft man in a shiny suit.

Jackson just stood there, waiting to see if he'd said enough.

'Alright, you can come in then, but not yet, we're not ready. Go away and come back in a couple of hours, and before you go put that thing in the shed there.'

Massive had just jumped down from the Albion's cab. On overhearing Marlene's instruction, he climbed back on board, started up the engine and began reversing the wagon into the ramshackle garage; the doors were still open since the vehicle had been driven out nearly three weeks previously.

Broth

They all got into the BMW, and Driss drove them off the premises.

'Where the fuck shall we go then?' asked Driss.

'Oh, let's find a pub or something,' said Jackson, visibly relieved by how the encounter had just progressed. His promise to Marlene had not been untrue; the reversion agreement had been properly drafted and only required her signature. But he hadn't told her about the contents of the small print, the detail wherein resided some devilish clauses about continued mental capacity, proper and legal upkeep of the property, and payment of ground rent to the new equitable owners. Together with other convolutedly worded conditions, these obligations imposed a heavy burden on the old lady who would become a mere tenant of her own home.

'What, us? In a pub? Round here? You gotta be kiddin' man. We'll get fuckin' lynched, man, dis is fuckin' redneck country!' And they all laughed, including Jackson.

218

Passey was a troubled man. The Galleons Reach shoot-up had been easy enough to investigate, albeit a bit messy. All the suspects were either banged up or out on bail awaiting trial and it didn't look like there were any loose ends. Apart from one: Freda Larssen. The linked series Beretta found in her freezer tied her nicely in with the Braganza Boys and, by extension, five shootings that included four murders. Rather too nicely. Far too nicely, in fact. Her allegation that the gun had been planted by a cop with a questionable reputation had a horrible ring of truth about it. But another truth – an actual one – was that she was a nutter and a nasty piece of work, and there was additional circumstantial evidence that pointed to her being involved with the Pope brothers and their crew. However, it still didn't quite stack up. So, in the best tradition of the arse-covering senior ranks, Passey had put in a call to the Professional Standards Directorate, just to give them the 'heads up' in case they were interested.

They were. The Dane was being held in a secure mental unit at Wormwood Scrubs, and Reeve and Durman were on their way to visit her on the basis that she was a possible source of intelligence that would help the PSD root out corruption amongst London's finest. Even if she were subsequently deemed to be unfit to stand trial, with carefully caveated filtering any information she imparted could still be used in a tangential investigation into 'misconduct in public office', the favoured catch-all charge used against bent coppers. It carries a possible sentence of ten years and can only be tried in the Crown Court.

The two rubber-heels signed in through security and were shown into a windowless interview room in the bowels of the Victorian prison. Larssen awaited them. Passey had warned Reeve about the Dane's volatility, but there'd been no need.

She smiled as they entered. 'Good morning, officers, how nice of you to visit me. Please sit down.'

They did so, on two chairs on the other side of the small table behind which the woman sat. As usual, all the furniture was bolted to the floor. 'I would like to shake hands but, well…' she finished the explanation by nodding down at the handcuffs she wore over the baggy sleeves of her prison-issue grey cotton tracksuit.

'That's okay, Miss Larssen, we understand. I'm Detective Superintendent Colin Reeve, this is Detective Sergeant Gill Durman.'

'Welcome to my temporary home,' said the Dane, without irony.

Reeve got on with it. 'Right, Ms Larssen, first of all, thank you for agreeing to see us at such short notice. This is to be an informal interview, we aren't recording you and you're not under caution, so nothing you say can be used in evidence against you. We're from the Professional Standards Directorate and we just want to find out if you have anything to share with us about an officer called Douglas Napper. We are given to believe that you are, er, somewhat unhappy about his behaviour.'

Larssen regarded Reeve thoughtfully, like she was assessing this new player in the game.

'Yes, Superintendent, and I thank you for this opportunity to make a few suggestions as to how you might progress your investigation into the corrupt policeman.'

She was about to go on, but Reeve intervened. 'You can put it like that, if you like,' he said, with a slight shrug and a thin smile.

'Yes, I think I can. That way we can pretend to be on equal terms.' The Dane frowned as she spoke and stared down at her handcuffs.

'How well do you know the Pope brothers?' asked Durman, keen to start at the beginning to give the interview context.

'Not at all. They accosted me outside my house a few months ago, and I think one of them got arrested outside my office soon after that. I saw them at Tom Rankin's place once, but not to speak to, and that's about it, nothing more. The suggestion that I'm in some sort of, er, how do you say it, *cahoots* with them, is ridiculous.' She spoke evenly, reasonably.

'Do you still maintain that the gun found at your address was planted by PC Napper?' Passey thought he might as well cut to the chase.

'Yes.'

'Have you any idea why he would do that?'

'No, not really, I thought he and I were getting on well. We had sex on one occasion, and I think I can prove that forensically.'

The officers hadn't been ready for this one; they both stared at the Dane, neither wishing to be the first to ask the obvious. But Durman obliged.

'How can you prove it?'

'There's some tissue paper in my freezer, nicely folded by me, if you get your scientists to examine it you'll find Police Constable Napper's semen, and therefore his DNA.'

'Have you told anyone else about this?' asked Reeve.

'No, I've refused to be interviewed so far, you're the first officers I've spoken to since I was arrested. It seems to me that you're from the right department to be trusted with this information.'

'You'll know that we found the firearm in your freezer, if you're saying that Napper put it there, then...'

Larssen anticipated Reeve's question and interrupted. 'Then he would have removed the tissue paper when he planted the gun, possibly, but probably not, it was stuffed right at the back of the freezer, under an ice tray.'

Reeve turned to Durman. 'Go and make a call, Gill, get another search done, on my authority. I'll sign off the authority later.' Durman rose, tapped on the door and was allowed to leave the room.

Larssen was now fiddling with her handcuffs; her demeanour was still relaxed, detached even.

Reeve asked, 'Could you describe your relationship with Doug Napper? Was it in any way emotional?'

'No, not emotional, more playful. I was toying with him, he couldn't resist me,' replied the Dane, allowing a smile to play on her lips. 'It was just a bit of fun, that's all, except that...'

'Except that what?' pressed Reeve as he fought off the urge to worry about being alone in a room with a psychopathic alleger of police misconduct.

'Except that I was trying to use him, trick him into working for me so I could get information from him.'

'What about?'

'The police investigation.'

'Which police investigation?'

'The one about the Rankin property in which my company had a financial interest.'

The Superintendent regarded the woman with a mixture of interest and suspicion. This was not the raving lunatic he'd expected.

Durman returned and sat down. Reeve brought her up to speed. 'Miss Larssen has just told me that she was using PC Napper to get her information about the police investigation into Stanwell Moor—'

'And anything else that would help me with my business,' added the prisoner, helpfully.

Durman wanted to focus. 'You say you don't know the Pope brothers, and for the time being let's say we accept that—'

'I don't.'

'Let her finish, please,' helped Reeve.

'Sorry.'

Durman continued. 'We have it on good information that you were going to pay them to take responsibility for the cocaine found at the Rankin address, is that true?'

'Not exactly, no. They offered to tell the truth about those drugs if I could give them financial assistance. They approached me through their solicitor.'

'Katrina Swan?'

'Yes.'

'What did you think about that approach? What was your reaction?'

'I was surprised, but it made sense. It was a good idea. Her clients saw an opportunity, or at least that's what she told me. I never actually met them to discuss it.'

'So, it could have been her idea. They could have been working for her, perhaps?' Reeve was thinking outside the box, looking for an opportunity of his own: have a pop at a defence lawyer – always good sport.

468

The Dane had thought of this. 'That's unlikely. Swan would never have known about the Stanwell Moor property if the blacks – sorry, the Pope brothers – hadn't told her. They knew about my interest in the place, they'd seen me there and Rankin must have told them.'

'But—' Durman tried to chip in, but Larssen was on a roll.

'But I reckon she must have been advising them because she told me that they knew all about the law that lets you guys take away property under the Crime Proceeds Act, or whatever it is. According to her they knew that if they owned up to the cocaine being on the property then Rankin would not have the property seized by you and then we could carry on with the repossession and I could make my money.'

Both officers fell silent for a few seconds, digesting the Dane's reasonable logic. Durman wrote some notes, Reeve nodded sagely. 'Okay, that's a very interesting theory.' He paused, then went on. 'Right, Freda, I'm going to make a suggestion.'

219

Napper was considering his options. The worst possible outcome was that he would be sacked for gross indiscipline – but he doubted it. As for the criminal offence of misconduct in public office, he was confident that there was nowhere near enough evidence against him. Cops had been associating with suspects since time began; it went with the territory and it had to be proved that such an association was for corrupt purposes. As for Larssen being a suspect – and she certainly ticked that box now – well, she wasn't a suspect when he was visiting her. There was no way he could have known she had that gun in her freezer, unless they could prove that he'd planted it, which he knew they couldn't.

He lay on the unmade bed in his chaotic room. The effects of the psilocybin he'd ingested the night before were wearing off and he was enjoying the clarity of thought that was often a residual effect of the drug, once the hallucinations had subsided.

He knew it was the day of Rankin's funeral and the restricted duties he'd been placed on, together with various warnings, meant that he was fully expected not to dare be anywhere near it. Some chance of that, he thought, a smirk on his sleep-caked face. It was 10am, four hours to plan and make the journey to the far west of London. Plenty of time. He just had to be there, had to see it.

He called Blake. 'Mornin', how is it?'

'Morning, how is what?' replied the lawyer, genuinely not knowing which particular 'it' his friend was referring to.

Napper took the point. 'Er, well, I suppose we could start with you getting paid by Jackson.'

'It'll come, I'm pretty sure of that. We've put together a deal with the bank so that the old girl gets to keep her house until either she pegs it, goes round the twist, or breaks any one of several conditions that are virtually impossible to comply with, then they swipe it off her.'

'I thought they were in a hurry to sell the land for development.'

'Well, they could always renegotiate with the old girl, pay her extra to get her out quicker. That option still exists outside of the reversion deal, but the main idea is to keep Larssen out of the picture.' This wasn't the first time Blake had had to go through this with the copper and his patience was getting stretched. 'Why are you so fucking interested anyway, Nappy, just keep your head down and out of the way, you scruffy fucker!' This was rich, coming from a man sitting in his office wearing nothing but boxer shorts.

'I want to see a bit of justice. The poor woman's lost her husband, she doesn't need to lose her home—'

Blake burst out laughing. 'Don't fucking give me that! Stop trying to be the White Knight – I know you better than you know yourself!' The spittle flew from the fat solicitor's mouth as he chortled.

'Are you going to the funeral?' ventured Napper.

'What? No way, mate, I've got work to do, and I don't think you should turn up there either. You're in enough shit.'

Napper cut the call and heaved himself out of his pit.

220

Jackson led his black-tied boys into the cafe. 'All Day Breakfasts' was handwritten on the wall menu behind the grubby counter, to the exclusion of anything else. The half dozen or so morose locals who occupied some of the plastic tables looked up, watching the incoming entourage with open suspicion. The big Pole behind the counter did likewise. Had it not been for the presence of Jackson, he'd have turned them round on a sixpence. 'Yes?' he grunted to the white man.

'Five coffees, please,' said Jackson, assertively.

'Sit down, I will bring,' said the Pole, locking eyes with Driss.

'Cool it, bro,' growled Kribz, seeing his brother's racism radar activate.

The unwelcome group sat down near the window, having to shuffle along two fixed bench seats on either side of an unwiped table.

'It's fuckin' filthy,' commented Massive with a grin, like he was delighted. 'At least in Brixton dey keep t'ings fuckin' clean.'

'Yeah, man, this place is shit, man,' agreed Numbers loudly, keen to be part of the conversation.

Jackson nipped this in the bud. 'Okay, guys, can we calm down please? We don't want to be attracting too much attention to ourselves here, we're kind of out of bounds.' He made a little show of swivelling his eyes as he spoke, lowering his head as if taking cover.

471

Kribz nodded. 'Yeah, we don't want no kick-off with a bunch of fuckin' hillbillies.' He tried to keep his voice low, but failed; its baritone clarity carried his words across the cafe, causing the heads around a table on the other side of the room to turn.

'Hope you're not talkin' about us, fellah!' said one.

'Yeah, what the fuck are you lot doin' in 'ere anyway?' said another,

The B Boys all froze and stared down at their table. The coffees arrived, accompanied by a warning from the owner. 'I suggest you guys just drink this, pay me, and get the fuck out of here.' The big Pole spoke loud enough for the gang of what looked like very fit scaffolders to overhear.

'Yeah, nice one guv'nor, better make sure they do pay you an' all, don't fuckin' trust the black bastards!'

That did it: Massive just managed to get his arm around Driss's neck to stop the younger Pope from jumping to his feet. But Jackson stood, palms raised. 'Right, just calm down, we don't need any trouble, in fact it's the last thing you lot need. Come on now, no more talking.' They did as they were told and Jackson had no need to remind the Popes about their bail conditions.

221

Napper had a valid reason for being in Stanwell Moor village. Well, sort of. His Land Rover had been parked up in a quiet back road for months and, if challenged, he would say he'd come to retrieve it.

The old jalopy was filthy; he could hardly see through the windscreen and had to urinate on an old rag and wipe it just enough for visibility. It started first time. 'Nice one, me beauty!' he congratulated loudly, above the noise of the diesel engine. He engaged first gear and began trundling around the village. Old bangers were a familiar sight in these parts; suspicion would not be aroused.

He drove past the gateway of the Rankin homestead at a reasonable speed, but slow enough to take in the sight of several vehicles parked up in front of the house and get a glimpse of food and drink being carried in through the front door by some women. His intel had been right: 'wake day' – the Irish liked to see their loved ones off in style.

On his second recce around the village, he saw Jackson's big Beemer outside the cafe. He'd long since memorised the registration number in the course of his ordinary duties – it hadn't been difficult: CJ101 – and his adrenaline surged. This was going to be fun.

222

The absence of air traffic gave the dogs primacy on the noise front. The smell of food was driving them mad and Marlene took time out from the arrangements to feed them.

'There you are, you feckers, that'll keep you quiet,' she muttered, throwing a few handfuls of raw sausages and burgers into the pens. There were only a dozen dogs remaining, including Lois and her pups, and she'd made a mental note to ask the black boys to arrange their removal; she had no need for them and they'd brought her nothing but very bad luck. 'You lot have no idea what you did to us, but it wasn't your faults I suppose,' she mused, tears welling up before she pulled herself together: *'Come on now Marlene, there's nothing in feckin' sentiment.'*

Satisfied that the hounds were happy, she trundled back across the patio, inspecting the growing spread of food and drink as she went and thanking the Mother of God for the weather and the air traffic controllers' strike. It was in her family's tradition to have the wake before the funeral and Tom Rankin lay in state in the rarely used front parlour of the house. The floral tributes were extravagant to the point of vulgarity, almost totally obscuring the open wickerwork coffin. Pleased with the progress of her helpers, the widow slowed her pace as she walked into the parlour to talk to her husband.

Tom's face was a picture of peace; the embalmers had seen to that, and he was dressed in the 'Sunday best' that he'd never worn before.

'Aye, Tom,' she scolded, 'you were determined to go out with a bang, were you not, and you right as hell did that, my awful man!' Her tone softened as she spoke; she couldn't keep this bravado up for much longer. Get today and tomorrow out of the way, she thought, and then we'll see what happens. She looked out of the window to check for activity out front: nothing seen. The horses had been booked but wouldn't be pulling their hearse into the drive for a few hours yet.

223

Although banged up in solitary for 23 hours each day, Zamir had used his influencing skills in the exercise yard to send out a heavily encrypted message demanding he be told of the date of Tom Rankin's funeral. The speed at which he'd got his reply – a date neatly written in miniscule numbers along the side of a hand-rolled cigarette – had made him smile. You didn't need the internet in remand prison where visitors were allowed at least weekly. He'd supplied Bora with the information and knew that would convince her of his determination and his authority. He was still the boss and she had no choice but to respect him. 'Look, I've even found out the date for you, now you have to do the right thing, or we'll miss our chance and you'll have the guilt on you for—'

'Alright, alright!' she'd said.

Bora had no troops to draw on, and she was determined to leave Mergin well out of it. So, she was alone in the Vauxhall Astra she'd hired for the day – no more attention-grabbing black Lexus for her. She motored quietly around Stanwell in her nurse's uniform and an NHS shoulder bag on the passenger seat. It contained more than a pack of disposable rubber gloves and a few obsolete patients' notes.

She shivered, not for the first time trying to think why she'd succumbed to Zamir's sway. She had a vague awareness of the power of blood, of how shared DNA could diminish free will, something she'd got a glimpse of in the numerous books she'd had to read during her nurse training. But according to some texts, it took thirty generations for a trait to become hereditary, atavistic, yet she could only trace herself back three, so there was something else at play. Balkanisation, perhaps: the name given to the phenomenon by which a sub-culture of sociopathy can take root and grow in a population riven by war, oppression and poverty, firstly bonding its members against the outside world, then blunting their ability to believe in or abide by the laws and norms of others. Whatever: she was here, risking everything. Madness.

Needing to stretch her legs – the drive from Barking had been arduous – she pulled over and parked up in the tatty high street. Switching off the engine, she was hit by how quiet the village was; but not *nice* and quiet, more like *deadly* quiet: despite the bright autumnal weather, there was a heaviness in the air, an expectancy. She tried to put the feeling down to her own nervousness, but it lingered; something wasn't right. The big BMW parked outside the greasy spoon was a clue, an incongruity. She got out of the Astra and walked, slowly but not too slowly, along the pavement towards the cafe, but on the opposite side of the street. She pretended to fiddle with her mobile for cover, but with eyes swivelling, hurting in their sockets. The Beemer wasn't a cop car, of that she was sure, and if it was a Gheg-mobile she'd have been told about it. No, neither of those, but in this Godforsaken shithole it was bang out of place; had trouble written all over it.

Even if she could have seen through the grease-smudged window with its makeshift signage, the interior of the cafe was poorly lit, its seated occupants appearing as dark figures hunched over the tables. But Bora was stood in the sunshine: floodlights couldn't have improved her exposure.

'Fuckin' shit, Jesus fuckin' shit, man.' Numbers' voice was low, tremulous, his eyes bulging at the object of his fixation. Jackson, thumbing his phone, was oblivious, but the others followed their brother's line of sight, acutely sensing the boy's sudden fear.

'S'up, bro, whadya seen?' demanded Kribz, suddenly tensing.

'It's her, innit, fuckin' Bora, Mergin's fuckin' big auntie or cousin or fuckin' sister.' Numbers' lips barely moved as he spoke. He was slack-jawed, unblinking, small hands forming pale-knuckled fists on the table.

'Who, her stood over there? She's a fuckin' nurse, bro', whadya chattin' 'bout?' Kribz blinked back and forth from Numbers' stricken face and the woman standing reading her phone thirty yards away.

'I'ze tellin' you it's her, man, no fuckin' doubt 'bout it.'

Jackson was also looking now, but not knowing – and not particularly wanting to know – what the hell was occurring. 'What's going on, boys?' He felt obliged to take an interest.

The B Boys ignored him. 'Nah,' said Driss, 'that ain't the Albo woman that was in that car park that day, if that's who you mean.' The younger Pope had turned around in his seat and was squinting through the window, shaking his head.

'You wasn't tortured by her for two fuckin' days, bro. Truss me, it's *her*.'

'Well, you know what, if it is her an' she's got her posse wid her, I'ze fuckin' outa here,' said Massive.

Jackson was getting worried. 'Would somebody mind telling me what's going on?' It was dawning on him that serious trouble loomed. He'd had the Galleons Reach shoot-up briefly recounted to him a couple of times and certainly didn't want to be anywhere near an action replay.

The B Boys were unarmed, and all were having the same thoughts about the bag that Bora hoisted onto her shoulder and pulled across the front of her midriff as she looked left and right before stepping off the kerb to cross the road between them.

'You sure it's her, man?' said Kribz, a mounting urgency in his voice. He hadn't got a good look at the woman back at Galleons, but sure as hell knew what she would be capable of.

For an answer Numbers half rose, got his feet up on the fixed plastic seat, vaulted over the table and started heading at a crouch towards the rear of the cafe. Jackson felt the colour drain from his face as the other three wordlessly followed their youngest member, like animals heeding a survival signal.

Bora could see through the window now and the sight of the retreating gang confirmed her instinctive guess. A Beemer in this toilet? Had to be blacks, and they were running away, so it had to be *them*! She pulled the Glock from her bag, pushed open the door, raised it and fired. Thrice. Jackson sat stock still and felt the warmth of his urine as it filled the plastic seat beneath his buttocks.

The handful of locals had seen their fair share of Netflix shoot-ups and knew what to do; they all hit the deck. But one fat bastard who wasn't quick enough screamed as he took a bullet in the shoulder before going down like a sack of shit. Bora hadn't fired a gun in anger since she'd been a teenager and the other two bullets went high, sending lumps of plaster and shards of fluorescent tube lighting in all directions. She didn't get to pull the trigger a fourth time: the gang had gone, past the end of the counter towards the toilet and out the back of the premises. She knew better than to try to follow.

The big Pole was rising from behind the counter, slotting a cartridge into the barrel of a sawn-off shotgun. 'Get out! Or I'll fucking blast you to hell!' he roared.

Bora re-bagged the Glock and backed out of the door, resolving not to run. The street was as still as it had been, deserted but for a few disinterested pedestrians and light, insignificant traffic. Nothing much ever happened in Stanwell Moor and the three loud crashes of the Glock would have been put down to a car backfiring or a skip falling off a wagon. Anyway, it was the sort of place where people minded their own business.

She walked back to the Astra, unshouldered her bag, got into the vehicle and drove slowly off. Any CCTV would not see a fleeing getaway car, just a district nurse doing her rounds. But her father's killers knew she was there and the element of surprise was gone. She would never get into that wake now; she'd blown it, unless...

She did a ninety degree turn along the first side road off the cafe side of the high street, hoping to get sight along the access road that would surely lead to its rear. She found it all right, but a delivery wagon blocked both her view and any chance of driving along it.

'Where the fuck do we go now?!' panted Driss. It was like the B Boys had guessed Bora's next move and had known better than to go in either direction along that access road behind the cafe; they'd instead run straight across it, over a brick wall, onto a shed and down into the rear overgrown garden of a terraced house, one of a row with no visible gaps between them. They all crouched, apart from Kribz who'd needed help and stood in pain, his leg injury still a hindrance. Then he shared his thoughts.

'Right, listen, we ain't done nothing wrong, we wuz attacked an' ran. We got witnesses, including fuckin' Jackson, our fuckin' bail bonder, so we'ze goin' to the fedz.'

Numbers was nodding, but Driss wasn't so sure. 'Hang on bro, me and you'ze got bail conditions not to leave the boro' of Lambeth—'

'That's Jackson's problem, he should of thought of that before he brought us here. We wuz only 'elpin' out, innit. We had to bring the wagon back and stuff, an' show some respect innit, we wuz doin' nuthin' wrong.'

'I ain't got any bail conditions,' grinned Massive. He was right – the big negro hadn't even been charged with any offence following Galleons Reach. He'd been released pending further enquiries, although he wasn't totally off the hook because he still stood a chance of the CPS roping him in on a joint venture charge.

'Good thinkin', man,' said Kribz. 'Go back into the caff, Mass, go an' tell the fedz what 'appened. If they'ze not already there dial 999 an' get them there. Tell them we've fuckin' legged it, that you don't know our names, anything, that we was jus' getting a lift to the wake thing, whatever. Jus' make sure they know that that fuckin' Albo woman is prob'ly gonna be there poppin' that piece of hers. They'll 'ave the fuckin' place surrounded in no time, innit.' Kribz delivered this strategy standing but bent over, hands on knees. The others were still crouching, nodding. Numbers was rubbing his hands where he'd been stung by nettles.

And then the sound of two-tones: no need for the 999 call. Massive climbed back over the wall.

224

Someone else had hired a car for the day, but it wasn't a Vauxhall Astra. Larssen drove the white Audi Q6 off the M25 slip and down into the village. Her bail conditions had been surprisingly light, probably because the court was reluctant to impose anything that could be seen to interfere with the recuperation of her mental health. The CPS was also running scared: from the outset she had made it clear that her defence would be based on the allegation that Napper – a cop whose credibility was steadily diminishing – had planted the Beretta in her apartment and that he'd done this out of spite as a scorned lover. In the light of Napper's admission that he had made unauthorized visits to the woman, the prosecutors were nervous that a jury would later give her the benefit of the doubt. This unease, together with a psychiatrist's report to the effect that incarceration could be extremely damaging to the defendant's capacity to stand trial, translated into rather lacklustre objections to her being released on bail. Well, that was the official line of reasoning, should accountability ever be called for. What also helped the judge to grant bail was some information in a sealed document handed to him in his chambers before the hearing by Detective Superintendent Colin Reeve of the Professional Standards Directorate.

So now here she was, her obsession with regaining beneficial possession of the Rankin property undiminished and now accompanied by a savage quest for revenge. Swan had brought her up to date with events, including the funeral and wake arrangements as provided to her by her clients the Pope brothers, who had rightly thought it best to inform their solicitor of their planned movements. Swan had warned Larssen not to go anywhere near Stanwell Moor, knowing damned well that there wouldn't be the slightest chance of the Dane missing the party.

Larssen parked up in a street of shabby local authority bungalows. She'd driven round the neighbourhood for half an hour and had lost no time spotting Jackson's car parked stupidly in the high street, but she'd missed the action in the cafe and hadn't heard Bora's gunshots. She looked at her watch and hunkered down to wait for the call.

When it came she didn't recognise the number; the caller was using a burner. She knew it was him, but asked anyway: 'Who is this?'

'Take a woild fuckin' guess.'

'What do you want?'

'I want to know how the fuck you got bail but I think I can guess the answer to that one, so the next question is – where are you?'

'You should be able to guess the answer to that question also, Douglas Napper and, as we're playing a guessing game, I *guess* that I am quite near to where you are.'

'And where's that then?'

Larssen had repeatedly told herself to stay calm and in an approachable location: *let him come to me*. She wore an ankle tag, a condition of her bail, and correctly suspected that she would be under constant surveillance. She additionally assumed – again, correctly – that her phone had been bugged with eavesdropping software before it was restored to her on her departure from prison. But being passive had never been her forte.

'Where exactly are you?!'

'Why, you gonna 'ave me shot?'

'No, I would just like to talk to you face to face, ask you why you did this to me.'

'Where are *you*?'

'Oh my God!' Exasperated, she tried sarcasm. 'Having a drive in your beautiful English countryside. Fancy a nice cup of tea somewhere?'

For a police officer to meet a person on bail is a serious disciplinary offence, and Napper had to assume that the woman was aware of this. He was in enough shit as it was, but if she was going to try something, anything to disrupt what had been achieved – and he knew her capabilities – then it would be negligent of him not to try to stop her. Not that avoiding allegations of negligence was his motivation of course, but it would have to suffice as an official line of argument during the inevitable maelstrom of scrutiny that would be heading his way when – not if – this madness concluded.

481

'Stanwell Moor. Main street.' He spoke the words with an air of resignation; he'd crossed a red line, no going back now.

By the time Larssen and Napper drove towards each other from opposite ends of the street, the cafe was swarming with police. Napper recognised the Dane as their vehicles crossed, so he swung the Land Rover around and followed her. Larssen immediately became aware of him in her rear-view mirror and led the way.

225

Jackson couldn't keep still. He'd slid out of the cafe when Massive had walked through from the back to wait for the police. The Polish owner had dialled 999, and Massive had also done so. The B Boy's call had served its real purpose; it had been received and, more importantly, logged – moral high ground taken; they were the victims. Jackson made for his car. It was another hour before he dared go back to the Rankin place; he needed the papers signed and annoying Marlene by arriving too early was a risk he couldn't take. But this latest little episode had knocked the whole plan cock-eyed. His minders were getting shot at before they even got there and now he suspected that the police would be wanting to know what they were doing in Stanwell Moor in the first place – if they got to speak to them, that was.

He needn't have worried on that point. With Massive giving the victim's narrative – the truth, in fact – about an Albanian gang sending in an assassin dressed as a nurse who was on the loose in the village, the police had more to worry about than chasing down a bunch of lads in breach of their bail conditions.

And Massive put on a convincing act. 'We was helping with some removals, we delivered a truck.... dunno, near here, can't remember the address... my buds've gone, boss, took off, innit, but I t'ink it was me she was after. I recognise 'er from Brixton, she's Hellbanianz innit, tried to cap me before once... I dunno...' and so the big fella played for time, managing for once to keep a straight face as he spoke so the cop on the other end of the line couldn't hear his grin. What he said was all rubbish of course, totally uncorroborated, but an effective distraction; *smoke'n'mirrors, innit*. On Kribz's strict instructions, there was no mention of the wake.

The police went through the motions: forensic examination of the cafe, high street sealed off, door-to-door search for eyewitnesses (in Stanwell Moor? Not a chance), CCTV footage from the single local authority camera mounted at one end of the street: faulty – negative result. But the short-wave radio traffic had generated a frenzy of activity and swarms of police were making their way to the village and its surroundings.

226

Briggs had been told not to bother trying to attend Rankin's wake and funeral on account of there being nothing to gain from it. Larssen's and the B Boys' release on bail had not been deemed to present sufficient risk as to require a very unwelcome police presence at a Gypsy event.

But when he got wind of the cafe shooting, and the name of the reporting witness, he felt the need to cover his arse by alerting senior management to the significantly raised threat level.

'With respect, guv'nor, I think we should at least get some armed units out there, or we risk a re-run of Galleons Reach,' he said, affecting a conscientious urgency he didn't feel. Mason, sitting beside him in the Walworth CID office as he made the call to Passey, was smirking, knowing exactly what the acting detective sergeant was up to.

Passey, still twenty miles away in Barking, was on the career damage limitation wavelength and couldn't disagree with Briggs.

'Yeah, okay, email me everything you've got and I'll get the ball rolling, Aaron, thanks.' The Superintendent cut the call and set to work joining the dots.

'What's happening guv?' asked a middle-aged DS who'd caught the back end of the conversation.

'We've got fun and games looming out near Heathrow. Can you get Flying Squad control to muster a couple of Trojan wagons? We've got about two hours.'

'Yes, guv'nor.'

227

Neither Larssen nor Napper had any right to be in Stanwell Moor. Both were under official instructions not to go anywhere near the place, Larssen from the court by way of her bail conditions and Napper from the DPS under the rules of his suspension whilst under investigation.

The DPS had assumed the cop would stay under the radar and tread very carefully; the allegation that he'd planted the linked series Beretta was serious, but unverifiable by forensic evidence, so any disobedience on his part could be used to bolster the case against him. Consequently, they were casting their net wide and tight, just in case he slipped up. They had no choice: to do otherwise could later be construed as not taking the allegation of evidence-planting seriously.

Napper had also made an assumption; that the DPS didn't know about his clapped-out Land Rover. He was right; he'd checked it over when he picked it up – not a sign of interference, and the insertion of a tracking device would certainly have left signs that he would have noticed.

Questionable sanity aside, Larssen saw no need to be cautious and a good reason not to be. Reeve hadn't briefed her to be a honey trap – the DPS just didn't do that sort of thing – but the Dane suspected that they hoped she would make contact with Napper, or the other way round and, as usual, her feral instinct had served her well.

Reeve and Durman had watched the tracker dot as she travelled out from central London on the M4, and now sat attentively as it seemed to patrol the on-screen map of Stanwell Moor, stopping, turning, searching, and then stopping.

'High Street junction with Beech Close,' said Durman over the encrypted radio.

'Received, on way,' responded the surveillance officer, and then to his colleague behind the wheel of the observation vehicle, a white Ford Transit, inconspicuous in the working-class neighbourhood, 'Okay, you heard, let's go, nice and slowly.' The back of the van was decked out with video kit that received pictures from covert cameras on its front, rear and sides. The lone operator sat in a swivel chair bolted to the floor and watched the split screen monitor. Not that she had to do anything: the pictures were automatically transmitted to the DPS office in Pimlico, central London.

'What the hell is that?' said Reeve.

'Looks like something off Jed Clampett's farm,' replied Durman. They were both staring at the filthy vehicle that had just come into view as Larssen pulled up behind it.

'Do a VRM check,' said Reeve, flatly, unnecessarily; Durman was already tapping out the Land Rover's registration number.

'Comes back to a lady with an address in Cruz Hill, near Epping. She's informed the DVLA that she's no longer the owner.'

'And who lives out near Epping?' grinned Reeve, turning to Durman.

'Our very own PC Douglas Napper.'

'Is that him at the wheel?'

'Can't see, too much dirt on the windows.'

'And there she goes. That's it, Freda, do your stuff, my love.' Reeve was still grinning. Durman frowned: she didn't like gloaters and hadn't put her boss down as one. It disappointed her that Reeve had developed an appetite for nailing Napper who, in her view, was an unconventional but nonetheless hard-working copper.

The obo van had been manoeuvred into a luckily vacant space on the opposite side of the road, and the view on the DPS screen was 'clear and unobstructed', to use the jargon that would feature in the surveillance log.

228

It took Larssen two or three tries before she managed to figure out how the door of the Land Rover opened, so by the time she climbed into the vehicle she was cross and flustered.

'What the fuck is this shitty thing?' she shouted at Napper, who just sat very still behind the wheel, unfocused eyes fixed ahead of him. He couldn't believe this: she was acting like he was under her control, like it was normal, like he'd just been waiting to pick her up from a shopping trip. The woman was looking all around the inside of the vehicle. 'Could you not have washed this? It makes me feel sick!'

Then he turned his head slowly to look at her. She met his gaze. 'Well?'

'Well what?'

'Are you going to help me?'

'How am I goin' to do that?'

'By coming clean and admitting you planted that gun in my freezer,' she snarled.

He turned back to face the inside of the windscreen. 'I don't know what you're talking about,' he said, for the benefit of the transmitter he had assumed she was wearing. And for good measure: 'Why are you alleging this against me?'

She stared at him. One side of her face twitched faintly. She had lost weight in prison and her hair was newly shorn; she looked hard; her craziness exposed. The baggy black tracksuit she wore made her look even more like an emaciated crackhead. 'Are you fucking serious? Are you denying that you planted that gun in my place? *Look at me!*'

He turned his head again, stared into her pale blue eyes, and said, 'Yeah, I'm denyin' it. I never 'ad nothin' to do with that gun bein' in your place, s'got fuck all to do with me.'

'Who the fuck put it there, then?!' screeched Larssen. Her hands were clasped together and she was shaking, rocking back and forth, like she was having serious trouble stopping herself from attacking Napper.

'Fucked if I know,' shrugged the cop, turning back to the windscreen.

'Are you saying that it was the officers who searched my place?'

'I'm not saying nothing like that.'

'It wasn't Briggs, they found it before he even got there.'

Napper stayed silent; she was floundering, looking for alternatives.

Then she changed direction, sighing: 'Perhaps you could help me understand.'

'Understand what?'

'What I've done to deserve this.'

'What do you mean?' He was genuinely curious.

'Think about it, I haven't killed anyone, I haven't stolen anything, I haven't really broken any laws,' she paused and he thought her heard her sniff, she went on with a weaker voice, her face turned away from him: 'Being a bitch isn't illegal, you know, I've done my research.'

Napper felt something stir within him. She had a point and he felt its sharpness beginning to penetrate. Time to end the meeting.

'Will you get out of my vehicle now please?' His enunciation was clear, precise, for the benefit of the listeners.

'You are a piece of English shit,' her voice was suddenly strong again, she opened the door and nearly fell out of the Land Rover. She slammed the door so hard the catch failed to engage and it bounced back and hit her in the face. She staggered backwards into the road; an oncoming car had to swerve violently to avoid her.

'I think they've just had a little tiff,' said Durman.

Reeve was still grinning. 'Yeah, but it doesn't matter. He's still gone there and met up with her, stupid twat. Now he's well fucked.'

'Not really, guv,' countered Durman. 'She approached him. She got into his vehicle, not the other way round.'

Reeve regarded his DS balefully, but said nothing.

Larssen got back into her own vehicle and swung it round in the high street without looking, nearly causing another accident. She drove off in the direction of the Rankin property.

Napper sat still and assumed the white van on the other side of the street was what it was. He ran mentally through what had just occurred; the woman had accosted him, he'd spurned her, sent her packing. No worries.

229

Tom Rankin wasn't exactly grinning, or smiling really, but there was certainly a hint of mischief on his embalmed face, a hint of that cheeky little smirk he wore when he'd been up to tricks, hatching plots and staying one step ahead of the game.

Marlene was having another few minutes alone with him, before she allowed the stream of keeners in to do their stuff.

'You stupid old fecker, Tom Rankin. You was determined, wasn't you, to do this to me, leave all this shite for me to sort out, an' you never even gave me any little'uns to help me. I swear to this day that that was your fault, refusing to go to the doctor an' all, but there we have it, it's done now. You've feckin' gone an' left me to it, as feckin' usual.'

Having finished her scolding, she turned and left the room, leaving the door open behind her. By then over a hundred people had gathered in the house and grounds, and the booze had been flowing for the best part of three hours. The unmetalled road leading to the place was packed with vehicles parked bumper to bumper; Marlene had ordered the front drive to be kept empty to accommodate the hearse which would soon arrive to take her husband to the crematorium.

The dogs had been excited by the arrival of the guests and the ensuing noise and activity, not to mention the smell of the raw meat destined for the barbeque. And they'd been spoiled rotten, despite Marlene's entreaties to the contrary; sausage after burger after steaklet had been surreptitiously chucked into their pens. By the time the actual cooking started they were thoroughly satiated and subdued.

So, Lois turned a few heads when she suddenly started barking, her ears pricked and pointing to the big shed at the back of the Rankin landscape, the doors of which had been patched up and kept precariously in place with a few lengths of rope, just to look tidy. Marlene was still inside the house and unaware of the dog's excitement. Those out in the garden put it down to a fox or a cat or something beyond the rear perimeter fence. Nobody thought to investigate: alcohol induces complacency.

The average dog has a hearing distance twice that of humans, and when it comes to picking up its master's voice – or in this case voices plural – you can add another fifty per cent. Growing up from a pup to adulthood in the Elephant, Lois had developed a very keen ear for the hushed, conspiratorial tones of her two masters. So, when Kribz hissed, 'Shut the fuck up!' at Driss, the dog knew exactly who was behind that shed.

The perimeter fence had not been repaired and they stood looking at the hole they'd escaped through three months previously; it seemed a lot longer ago than that. They could hear the hubbub of swelling social occasion and, following

Kribz's whispered rebuke of his brother, Lois barking, but didn't attribute the sound to their bitch.

The B Boys had known better than to try to link up with Jackson on the street: he was their bread and butter, not to mention their bail surety, and getting him popped by a crazy Albo who, for all they knew could be teamed up with others, was a direct route back to the boob. But, for the same reason, they also had to stay alongside him, remain useful to him, so they had to get into that funeral wake somehow. Well, that was the rational reason for their determination to gain access to the site. They also needed to be where the action was. To slink away and avoid trouble just wasn't an option: not their style at all. Kribz figured that the point of least resistance was the rear entrance, and now all they had to do was mingle – yeah, right, a bunch of black gangbangers in amongst a much bigger bunch of Irish travelers: not easy, but once they were in, he reckoned, they would be safe from that marauding bitch with the gun.

Jackson had not seen Larssen patrolling the high street, but had changed location anyway, not wishing to be corralled by the police as a witness to the cafe shooting. He'd managed to find a parking slot about a hundred yards from the Rankin place and was now sitting pensively in his car, going through the estate possession transfer papers for the umpteenth time. Blake had assured him that they were fine and would secure equitable ownership of the property. All he had to do was get Marlene's signature, hopefully while she was still reasonably sober.

He worried that he was alone and unprotected and wrongly assumed the B Boys had legged it back to south London. They all wore ankle tags, but he'd got permission from the prison authorities to have them with him during lawful business and strictly under his control and supervision. So, the current situation didn't really come up to standard and he himself was now involved in their breach of bail conditions and risked losing his £10k surety bond. *All these fucking worries*, he thought, and for what? A shithole near the airport. But the Rankin land was his pension and the money he stood to gain was worth the punt. He looked down at the papers on his lap again, and then at his watch; another ten minutes and he would go for it.

230

Bora had changed clothes, reloaded her Glock and abandoned the hire car. The Hellbanianz network had been buzzing and she'd done her homework, adding her findings to what Zamir had told her across the table in the visiting room at Belmarsh.

She wore a set of dark green overalls and, ludicrously given her mission, a yellow high-viz vest. On one of her recces in the preceding days she'd seen similarly attired staff, from the Environment Agency or some such thing, going about checking the fences of the reservoirs that surrounded and isolated Stanwell Moor village. She hoped she was hidden in plain sight. She had a good view of the rear of the Rankin shed from where she stood behind a clump of six-foot-high hawthorn bushes at the foot of the steep reservoir embankment. She watched as Driss helped his brother up and through the rear window of the shed, then followed. She saw how the other two hung back, crouching low, waiting for instructions. They would do, or even just one of them, she thought, as she started advancing to improve her chances of a clean shot. But then they followed the brothers through the window. Chance missed, she had to move in.

The inside of the shed still reeked, mostly of disinfectant but with a hint of burnt wood and, disgustingly, cooked meat. Or was that the smell of the barbeque party? On the other side of the flimsily repaired big doors, the Popes could hear that it was now in full swing.

231

The sight of Jackson's car in the village main street had distracted Larssen immensely. The purpose of her trip to this godforsaken place had been to get alongside Napper, discredit him, trick him into somehow incriminating himself. She realised that she'd been naïve to even attempt this and knew that the meeting with him had achieved little, if anything. But now she knew there was something else going on and her desperate nose had caught the whiff of opportunity.

The Dane had made good use of her unexpected liberty and had hoovered up the intel, largely from Palmer who'd continued running what was left of the business back at the office. She knew that the company was back under Jackson's control and would stay that way, unless she found a way to object, which would include getting herself acquitted of the firearms offence. She knew that there was a better than evens chance that the CPS wouldn't progress the Proceeds of Crime Act forfeiture against Rankin's widow. Swan had told her about the funeral wake and the fact that the two leading members of the Braganza gang had been strangely befriended by Jackson who'd stood as bail surety for them. And now, Jackson's rocking up in the neighbourhood on this auspicious afternoon was a big surprise indeed.

She'd followed her antennae and, like so many times before, the dividends surprised even her. *You're so fucking good,* she thought, but the self-congratulations didn't quell the frantic crackle of electricity that was powering her mind. The blistering speed at which her brain made connections, cross-connections and convoluted associations all but took her breath away.

She decided to do a drive-by. Being in Stanwell Moor she could justify in order to compromise Napper, as per what she could claim to be the tacit expectations of Reeve and Durman, but now that was done, she needed to get clear, go home and lay low like a good girl. Going within shouting distance of the

Rankin place could be a step too far, and risk her bail being withdrawn on account of her being accused of interfering with witnesses. Marlene was one such example in that she could be called to give evidence of the Dane's previous harassment of her husband, potentially useful as circumstantial proof of her connection with the Pope brothers.

She took it none too slowly and gunned the car down the unmetalled road like she was trying to get somewhere, as opposed to doing a hunch-based recce. She passed Jackson's car at just a shade under thirty miles an hour, spraying dirty gravel up the side of the BMW, causing its occupant to look up from the papers on his lap. He didn't see Larssen behind the wheel of the speeding vehicle, but she saw him – and got a split-second glimpse of what he was doing. And then of course she had it: the bastard was going to serve papers on the widow. Or at least he was going to try, and seemed to be waiting for something, or someone.

Larssen pulled over when she'd got round a corner and out of sight. Her thoughts were at once spiteful and desperate. Stopping Jackson now would only delay the inevitable: the papers – undoubtedly to do with the property transfer – could be served on Marlene Rankin at any time, and she could only think that Jackson had chosen the occasion of Rankin's funeral so he could catch the widow when she was off-guard and vulnerable. Grubby, yes, but then that was Jackson all over. Disrupting the transaction was pointless: she had to disrupt that thing called Claude Jackson. Her hatred writhed within her, an incubus determined to express itself through her words, actions, and the very pores of her being. She would have her way somehow, or at least an approximation of it, something to sustain her through the years of imprisonment she feared she faced.

232
The Superintendent at Heathrow, a youngster in his first

command role, knew better than to attempt a raid on a Gypsy funeral, regardless of intel about firearms or wanted persons or anything else. Police encroachment would be like tossing a match onto an ammunition dump. The plan was simple containment and Trojan Units were positioned strategically, but well clear of the Rankin homestead, ready for deployment as a mop-up exercise, as opposed to meaningful intervention.

Napper sat in his dirty old Landrover and came to the correct conclusion that this was what would be happening. If it kicked off at the wake like it did last time it would be a repeat performance, without him – and old Tom, of course – and the Met would just mop up afterwards. His instinct was to have a plan, though, especially since there was a good chance of him being out of work soon. Nothing to lose.

Reeve couldn't take his eyes off the monitor. Larssen's little green dot was beavering away, moving this way and that, checking possibilities, searching for openings. 'Go on, there's no stopping you, is there? You just can't help yourself,' he whispered.

'Talking to yourself, guv'nor?' asked Durman as she returned to the desk with two coffees.

'First sign of madness,' said Reeve with an embarrassed chuckle. Durman regarded her boss disdainfully, thinking how, when opportunities presented themselves, people could change so quickly. She knew Reeve wanted one last promotion before he retired, to get his pension enhanced. She also knew that taking down a corrupt cop, even a lowly one like Napper, wouldn't do his plan any harm at all.

233

From fifty yards away, Larssen watched Jackson get out of his car and make his way to the open gate of the Rankin property. She noticed that, although slow, he was barely limping. He moved cautiously, purposively. The documents in his hand were folded lengthways, for ease of presentation.

He pressed the doorbell and added a couple of raps on the big brass knocker for good effect. Then his phone buzzed.

Kribz needed instructions; he and his little posse were unsighted in the shed, and unarmed. They hadn't a clue what they were heading for, although the sounds from the garden were unthreateningly those of an autumn barbeque party.

'What's 'appenin', Mr Jackson? We'ze got through the back, waitin' for you, innit.'

'I'm waiting for Mrs Rankin to answer the door. Does she know you're there?'

'No, we're in the shed, outa sight.'

Jackson felt it best to keep it that way.

'Okay, just stay where you are, I'm probably better off doing this myself. I'll call you if I need you.'

Marlene opened the front door and regarded Jackson thoughtfully, before nodding curtly to allow him to enter and follow her through the house. It was like he'd shown respect and the appropriate time had come. She led him into the rear living room from which he saw the full-swing party through the open French windows.

Then came the double crack of Bora's gun and Massive's scream as one of the bullets shattered his elbow. The other bullet flew wide as the B Boys launched themselves down and forwards. The broken shed doors offered no resistance and crashed open as the four scrambled and rolled frantically out into the sunlight as Bora came through the shed behind them, firing another two shots off wildly.

The drunken congregation had parted like the Red Sea, shrieking and cursing, trying to find cover behind tables and dog kennels, giving the widow a clear view of Bora in her high-viz jacket, half crouched in the gaping shed doorway, gun in hand, head swivelling in search of her prey.

Kribz was crawling commando-style towards the dog kennels: he'd had an idea, albeit fuzzy and malformed. Numbers and Driss were curled up under a food-laden table.

Massive had rolled around for several seconds, in total shock, before he'd managed to squirm his way behind a stack of beer crates.

Bora saw Marlene raise the Purdy to her shoulder with remarkable composure. The old woman hadn't used a shotgun since she'd hunted pigeons in her teens, but her posture focused Bora's attention and the Albo woman quickly took aim with the Glock – but not quickly enough. As Marlene let rip with the shotgun, Napper hit Bora from behind like a juggernaut, got her around the neck with one arm and used the other hand to disarm her. Most of the lead pellets flew over both their heads, but a few skimmed the top of Napper's scalp, ripping it open. The cop hardly felt the glancing impact: white-hot adrenalin gave him the strength of two men and restraining the winded woman was effortless. As he lay on top of her the blood from his wound gushed down onto the side of her contorted face. 'You're under arrest, moi little darling,' he said quite calmly as he threw the Glock to one side, out of her reach.

Then Kribz let the dogs loose. The pups were only six months old, but they were big, muscular, totally unsocialised and already fired up by the gunfire and bedlam. Lois tried to lead them out and keep them in check, but their exhilaration and need for exertion propelled them into the cowering clusters of people. A big Gypsy man grabbed a shovel and took a swing at one pup as it bounded towards him, connecting soundly with the animal's head. The yelp made Lois change direction and she launched herself at the assailant, fastening her teeth firmly into his fleshy upper arm. All but the injured pup joined her and the big guy went down, flailing at first, then rolling himself into a ball, yelling for help. Men and women alike piled in, hitting the dogs with anything they could lay hands on.

Having seen Napper toss Bora's gun, Driss took advantage of the chaos and made a dash for it, crouching then rolling away behind an empty kennel, the weapon in his hand. Napper just held on to Bora, laying on top of her, whispering sweet nothings into ear. 'Let's just lie still, moi lovely, this'll all pass over in a minute.' Her face was soaked in his blood. She squeezed her eyes tight shut and, for a few seconds, wished she was dead because her life as she knew it was over.

234

On seeing Larssen's anklet tracker dot move into the Rankin driveway, Reeve called Passey.

'Duncan, it's Colin Reeve.'

'I know. What's happened?'

'Larssen's gone out of line. We've lost control, it's back over to you.'

Typical PSD, thought Passey. 'Now there's a surprise. What's she up to?'

She's heading into a place we told her not to go to—'

'What, the Gypsy funeral?'

'Yes, and Napper's nearby. We've got footage of them meeting up. Something's going off, mate.'

Passey liked the 'mate' bit – not. 'Okay, I'll take it back from now, but you lot get fucked off out of there, okay?'

'We've only got an obo van—'

'I don't care, just get it out of there. If I've got control it's got to be total,'

'All yours, mate.'

Passey cut the call and made his next one to Flying Squad control. In under a minute the inspector in charge of the armed Trojan units was dishing out deployment orders and a personnel carrier started moving in.

235

Jackson just stood there, quite still and silent, about ten feet behind Marlene. He looked out over her shoulder at the mayhem across the patio, and then at Kribz and Driss running towards the house. Marlene saw the gun in Driss's hand and began to raise the Purdy.

'No! They're my guys!' blurted Jackson as he started to hobble towards the old woman. Too late: the blast from the shotgun drowned his words and Kribz would have taken a face full of lead had his leg not given way at the instant Marlene pulled the trigger. He went down on one knee and the pellets flew over his head.

'That's both your barrels, Mrs Rankin!' yelled Driss gleefully as he continued running towards the widow. Jackson had got her and was reaching round her to grab the Purdy and prevent her from reloading. To do so he tossed aside the sheaf of papers he was carrying. They landed on Tom Rankin's empty armchair. Larssen, unseen behind him, moved forward and picked them up.

'I'll take these,' she said.

Having wrenched the Purdey from Marlene's grip, Jackson swung round to face Larssen. The Dane grinned as she stowed the papers inside her coat.

'No, don't be stupid! Give me those, you damned bitch!' Jackson croaked the words as he lurched towards his former business partner.

'Get out of my feckin' house, the pair of you!' screeched Marlene.

'Give back those papers, now,' came the stern order from Kribz, who'd made it to the open French doors and was pushing his brother out of his way. He took Bora's Glock from Driss and pointed it directly at the Dane.

'Oh, it's you. What are you going to do if I don't? Murder me in front of these witnesses?' Larssen cocked her head to one side as she posed the question, raising her voice just enough to be heard above the approaching police sirens; that noise was soon drowned by a louder one, overhead.

Passey knew how volatile Gypsy funerals could be at the best of times, never mind when there'd already been a shooting incident nearby, and a violent urban street gang mixed in with it.

'Feck me! That thing can't land here!' exclaimed an astonished drunk as he fended off one of Lois's big pups that was trying attach itself to his ankle. The aircraft got down to a hundred feet and just hung there, the downdraft and cacophonic clatter of its rotors dispelling the cowering congregation into the corners and sides of the fenced off land, food and paper plates flying everywhere in the windstorm.

Kribz had his back to the French doors, determined not to be distracted. 'Give him back those papers! Fuckin' now!' he shouted at Larssen.

'It doesn't matter, let her have them, I've got copies – put that gun down!' whined Jackson. He held the Purdy, awkwardly. Marlene, exhausted, slumped into her husband's armchair. 'Oh Mary mother of Christ,' she moaned, her day's work in ruins.

There was then a surreal pause, an interval in which everyone in the room seemed to consider their positions. There was no way Jackson was going to get those papers signed by the widow now, Kribz had a loaded gun in his hand, Larssen was in serious breach of her bail conditions and the police were about to gatecrash the party. Then Massive staggered through the French doors, holding his elbow and helped by Numbers.

'We gotta get out of here!' yelled the youngster, and it was like he'd taken charge. Kribz came to his senses and threw the Glock into a corner of the room. 'Yeah, come on,' he grunted, keen to regain leadership, and the B Boys began walking through the house towards the front door.

Four white horses, resplendent in black plumage and polished tack, hauled the liveried wooden hearse at an unhurried trot. The animals were well trained and totally unfazed by the yelps and blares of the sirens behind them.

'Police, get out of the way!' shouted the sergeant over the PA system of the Trojan personnel carrier.

The top-hatted undertaker sat high up on the carriage and kept his reins slack, refusing to give way. The horse-drawn hearse was bizarrely dictating the pace of the police vehicle and the roadway to the Rankin place, congested by the numerous parked vehicles, was too narrow for the cops to overtake. They gave up and turned off their noise.

'What's the news from the air?' asked the Trojan sergeant. His radio operator got an update and quickly replied, 'As far as they can make out it's just a crowd of well-dressed Gypsies havin' a barbeque and playing around with dogs.'

The sergeant shrugged. 'No rush then, just stay behind the hearse.'

The B Boys emerged from the front door just as the horses drew level with the driveway entrance. Looking over the hedge, Kribz could see the top of the Trojan carrier behind it. He made a decision.

The scene inside the house was still one of suspended animation. Larssen knew better than to go for the gun Kribz had just chucked – she was in enough trouble as it was. Above the clatter of the helicopter, Jackson shouted, 'It's my deal now, Freda, you're out of the picture. Just give me those papers so that Mrs Rankin can sign them.'

'I'm signing feck all, so the lot of you can get out my house and let me bury my husband. You're all the feckin' same, all as bad as each other, like lumps of bad meat in the same pot of stinkin' broth!' Marlene's voice was croaky, choked with emotion and hurt.

'Quite right, Mrs Rankin,' smirked Larssen.

And it suddenly dawned on Jackson that the old woman had a point; that he, Larssen, the Albanians and the urban street gang he'd found himself teamed up with were all now tarred with the same brush, all up to their throats in lies, treachery and murderous violence.

The undertaker looked at his old pocket watch: too soon yet – another three minutes. He was enjoying holding up the police and watched with interest as the helicopter rose into the sky, dipped its nose and sped off and away. Cheekily, he lifted his black top hat and waved it in a mock salute to the departing aircraft. 'Away you go, you Gorga menace, you didn't frit my lovely creatures,' he muttered, and four sets of ears swivelled around as if to acknowledge the compliment, whilst waiting for further instructions.

The short, eerie silent that then followed was shattered by the sudden roar of the Albion. Even the horses jolted, unsure of the source of the noise. The two leading animals had to jump backwards a foot or two as the wagon thundered out of the gate like a furious escaping beast. Kribz was behind the wheel with the injured Massive alongside him, shouting instructions. 'You gotta double the clutch, man, or it won't engage!' laughed the big man through the agony of his elbow injury, his leader wrestled with the shuddering gearstick at the same time as wrenching the steering wheel hard round to the left to avoid going straight through the hedge opposite the Rankin gateway. He made it, found second gear and the lorry roared off along the lane towards the M25.

'What the fuck!' The sergeant in the Trojan carrier picked up the radio handset: 'All units from Trojan 51, HGV just decamped from location, heading east towards motorway intersection. Do we have any units in that location?'

The response came back in the negative, and the sergeant wished he'd deployed differently.

'We can't follow it, we're stuck behind a horse-drawn fucking hearse,' he reported, watching Numbers and Driss waving their goodbyes from the back of the Albion.

Someone else was stood watching the gang's noisy departure. Katrina Swan had paid off her Uber driver two hundred yards back down the lane and had trudged along it and past the waiting Trojan van and the hearse. She'd just about reached the open gates of the Rankin place when the Albion had lurched out and torn away. When she walked through the front door of the house the scene was more or less what she'd expected, particularly the standoff between Larssen and Jackson.

'Am I interrupting something?' she asked loudly, confident that she had indeed just done so.

'What are you doing here?' Larssen's voice was strained, slightly breathless, like this interference was the last thing she needed.

'I've come to see you, Freda, to give you some information.'

'And what might that be, Katrina?' Larssen turned slowly but pointedly to face the lawyer, like she was more than ready to deal with another confrontation head on.

'That I can no longer represent you, and that I've reported you to the police.'

'What for?' Larssen tried to smile, but her lip curled.

'Conspiracy to pervert the course of justice will probably be the defining offence, but that's not for me to decide.'

'What? What are you fucking talking about?'

Swan was solid, standing her ground. 'You assured me that you had no prior dealings with the Pope brothers. What I've just—'

'I fucking haven't!'

'What I've just witnessed confirms my suspicions that you've been involved with them all along—'

'That's shit and you know it!'

'They are my clients. I have a duty of care to them and I now have no doubt that you've been corrupting them.' Swan spoke authoritatively.

'What?! And you come here to tell me this? How did you know I was here?' Larssen was shaking, her voice a strangulated screech.

'I didn't know, I guessed,' said Swan, but her eyes flicked towards Jackson as she spoke.

Larssen spun round at her former business partner. 'You bastard! You filthy bastard!' she screamed and launched herself at him, her nails finding purchase in his chubby face and neck. Knocked immediately off balance, Jackson went down, trying to fend off the clawing banshee.

Having seen the escape of who he rightly assessed to be the Popes and their helpers, the Trojan sergeant did a quick risk reassessment and decided that it was safe to enter the property.

'Right you lot, in we go on foot. We'll leave the carrier here.' The eager cops were out of the van in seconds and running around the hearse and into the driveway of the Rankin house. The front door was still open.

'Police!' shouted the sergeant, unnecessarily, his Heckler raised at his shoulder and ready to fire. His troops were fanning out behind him, checking the ground floor and stairway.

Larssen released her grip on Jackson and turned to face the new threat.

'Get away from him, lie down and keep still!' barked the sergeant. Two cops walked quickly past him and out into the garden to train their weapons menacingly at the stunned and dishevelled congregation. Even the dogs were subdued.

Another police vehicle had pulled up behind the Trojan van. It was the turn of Briggs and Mason to walk around the horse-drawn hearse and enter the house.

'All under control, sergeant?' asked Briggs, almost nonchalantly.

'Who are you?!' demanded the sergeant, without looking at the newcomer and still swivelling his weapon, checking for hazard.

Briggs didn't have to reply. 'Well, well, it's *detective* Briggs, come to save the day!' announced Larssen.

'Nah!' interrupted Napper as he shoved the now handcuffed Bora Gozit through the French doors and into the room. 'It was me who saved the fuckin' day!' The Cornishman, his bloodied face wide-eyed and grinning, had snatched his prisoner back from a couple of Trojan cops who'd done the handcuffing, and was determined to parade his trophy.

'This is how you do it, Briggsy, this crazy bitch would have taken the lot of us out if oi hadn't been roight behind 'er, and best you check out why *she's* fuckin' here!' He used his free hand to point dramatically at Larssen, before continuing to push Bora through the house and out towards one of the many police cars that were arriving in droves.

236

It was just gone midday and the Coach and Horses was still empty, save for two unkempt men about to embark on a serious mission. The following seven hours would feature the exchange of an inward stream of alcohol for an outward torrent of expletive-laden pronouncements, proclamations, and insults.

Napper and Blake had their separate reasons to celebrate. Not only had the Cornishman kept his job, he'd also been recommended for a Commissioner's Commendation for bravery and the CPS enrolled him as a prosecution witness in their case against Larssen, the Dane having been charged with attempting to pervert the course of justice, in addition to unlawful possession of the linked series Beretta. The shrinks had finished their assessment and she'd been certified competent to stand trial.

The Pope brothers had denied all knowledge of the cocaine stash at Stanwell Moor and their solicitor had declined to assist the police against them, professionally suggesting that it must have been Larssen who had instigated their offer to take responsibility, a scenario that suited everyone. Katrina Swan had always had a hopeful eye on this outcome but had never admitted it to herself. Just maybe, much later, she would very privately concede that helping an asset stripping thief along the road to poetic justice would be the pinnacle of her legal career.

So, Swan was exhausted but at peace with herself as she walked into the pub and approached her fellow lawyer and his buddy cop.

'Well, look who it is,' slurred Blake – it was now gone two in the afternoon – 'it's our champion of the great unwashed!' The pitch of his voice was on the rise, usually the prelude to a fit of tasteless glee.

'Gin and tonic please, large,' replied Swan, determined not to be drawn.

'I'll get that,' said Napper.

'No, I'll get it, it must be my round.'

The new voice belonged to Claude Jackson, who had just walked unsteadily through the door.

'Fuck me,' chortled Blake, 'it's the richest one-legged pirate since fucking Long John Silver!'

'At least I'm no longer the parrot on the pirate's shoulder,' was Jackson's riposte; he was smiling, relaxed.

'That's right, mate,' agreed Blake, 'the owner of that shoulder is now nicely out of harm's way.'

Larssen's bail had been unsurprisingly withdrawn and the *grande finale* at the Rankin house had rendered her of no further use to the DPS, Reeve's investigation of Napper having been abruptly discontinued.

'Well, for the time being, anyway.' Jackson addressed the rest of his sentence to Napper. 'Let's see how her trial goes.'

Broth

Napper shrugged and said nothing. Blake changed the subject.

'And how's the gang, Jacko? I understand you had to up your surety a few notches.' Napper had told Blake how the CPS had insisted that the Popes' bail conditions be tightened, including doubling the sum of Jackson's recognisance.

'Yup, twenty grand each now, so the bastards had better behave themselves or I'll withdraw my surety and they'll be back inside until their trial.' This time Jackson delivered the last part of his sentence to Swan, who was taking some very large sips of her gin and tonic.

'They know the score,' she said, 'and, anyway,' – she paused for another gulp and got the men's avid attention – 'the CPS have dropped the firearms charge against the older Pope brother,' – another savoured sip – 'something about them not wanting to use Lashford's evidence in court and that Chris Pope's taking of the Albanian boy as hostage had tacit police approval.'

Blake hadn't known about this bit; incredulous, he turned to Napper. 'Is this true, Doug?'

'Not sure meself, mate, that's why I haven't mentioned it. All I've heard is that Gerry Lashford's chucked a sicky, stress oi think, they're prob'ly gonna retire her.'

'On a full pension, I presume?' said Swan, witheringly.

'Probably,' replied Napper, 'along with an enhancement for psychological injury.'

Jackson snorted. 'Bloody marvellous, isn't it? More public money down the drain.'

Blake let fly with a sprayed combination of Kronenbourg and spittle, shrieking, 'Hah! You've got a fucking nerve, Jacko. I bet your tax returns are like something out of Walter Mitty!'

And they all laughed.

237

Kribz and Driss were not accustomed to manual labour.

'I've got blisters bruv, look,' said the younger bro proudly.

Kribz inspected the proffered hand, which had for the previous two hours been wielding a sledgehammer. 'Jeeze, bruv, looks 'orrible, best get Mrs R to put a bandage on that.'

The pair had spent the morning fixing the doors of the big shed and constructing a fence for what they intended to be a new dog enclosure. It was all part of an unwritten deal they'd struck with Marlene Rankin wherein they would rent the land to the rear of the house and use it to breed dogs under the licence she'd had as a formality transferred from her deceased husband's name.

'Yeah, let's go in now, the tea should be ready.' Marlene's call five minutes earlier had followed the sound of the kettle whistling.

The brothers trudged over the grassed area, across the patio and through the French doors which were open, despite the wintry weather.

Kribz went in first and stopped dead after three paces. 'Fuckin' hell!'

'What?' said Driss, before following his brother's line of sight.

Marlene Rankin lay face down on the floor, lifeless. The boys rushed towards her, neither having a clue what to do. They turned her over so that she lay on her back. Kribz put his ear to her mouth. Driss pulled out his phone and dialled 999 for an ambulance. They knew it wouldn't need to hurry.

Epilogue

HMP Bronzefield is a state-of-the-art women's prison located just to the west of London. Like many of the six hundred inmates, Freda Larssen had her own cell, or 'Room' as they called the eight-by-five cubicles. Her window was east facing and the elongated shadowgraph of its pleasantly curvy bars – but bars all the same – cast by the early morning sun was always of interest to her as it moved almost imperceptibly across the floor, then her bed and then the wall.

She had been there for just over three months, having drawn a five-year sentence after the medical experts had decided she was fit to stand trial at Southwark Crown Court. The jury of eight women and four men had then rejected her claim that the Beretta found in her freezer had been planted by a police officer who had demonstrated courage and fortitude through the complex investigation of a series of incidents arguably instigated by her own unscrupulous business practices.

Those who live in greenhouses shouldn't throw stones, as the saying goes, and Larssen's insistence on alleging that PC Napper had planted the weapon in her flat had been a direct attack on the officer's moral integrity, allowing the prosecution to respond with a similarly couched counterattack. Consequently, the jury heard all about Larssen's dishonesty in respect of her attempted confiscation of the Rankin homestead and her virtual theft of Claude Jackson's half of the shared company. Not evidence to support the charge of possession of a firearm of course, but nevertheless admissible to rebut her claim of being a thoroughly decent citizen with a licence to impugn a brave young bobby.

During the pre-trial preparations, the CPS had disclosed to the defense lawyers the fact of the Beretta having linked series status, even though to keep things simple this material was unused in the case against Larssen. Unsurprisingly, the defence team did not seek to argue: to have had the weapon's antecedent history laid bare would have worsened Larssen's chances of acquittal. And it turned out that the odds had been bad enough and the jury returned a unanimous guilty verdict after less than an hour of deliberations.

She'd been told that there was no point in appealing, either against conviction – the evidence had been compelling, or sentence – five years was the statutory minimum for the offence she'd been convicted of.

So, the Dane had settled into prison life, and Bronzefield wasn't too bad. She had a gym, edible food and, above all, time to think. If she stayed out of trouble, she would be out in two and a half years, possibly sooner with an electronic ankle tag.

Yes. Time to think. And be angry. And nothing angers the human heart more than injustice. Her prison time would be short – and then *her* time would come.

About the Author

Hugh Duncan Munro was born in Northumberland in 1954, graduated from Aston University in 1976 and spent the following 40 years in military intelligence, law enforcement, teaching, and the lowliest echelons of the legal profession.

He lives in London and works as a freelance ghost-writer and private investigator. He supports Newcastle United Football Club.

Printed in Great Britain
by Amazon